D1172887

NO
SURVIVORS

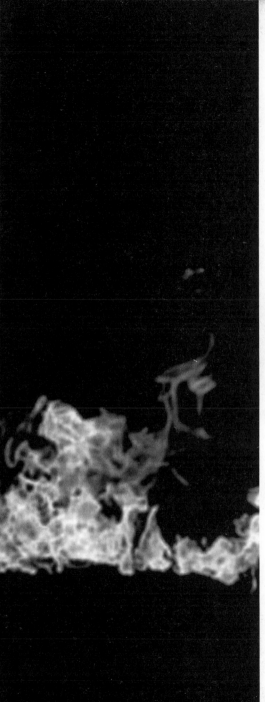

NO
SURVIVORS

An Accident Man Novel

TOM CAIN

VIKING
CANADA

VIKING CANADA

Published by the Penguin Group

Penguin Group (Canada), 90 Eglinton Avenue East, Suite 700,
Toronto, Ontario, Canada M4P 2Y3 (a division of Pearson Canada Inc.)

Penguin Group (USA) Inc., 375 Hudson Street, New York, New York 10014, U.S.A.
Penguin Books Ltd, 80 Strand, London WC2R 0RL, England
Penguin Ireland, 25 St. Stephen's Green, Dublin 2, Ireland (a division of Penguin Books Ltd)
Penguin Group (Australia), 250 Camberwell Road, Camberwell, Victoria 3124, Australia
(a division of Pearson Australia Group Pty Ltd)
Penguin Books India Pvt Ltd, 11 Community Centre, Panchsheel Park, New Delhi – 110 017, India
Penguin Group (NZ), 67 Apollo Drive, Rosedale, North Shore 0745, Auckland, New Zealand
(a division of Pearson New Zealand Ltd)
Penguin Books (South Africa) (Pty) Ltd, 24 Sturdee Avenue, Rosebank,
Johannesburg 2196, South Africa

Penguin Books Ltd, Registered Offices: 80 Strand, London WC2R 0RL, England

First published in Canada by Penguin Group (Canada), a division of Pearson Canada Inc., 2009
Simultaneously published in the United States by G. P. Putnam's Sons,
a division of Penguin Group (USA) Inc.

1   2   3   4   5   6   7   8   9   10 (RRD)

Copyright © Tom Cain, 2009

*Publisher's note: This book is a work of fiction. Names, characters, places, and incidents
either are the product of the author's imagination or are used fictitiously, and any
resemblance to actual persons, living or dead, events, or locales is entirely coincidental.*

Manufactured in the U.S.A.

ISBN 978-0-670-06740-4

Library and Archives Canada Cataloguing in Publication data available upon request to the publisher.
American Library of Congress Cataloging in Publication data available.

Visit the Penguin Group (Canada) website at **www.penguin.ca**

Special and corporate bulk purchase rates available; please see
www.penguin.ca/corporatesales or call 1-800-810-3104, ext. 477 or 474

PREFACE:

These Are the Facts . . .

On September 6, 1997, the Princess of Wales was laid to rest on an island in the Oval Lake at Althorp, her ancestral home.

On September 7, 1997, General Alexander Lebed, former National Security Adviser to Russia's President Yeltsin, appeared on the prime-time American television news program *60 Minutes*. He revealed that his government no longer knew the whereabouts of many of their small-scale nuclear weapons, commonly described as suitcase nukes.

"More than a hundred weapons out of the supposed number of two hundred and fifty are not under the control of the armed forces of Russia," Lebed said. "I don't know their location. I don't know whether they have been destroyed or whether they are stored or whether they've been sold or stolen. I don't know."

On February 23, 1998, Osama bin Laden used the London-based newspaper *Al-Quds Al-Arabi* to issue a declaration of war against what he termed "the crusader-Zionist alliance." Bin Laden declared, "[The] crimes and sins committed by the Americans are a clear declaration of war on God, his messenger, and Muslims. . . . On that basis, and in compliance with God's order, we issue the following fatwa to all Muslims: The ruling to kill the Americans and their allies—civilians and military—is an individual duty for every Muslim who can do it in any country in which it is possible to do it."

On October 20, 1999, the FBI released Project Megiddo, a long-term investigation into fundamentalist Christian cults who "believe the year 2000 will usher in the end of the world and who are willing to perpetrate acts of violence to bring that end about." In its section on "apocalyptic religious beliefs," it noted, "Many extremists view themselves as religious martyrs who have a duty to initiate or take part in the coming battles against Satan." The report also commented, "There is no consensus within Christianity regarding the specific date that the Apocalypse will occur. However, within many right-wing religious groups there is a uniform belief that the Apocalypse is approaching."

This much is true.

Everything and everyone else in this book is pure fiction.

NO
SURVIVORS

PROLOGUE:

March 1993

1

The airport mechanic was a shade under six feet tall, and the body beneath his overalls and padded cold-weather vest was lean and athletic. The single line that bisected his strong, dark brow suggested a determined fixity of purpose, and his clear green eyes conveyed a calm, almost chilly intelligence. A woolen knitted cap covered his short brown hair. The lower part of his face was hidden behind a beard.

There was a badge on his chest. It gave his name as Steve Lundin.

The badge was fake. The mechanic's real name was Samuel Carver.

No one in the hangar batted an eyelid when Carver unscrewed the hatch at the tail end of the executive jet and hauled himself up into the rear equipment bay for a standard preflight inspection.

This area was not reachable while the jet was airborne. It was simply a place filled with ugly but functional components, much like the basement of a building. Things like bundles of wires linking the plane's electronic circuits, the cables and hydraulic lines that controlled the rudder and elevators, the accumulator holding the hydraulic fluid that got pumped out through the system, the pipes that carried super-heated, high-pressure air off the engines and sent it for use in the plane's cabin heating system. None of these things were much to look at, or remotely exciting, until, of course, they went wrong.

The air pipes were what interested Carver. They were covered in thick silver-colored cladding, held with plastic clips, and they formed a network through the plane via valves and junctions, pretty much like a domestic water system. So he messed with the plumbing, loosening one of the junctions so that the hot air would leak from it. The junction in question was barely a hand's breadth away from the hydraulic accumulator.

By the time Carver closed the equipment bay hatch and walked away, the fate of the aircraft was sealed.

There was a TV on in the passenger lounge, the CNN reporter having a hard time holding back his tears as he stood in front of a blackened, burned-out church.

"We can't show you what it looks like inside the smoking charnel house behind me," he said, an undertone of barely restrained passion coloring his lyrical Irish brogue. "The scenes are too appalling, too sickening. The charred and mutilated corpses of four hundred innocent women and children lie in there. The scent of their burned flesh fills the air all around.

"While Western politicians turn their eyes away from this insignificant corner of West Africa, a ten-year civil war has descended into genocide. The rebel forces mounting this ruthless campaign are better-trained and equipped than ever before. Their leaders are showing levels of organization and strategic planning far ahead of anything they have displayed before. Somehow, somewhere, these merciless killers have acquired new resources, new expertise. And so, as the village's few survivors search among the corpses for their loved ones, one question comes inevitably to mind: Who is backing the rebels? For whoever they are, and whatever their motivation, they have the blood of an entire people on their hands."

"Shit, this boy's a friggin' comedian!"

Waylon McCabe slapped a hand against his thigh as he addressed the three other men in the room. Most of the time McCabe's eyes were cold, narrow slits in wrinkled folds of leathery skin that seemed permanently screwed up against the glare of his native Texan sun. Now he was letting his guard down, opening up a little, taking it easy with his buddies.

"Man, I swear he's about to cry, just to show how sensitive he is. But I'll bet he don't care about a bunch of dead niggers, any more 'n I do. He's just in it for hisself, thinkin' on the prizes he's gonna git for being such a damn humanitarian . . . hell, he might make almost as much money outta this war as me."

"I seriously doubt that, boss," said one of the other men, swigging from a bottle of Molson Canadian.

"Well, I don' know, Clete," replied McCabe with a grin. "Sure, my diamonds'll pay better. But you gotta consider the costs. He ain't had to ante up for guns 'n' ammo, instructors to train them native boys. . . . Here, throw me one of them beers afore I die of thirst."

McCabe was a long way past sixty, but for all the lines on his face, he was still tougher and possessed of more energy than most men half his age. He had spent the past three days on the northern coast of the Yukon and Northwest territories. From there on up to the North Pole it was pretty much just ice. Now he was sitting in a private room in the terminal at Mike Zubko Airport, right outside the town of Inuvik, waiting on the plane that would take him home.

He was trying to decide whether to pursue his hunch that there were significant oil deposits in the region. The major corporations had all pulled out of the area. Oil was cheap, extraction would be expensive, and the local Eskimos—Waylon McCabe was damned if he'd call them Inuits; screw them if they felt offended—were getting uppity about their tribal lands getting despoiled. The way they saw it, the upside wasn't worth the aggravation.

McCabe, however, looked around the world at where all the oil was, and where all the trouble was, and saw they were all pretty much the same places. Sooner or later, between the towel heads in the Middle East and the Commies down in South America, supplies would be threatened. Meanwhile, there were billions of Chinese and Indians buying automobiles and building factories, so demand could only go up. High demand and insecure supply would mean rocketing prices, and fields that were only marginal now would become worth exploiting. At that point, who gave a damn what a bunch of seal hunters thought? A few bucks in the right pockets and that problem would be solved. And anyone who refused to take the money would soon find out they'd made the wrong decision.

There was a knock on the door, and Carver walked into the room. His normal relaxed stride had disappeared. The way he carried himself was tentative, his expression hesitant and nervous. He gave the clear impression that he felt uneasy in the presence of a man as wealthy and powerful as McCabe.

"Plane's checked, filled up, and ready to go," he said. "Don't mind me saying so, sir, you'd best be on your way. There's weather coming in."

McCabe gave a single, brusque nod that at once acknowledged what he'd said and dismissed him from the room.

Carver paused briefly in the doorway, though nobody seemed to notice or care.

"Have a good flight, sir," he said.

2

The plane was routed out of Inuvik to Calgary, three hours and fourteen hundred miles away to the southeast, most of it over mountainous wilderness.

The moment the engines were fired up, air started leaking from the pipe, gaining all the time in temperature and pressure. It was directing its heat right onto the hydraulic accumulator, which was filled with very sensitive, highly flammable fluid. As the minutes rolled by, and the plane rose to its cruising altitude at around thirty thousand feet, heading out over the Selwyn mountain range, that fluid got hotter and hotter. Finally, about forty minutes out of Inuvik, the temperature became critical and the accumulator burst open with an explosive blast that shook the rear of the plane. The airframe was strong enough to withstand the detonation, but the flames from the burning fluid greedily found more fuel in the plastic sheaths around the wires, the ducting within which the circuits were bundled, the cladding around the air pipes—all manner of combustible materials.

The crew barely felt or heard the explosion over the juddering of air turbulence and roaring of the jets. The first thing the pilot knew for sure was the warning light telling him that fire had taken hold in the rear equipment bay. The second was that there was nothing whatever he could do to put it out. From this point he had a maximum of seven to eight minutes before the flames ate through the control systems for his rudder and elevators.

The moment McCabe's jet left the ground, Carver got into the three-year-old Ford F-250 heavy-duty truck he'd bought for cash two weeks ago in Skagway, Alaska, and headed to the nearest gas station. In the restroom, he shaved off Steve Lundin's beard and took off his overalls, which he dumped in a trash can out back. Then he turned south, onto the Dempster Highway. A short while down the road, the asphalt ran out. For the next 450 miles, crossing one Arctic Circle, two time zones, five rivers, and several mountain ranges, he'd be on nothing but rough shale and gravel.

They told you this kind of thing in Inuvit, the sheer, overwhelming scale of the local geography and the incredible absence of other people being the region's proudest features. The Yukon Territory alone was almost as big as Spain, but had just thirty thousand people in it. But the Northwest Territories, next door, made Yukon look as impressive as a suburban backyard. Its forty thousand inhabitants were spread across an area bigger than Spain, France, Holland, Belgium, and England put together.

Carver was perfectly happy to listen to these boastful recitals. He liked facts. He found their certainty reassuring, something reliably nonnegotiable in a world of compromise, betrayal, and unpredictable emotion. They took his mind off the thing that was eating away at his conscience, the thought of all the other people on the plane who would die with Waylon McCabe. Carver was used to the concept of collateral damage. He understood that the innocent often died alongside the guilty. He grasped, too, the human mathematics that said it was better that a handful of people should die in a plane crash than hundreds of thousands be wiped out by acts of genocide. He could even tell himself that the people who worked for Waylon McCabe probably knew what he was doing and had profited from his actions. That didn't mean he had to like any of it.

His secretive employers, who called themselves the Consortium, would not have been impressed by his principled qualms. They saw themselves as moral guardians in an immoral world, righting wrongs that defeated politicians, policemen, and armies, hidebound by laws and rules of engagement. The McCabe job was Carver's third assignment. A former Royal Marines officer who had fought with the corps' Special Boat Service, an elite within an elite, he had resigned his commission in disgust at the futility of his unit's efforts. The dictators he and his men had fought were still in power. The terrorists were treated like statesmen. The traffickers in drugs, guns, and people had never paid for their crimes.

He could kill a man face-to-face, with a gun, a knife, or his bare hands. But his employers preferred a more subtle, deniable approach. So Samuel Carver provided them with accidents, like the one he'd just prepared for Waylon McCabe.

3

The pilot had shut down the engines to slow the progress of the fire, and the only sound was the eerie rush of the air outside. The flight attendant, perched on her flimsy fold-down seat, was biting her lip and trying desperately to suppress a tidal wave of panic, barely held in check by her training and professional pride. She was smoothing down her skirt with jerky, distracted movements that suggested she was unaware of what she was doing. But, looking back down the cabin toward the rear, she was the first to see the smoke as it seeped into the compartment, insinuating its way through air vents and between the gaps in floors and partitions like a plague of ghostly, toxic snakes. The smoke was shot with bilious yellows and dirty browns, a stew of chemicals given off by all the materials burning in the back of the plane. As the cabin filled with it, the passengers started to cough and retch.

"Oxygen masks . . . !" croaked the attendant, hammering her fist on the flight-deck door, forcing the words out between desperate attempts to breathe. The copilot turned his head, caught a whiff of smoke, and immediately hit the release switch that opened the trap doors above each seat and let the masks dangle down by the passengers' heads. Then the crew put on their own masks. They worked fine. The passengers were not so lucky.

There were six passenger seats in the cabin, plus the attendant's position, making a total of seven masks. One of them did not deploy at all. Two dropped, but supplied no oxygen. That left four masks among five people, and a life-and-death game of musical chairs began.

The attendant's mask was functioning. So was McCabe's. He'd inhaled a whole load of crap by the time he got it on, but finally he was breathing sweet, pure oxygen, and the heaving in his chest began to subside.

The other three men started scrambling through the ever-thickening smoke, shouting, screaming, and coughing in their desperate search for clean air. One managed to kick, punch, and elbow his way to a chair that had a working mask. Another was overcome by the smoke and sank to the floor, bent double on his knees, where he took his last few breaths. Then he collapsed, stone dead, in the aisle.

The fourth man, meanwhile, had finally found a working mask, but his brain seemed unable to give his hands the necessary instructions, his fingers fumbling helplessly as they tried to stretch the elastic strap over his head. He was coughing so hard now that he was bringing up blood, a scarlet spume that foamed from his mouth, bubbling and wheezing until he, too, was still.

And all the while, the plane kept dropping through the sky, the wind howled and buffeted around it, and the cables controlling the elevator flaps were eaten away by the flames.

The flight crew, meanwhile, were too busy to be afraid. There was barely any light in the sky now, and the mountains through which they were descending were just black silhouettes, outlined against a deep blue horizon. They were seven thousand feet up, less than five thousand feet above the lowest ground in the region, giving them maybe ten miles to play with at most, and no way to go but down. They'd dumped all their fuel to save weight and reduce the risk of any further fires. They'd deployed the undercarriage. All they were missing was their landing site. Then one last faint glint of light reflected off a sheet of flat white ice, and they saw a frozen lake up ahead.

It looked like a giant pair of spectacles. Two large, open areas at either end formed the lenses, linked by a curved channel. A small island stood right in the middle of the left-hand, westernmost lens. But it was too close and they were still too high. They were going to overshoot.

The pilot muttered a string of expletives into his oxygen mask and pushed the plane into an even steeper dive. He'd wanted to come in at a steady, shallow glide. Now he had to swoop down toward the lake like a dive-bomber, pull up at the final moment, and pray that the controls could take the strain.

Down the plane plunged, closing in on the lake, till the cockpit windshield seemed filled with nothing but ice.

They were over the first round lens of the lake now, still five hundred feet up, the pilot frantically pulling at the joystick to get the elevator flaps to lift, and pull the plane out of the dive.

In the rear equipment bay, the cables connecting the pilot to the elevators had been burned and frayed to little more than wire strands, and all the time, the demand for more lift was putting more pressure on the cables, stretching them tighter.

The nose wouldn't come up. They were going to crash straight into the ice.

The cables were unraveling.

The ice was barely a hundred feet below them.

And then, at last, the plane pulled out of its dive, the descent flattened, and at that precise moment the final strands of cable snapped, the elevators lost all control and the plane fell the last fifty feet onto the frozen lake in a spectacular belly flop that buckled the undercarriage and sent the craft skittering across the ice like a giant hockey puck.

Somehow it found a straight-line path across the curved channel between one half of the lake and the other. But the impact had been enough to throw the attendant from her flimsy seat, ripping her mask away from its moorings, and throwing her in a flurry of arms and legs down the cabin, between the chairs, till she collided with the back wall and slumped motionless to the ground.

In the final instant before the plane had landed, an image flashed across Waylon McCabe's mind, a memory from his childhood, Sunday morning in the church house, his mother singing a hymn in her harsh, reedy voice, his father's voice a low, tuneless drone. He could smell their clothes, a bitter scent of sweat, dirt, poverty, and defeat. McCabe had not been back to that church in fifty years. He'd left it far behind the day he had watched his mother being buried and had quit his hometown for good.

The image vanished as he realized they'd got back down to earth in one piece. The impossible had happened. He'd made it.

Then the tip of the starboard wing caught against the rock face of the island, which jutted up out of the ice in the middle of the lake. The wing sheared right off and sent the rest of the plane spinning off at a new angle.

It came ashore in the center of a small cove, riding up the frozen beach till the port wing hit a massive boulder, crumpled, and left the fuselage arrowing into the rocks and trees, burrowing a deep trench through the thick winter snow and trampling the smaller saplings until the nose of the fuselage hit a much older, bigger pine.

The point of impact was slightly off center, to the pilot's side, and he was squashed like a bug on a windshield as one half of the flight deck was obliterated and a huge gash was torn down the side of the plane. McCabe's last surviving companion was flung out into space, still attached to his chair, till he came to rest, impaled by a tree branch, fifty feet away.

The final intact section of the plane caromed off a rock outcrop. The rest of the flight deck disintegrated, taking the copilot with it, and the main length of the cabin simply snapped in two, like a broken twig. The last of the smoke escaped into the subzero air. And Waylon McCabe slumped, eyes closed, in his chair.

There was an emergency locator beacon on the plane. A helicopter was heading out of the nearest settlement, Faro, within half an hour of the crash. The rescue team was winched down to the ground while the helicopter hovered overhead, illuminating the main crash site with its spotlights. One by one the corpses were discovered and then, when all hope seemed lost, there came a shout: "We got a live one!"

Waylon McCabe briefly regained consciousness as his stretcher was being winched up toward the helicopter. As he rose though the air, up into the heavens, his eyes were dazzled by shafts of light, his ears overwhelmed by what sounded like the fluttering of a million angels' wings. The first words he was aware of hearing came from a paramedic: "It's a miracle you survived."

That's what the doctors said, too, when he'd been airlifted to the nearest hospital. The news reporters who besieged the modest facility, his lawyer and financial director, who flew in from his corporate headquarters in San Antonio, the flight attendant who fussed over him as he was flown back home to Texas—they all used that same word: *miracle.*

FIVE YEARS LATER:

January 1998

4

S amuel Carver's room had a million-dollar view, clear across the water to the snowcapped peaks that rose in serried ranks beyond the southern shore. While the mountains stood solid and immutable, the skies above them displayed an infinite variety of light, color, and temper, concealing the glorious landscape one moment, illuminating it the next. On a clear day, a man could stand at that window and see all the way to Mont Blanc. He could practically reach out and touch the black runs.

But Carver wasn't standing. Having visited death upon so many, he was now condemned to a half-life, trapped in a solitary purgatory. He was lying in bed, his body twisted in a fetal curl. The room was centrally heated, but his shoulders were hunched against the cold. It was silent, yet the palms of his hands were cupped over his ears, his fingers clawing at the back of his skull. The light was gentle, but his eyes were screwed tightly against a scorching glare.

Then he began to stir. He jerked his back straight, then arched it, throwing his head up the bed and opening his mouth, uttering soft, wordless moans, while his limbs thrashed in random, spastic movements. His twitching became more frantic and his cries grew in volume.

By the time Carver woke, he was screaming.

"Wake up, wake up!"

Alexandra Petrova placed her hands on Carver's shoulders and tried to free him from the nightmare's grip, gently shaking him back into consciousness. His body felt weak and flabby, softened by months of inactivity. His face was rounder, his features less clearly defined as the bones disappeared behind pouches of flesh. His eyes were red-rimmed and fearful.

The screams petered out, replaced by a confused, semiconscious muttering and then the familiar sequence: the panicked, darting looks around the room, his body half raised from the bed; the gradual relaxation, sinking back onto his pillows as she stroked his hand and reassured him; finally the answering squeeze, the attempt at a smile, and the single whispered word, "Hi."

And then another, "Alix."

It was Carver's name for her, the one he'd used in the days they'd spent together, before his months of confinement in this private clinic on the shores of Lake Geneva. It was a sign that he recognized her, and was grateful for her company, though he could not yet recall what she had meant to him before. But then, he did not know who Samuel Carver truly was, either: what he had done and what others had done to him.

"Still the same dream?" she asked.

He squeezed his eyes shut for a moment as if to drive the last fragments of the horror from his mind, then answered, "Not the same dream. But the same ending, like always."

"Can you remember what happened at the beginning of the dream this time?"

Carver thought for a while.

"I don't know," he said.

He sounded indifferent, not quite seeing the point of the question.

"Just try," Alix persisted.

Carver screwed up his face in concentration.

"I was a soldier," he said. "There was fighting, in a desert . . . then it all changed."

"You were probably dreaming about something that actually happened. You really were a soldier."

"I know," said Carver. "You told me before. I remember that."

He looked at her with eyes that sought her approval. For the umpteenth time, she tried to persuade herself that the man she loved was still in there somewhere. She imagined a time when the blankness in his eyes would be replaced by the fierce intensity she had seen in them on the night they met, or the unexpected tenderness he had revealed in those stolen hours when they had been alone together, keeping the world at bay.

They'd both been in Paris, working the same assignment, the night of August 31, 1997. Carver had been standing at one end of the Alma Tunnel, waiting for a car. She had been riding pillion on a high-speed motorbike, firing her flashing camera at the Mercedes, goading the man at its wheel to drive ever faster, whipping him on toward death in Carver's hands.

The moment they met, she was pointing a gun in his direction. Seconds later, he'd pinned her to the pavement, his knee in the small of her back. Half an hour later, she'd followed him into a building, knowing he'd rigged it with explosive charges, knowing that those bombs were about to go off, but trusting absolutely in his ability to get them both in and out alive.

Now here they were in Switzerland, almost five months later, two people who had been forced into acts of terrible violence, but who, in their few precious moments of shared tranquillity, had each seen in the other a hope, not just of love, but of some small measure of redemption.

For Alix had secrets of her own. On her journey from the drab provinces of the Soviet Union to the gaudy luxuries of post-Communist Moscow, she, too, had compromised her soul. Just like Carver, she longed for an escape. But the past had clung to her and Carver alike, and it had exacted a bitter price on the night of torture and bloodshed that had subjected Carver to agonies so extreme that they had ripped his identity away from its moorings and buried his memories too deeply to be retrieved.

Alix had even begun to wonder if she really did love him anymore. How could you love a person who no longer knew who you were, or what you and he had meant to each other? She had once loved Samuel Carver—she was sure of that. She would still love that man if he were with her. But was he that man any longer? Was he any kind of man at all?

Alix fiddled with Carver's pillows, plumping them up and rearranging them, pretending to make him more comfortable but really just trying to distract herself from her thoughts, and the guilt she felt for even allowing herself to consider them.

From behind her came the sound of a discreet cough.

A man was standing in the doorway, wearing a somber dark-gray suit and a tie whose pattern was so muted as to be virtually invisible.

"Mademoiselle Petrova?" he said.

5

"Good afternoon, Monsieur Marchand," Alix said, making a conscious effort to stand up straight and smile as cheerfully as her stress and fatigue would allow.

She spoke French. That at least had been one positive achievement over the past few months. She had a third language to add to her native Russian and the English she'd been taught by the KGB a decade ago. The same agency had trained her to charm any man she wanted, but Marchand seemed resolutely immune to what was left of her old powers. He was the clinic's finance director. His sole concern was the bottom line.

"Could you spare me a moment, Mademoiselle Petrova?" he said, managing to combine an obsequious, oily politeness with an unmistakable hint of menace. He waited until she had followed him out into the corridor, out of Carver's hearing, then spoke again.

"It's about Monsieur Carver's account. The payment for last month will soon be overdue. I trust there is not a problem. You should be aware that if patients are unable to settle their accounts, it is the clinic's policy to terminate their treatment."

"I quite understand," said Alix. "There is no problem. The account will be settled."

Marchand gave a curt nod of acknowledgment and farewell. Alix watched him walk away down the corridor. Only when he had turned the corner and was out of sight did she go back into Carver's room and slump down in the visitor's chair, holding her head in her hands.

Somewhere Carver had a fortune, the profits of his deadly trade, banked in an anonymous offshore account, or stashed in safe-deposit boxes and private hiding places. The money would keep Marchand satisfied for years, but only Carver had ever known where it was. And now he had no clue that it even existed.

He had at least been blessed by one benefactor. Thor Larsson, the tall, skinny, dreadlocked Norwegian who was Carver's technician, computer expert, and closest friend, had given Alix access to Carver's flat. Using money paid to him by Carver, he had done his best to meet the sanatorium bills. But now that money was running out and Larsson had nothing more to give.

Alix would happily have paid her share, but she had no formal identification papers and no work or residency permits, and thus no way of getting a respectable job. In any case, she spent every day at Carver's side. All she'd been able to find was a late-night waitress gig in a sleazy *bierkeller,* whose owner was only too happy to turn a blind eye to Swiss employment law if he could hire pliable, immigrant women on the cheap. As he liked to remind his girls, Switzerland had no minimum wage. Alix just about made ends meet from her tips, but she couldn't hope to pay Carver's bills as well. Not if she stuck to waitressing.

6

L ev Yusov was fifty-two years old, though to Western eyes he would have seemed at least a decade older. He smoked too many coarse, unfiltered cigarettes. He drank too much cheap vodka. His single-room apartment lacked ventilation in the summer and heating in the winter. The walls were peeling and the window frames were rotting. But Yusov was no worse off than anyone else in the 12th GUMO.

The workers of Russia's 12th *Glavnoye Upravleniye Ministerstvo Oborony*, or Main Directorate of the Ministry of Defense, were just like every other employee of the once-mighty state. Their wages were pitiful, when they were paid at all. Their living conditions got worse by the day. The staff at one 12th GUMO base had recently gone on a hunger strike, demanding to be paid the money and benefits that they had been owed for months. Even officers had started protesting that they couldn't get by without taking a second job.

This dissatisfaction was significant for one very simple reason. The 12th GUMO was the organization responsible for the administration, storage, security, and safety of Russia's nuclear weapons. When its people became angry and resentful, they were in a position to cause serious trouble. And for Lev Yusov, anger and resentment were his default states of mind.

A lifetime spent in the service of the Motherland had left him little more than a glorified filing clerk, sitting behind a counter in a provincial depot, checking papers in and out, taking orders from officers no better than him, or—which was even worse—their stuck-up personal secretaries. He knew he was just an anonymous old drudge in their eyes, an insignificant functionary whose only means of exercising power lay in his ability to be unhelpful. Yusov exercised that power to the full.

Woe betide the request that was not made exactly as the regulations required, or the form that was incorrectly filled in. His capacity for nit-picking, obstruction, and sheer bloody-mindedness, honed by decades of experience, had become legendary. No one went down to Yusov's grim, windowless basement kingdom if they could possibly avoid it. No one socialized with him or passed the time of day. And so, when Alexander Lebed went on American TV, talking about missing nukes, and set off a frenzy of backside-covering within the 12th GUMO, as senior officers desperately strove to find out whether these bombs existed and, if so, what had actually happened to them (before passing the buck as far and as fast as they possibly could), no one thought to ask Lev Yusov whether he had any files on the subject, tucked away on the rows of shelves that stretched into the darkness behind him.

This exclusion was just one more drop in the acidic lake of Yusov's bitterness. The more he was ignored, the more he sat and pondered about all the documents that had passed before his eyes, documents that he cherished as his most precious, meticulously cared-for possessions. Something was nagging at the corner of his mind, an uncertain memory of a computer printout handed to him many years before, when half the ambitious young whippersnappers who now bossed him around were still in short trousers. It had contained a stream of numbers, and had been folded up and put in a cardboard envelope. This file had no name, just a reference number. Nor had there been any description of its contents. The man who had handed it to him had insisted he had no idea what it might be—just another piece of bureaucratic flotsam that had washed up in his department.

Four months of furtive but infinitely patient rummaging passed by before Yusov found the envelope. It was marked TOP SECRET and date-stamped with the 12th GUMO insignia.

He took out the computer printout. The paper was flimsy, the dot-matrix printer ink fading to pale gray, but he could still make out 127 entries arranged vertically over six pages. Each entry consisted of three number groups. The first two groups contained either ten or eleven digits, divided into three subgroups, of degrees, minutes, and seconds. The third group contained eight digits in a single sequence. One complete entry read: 49°24'29.0160"94°21'31.047"99875495.

Lev Yusov had spent his entire working life in the 12th GUMO. The first two number groups were easily understood: He knew a set of map coordinates when he saw them. Normally, such coordinates would describe a weapon's target: either the location at which it was aimed or the one it had actually hit. But what if these numbers referred not to targets, but locations? The missing weapons described by Alexander Lebed were portable. They must have been taken somewhere. Perhaps these numbers revealed where.

As for the last eight digits, Yusov assumed they referred to some sort of arming code. He knew that no nuclear weapon, be it an intercontinental missile or a single artillery shell, could be detonated without specific instructions. These numbers would provide the correct combination for each individual bomb.

Late at night, his hand clutching a half-empty bottle, Yusov considered the significance of what he had found. If he was right about the meaning of those numbers, then they were his way out of his shit flat and his shit job, and the shits he had to work with.

Someone, somewhere would pay a fortune for that list. For anyone who possessed it and the means to get at the bombs would have the whole world at his mercy.

7

War in the desert was supposed to be all about heat, sweat, and choking clouds of dust. But that was when the sun was up. This was a winter's night. Carver felt deep-frozen, colder than he had ever been, and the chattering of his teeth drowned out the scrabble of steel against dirt from the spades of the men digging down into the earth.

From where Carver stood, the holes were simply patches of blackness in the blue-gray expanse of the starlit desert.

There were seven of them, the size and depth of open graves awaiting their coffins. Or maybe this was what a goldfield looked like when the first prospectors arrived and started burrowing down for their fortunes. Carver and his men were prospecting, too, searching for the fiber-optic cable, buried somewhere beneath their feet, that kept the Iraqi dictator in touch with his troops.

Carver's team from the Special Boat Service had been allotted two hours on the ground to break that link. There were fifteen minutes left. And still no sign of any cable.

Carver shook his head in helpless frustration. There was just time to dig one more hole. He was trying to work out where to put it when there was an explosion of deafening white noise, hissing, and crackling in his ear. He could just make out a voice, almost buried beneath the distortion: "We've got company, boss. Couple of companies of mechanized infantry, heading directly at us."

"Do you think they've seen us?" Carver asked.

He was already on the run toward the perimeter, needing to see for himself, but the ground seemed to have softened, sucking at his feet like quicksand. His progress was way too slow. He wasn't going to get there in time. Meanwhile the noise in his ear was getting louder. He wanted to tear off his headphones, but now the lookout's voice was bursting into life again. "They've got mortars. Here we go . . ."

The desert silence was broken by a series of distant percussive crumps, followed by whooshes, like fireworks streaking into the sky. A few seconds later, magnesium parachute flares burst over the landing zone, scorching Carver's eyes and leaving the fifty-foot-long Chinooks as exposed in their burning white light as a pair of naked lovers surprised by an angry husband.

Now there were mortar rounds falling all across the landing zone and cannon fire cracking through the night air. Carver could hear a new voice now, one of the chopper pilots, his voice tightening as adrenaline flooded his nervous system: "We're like coconuts in a shy here. I'm starting up the rotors. You'd better get your men aboard sharpish."

Carver started issuing orders. He was shouting into his intercom, but he must not have made himself heard because the men weren't moving and even though the chopper rotors were turning at top speed, they didn't seem able to lift off the ground, and suddenly the whole landing zone was filled with Iraqis. He couldn't work out how they'd got there so fast, or why they were speaking Russian at him. He thought he recognized their faces, but they kept blurring out of focus. He pulled the trigger on his submachine gun, but no bullets came out, even though the magazine was full.

This wasn't right. This wasn't what was supposed to happen. The Chinooks were meant to take off with all his men aboard. Then the explosives would blow and cut the cable, turning an imminent fiasco into a last-minute triumph. But that wasn't happening at all, because now his men had all disappeared and he was alone with the Russians, and they were taking him through a door into a room where there was a log fire burning in an open grate. And he didn't have his combat gear on anymore, in fact he was stark naked except for a black nylon belt strapped around his waist.

There was a man in front of him, sitting in a chair, and next to him there was a woman, an incredibly beautiful woman in a silver dress. Carver cried out to the woman to help him, but she couldn't hear him, either. And that was wrong, too, because she was supposed to love him. But she didn't love him at all. In fact she was laughing at him, and all the men around her were laughing at him, too, and now the woman was looking at him with a new face, twisted, ugly, and hate-filled, and she was screaming, "Hurt him! Hurt him! I want him to suffer!"

The laughter was getting even louder and one of the men was pointing a small black box at Carver, holding a finger above a single white button. And suddenly Carver was filled with a fear that tore at his guts and dropped him to his knees, begging for mercy, though his pleas came out as wordless whimpers because he knew what was coming now—the same thing that always came at the moment that the man with the box pressed the button.

Then the finger moved down. And the agony began again.

8

"**Y**ou must let me help him, you know."

Dr. Karlheinze Geisel was the psychiatrist assigned to Carver's case. He turned away from the bed where his patient was writhing in torment, and spoke to Alix in a voice whose overlay of sympathy could not disguise his frustration.

"Come," he said, and led her out through the clinic to his consulting room.

"What do you want me to do?" she asked, when the door had closed behind them.

Geisel did not answer until they were both seated. Then he said, "You already know the answer to that question. You must tell me exactly what happened to him. How else can I provide the best treatment?"

Alix said nothing. She glanced away, brushing a strand of blond hair away from her face. Finally she turned back toward Dr. Geisel, looking directly at him.

Geisel was all too accustomed to the effects on those whose loved ones suffered serious illness. Miss Petrova had been worn down by the months of worry and uncertainty. Her face was thinner, more drawn than it had been; her complexion was pale, the skin dry and unattended; there were deep, dark rings around her eyes. But, my God, he thought, what eyes.

They were pure sky-blue, but as he looked more closely—purely in the interests of dispassionate analysis, he told himself—Geisel noticed a slight asymmetry. One lid was very slightly heavier than the other and the two eyes were fractionally out of line. This imperfection in an otherwise flawless assembly—her lips were full, her cheekbones high, her nose straight and neat—served to add to, rather than detract from, her beauty. Without it, she would merely have been very pretty. With it, she was mesmerizing.

"I understand," she said, "but I can't discuss it . . ."

"Let me be frank," he said, steeling himself. "For months you have refused my questions. But if Herr Carver is to have any hope of a recovery, I must have the information I need to treat him. You must understand—I am very used to dealing with patients who require extreme discretion. What you say to me goes no farther. But I need to know."

"If I tell you, can you make him get better?" she asked.

"No, I cannot promise that. But I can promise you this: If you do not tell me, I have no hope of helping him. The longer you remain silent, the more certain it is that Herr Carver will remain like this forever."

"I'm only trying to protect him."

Her voice was little more than a whisper. She was trying to persuade herself as much as him. Her anguish was so stark that Geisel's human instinct was to reach out and comfort her. But his professional self knew that he must do and say nothing. She had to have the space to find her way to her own decision.

Alix suspected that the timing of his approach was no accident. He must have known that she had been visited by Marchand yesterday, and had realized at once what that must mean. Carver's bills had not been paid. Unless they were, he would surely be forced to leave. So now there was a ticking clock counting down to Carver's expulsion, making the need for a cure even more desperate.

Alix struggled to defy the inexorable logic of her situation. Finally, she came to her conclusion.

"All right," she said. "I will tell you. . . . I tried to escape from a man, a Russian, like me. He was very rich, very powerful."

"Was?" asked Geisel.

Alix ignored the interruption and what it implied. "He sent his men to take me back. Carver . . . Samuel found out where I was and came after me, to Gstaad. He hoped to exchange me for . . . certain information. The man who had taken me had no intention of making the deal. His men took Samuel and . . ."

She seemed unwilling or unable to finish the sentence.

"He was harmed?" asked Geisel.

"Yes. They stripped him, blindfolded him, and put him in handcuffs. Then they . . . excuse me . . ."

She stopped for a moment to compose herself, blinking rapidly and clearing her throat.

"Sorry," she said.

"You were saying . . . ?"

When Alix spoke again, she sounded dispassionate, almost matter-of-fact. "They placed a belt around Samuel's waist. It was linked to a remote control. When the remote control was switched on, the belt gave him an electric shock, very strong, enough to make him fall to the floor and jerk around, with no control over himself. They made him do this in front of me, at my feet, to make him ashamed."

"How many times did this happen, the shock?"

"Three or four times for sure, maybe more that I didn't see."

"Was that all?"

"No, that was just the start. Afterward, they took him down to a room and tied him to a chair. The room was painted white: every wall, the floor, the ceiling, all white. It was very cold, too. They gagged his mouth with a leather strap. They taped his eyes open, so that he could not close them or even blink. They put headphones over his ears. Then they turned on lights, bright lights, right in front of his eyes. And they put noise through the earphones, so loud, without stopping. That was how I found him. He had been like that for almost four hours . . ."

"I see . . ." murmured Geisel, thoughtfully. The story was horrific, but he tried not to be shocked by what he had heard. At that moment, in the context of his consulting room, it all had to be looked on as information that might help him reach a more accurate diagnosis. Only that evening, sitting at home with a drink in his hand, might he go back and contemplate Carver's ordeal in more human terms.

"Now I understand the fear that consumes him," he continued. "His conscious brain has blanked the torture from his mind, but his subconscious dreads its repetition. Still, there is one aspect of your story that puzzles me. . . . If he was tied to this chair, completely unable to move, how did he escape?"

"I cut him from the chair," said Alix.

"But there was this man you spoke of, with other men under his command . . ."

"Yes."

"So how did you . . . ?"

"I am not your patient," said Alix. "Our conversations have no legal privilege."

"Quite so. . . . Still, with one woman and many men, I'm sure that whatever you did, it must have been in self-defense."

"Exactly. It must have been like that."

Geisel nodded to himself, coming to terms with what he had just heard.

"There's something else," Alix added.

"Yes?"

"I want you to understand the man he was . . . before all this."

She paused for a moment, trying to find the right words. Then she remembered that night in Paris again, and looked away from Geisel, her eyes unfocused, her concentration turned inward.

"When I first met Samuel Carver, I was trying to kill him. An hour later, I followed him into an apartment. We both knew that it had been booby-trapped. The explosives were set to detonate within thirty seconds. But I followed him into that apartment, I chose to do that, because I trusted him completely to keep me safe, and I wanted to be next to him. . . ."

Alix turned her eyes back on the psychiatrist, then glanced away again. She was almost talking to herself when she said, "I just want to be next to him again."

"I understand," Geisel replied. "And thank you, Miss Petrova. I know how hard it must have been, summoning up such painful memories."

He stood up and held out his hand to her as she rose. They shook. He did not move away, though, but kept looking at her, as if she were his patient.

"You have been through a deeply traumatic experience, too," he said. "You will need to talk to someone. Please, if you wish to arrange a consultation, do not hesitate to ask."

He smiled. "Then you will be my patient, and you can speak as openly as you like."

"Thank you, Doctor. I'll bear that in mind. Now, if you will excuse me, Samuel will be waking soon. And he needs to see me there when he does."

9

Far away in Russia, Lev Yusov was sitting in a dingy bar called Club Kabul trying to explain the significance of an apparently worthless strip of computer paper covered in numbers to Bagrat Baladze, a swarthy, mustachioed, shiny-suited psychopath in his early thirties. What with the noise in the club and the significant quantities of vodka that both men were consuming, it was not easy to convey the value of this document, particularly since Yusov was not willing to reveal its physical whereabouts until Bagrat committed to the deal.

"How can I agree to pay without seeing what I am paying for?" asked Bagrat.

"If the document is real, what will you pay me?"

"Five thousand, U.S."

Yusov had hoped for more. He knew the list would be worth millions by the time it reached its final destination. But in a land where American currency held far more value than local rubles, five thousand dollars was more than he would earn in ten years.

"Ten thousand," he said.

"Don't waste my time, old man," said Bagrat, getting to his feet. "You asked what I would pay. I told you. Go screw yourself if you're not interested."

"All right, all right!" yelped Yusov, watching his jackpot leave the table. "Five thousand."

Bagrat turned to one of his henchmen. "You see? He has the wisdom of the old." He sat back down and pulled a wad of cash from his jacket. He placed it on the table between them.

"Here is the money. Now where is the list?"

Yusov reached a hand behind his back and pulled the envelope out of his trousers. He opened it and took out the list.

"Look," he said. "First the latitude, then longitude, then arming code. You could fight a world war with the weapons on this paper."

Bagrat considered this proposition, then nodded. "Okay, we have a deal. Take your money."

He pushed the wad of cash toward Yusov, who grabbed at it with an eagerness that betrayed his desperation. He looked as if he wanted to make a run for it before the gangster could change his mind. But Bagrat put a hand on his shoulder.

"No need to rush," he said. "I have more business to do, but you should stay and celebrate. Enjoy yourself . . . on the house."

Bagrat picked up the envelope and left. On his way from the table, he shouted at the barman. "Bring vodka for my friend . . . the special vodka, got that? The best!"

Moonshine vodka, or *samogon*, is a noxious spirit, brewed in illegal stills all across Russia. Its ingredients include (but are not limited to) medical disinfectant, brake fluid, lighter fuel, cheap aftershave, and even sulfuric acid. Thousands of Russians have died over the years from drinking it, and many more have suffered blindness and chronic liver disease, so that doctors and coroners are not in the least surprised when they come across another case.

Bagrat Baladze had therefore thought twice before throwing away a particularly evil batch of *samogon*, acquired from a local bootlegger, even though its excessive toxicity had made it unsalable, even to the most desperate drunk. It occurred to him that he had stumbled on an ideal murder weapon.

When Yusov collapsed, an empty bottle at his side, he was carried to a waiting car, which drove to a quiet back street near his block of flats. The American currency was recovered, then he was dragged from the car and deposited on the pavement. The following morning, when his dead body was reported to the police, Yusov was carted off to the morgue. The postmortem was barely even cursory. No police investigation was made. The death of another insignificant drunk was not exactly a priority.

At the 12th GUMO offices, Yusov's passing was celebrated, rather than mourned. A new, younger, more cooperative clerk took over his duties.

The clerk had no idea that the missing file had ever existed, let alone been sold to an ambitious gangster who was, even now, trying to work out how he could use it to leapfrog several rungs up the criminal ladder.

There were, Bagrat knew, middlemen who specialized in setting up deals between Russians in possession of weapons—conventional, chemical, biological, and nuclear—and the wealthy customers who craved them. It was his task now to find one of these traders without alerting other, more powerful criminals to the item he was trying to sell. If the word got out, they would dispose of him as swiftly as he had dealt with Yusov.

So Bagrat Baladze began making inquiries. And the world took a first, blind step on the road to Armageddon.

10

Alix took the bus back into Geneva after another long day at the clinic, then walked across the Rhone River and uphill, through the narrow, cobbled streets of the Old Town, lined with centuries-old houses as tall and thin as books on a shelf. The windows of the chocolate shops were filled with heart-shaped boxes. The boutiques and designer stores were given over to lingerie and seductive dresses. The banks watched over them all, knowing, as always, that everything, including love, had its price.

She stopped for a moment to look at a mannequin in a short black party frock and shoes that were little more than a pair of teetering heels and a couple of slim leather straps.

She had once dressed like that, choosing her clothes with the confidence that came from being sure of their effect. She wanted to be that woman again, with a drink in one hand and her handsome man in the other. But the reflection in the shop window showed a sorry creature, wearing a charity-shop coat and cheap, unflattering denims. Somehow, in the next hour or so, she had to paint on a facsimile of what had been her natural beauty, a fake that would be good enough to fool the *bierkeller* customers, drunken men with groping fingers who expected a visual treat to accompany their overpriced drinks.

She got back to Carver's flat. The rooms were emptying fast as the furniture was sold to meet the sanatorium's endless demands. She missed the huge Chesterfield sofa and the antique leather armchairs that had been all the more inviting for being softened and worn by decades of use. His beloved widescreen TV and hi-fi system were gone, too, along with all the paintings, save one. It hung above the fireplace in the living room, a bright, impressionistic depiction of a Victorian day out at the beach, the women lifting their skirts and the men rolling up their trousers, a tableau of innocent pleasures.

Alix only had to look at the picture to remember the afternoon when she had first seen it. She'd been wearing one of his old T-shirts and had curled up in an armchair as cozily as a sleepy cat, watching Carver as he walked through the dusty beams of afternoon light that angled in through the windows of his top-floor flat. He'd walked with an easy, animal grace, then leaned across her chair. She'd felt his eyes skimming over her before he handed over one of the cups of coffee he'd been holding. He'd seen her looking at the picture.

"It's Lulworth Cove," he said, "on the Dorset coast, west of my old base."

"It's very beautiful. What was this base?"

Carver had laughed. "I can't tell you that. You might be a dangerous Russian spy."

She'd smiled and said, "Oh, no, I'm not a spy. Not anymore." She was telling the truth. That afternoon in Carver's flat, for once in her life, she'd been a normal woman, surrendering to the blissful indulgence of falling in love.

That dream had been torn away from her. There was no point in clinging to some pathetic, girlish illusion of romance. In the real world there was no such thing, just an endless fight for survival, a fight that had no concern for scruples or principles. When everything else was stripped away, there were only two issues to consider: how badly she wanted to survive, and what she was prepared to do in pursuit of that survival.

11

Kurt Vermulen's cell phone started buzzing right in the middle of dinner. He flipped it open and took a look at the name on the screen. Then he turned to the three other people sharing the table at an Italian restaurant in the Georgetown district of Washington, D.C., a rueful half-smile on his face, and said, "I'm really sorry—got to take this one."

Yet, as he said, "Hang on," into the phone and got up from his place, making his way to the door, the truth was he felt relieved.

Bob and Terri had meant well, setting him up at a dinner for four with Megan, a single, thirty-nine-year-old lawyer. She was a hot date: attractive, smart, and happy to leave her litigator's aggression in the courtroom. He was pretty sure she liked him, too. That was the problem.

Eighteen months had passed since Amy died, and he still couldn't get his head around the whole dating game. They'd met the summer before they went to college, 1964; two kids who'd bumped into each other in a Pittsburgh music store, both trying to buy the last copy of *A Hard Day's Night*. And that was that—the start of thirty-two years together, their one regret that they hadn't had children, till Amy got breast cancer and suddenly, the one thing he'd never expected, he was the one left alive and alone.

All that time, her presence in his life had been one of the things that defined him, as much a part of his identity as his blue eyes or his sandy hair. Now that she was gone, he felt incomplete. But even worse than that, he couldn't figure out how to make himself whole again. With Amy, everything had been natural. So much was understood, unspoken. But now it all had to be explained from scratch, and he wasn't sure he was up to that just yet. Sure, he'd been with a couple of women. He wasn't a monk. But someone like Megan deserved better than a casual fling. And Kurt Vermulen didn't know that he could give it.

Not when he had the fate of the world on his mind.

He was outside the restaurant now, stepping onto Wisconsin Avenue, feeling the quick chill of a January night. "Okay, Frank, I can talk now—what's the news?"

"Not good, Kurt. I raised your concerns with the Secretary of State, but the feeling, right around the department, is that they just flat-out disagree with your assessment. Don't get me wrong—everyone really respects what you've accomplished, but they just don't see the situation the way you do."

"What? Don't they believe what I'm saying?"

"Not really. But even if they did, no one wants to know. I mean, we've made our position clear, as an administration. We've picked the horse we're going to ride and it's too late to change it now."

"Well, you picked the wrong one."

"Maybe, Kurt, but everyone's happy with the decision—State, the Pentagon, Langley—you're the odd one out on this. Look . . . we all know you've had a rough time the past couple of years, so why beat your head against the wall on this one issue? No one sees it as a priority going forward. Don't throw away a reputation you've spent decades building up over a bunch of crazies. Trust me, man, they're not worth it."

"Thanks for the advice, Frank," said Vermulen. "Give my regards to Martha."

He snapped the phone shut, as if that physical act of closure could contain the frustration burning inside him. All his career he'd been an insider, a man whose analysis was respected, whose judgment was trusted. Now he was out in the cold, saying things that no one wanted to hear. Sometimes he felt like one of those movie characters who get shut away in an asylum, even though they're sane. The more he shouted he wasn't crazy, the more everyone thought he was. Was this how Winston Churchill had felt, telling his people that the Nazis were a deadly menace when all anyone wanted was peace at any cost?

He shook his head at his own presumption. Comparing himself to Churchill: Maybe he was going nuts. Meanwhile, there was a good-looking lawyer waiting inside the restaurant, expecting him to make some kind of sophisticated, grown-up pass at her. Screw global security—that was the first problem he had to solve.

Vermulen was about to step back inside when a man caught his eye across the far side of the road. He was medium height, skinny build, wearing a brown leather jacket, the gray hoodie underneath it hiding his face. There was nothing unusual about that, not in January. Nothing unreasonable about him walking fast, either, keeping the blood circulating. There was just something about the way he was doing it, pushing past people on the sidewalk. He didn't look like he had anything good on his mind.

Vermulen saw the glint of steel in the streetlight as the man pulled a knife from his pants. He saw the woman looking at some shoes in a store-window display. He knew at once, with absolute certainty, that she was the reason the man had drawn his knife.

And then he was running across the road, dodging the traffic, praying he could get there in time.

The man had come up to the woman and grabbed her arm and was snarling threats and obscenities in her ear. Vermulen saw the shock take hold, leaving her wide-eyed and paralyzed, unable to obey the mugger's instructions, her mouth open but no sound emerging.

He shouted out, "Hey!" Just a noise to distract the guy.

The cowled head turned and Vermulen felt the raw, drug-fueled rage in the man's eyes, then the jittery panic that filled them as the mugger realized he was under threat.

The man slashed with his knife, slicing through the strap of the woman's handbag and the sleeve of her coat. He grabbed the bag and started running.

There were people all around. They were looking at what was happening, shying away, not wanting to get involved, some scattering as Vermulen burst through them, carried on past the woman, and pursued the man up the street.

He took maybe twenty quick strides down the sidewalk, then pulled up. It would make him feel good to catch the dirtbag and teach him a lesson. But there was a woman standing frightened, alone, and quite possibly wounded. She was the priority now.

He turned back to her, walking slowly, trying not to add to her fear and distress.

"Are you okay? Here, let me look at your arm," he said, when he reached her.

And that's when she burst into tears.

"I'm sorry," she said between sobs, as though it were she who had done something wrong.

Gently, he helped her ease her arm from the sleeve of her coat. Her blouse had been cut right through and there was a little blood on her arm, but it didn't look too serious.

"You're lucky—just a scratch," Vermulen said. "We can get you to an emergency room, to be on the safe side. Or would you rather go straight home?"

"I just want to get back to my hotel," she said, and started crying again. "I'm sorry," she repeated.

"Don't be. You've had a shock. It's natural. Where are you staying?"

"The Georgetown Inn," she said. "It's only a couple of blocks. That's why I thought it would be okay to take a walk, you know? I mean, just around the corner, get some fresh air . . . Oh, God . . . My bag, I had everything in there. . . ."

"Here, I'll walk you back," he said, taking her good arm.

It took only a couple of minutes. Along the way they exchanged names. The woman was Sandra Marcotti, in town for a meeting with a firm of lobbyists. At the hotel, Vermulen spoke to the front desk, explained what had happened, and left his contact details. Then he gave the woman his business card, and shook her hand, quite formally.

"Good night. You take care now, ma'am. If there's anything you need, anything at all, just call."

As he left, Sandra Marcotti looked at his card for the first time. At the top it said, VERMULEN STRATEGIC CONSULTANCY and then, below that, LT. GEN. KURT VERMULEN DSC, PRESIDENT.

My God, she said to herself. He's a general.

Back on the street, Vermulen got out his phone, intending to call his friends and explain his absence. Before he could dial, he noticed a flashing icon, telling him he had a message waiting.

It was a woman's voice, a southern accent: "Hello, Lieutenant General Vermulen? This is Briana, from the president's office at the Commission for National Values, here in Dallas. I know you expressed an interest in addressing our organization. Well, we have a meeting of our charter members coming up in Fairfax, Virginia, day after tomorrow, and one of our speakers has dropped out. I appreciate it's awful short notice, sir, but if you could take his place, we sure would be grateful."

Vermulen listened to the rest of the message, which gave contact details for confirming his appearance. As he walked back toward the restaurant, he looked a whole lot happier than he had walking out.

12

Finally Carver was making progress. The last few mornings he'd managed a short stroll around the gardens that surrounded the clinic. Alix went with him, patiently telling him the names of all the people they met, the same names she'd told him just the day before. They played little games to see if he could find his way back to the main entrance from different parts of the grounds. On the rare occasions he succeeded, or recognized a passing face, Carver lit up with boyish glee at his own achievement. But just as often, something or someone spooked him. All that was needed was a sudden loud voice, a car backfiring, even the low winter sun dazzling his eyes, and he was plunged into a cowering, weeping anxiety that had nurses dashing over to administer sedatives and return him to his room in a wheelchair.

There came a point, as she watched his slumped body being wheeled away after another panic attack, when Alix realized she couldn't go on like this, doing nothing. It wasn't just the need for money, however acute; it was a matter of self-preservation. She had to find a way to make him better, not just for him, but for her, too: for them. With every day that went by, she could feel herself falling a little more out of love, and she hated it. Her feeling for Carver was the one true emotion in her life. To lose that would be to lose everything.

She left Carver unconscious in his bed and went back to the apartment, determined to take charge of her destiny and maybe to take charge of his. As she washed the smell and depression of the clinic from her body and hair, she reminded herself of the well-trained, resourceful agent she had once been. What would that woman do? Simple: She would steel herself, and get on with her job.

By the time she'd made lunch, she'd decided.

She dressed in the cleanest, least shapeless pair of jeans she could find, a plain white T-shirt, and her winter coat, with a scarf around her neck and a beret over her hair. She slipped her only pair of shades alongside her purse in her shoulder bag. She took a small pair of wire cutters from the household tools Carver had left in a kitchen drawer. She was ready for action, she had a plan, and just having that sense of focus, the spur of determination, made her feel better than she had in months.

Her first KGB operations had taken place in smart hotels, whether in Moscow or Leningrad. She knew how those places worked, and felt at home amid the flow of workers and guests. That's where she'd go to work now.

Her first choice was the Impérial, one of the city's classiest establishments. It attracted wealthy foreign tourists and businessmen to its rooms, and the bankers and diplomats of Geneva to its bars and restaurants. It was the perfect environment for Alix to rediscover her old magic. First, however, she had to dress for the performance, and since she lacked the means to buy the right clothes, she would have to find another way of acquiring them.

She walked right by the front of the hotel and went around the block to the staff entrance at the rear. The entrance was wide enough to admit vans into an unloading bay. To one side there was a small hut. Time clocks were fixed to the wall beyond it, where the cleaners and catering and maintenance staff clocked in and out. Alix went up to the porter standing guard in the hut and spoke in her worst French and strongest Russian accent.

"Excuse, please," she said.

The porter was reading a tabloid newspaper. He ignored her.

"Excuse," she repeated. "Have appointment with housekeeper, fifteen hours, for get job chambermaid."

The porter reluctantly dragged his eyes to the date book in front of him.

"Name?"

"Yekaterina Kratochvilova," said Alix, speaking quickly in an incomprehensible gabble of syllables.

The porter gazed helplessly at the open page, an angry frown on his face. He clearly hadn't a clue what she'd just said.

"Not here," he said. "Come back another time."

"Impossible! I make appointment. Please to look again, Yekaterina Kratochvilova."

A couple of uniformed maids walked by, turning their heads to see what the fuss was about. Alix caught their eye.

"Maybe you help," she called to them. "I come see housekeeper, have appointment. She can see me now, yes?"

The maids looked to the porter for guidance.

"It's not my decision," he insisted. "There's nothing in the book."

Alix gave the two women another pleading stare. She'd timed her performance carefully. By three in the afternoon, any guests that were leaving a hotel would have checked out and their rooms prepared for the next occupants, but few of the coming night's guests would have arrived. It was the quietest time of the working day, when even the busiest housekeeper might be able to see an unexpected job applicant.

One of the maids took pity.

"I'll go and get her," she said.

"Thank you, thank you," Alix gushed, while the porter looked on indifferently.

The maids disappeared.

Alix took a couple of steps backward, out of the light.

The porter returned to his tabloid.

A middle-aged woman appeared at the far end of the passage, tight-lipped and stern-eyed, her steel-colored hair pulled back in a bun, reading glasses hanging from a gold chain around her neck. She was talking to the chambermaid, clearly irritated by the intrusion.

It took Alix no more than a couple of seconds to fix an image of the housekeeper in her mind's eye. Then she slipped away from the entrance, unseen by anyone as she left. By the time the housekeeper got to the hut, she was long gone.

13

Kurt Vermulen looked around the banquet hall where the Commission for National Values was holding its private meeting. The room was located on the fifth floor of a modern hotel close by a shopping mall on the outskirts of Washington. The interior designer had gone for a gentlemen's club effect, with dark paneling, lights in ornate sconces, and vintage oil paintings in gilt frames. Vermulen hoped the men he'd come to address weren't equally phony.

The meal had been cleared away, and the speeches were about to begin. Vermulen, however, would have to wait his turn. For now a stocky, pugnacious man, in a sober black suit, his shock of silver hair glinting in the glow of the chandeliers, was making his way to the podium, which had been placed on a low stage just behind the top table.

His name was Reverend Ezekiel Ray. Across a swath of states in the South and Midwest he could draw crowds to hear him preach that would put platinum-shifting rock acts to shame, but today there were no more than eighty men present. No women had been invited, and the only brown faces in the room belonged to the waiters.

This select congregation belonged to the innermost core of a secretive organization, invisible to the public eye. Its membership constituted some of the heaviest hitters in American conservatism: politicians, preachers, lobbyists, strategists, lawyers, academics, and business leaders. Their congregations ran into millions, their fortunes to tens of billions. They could bankroll candidates, or boycott TV stations. Though they were, for the time being, denied control of the White House, they still wielded enormous, if well-disguised influence on their nation's politics.

The "national values" with which the commission was concerned were defined in a very particular way. They felt that it was immoral, even blasphemous, to keep God out of government. Their God, however, was a very specific, Baptist Christian deity, and they regarded the followers of Islam with a fear and hatred equaled only by the loathing that Islamists felt toward America's satanic, crusader culture.

These were not Kurt Vermulen's values. He believed in God, but his faith was a personal, private affair. When it came to the country for which he had so frequently risked his life, he believed that the Constitution was a more important document than the Bible, and that the nation's Founding Fathers knew what they were doing when they argued for the separation of Church and State.

At this moment, he wasn't in the position to debate such philosophical niceties. He needed every friend he could get, and if that meant talking to his audience in their own language, he would do it. So Vermulen aimed to pay careful attention to Ezekiel Ray: to both what he said, and how.

For a while, Ray stood in silence, acknowledging the applause that had greeted his arrival at the podium. He waited till it had risen to a crescendo before he bowed his head and clasped his hands in front of him, murmuring the words of Psalm 19: " *Let the words of my mouth, and the meditation of my heart, be acceptable in thy sight, O Lord, my strength, and my redeemer.'* "

His audience responded with a murmured "Amen." Again, the preacher let the silence build, holding himself in a pose of prayer and contemplation until he suddenly stood tall again and flashed a smile that lit up the room as brightly as the chandeliers.

"My friends," he began, "I bring you joyous news of our Savior's return! This is news of exultation for those who are brothers and sisters in Christ. But it is news of pain, and death, and eternal torment for those who have turned away from Christ, those unbelievers who mock the Lord and wallow in the sin and temptation offered by the Antichrist.

"You know the news I'm talking about. You have the words of the first letter to the Thessalonians, chapter four, verses sixteen and seventeen, engraved upon your heart. *'For the Lord himself shall descend from heaven with a shout, with the voice of the archangel, and with the trump of God: and the dead in Christ shall rise first:*

" *'Then we which are alive and remain shall be caught up together with them in the clouds, to meet the Lord in the air: and so shall we ever be with the Lord.'* "

Many of the congregation had mouthed the words as they were spoken, and murmurs of approval greeted their conclusion.

Ray nodded in acknowledgment. "Gentlemen, we only have to look around us today to see those who are pious, God-fearing, and living a life of decency and morality. But if we turn on the television, or read the poisonous words of the media elite, we see those who *mock* the word of God . . . who sneer at those who believe . . . who degrade the holy institution of matrimony . . . who wallow in decadence and fornication.

"Believe me, they will soon be cut down by the sickle of Christ, and all the followers of the Antichrist with them. For their day of reckoning is coming soon, as the word of the Lord makes plain.

"Consider the second epistle of Timothy, chapter three: *'In the last days perilous times shall come. For men shall be lovers of their own selves, covetous, boasters, proud, blasphemers, disobedient to parents, unthankful, unholy, without natural affection . . . despisers of those that are good . . . lovers of pleasures more than lovers of God.'*

"The Gospel of Matthew, chapter twenty-four, warns that *'nation shall rise against nation, and kingdom against kingdom . . . And many false prophets shall rise . . . iniquity shall abound.'*

"Sounds familiar. Sounds like the world today. So now we wait for the final warning that the end is nigh, the arrival upon the earth of Satan himself. Gentlemen, you must be on your guard. For Satan will come soon, and when he does come we must make ready for war.

"We know where that last, great battle will take place, for it is written that *'he gathered them together into a place called in the Hebrew tongue Armageddon.'*

"As you know, this place truly exists. It is the hill of Megiddo, which stands in the land of Israel. And you can visit this place. You can see it with your own eyes.

"But do not be afraid of this great battle. For the Christ who will return in glory is a mighty Christ, a warrior Christ, riding on a white charger, a Christ who will make His enemies tremble. So be joyful that He comes. Be happy that you will be saved. But be prepared for that final conflict between good and evil.

"For He is Christ . . .

"He brings us rapture . . .

"And He is on His way!"

As the shouts of "Amen!" rang around him, and the Reverend Eze-kiel Ray settled back down in his seat, accepting handshakes and back-slaps from the men on either side, Kurt Vermulen clapped politely. He was assessing the room as he'd so often assessed a battlefield, looking for strong points and weaknesses, calculating threats and opportuni-ties, seeking out hidden dangers. Above all, he was considering the men he was about to face. He knew now exactly what his audience wanted to hear. But could he give it to them?

He was about to find out.

14

I t was half past six, and Alix was sitting on a bus, three rows behind the housekeeper, as she made her journey home. She would, Alix knew, be carrying her own personal set of keys to virtually every working room in the hotel, as well as a pass card guaranteeing access to every guest room. Chambermaids had pass cards, too, but they were kept on cords tied around their waist so that they could not possibly be dropped or mislaid. Only staff as senior as a housekeeper were entitled to put their keys in a handbag. Somehow Alix had to get inside that bag.

It happened in a neighborhood supermarket. Alix watched as the housekeeper paused by the first aisle, reached into her bag to get her shopping list and left it open as she put on her reading glasses, then ran her finger down the piece of paper, mentally ticking off everything that she had to buy.

Alix walked by her, glancing down at the bag. There were two sets of keys clearly visible: a small ring with her car and front-door keys, and a much larger bunch of hotel keys, one of which looked like a credit card. That was the one Alix wanted.

But for the next ten minutes she had to wait, her frustration growing, unable to find an opening. The housekeeper had almost reached the checkout when she suddenly stopped dead in the middle of an aisle. She replaced her glasses on her nose, consulted her list again, hissed crossly at her own forgetfulness, and scuttled away to another aisle, leaving her cart behind her.

Alix walked steadily toward the cart. Making no sudden movements, she reached into the bag with her wire cutters and snapped the link that attached the housekeeper's pass card to her key ring. She palmed the card and put it in her own shoulder bag. At the checkout she paid for a lettuce and a jar of Bolognese sauce, then disappeared into the night.

15

Kurt Vermulen looked out from the glare of the podium into the darkness of the room beyond. He had one last chance: one shot at getting the backing he needed to make his country aware of the threat building against it in mountains and deserts thousands of miles away. The nervous energy was building inside him, adrenaline parching his mouth. Then he began.

He delivered a warning of a war that could engulf the world, a conflict to the death between religions and civilizations. And it was, he said, a war that America had brought upon itself.

"I was there when it all began," he said, his voice low-pitched but intense. "I saw our fatal mistake."

He took them back to the late summer of 1986 and the first secret shipments of Stinger antiaircraft missiles by the United States to the mujahideen, the resistance fighters battling the Soviet invasion of Afghanistan. "They called this fight the *jihad*, which literally means 'the effort,' or 'the struggle.' To them it was a battle against the enemies of Islam. It was their duty to fight in the service of their God."

Vermulen was not an orator. He was a man of action, and he spoke simply, without any of the vocal flourishes of a preacher like Ezekiel Ray. But he could feel the atmosphere in the room change as he talked about men who fought for God. This was language that the men in front of him understood, even if theirs was a different deity.

"These jihadists were given our most deadly weapons, and they were trained to use them by U.S. military advisers under my command. We thought we were teaching them to beat Commies. We forgot that we were also training them to beat us. And it wasn't till the Red Army was finally kicked out of Afghanistan in 1989 that we figured out that these warriors of the jihad didn't like Americans, or Christians, any more than they'd liked Russians. And by that point, a register had been taken of all the men who had fought as mujahideen. It was a list of names and contact details, and it was called 'the base,' or in Arabic, *al-Qaeda.*

"A year later, in August 1990, Saddam Hussein, dictator of Iraq, the Muslim leader of a Muslim nation, invaded Kuwait, another Muslim nation, and took his armies right up to the borders of Saudi Arabia. And I guess you all know how they worship there."

There was a ripple of laughter through the room, a relieved release of tension. When it died away, Vermulen said, "We beat the bad guy, gave the Kuwaitis back their country, and helped our Saudi allies. But the men of al-Qaeda and their allies in Egyptian Islamic Jihad didn't care about that. Far as they were concerned, the presence of infidel Americans in the same country as the holy shrines of Mecca and Medina was a sinful pollution. They hated us for being there and they have never forgiven us.

"So, we know these folks are out there. We know their stated intentions to fight against us, our faith, and our way of life. They have already attacked U.S. forces in Sudan, Saudia Arabia, and Aden. But it was not enough for them to kill Americans. They wanted to strike directly at America itself. You know that on February 26, 1993, Islamic terrorists detonated a fifteen-hundred-pound bomb underneath the World Trade Center in New York City. The guys who carried out that bombing had links to al-Qaeda and also to our own intelligence services. The Trade Center conspirators used a bomb-making manual originally supplied to them by the CIA. They also had access to combat manuals from our own Special Forces Warfare Center. We taught these guys to blow us up and we're still doing it.

"Just look at the civil war that has torn apart the European nation that was once Yugoslavia. Islamic jihadists trained and armed by U.S. corporations were active in Bosnia, and are joining the conflict currently starting in Kosovo. Al-Qaeda and Egyptian jihadists are operating in Albania and throughout the former Yugoslavia. Their aim is to use that war as a means of opening a back door into Western Europe. Yet the Pentagon, the State Department, and the CIA remain in total denial about the threat they pose. Gentlemen, this is madness."

For the first time, Vermulen was raising his voice and putting extra emphasis into his words. He had paced his speech like a long-distance runner waiting till the final lap before he put in his big effort.

Sitting at a table in the far corner of the room, Waylon McCabe was impressed. He was beginning to understand how Vermulen had earned three stars before his fiftieth birthday.

"I fear that we are witnessing the first skirmishes in a great war between faiths that could determine the state of the world for decades, even centuries to come," the general continued. "The soldiers of Islam won't use tanks or rockets, but bombs, strapped to their own bodies. For they are prepared to sacrifice everything, including their own lives, while too many of us lack the courage or the will to sacrifice anything at all.

"Our society is soft. Our leaders dare not confront the electorate with the truth. They do not even want to hear the truth themselves. And so I come to you, the members of the Commission for National Values, because I know you will appreciate the stakes for which we are playing.

"We are sleepwalking toward disaster. And if we do not wake up, our values, our freedom, and our faith will be murdered while we sleep.

"Thank you."

As Vermulen stepped away from the podium, he sighed with relief, and felt his shoulders drop inches as the tension finally drained away. He'd been back at his table for a couple of minutes, sitting silently, too mentally spent to make conversation with the other men at his table, when he felt a tap on his shoulder.

He turned in his seat to see an elderly man in a suit. But this was no amiable, silver-haired geezer. The face that looked down at Vermulen was as tanned and desiccated as a headhunter's trophy, pierced by eyes that burned with a feverish intensity. And though the body beneath was clad in an expensively tailored suit, Vermulen could sense that it was as lean and tough as beef jerky.

The man bent down and spoke in a rasping, dry-throated Texas accent.

"Liked what you had to say, General. The name's McCabe. I believe I could help you some. Maybe we could talk about that."

Then he turned away with a hurried "'Scuse me," and hunched over with a hand to his mouth as his whole body was wracked by a fit of coughing that seemed to tear at his lungs like a ravenous predator, ripping his chest apart.

16

Alix put on her shades, then strode right into the Hotel Impérial as if she owned the place. Confidence was the key to acceptance. Aside from the occasional casual glance as she went by, no one paid the slightest attention as she walked toward the main staircase and made her way to the first floor of guest rooms.

She walked to the end of the corridor, checked to see that there was no one else around, and knocked on a door.

"Entrez!" came the voice from within, the word spoken in a British accent: *"Orn-tray."*

Before she could get away, the door opened. A middle-aged man was standing there, fresh from the bathroom, a towel around his waist. He raised an eyebrow and looked her up and down.

"Yes? Can I help?"

"Sorry," she stammered. "Wrong room."

"Well, do come in anyway," he said, oozing an unwarranted confidence in his powers of seduction.

She shook her head and scurried away. The man stood and watched her, then retreated into his room.

She tried a second time, at the other end of the corridor. There was no reply. She slipped the pass card down the slot in the lock and a green light appeared by the door handle.

The room was unoccupied, the beds undisturbed, the closets empty.

The third room's guest wasn't in, but he was a lone male, with nothing that Alix could use.

Finally, in the fourth room she tried, she struck gold. A couple was staying there, the name SCHULTZ inscribed on their luggage tags. It looked as if they'd already gone out for the evening. There were daytime clothes scattered on the bed and chairs, damp towels on the bathroom floor, and Chanel makeup strewn around the marble basin. The woman had packed for a busy social life, because whatever she was wearing this evening, there were two more evening gowns hanging in the closet. The frocks weren't Alix's style, but the pretty pair of high-heeled black leather sandals, perched on a rack below them, fit just fine. By the time she left, five minutes later, the shoes were in her bag and her face had a freshly applied coat of foundation and blush.

On the second floor, she knocked on a door, received no answer, walked in, and found a couple making love. They had the lights down low and soft music playing. She'd raced from the room before they'd even realized she was there.

Five rooms later, she emerged with a black silk corset on under Carver's coat, and glossy scarlet lips, courtesy of another woman's Christian Dior. On the third floor Alix made excuses to an African woman about her own age and, a few doors down, a Chinese businessman hard at work at his laptop. But another room she tried provided a black skirt that clung to her in all the right places and a pair of sheer black stockings to wear beneath it.

She had been pondering the question of jewelry as she worked her way up the hotel. In one of the rooms there were a pair of simple diamond studs that would have finished her outfit off perfectly. But stealing someone's diamonds seemed a step too far, both morally and practically. You don't call the police if you can't find a skirt. But you press the panic button when your rocks go missing.

She went up another floor. When she got there, she had to use the housekeeper's card just to get out of the elevator.

On the ground floor, in the office behind the main reception desk, the hotel's duty manager was checking the latest telephone logs, trying to sort out a complaint from a guest who swore he was being overcharged. A computer printout monitored all guest-room activity, including the use of phones and key cards. The duty manager couldn't help but notice that one staff pass card was being used to gain access to numerous rooms, on at least two floors. The printer chugged and spat out another entry. The same card, this time exiting the fourth-floor elevator.

The manager sighed irritably. This distraction was the last thing he needed. He checked the pass-card number. It belonged to Madame Brix, the senior housekeeper. She had left work almost two hours ago, and it was unthinkable that she would knowingly allow anyone else to use her card.

He picked up the phone and called for the head of security.

17

s she looked in the full-length mirror, plumping up her freshly
sprayed hair, adjusting the way her breasts sat in the corset, and
examining the cut of the waist-length black jacket she'd just pur-
loined, Alix felt reborn. For the first time in months she recognized the
face looking back at her in the glass and took pleasure in her appearance. It was like meeting a bunch of long-lost friends, not just her looks,
but her feelings of self-assurance, and even power. The dowdy, down-
trodden woman she'd been that morning had vanished. This was the
real Alexandra Petrova.

Satisfied that her makeover was complete, she put her old jeans,
T-shirt, scarf, hat, and bag into one of the hotel laundry bags that were
hanging in the suite's closet. She couldn't really afford to let them go,
but they were a necessary sacrifice. Only her coat, and the purse she'd
stuffed into one of its pockets, would stay with her. Next, she went into
the suite's bathroom, took a tissue from the dispenser, wiped down any
surfaces she had touched, then flushed it down the lavatory. She pulled
out one more tissue from the dispenser, to use on the door handle, then
left the suite, carrying her coat and the laundry bag.

The suite was right at the end of the corridor, by the emergency exit.
As she passed it, Alix thought she heard footsteps. She opened the door
a fraction and listened. Yes, there were definitely footsteps, several of
them, coming up the stairs, still some flights below. She muttered a Russian expletive under her breath. The housekeeper must have reported
her missing key. They were after her.

She glanced down the corridor. If there were men coming up the
stairs, others would be using the elevator. She prayed she had enough
time. Leaving the coat and bag by the door, she dashed back into the
suite. A pair of French windows led from the sitting room to a balcony
with views across the city. She flung the glass doors wide open, then ran
to the bathroom, wrapped the key card in toilet paper to make it sink,

and flushed that, too. Then she bolted to the door, leaving it open as she went.

The footsteps from the stairway were much louder now. They couldn't be more than a floor below her.

Alix started walking toward the elevator. Along the way, she draped the laundry bag around the door handle of another room. The house-keeping staff would pick it up and clean everything inside, removing any trace of her identity.

When the elevator doors opened and the hotel security chief and his men stepped out, she was there to meet them. Every single one of those men saw a hot blonde casually leaning against the corridor wall with her hands behind her back and her tits poking out of a sexy corset. Not one of them saw a thief holding a coat. By the time the doors of the elevator had closed behind them, she had slipped by and was pressing the button for the ground floor.

Alix sauntered into the hotel bar. The men's gazes warmed her like sunlight, making her blossom. The women's eyes were a challenge she was ready to overcome. Her back was straighter, her head held more proudly, her walk just a twitch more flirtatious in her tightly cut skirt and teetering heels. She thought of the last time she'd done this and the night that had followed. Then she ordered a kir royale.

"Please charge it to Room one thirty-eight," she told the barman as she took a stool by the counter. "The name is Schultz."

She cast a practiced eye around the bar, looking for the best marks. A man sitting alone at a table, just across the room, caught her eye. His dark hair, slicked back across a tanned but balding crown, was just graying at the temples. His dark-blue suit was immaculate, his silk tie perfectly chosen to complement the sky-blue cotton shirt. The watch was a gold Mariner model, on a polished brown leather strap. He was, in short, the epitome of sophisticated, middle-aged European wealth. And he was looking at Alix with a smile playing around the corner of his mouth that suggested he knew exactly what she was up to. And he didn't mind at all.

She pretended not to pay him any attention. But from the corner of her eye, she saw him summon a waiter and hand him a piece of paper.

Half a minute later, a freshly sparkling glass of kir appeared beside her. Slipped beneath the glass was a note. It simply read, *Ponti, 446, 10 mins.* By the time she turned around to acknowledge the message, his table was empty. She was impressed. This man was as practiced as she was.

So now the deal was on the table. All she had to do was go upstairs and fulfill her side of a civilized, adult transaction. All her years of experience, and his own calm assessment of the situation, suggested that Ponti would prove an adept, experienced lover. He would not be grudging or ungenerous. If the night went well and he was a regular visitor to the city, he might very well suggest a more regular arrangement. Her financial security would be assured, and with it Carver's treatment. As these arrangements went, it would be as good as she could possibly expect.

And that was what made her realize that she simply could not go through with it. She couldn't fool herself anymore. Even more important, she couldn't save Carver on those terms. She tried to imagine what he would think if he knew what she was doing. Would he tell her to go ahead?

The question was no sooner asked than answered.

She left the bar, picked up her coat from the cloakroom, and walked from the hotel, feeling utterly deflated.

All her newfound confidence had disappeared, leaving her even more bereft than before. She had tried to determine her own future, and save the man she loved, but her efforts had been futile. Her defeat was absolute.

18

The years since Waylon McCabe's fall from the sky had treated him well. His image had been transformed by his religious conversion. Gone were the accusations of brutal business practices, political corruption, and environmental vandalism. Now McCabe was hailed as a philanthropist, donor to a billion-dollar charitable endowment, and a man of profound religious principles. In the official report, compiled by Canada's Civil Aviation board, the crash had been classified as an accident. But McCabe didn't believe that for one second. Someone had been out to get him, and they'd damn near succeeded.

If he had to put money on it, he'd bet it was that mechanic—LUNDIN was the name on his badge—coming into the airport lounge, practically begging him to get on that plane. He'd been up to Inuvik plenty of times, but he'd never seen that mechanic before. Probably never see him again, either, which was a pity.

He'd have liked to shake the man's hand.

Recently, however, things had changed. Now he wasn't feeling quite so charitable. A shadow had fallen over his life, casting him in a darkness that filled him with dread. Just thinking about it made his heart pound and his mind panic. He was glad of the distraction when he heard the knock on the door. By the time he opened it to greet Kurt Vermulen, McCabe was back in control, displaying no signs of unease, his usual, impregnable self once again.

He motioned Vermulen to sit down and poured him a whiskey. Then he served himself and relaxed into the chair opposite. As he sat, his trouser legs rode up to reveal the ornate leatherwork on his five-thousand-dollar custom-made black boots from Tex Robin of Abilene. His suit might come from some fancy tailor in New York City, but his boots were pure Texas.

"So, you think this al-Qaeda is a real threat?" McCabe asked, opening the conversation.

Vermulen nodded. "I think it constitutes a clear and present danger to the security of the United States and our allies, yes."

McCabe had been born-again for five years now, but he had never stopped thinking like a businessman. He still saw the world in terms of transactions.

"So why don't we sit down with them, figure out what they want, try to make a deal?" he asked.

"There is no deal to be made," said Vermulen, with absolute certainty. "They aren't interested in negotiations. You can't reason with them, can't appease them or change their minds. They know what they want and they won't settle for anything less."

"And that is . . . ?"

Vermulen had the list hardwired: "The removal of all U.S. troops from Saudi soil, the destruction of Israel, the toppling of all Middle Eastern governments with friendly ties to the West, and the setting up of a global Muslim state governed by Muslim religious law. They call it the Caliphate."

"These people must have a leader," said McCabe. "Who is he, what's he like?"

"They call him the Sheikh." Vermulen swirled the whiskey in his glass, contemplating the patterns of light shining through it as he collected his thoughts.

"When I knew him, back in Peshawar, he was about thirty, still a young man. He had dark hair, a thick beard. He was tall and very slim— very rich, too, a sophisticated, educated guy, with relatives who are living, right now, right here in the States. But he dressed in simple robes and barely ate anything: A loaf of unleavened bread, some yogurt, and a handful of rice—that was like a feast. His people knew that if they were going hungry, so was he. He's an inspirational orator, a natural commander, strong and fearless in combat. I mean, I believe he's evil, all right, but I've got to tell you, this is one impressive individual."

McCabe's face gave nothing away. Inside, though, he was exultant. His instinct had been right: Vermulen was describing the Antichrist. The prophecies were coming true. A path was lighting up before him, a route to salvation and immortality.

"Let me get this straight," he said. "This Sheikh has a personal army. He can bend people to his will, he wants to destroy the Jews, he hates

Christianity, and he aims to see the rule of Allah across the world. Is that what you're saying?"

"That would be a fair summary. You see, to a devout Muslim, the earth is divided in two. First, there's the Muslim world, where they can pursue their religion in safety and follow Islamic law. They call that *Dar al-Islam,* which means the House of Peace. The rest of the world, that's *Dar al-Harb,* the House of War. And the radical, fundamentalist Islamic scholars maintain that those who live in the House of War have no right to live. In fact, it's a religious duty to kill them. And what they mean by that is, kill us, Americans."

"But you've tried to warn people . . ."

"As much as I can. I speak to contacts in Washington, the people I do business with every day. I just lay out the evidence, Mr. McCabe. Try to persuade them to see things the way I do."

"It ain't workin', though, is it, General? You're tryin' to make your case, but you don't have enough to convince the jury."

Vermulen grimaced. "Seems like it."

McCabe gave a sympathetic shrug, drawing Vermulen in, painting himself as the ally he needed.

"Well, I guess that's their problem, 'cause you sure convinced me. I can feel that war comin', and I want to help you raise the alarm. But you'd better think about how you're gonna make folks come around to your point of view. I mean, if you can't find the evidence you need, you're gonna have to go right ahead and create some. Wouldn't be the first time. Johnson did it with the Gulf of Tonkin, draggin' us into Vietnam. Hell, I'm old enough to remember when Roosevelt did it at Pearl Harbor."

"I don't think that was anything other than enemy action."

"Whatever you say, General, but plenty of folks say otherwise. Fact remains, you need a Pearl Harbor of your own, somethin' spectacular, a moment of revelation that's gonna make the whole world sit up and focus on the threat we face."

McCabe was focusing the entire weight of his personality on Vermulen, bringing to bear all the persuasive, almost seductive powers of negotiation acquired over a lifetime of buying low, selling high, and always coming out on the right side of the deal.

"You know, General, you've got me thinkin'—heck, you've inspired me. We're gonna do somethin' great, you an' me, and I'll tell you when it's gonna happen: Easter Sunday, the day we celebrate the conquest of evil and death. If you're lookin' for a time to strike back at the Antichrist, go ahead and name me a better one."

McCabe did not wait for a reply before he went on.

"Let me see," he said, pulling a slim black appointment book from a jacket pocket and flicking through its pages. "Here we go . . . this year, Easter's April the twelfth, more'n two months away. So I suggest you think awhile on what I said. When you figure something out that can suit both our purposes, come and tell me about it. If I like what I hear, I'll pay whatever it costs to make it happen."

As he showed Vermulen to the door, McCabe said, "We're gonna work well together, General, I can feel it. That Sheikh's about to find out he ain't the only dog in this fight."

McCabe had said his final words with a grin, and ended them with a wheezing cackle, but as he closed the door behind Vermulen, his good humor vanished as if it had never been.

Alone in the room, with nothing and no one else there to distract him, the darkness fell on him again. His mind was filled with a secret terror as powerful as anything he had experienced as his plane fell from the Canadian sky.

Just a few weeks before, unable to shake the cough that had dogged him all winter, he had finally gone to see his doctor. Within hours he'd been referred to an oncologist at the M. D. Anderson Cancer Center in Houston. By the end of the week he'd got a second opinion, just to make sure, from the top man at Sloan-Kettering in New York.

Both said the same thing. McCabe had two inoperable tumors on his lungs. The cancer had also spread to his brain. The doctors weren't certain, but they thought the cancer might have been caused by the chemicals he'd inhaled inside that burning plane. McCabe could see the bitter irony in that: His assassin had got him after all. He had only months to live, nine at the outside, but he'd be hospitalized in six. He was heading downhill toward a yawning grave. And so the fear that gripped McCabe's heart and ate away at his mind was that he might pass before the great day came.

Of course, he believed in the resurrection of the body and the life everlasting. He reaffirmed that faith every week in church. But his faith was no defense when the thought of his own nonexistence gripped him in the darkest hours of the night. Despite the comforting words of the creed, he could not be certain of being woken from that last, great sleep. He wanted, more than anything else, to be alive, with his eyes wide open, on that great day when the Lord returned to His people. He longed to see the holocaust of which the Reverend Ezekiel Ray had spoken, when Christ would crush the grapes of wrath and the blood of His enemies would fill the valleys of Israel to the brim.

If that holocaust wasn't going to happen of its own accord, well, Waylon McCabe was damn well going to make it happen, even if it cost him every last dime he had. And Lieutenant General Kurt Vermulen, whose passionate conviction and desperate need to be believed had left him hopelessly vulnerable to McCabe's manipulation, was just the man to help him do it.

19

Mission Date: September 25, 1995
Location: Riverview Towers, Charoen Nakorn, Bangkok, Thailand
Target: Wu Chiu Wai, alias Tony Wu
Mission Statement: To eliminate a major drug trafficker, with established ties to U.K. and European heroin trade
Operative: Samuel Carver (Fee: US $350K)

Report: The target was known to play a regular weekly mah-jongg game with three of his closest associates, gambling for significant sums of money, with US $1m or more regularly changing hands in a single night. The participants also laid six- and seven-figure bets with one another on the results of soccer matches in Asia and the English Premier League, and horse races in Bangkok, Macao, and Hong Kong. It can reasonably be inferred that both match- and race-fixing took place as a direct result of these wagers.

The location of the game was a luxury penthouse apartment, on the twenty-fifth floor of a newly built apartment complex overlooking the Chao Phraya River, chosen by Wu for security purposes. It was the sole property on the top floor of the complex. The only internal access to the apartment was provided by a non-stop express elevator, with armed guards at both the ground and top floors. The apartment also possessed its own private water, power, and air-conditioning facilities, separate from those of the complex as a whole.

Freelance operative Carver determined that these security measures in fact made the apartment more, not less, vulnerable. He made his assault via the roof of the building, at approximately 1:45 A.M. on the morning of September 25. The weather conditions that night were severe, with thunderstorms and torrential downpours. These made the initial stages of the operation far more hazardous, but also provided useful cover.

Carver made his initial approach via helicopter (see separate accounts sheet for detailed cost breakdown of this and other expenses). It hovered over the Riverview Towers for less than five seconds. Using an SBS-standard two-inch hemp rope affixed to the roof of the helicopter, Carver descended to the roof at high speed, braking with his hands, clad in heavy-duty leather gloves, immediately before impact. Donning protective equipment, he then proceeded to the rooftop vent used to feed the apartment's air-conditioning system and inserted a canister of fentanyl gas, a fast-acting opium-based sedative.

Allowing five minutes for the gas to take effect, Carver climbed down to the external terrace running along one side of the penthouse and, having checked that Wu and his associates were sedated, used a glass cutter to break in through the plate-glass doors leading from the main living area, where the men had been gambling.

The only armed men on the premises were Wu, who carried a Glock 22 pistol, and his bodyguard, who was armed with a Steyr MPi69 submachine gun. All the other players had been searched prior to being allowed into the apartment.

Carver first ensured that all four gamblers were sitting upright around the gaming table. He then proceeded into the apartment's entrance hall and dragged the bodyguard, who was also unconscious, into the living area.

Next, Carver extracted Wu's Glock pistol from his shoulder holster, placed it in Wu's hand, and fired three shots: two into the wall directly behind the bodyguard's unconscious body, and one into the bodyguard's skull, where, being a low-caliber round, it lodged, killing the bodyguard instantly.

Using the bodyguard's submachine gun, Carver then fired a series of short bursts around the mah-jongg table, terminating all four men. He also ensured that a number of rounds missed their apparent targets and hit the plateglass doors, thereby destroying any trace of the hole he had made to gain access.

Having signaled to the helicopter that he was ready to make his exit, Carver then used the gamblers' cigarettes (all four had been smoking heavily) to start a fire in the apartment. He retraced his steps back onto the terrace and up to the roof. He had been winched back up into the helicopter before the fire alarm sounded in the apartment, triggering automatic sprinklers, which drenched the living area with water, greatly impeding the subsequent work of forensic investigators.

When police detectives were called to the scene, they concluded that the bodyguard had been hired to carry out Wu's assassination, but had been killed in the attempt. One zealous forensics officer has attempted to point out various anomalies in the blood-spray patterns and body positions of the victims, but his observations have been ignored. Local police authorities and politicians have been far too busy gloating over the death of a major gangster to worry about the finer details of his demise.

Conclusion: This was a daring plan, executed with exemplary resolve and thoroughness by an operative who acts calmly and with extreme ruthlessness in high-pressure situations. My judgment is that Samuel Carver can be trusted with our most important and sensitive operations, and I would not hesitate to call upon his services in future.

Quentin Trench, Operations Director

"Well, you called upon him, all right, didn't you?" muttered Jack Grantham to himself, as he put down the report, just one of the files seized when the Consortium had been discreetly, but permanently, shut down.

Grantham was a rising star in the British Secret Intelligence Service, otherwise known as MI6. His official record was one of constant achievement, flawless political judgment, and immaculate career management. He had, however, made one decision that could, if publicly revealed, ruin his career. That did not make it a bad call, simply one that had unavoidable downsides.

On September 3, 1997, Grantham had captured Samuel Carver, with the help of a colleague in MI5. By then he'd been fully aware of what

Carver had done a few nights earlier in that Paris underpass. He knew, however, that a public trial was in nobody's interest. So he had taken another route. Like a bureaucratic Mephistopheles, he had taken possession of Carver's soul.

"I own you," he said. "You have a debt against your name that can never be redeemed. But you can make reparations. You can do things for me, for your country. If you get killed along the way, tough. If you succeed, you've done some good to set against the harm."

Next, he let Carver fly to Switzerland to confront Yuri Zhukovski, the Russian oligarch who had been the silent force behind the Paris attack. Now Zhukovski was dead, and Carver had lost his mind.

It was, in some respects, disappointing that he had been placed so firmly out of action. It would have been useful to have a man like that available: off the books, and totally deniable. Then again, something would have gone wrong. Something always did. Meanwhile, Carver was in no state to tell anyone anything.

On balance, Grantham concluded, that was an excellent result all around.

FEBRUARY

20

Samuel Carver knew that he had once been a marine, but only because Alix had told him. She also said that he'd fought in the Special Forces, and explained to him what that entailed.

"I know how to do parachute jumps and swim underwater," Carver proudly told people at the clinic. "And I can fire guns and do explosions."

Yet he had no real concept of what those words meant, no sense of how it felt to do the things they described.

Carver didn't care. There was a smile on his face that was breaking Alix's heart.

He was taking a fitness class with half a dozen other patients. Some of them had become his friends. He had introduced them to Alix, these wrecked individuals as helpless and dependent as he was, each one making her feel like a mother confronted with a group of dysfunctional children. But of all of them, only Carver threw himself into it, heart and soul. He really tried, and when the instructor called out, "Good work, Samuel!" his face was suffused with a glow of happiness.

The old Samuel Carver would rather have died than live as this grinning simpleton.

So perhaps it was for the best that he had no memory whatsoever of his previous self. He had no awareness of the confidence he had once possessed in his abilities, nor the power that had come from his absolute faith in his ability to defend himself, protect those he loved, and hurt his enemies. His dry, sardonic sense of humor had vanished. He'd even lost his basic, masculine need for sex.

Alix was tortured by the thought, which slipped unbidden into her mind some days, that she, too, would have been better off if Carver had died. It was a cruel, hateful notion, but it reflected an undeniable truth. As much as she was devastated by his present condition, she was angered by it, too, and angry with him. There was no upside to their relationship anymore. She gained nothing from it, other than the knowledge that she would feel even more guilty if she should ever desert him.

Yet the new Carver was sweet, and this was the strangest of all. Alix had to remind herself sometimes that the man she missed, even mourned, had been a killer whose capacity for calculated brutality was only one step away from making him a sociopath. The childlike creature he'd become was entirely without malice, incapable of doing harm. Even his smile had swapped wickedness for innocence.

But what was to become of him? In her right hand, Alix held a crumpled envelope. It contained a letter from Marchand, the clinic's financial director. He acknowledged receipt of a little over five thousand Swiss francs, paid over the previous few weeks, but regretted that it was not nearly enough to cover M. Carver's bills. Sadly, he was left with no option but to issue a deadline. The outstanding sum had to be paid within the next seven days. After that point, the patient would be asked to leave and legal proceedings would begin, with the aim of recovering the debt.

21

Kurt Vermulen came away from his meeting with Waylon McCabe asking himself what he was getting into. He knew he was in no position to be choosy. After all those months of being ignored, he could hardly say no to an influential supporter with billions in the bank. But he wasn't naïve. He presumed McCabe had an agenda of his own, motivated by religion. For Vermulen, the problem of Islamist terrorism was first and foremost a security issue: He'd emphasized the Christian element in his speech because he knew it would play with the Commission for National Values. McCabe, however, had precisely the opposite priorities and sooner or later would want to go public with his views.

Still, Vermulen had to admit McCabe was right about one thing. It wasn't enough just to tell people about the threat of Islamist terrorism; he somehow had to show it, too. McCabe was proposing what the military called a false-flag operation, designed to provoke a response by means of deception. Vermulen didn't feel too comfortable about that. Even if the ends could justify the means, he had no idea what form those means would take. For a fortnight he tried to find a solution. And then, quite by chance, it fell right into his lap.

An old acquaintance, Pavel Novak, came into town and insisted on going to a hockey game, the Caps against the Blackhawks. So Vermulen found himself watching what to him just looked like psychos on skates beating the crap out of one another, while Novak punched him on the upper arm and yelled in his ear, "This, my friend, this is real sport!"

Vermulen wasn't too sure about that. Football was his game, and the Steelers his team. But then Novak was a Czech. He had grown up in the years when hockey was a symbol of national pride, one way the Czechs could defeat their Russian oppressors. In 1968, when Red Army tanks had rumbled into Prague to crush the Czech government's faltering steps toward democracy and free speech, Novak had been a junior officer in the VZS, the Czech military intelligence service. When he became a double agent, passing secret information to the Americans, he did not for one moment see it as an act of betrayal against his country. It was an act of defiance against Communist dictatorship, just like the hockey.

The first period ended and the two teams skated from the rink. Novak relaxed in his seat and his face took on a more contemplative air. He had short gray hair, gold-framed glasses, and a full gray mustache that drooped around the sides of his mouth, giving him a permanently downcast expression.

"You know," he said, "life is simpler when it is like a hockey game. There are two sides. They both want to defeat the other. Sometimes they fight. But always they accept that there are rules. Everyone knows where they stand. Do you understand what I am saying?"

Vermulen shrugged. "I guess."

"What I mean is, when you were on one side of the Wall, and I was on the other, both sides knew the rules. They had weapons that could destroy the whole planet. Many people thought it was crazy, but it was not so crazy. After all, none of those warheads went off. But now there are no rules. Now there are not two sides, but many sides. Now the game is falling apart and now I start to get worried."

Vermulen's eyes narrowed in concentration. He had spent several years attached to the Defense Intelligence Agency, the U.S. military equivalent to the CIA. Back then he'd been Novak's handler. A dozen years on, they were both retired, both operating in the private sector. Vermulen was a military lobbyist, a consultant to governments and corporations, an adviser in multinational arms deals. Novak worked out of Prague, a middleman between military, scientific, and intelligence interests in the former Soviet Bloc and the various clients around the world to whom they wanted to sell their respective skills or information.

"Many sides means many clients, Pavel. I'd say that was good for your business."

"Most of the time, yes," the Czech agreed. "But sometimes . . . You know all those stories that the Russians have lost one hundred nuclear weapons. Suppose I told you that those stories are accurate. . . ."

"So Lebed was telling the truth?"

Novak was about to reply when an earsplitting blast of rock music suddenly pounded from the arena's public-address system. He gave a grimace of discomfort and distaste, shook his head, as if in sorrow at the sullying of his sport, and leaned toward Vermulen.

"Yes, but he was wrong in one respect." Novak was practically shouting now, but was still inaudible to anyone more than a few inches away. Even Vermulen had to strain to hear him over the music. "He said that no one knew where the bombs were. That is not completely accurate. The information will soon be available, on the open market. There is a printout. It has locations, codes, everything."

That got Vermulen's attention.

"Do you have it?"

Novak frowned and cupped a hand to his ear.

"Do . . . you . . . have . . . it?" Vermulen repeated.

The music faded away as suddenly as it had arrived.

"Not yet," said Novak, with a sigh of relief. "But I have been approached by someone wishing to sell it, someone who knows of my reputation as, you might say, an honest broker."

"But this printout, if it's accurate, and it fell into the wrong hands . . ."

"The consequences would be unthinkable. Which is why I am asking myself, Do I want to be involved? Of course, the financial rewards would be very great. But if I were to help terrorists or drug cartels obtain such power, you know, I am not sure I could live with that. Yet how can I just turn my back and let someone else make this sale? The consequences would be just as bad."

"So what do you want me to do?"

"What you always did—take my information to those who need to hear it. You have many friends still at the Pentagon, even in the White House itself. Explain the situation. Maybe we can come to some arrangement, yes? After all, I must cover my costs."

"Okay, maybe I can help. But I need more information. These items, on this list, are they all in America?"

"Not all, no . . . I cannot be certain, but my impression is some are in America, others in Europe, maybe even Asia, too."

"Just NATO countries and allies?"

Novak raised his eyebrows, apparently amazed by Vermulen's naïveté.

"Ach, please, my old friend, I do not need to see the list to know the answer to that question. The Russians despised and feared the rest of the Eastern Bloc even more than their enemies in the West. They knew how much we hated them. I can guarantee you, without any doubt, there will be weapons in Poland, Czech Republic, Hungary . . . all the former Warsaw Pact nations. Yugoslavia, too."

Before Vermulen could take the conversation any further, there was another blast of music and a roar from the crowd. The two teams were reappearing for the second period. Novak's face lit up again. He leaned forward in his seat, all his attention on the ice, ready to follow every shift in the swirling, kaleidoscopic patterns etched by the skaters and the puck.

Kurt Vermulen, however, sat back, motionless and silent, ignoring the game. An idea had come to him, by no means fully formed, but rich in possibilities. It involved the list that Novak had mentioned and the bombs that it contained. But it had nothing whatever to do with anyone in Washington.

At the end of the game, the two men said their farewells and went their separate ways. Neither had noticed the man sitting a few seats away with a blue nylon knapsack on his lap. Once Vermulen and Novak had left the arena, the man checked the camera whose peephole lens was peering through the shiny blue fabric. The photographs still needed to be printed. But he had every confidence that they would come out just fine.

22

The one indulgence Alix still had left was the hot, scented bath she liked to sink into before she went to work. It was the cheapest way she knew of feeling good. But this evening she had to call Larsson first. She felt bad about depending on him. He'd already done so much for her.

"They've given me a final notice," she said when he answered the phone. "One week to pay. I don't know what to do anymore."

"There's no progress, then, no chance of him remembering where he's stuck his money?"

"In a single week, I don't think so. . . . But why do we need the clinic at all? I can care for him myself."

"How?" asked Larsson. "The man's still sick. He needs constant supervision, drugs, therapy. How can you afford that? Look, if there's really no other way, I could get a loan on my apartment."

"No, that's not fair. You've been a good friend to us, Thor, but even a good friend must look after himself. . . . Hell! I've got to go to work. We'll finish this some other time."

"I'm sorry, Alix. I wish I could have done more to help you."

"You have. You listened. You cared. That was what I needed right now."

She put down the phone. There would just be time to wash her hair before she left for the club. The bath would have to wait.

In an imposing Baroque office building on Lubyanka Square, in Moscow, the conversation between Alix and Larsson was recorded, transcribed, and passed on to a duty officer. He examined it, then leaned back in his chair and stared blankly at the ceiling, losing himself in thought as he considered his opinion and how best to present it. Finally he sat upright again and put a call through to his boss's assistant.

"I need to meet the deputy director," he said. "It is a matter of the utmost urgency."

23

Waylon McCabe owned five thousand acres of Kerr County, Texas, a private kingdom between Austin and San Antonio, shaded by ancient live oaks and watered by twisting creeks and landscaped ponds. Up in the hills, a few miles from the main compound, stood a private retreat that McCabe reserved for his special guests. That was where he took Kurt Vermulen when he wanted a private conversation.

"You said you had something for me. What you got?"

Vermulen looked him in the eye. "A nuclear bomb."

McCabe didn't know if he was being taken for a fool.

"Is this some kind of joke, General?"

"Absolutely not. There are more than one hundred of them, cached around the world. They've been hidden for at least ten years. But I can obtain the document that tells me where they are."

"You don't have it yet, though?"

"No, but I expect to take possession of that information, along with the codes needed to arm the devices, within a matter of weeks. At that point, it's just a matter of acquiring one functioning weapon."

"Then what do you plan on doing with it?"

"Put it in the hands of Islamic terrorists."

McCabe's eyes widened. "Are you crazy?"

"Don't worry. . . . I'll be giving it to terrorists we've invented. A video will be sent to news agencies around the world by a radical offshoot of the Islamic jihadist movement—an offshoot that does not exist, one that has been created for this operation. The video will threaten the detonation of a nuclear bomb in a major city. The bomb will be filmed in such a way that defense analysts will immediately recognize that it is genuine."

"Then what?"

"Then the world will see that Islamic terrorists have nuclear weapons and be forced to take the threat seriously."

"What if the President tells the American people not to worry? Says that ain't no bomb, folks, just some kinda fake. What then?"

"I don't envision that happening. The evidence would be too strong. But anyway, I plan to take steps to make sure the bomb is discovered. Before it detonates, of course."

McCabe looked skeptical.

"Same problem. Special Forces or the CIA find this thing, then they say it's a fake. General, if you want people to know what it is, you've got to make it go off."

"And hit a major city? Tens of thousands of people could die. We'd be no better than terrorists ourselves."

"Sure, if it went off in a city. But why do it there? These radicals'd have some kinda hideout, somewhere they can't easily be found. Maybe they'd be in the desert, or the mountains. Detonate your bomb out there in the boondocks, no one gets hurt, but you get yourself noticed, that's for damn sure. . . . Shit!"

He'd started coughing again.

"You should see a doctor about that," said Vermulen.

McCabe spat phlegm onto the ground.

"I got a chest infection. It'll pass. You just answer one last question: How much is all this gonna cost me?"

"I haven't budgeted it yet. But you'd have to allow several million bucks."

McCabe laughed.

"Several million? That all? Hell, I thought you were gonna ask me for serious money."

McCabe was impressed. He'd set Vermulen a challenge and the general had met it. That list of nukes would bring the war against the Antichrist a whole heap closer. So now he just had to find a place where a bomb could be the fuse that would make the whole world go up in smoke. Once Vermulen had been sent on his way back to Washington, McCabe went back to the estate house, where he'd installed a library of religious books. Then he poured himself a couple of fingers of bourbon and started his research.

His first thought was the hill of Megiddo itself, but it was just an outcrop in the countryside northeast of Tel Aviv, nothing much else around it. For sure it was the site where the final battle concluded. But it wasn't the best place to start a war. For that, he needed a place that was already a flashpoint, somewhere sacred to both Christ and Antichrist alike.

He was sitting at his desk, wondering where to look next, when something caught his eye, a letter he'd recently received, asking for donations to assist the preservation of the Temple Mount in Jerusalem. Recently, the evangelical movement had found common cause with the Jews because both of them hated the Arabs. Now the Arabs were being accused of disrespecting the Jewish relics on the Mount. A lot of folks had been upset by that.

McCabe's mind started turning over. He had little knowledge of Jewish theology and none at all of Islam. But he had as good an eye for an opportunity as anyone. He could see that different religions were already arguing over Temple Mount. That sounded worth his while to check out.

The significance of the Mount soon became very obvious. The Jews believed that the exposed bedrock on Temple Mount was the very Foundation Stone from which the world had been created, the center of everything. When Abraham had offered up his son Isaac in sacrifice, that happened on Temple Mount, too. Solomon had built his temple there, and he'd placed the Ark of the Covenant in the Holy of Holies right over the Foundation Stone. So that made the Mount the most sacred site in Judaism.

It was the Muslim angle, though, that really made McCabe's head spin. He looked on Muslims as godless heathens, but the thing that blew his mind was not how different the teachings of Islam were from those of Judaism, but how similar they were.

They believed in the Foundation Stone, too. The Dome of the Rock, the oldest Islamic building in the world, had been built right on top of it. Muslims also agreed that Abraham had come to the Mount, which they called the Noble Sanctuary. Difference was, they held that he offered up his other son Ishmael for sacrifice, and that Ishmael was an ancestor of the Prophet Mohammed.

Muslim scripture stated that the Prophet had been visited in Mecca by the archangel Gabriel, who brought an animal called al-Buraq, on which he rode through the night to the stone on the Mount. Then the Prophet ascended to heaven, and met Adam, Jesus and John, Joseph, Enoch, Aaron, Moses, and Abraham, before coming face-to-face with Allah himself.

McCabe couldn't understand how the Muslims could claim prophets and angels from the Holy Bible. And what was Jesus doing in their heaven? Bottom line, though, there were now two ancient Muslim shrines on the Mount—the Dome of the Rock and the al-Aqsa Mosque— which put it right up there with Mecca and Medina on the list of their holiest places.

Looking on a map of Jerusalem, McCabe also saw the Church of the Holy Sepulchre, built on the site of Christ's burial place. That was as important a shrine as existed in the whole Christian world, and it was just a few hundred yards away, in the heart of the Old City, well within range of any nuclear blast.

Suddenly the pain and fear of his disease was replaced by a glow of true contentment. Temple Mount was the flashpoint he'd been looking for. Nuke that, and all hell would break loose. Oh, yeah, that would do the trick, all right.

24

He was standing in the middle of the road and a black car was driving straight toward him. Its headlights were blazing right into his eyes, blinding him. He tried to close his eyes but his eyelids wouldn't move. He struggled to turn away, but no matter how hard he wrenched his neck, his head was held fast. He couldn't blink. He couldn't move. Now the roar of the engine was filling his head and he couldn't lift his hands to cover his ears and his brain was about to explode with noise and light and he wanted to scream, but he couldn't because his mouth was gagged and his teeth seemed loose against the leather strap. And he was cold, so terribly, terribly cold . . .

Carver came to, his pulse racing and his throat constricted by a pervasive, unfocused panic. For a while, he could not focus his eyes, so he reached out blindly for her hand . . . and felt nothing.

He frowned and shook his head quickly from side to side, banishing the last bad fragments of his nightmare from his brain. Then he opened his eyes . . . and Alix wasn't there.

Now he really had something to panic about. Carver told himself to calm down. There were very few things he knew for sure anymore, but one of them was that Alix came to see him every day. She had been there earlier, he was sure, and she'd be back again. It was just a matter of waiting. Maybe she was getting a meal or something to read. She did that sometimes, when she thought he was asleep. Yes, that was it. She would be back soon.

"Hello, Samuel." There was a woman at the door of the room. She was smiling at him and her voice was friendly. But she wasn't Alix. She was Nurse Juneau, bringing him food and medication.

She looked around as she came into the room, frowned to herself, then gave Carver another smile.

"Alix not here?" she asked perkily, then her voice took on a huskier tone: "At last, Samuel, we're all alone."

She looked at him over one shoulder teasingly. "After all this time—now what shall we do?"

She picked up one of his hands and stroked it.

Carver flinched at her touch. He found people confusing. He didn't always understand what they meant by the things they said. He couldn't work out what they were feeling when they spoke. Their intentions were unclear. He could see that Nurse Juneau was flirting with him, but he had the sense she was mocking him, too. He didn't like that.

He decided to ignore her and concentrate on what was on his mind.

"Where's Alix?" he croaked.

Nurse Juneau put the tray down across his bed and shrugged.

"I don't know, Samuel."

"Where has she gone?"

"I don't know. Samuel," Juneau repeated, with a little more emphasis, holding out a little paper cup in which sat three brightly colored capsules. "She's just not here."

She meant nothing by the remark. Nurse Juneau couldn't see anything wrong with Alix giving herself a break. The poor girl deserved it, the amount of time she spent in this room.

But her words hit Samuel Carver like a shock from the belt that had tortured him. He gasped. His eyes widened in shock. He gripped his sheets. Then he flung his arms upward, throwing off his bed linens and sending the tray flying as plates, glasses, and cutlery clattered down onto the floor.

Nurse Juneau was used to Carver's tantrums, his infantile fear of abandonment. But this time, she suddenly realized, his reaction to Alix's absence had a whole new intensity.

As she screamed in alarm, Carver got out of bed, with an energy she had never seen in him before, his eyes blazing, his face twisted with a primal, unfettered rage. She backed away, but he came after her. He wrapped his fists around her upper arms, gripping them so hard she winced in pain, then he stuck his face right up close to hers and hissed, "Where is she?"

His voice had lost any trace of childlike innocence. It carried the threat of real fury, ready to tip into violence.

Nurse Juneau shook her head. "I don't know," she pleaded. "I promise I'm telling the truth. I don't know where Alix has gone. But don't get upset—you know she always comes back. Always."

Carver threw her away from him, across the room. She crashed into the door frame, crying out with the pain of the impact.

"Alix!" shouted Carver, standing beside his bed. *"Al-i-i-i-x!"*

He stumbled across the room, almost tripping on the nurse's dazed body, and headed out into the hallway.

Stabbing bolts of pain cut through Carver's skull. His heart was palpitating. Images from his dreams were flashing before his eyes. But now, in this waking nightmare, everything was different. He knew where and when he had fought in that desert: a mission deep into Iraq in the midst of the Desert Storm campaign in 1991. He knew that he and his men had blown the cables and returned safely to base. And the woman in the dream was Alix. She'd been there, in that chalet outside Gstaad. But what else had happened there?

The memory would not come. Just another stab behind his eyes.

He made his way down the hall in his T-shirt and pajama pants, crashing into a cart laden with patients' medications, barging past the nurse who was pushing it from one room to the next, shoving a patient out of the way as he tried to get to the stairs that led to the exit and the outside world. The dream visions had gone now and he realized he was seeing everything around him with a new clarity, born of comprehension. It was as if there had been a thick glass wall between him and the world—a wall that had suddenly been shattered. He understood his surroundings, appreciated the function and significance of things and people that had been meaningless to him for months. Above all, he understood who and what Samuel Carver really was.

From behind, he heard hurried footsteps, scurrying down the hall. He turned and saw two of the clinic's male orderlies, men chosen as much for their physical strength as their caring natures, charging toward him. He tried to fend them off, but they ignored his flailing fists and charged right into him, knocking him over and pinning him to the ground.

A few seconds later, Dr. Geisel was kneeling beside him, holding a syringe.

"This is for your own good," he said, sticking the needle into Carver's upper arm.

Before the sedative hit him, Carver looked Geisel right in the eye.

"I know," he hissed. "I know."

Then the drugs hit his system and oblivion overcame him.

A minute later, as the orderlies were dumping Carver's inert body back onto his bed, Nurse Juneau approached Dr. Geisel. She was rubbing the back of her head. Her eyes were red-rimmed and welling with tears.

"Are you all right?" he asked.

"I think so," she said, wincing. "It is Samuel I am worried about. He seemed so shocked to be alone. I have never known him this bad before."

"You think so?" Geisel replied. "It seems as though the opposite is true, in fact. One shock has reversed another. The trauma may be his catharsis. Now, at last, he has started to get better."

25

The *bierkeller*'s dressing room reeked of stale smoke, hairspray, and cheap perfume. Alix stubbed out a cigarette and steeled herself to go back to work. She tugged at her short white stockings, snapping the elastic just above her knees. The waitresses all wore tarted-up Heidi costumes: a short red skirt with a petticoat frill at the bottom; a lace-up black bodice, and a skimpy, low-cut white blouse. She pulled the laces tight, tying the ends in a bow beneath her breasts. Then she put her wig back on. It was bright blond, with pigtails, tied at the end with little red bows. She took a deep breath and stepped out into the bar.

Alix scanned the room, apparently greeting the customers with a smile or a flirtatiously blown kiss, but in actual fact examining each of them, watching for any indications of those who were likely to be particularly drunk or obnoxious. On the far side of the room she saw a woman sitting by herself at a table for two, next door to the banker and his clients.

The woman was small and wiry. Her pantsuit—plain, but perfectly tailored—was as black as the hair that framed her face in a severe, geometric bob. The dim light of the *bierkeller* had turned her thickly painted lips from vivid crimson to the dark, rich purple of a ripe eggplant. For a moment, as she looked at Alix, her face was utterly expressionless—until their eyes locked and the woman smiled back at Alix and kissed the air, mimicking her gestures with a sort of contemptuous mockery.

Alix stopped dead in her tracks. She seemed unable to process the information her eyes were supplying. Then she gasped, darted her eyes around the room, turned on her heel, and fled back to the dressing room.

As Alix turned and fled, the woman in black caught the eye of two men sitting at a nearby table and nodded in the direction of the dressing room. They got up and started walking toward the door through which

Alix had just disappeared. The woman left thirty francs on her table and strolled to the main exit.

Alix hurried through the dressing room, barely breaking her stride as she grabbed her coat and handbag. She was pushing a fist through the arm of the coat as she burst through a second door at the back of the room and ran down a short corridor toward the staff exit. By the time she stepped out onto the street, she had pulled the coat tight around her and was huddling against the sharp winter wind, just like the other pedestrians scattered up and down the street, her collar up, one hand clutching the coat lapels tight around her neck.

Every nerve in her body was screaming at her to run, but she forced herself to walk at a normal pace. She had no hope of escaping her pursuers if it came to a foot race. Her only hope was to look inconspicuous.

She was about twenty yards down the road before she realized she was still wearing her wig. It wasn't such a big deal. The pigtails were tucked away out of sight. In the sulfuric glow of the street lamps, one blond head would look pretty much like another. But Alix was too tired, too stressed to make such dispassionate calculations on the run. She panicked and tore the wig from her head. She threw it into a public garbage can, then pulled away the nylon stocking cap from her hair, letting it fall to the pavement.

The sudden movement gave her away. Alix immediately heard the sound of quick, heavy footsteps behind her. She turned her head and saw two men striding toward her. One of them was speaking into a wrist mike. Desperately, she started to run, her ankles twisting every time her high-heeled shoes hit the ground. She stopped for a second to kick off the shoes, helpless as her pursuers drew closer, still marching, inexorably, as though they knew they did not need to break a sweat. Then she set off again in her stockinged feet.

The pavement was ice-cold and the soles of her tights tore through in a matter of seconds, but at least she could run properly now. She cut right onto another street, the rue du Prince. A group of men, clad in tight jeans and leathers, were clustered outside the entrance to Le Prétexte, the city's leading gay club.

"Help me!" Alix screamed, pointing an arm behind her at the two men. They were running now, too.

The men parted to let her through, then one of them, the club's bouncer, stepped into the path of the two men. He was massive, dressed entirely in black. His head was shaven, but the lower half of his face was covered with a thick, piratical beard.

"Hey!" he shouted. "What are you—"

One of the men chopped the bouncer to the ground with a single blow before he could even finish the sentence. The clubbers fled from the two men's path; then, once the men had gone, clustered around the bouncer's unconscious body.

Alix was on her own. She was in no shape to run. She smoked too much and exercised too little. But it was not far to the end of the street now, where it hit the rue du Rhône, one of the city's busiest roads. Half a dozen bus and tram routes connected here, and its pavements would be crowded with people. If she could just keep going, she stood a chance.

She dashed across the street, cutting across it diagonally to the corner, where it met the rue du Rhône. A car passed down the pavement behind her, briefly forcing the men to stop as it went by, buying her a few precious seconds. She looked up and down the main road, searching for a bus or a cab, and suddenly her luck changed. About fifty yards away, a taxi pulled away from the pavement, into the far lane of the broad one-way street. The driver flicked on his FOR HIRE light and Alix waved frantically.

The cab was driving forward, the driver seemingly oblivious to her desperate attempts to attract his attention. Behind her, the men had started crossing the road.

"Please . . ." Alix implored and then, in answer to her prayers, she saw the taxi's indicator flicking as it cut across the traffic toward her.

One of the men had spotted it, too. He gestured to his partner and they seemed to find an extra gear, sprinting even harder toward her.

Alix did not wait for the taxi to reach her. She dashed out into the road, ignoring the oncoming traffic, forcing the cab driver to brake in front of her. He flashed his headlights at her in protest, forcing her to put up a hand to shield her eyes as she dashed around the cab, wrenched open the passenger door, and threw herself onto the seat, yanking the door closed behind her.

Wheezing for breath, her eyes still dazzled, she managed to gasp the words, "Cornavin Station, fast as you can."

It was only when she sank back onto the seat, her chest heaving and her throat gagging, that Alix noticed that she was not alone in the back of the cab.

The woman she had spotted at the *bierkeller* was sitting, half turned, with her legs crossed and her right shoulder leaning against the side of the car. Her arms were crossed above her lap, with her right wrist resting on her left forearm, supporting the gun she was pointing directly at Alix.

"Good evening, my dear," said Olga Zhukovskaya.

She was one of the most powerful women in Russia, the deputy director of the FSB, the intelligence agency that was the direct descendent of the Soviet KGB. Yet she spoke with an affectionate familiarity that suggested long acquaintance, even a family tie.

Zhukovskaya had indeed been a kind of mother to Alix. She was still the wife, rather than the widow, of Yuri Zhukovski when she spotted Alix at a Communist Party youth convention in Moscow a dozen years before—a gawky provincial teenager, hiding behind thick-lensed spectacles. Yet the older woman's practiced eye had spotted a natural sexuality of which the girl herself was entirely unaware. And just as years of training can turn a raw recruit into an elite fighting man, so the gauche, unsophisticated Alexandra Petrova had been transformed by diet, exercise, surgery, and education.

Zhukovskaya had observed Alix bewitch generals, politicians, and industrialists. She had watched her own late husband—once, like her, a KGB officer; then a ruthless industrialist—fall under Alix's spell, and been content to let the relationship flourish as long as it suited her own purposes.

Alix had been magnificent. But now look at her—a tired, bedraggled creature in laddered tights and a cheap, tawdry costume.

For a moment, Zhukovskaya was tempted to let her go. Why waste time on someone who was already so close to the edge? But then she reconsidered. She had come a long way, after all, and gone to a great deal of trouble. There was no point in throwing away this opportunity.

Her head was tilted slightly, giving her a quizzical expression as she asked, "What made you think you could run?"

26

Mary Lou Stoller lived on Edmunds Street in northwest Washington D.C., on the block between Foxhall Road and Glover-Archbold Park.

At that point, Edmunds seems more like a country lane than a residential street just a few miles from the heart of a capital city. At the east end of the road, you can step right into the park, a rolling expanse of semirural woodland.

Mary Lou got home that afternoon around five. Her boss was out of town, so she'd left work early. It was such a lovely winter afternoon, with the low rays of the sun cutting through the bare branches and the fallen leaves crisp with frost underfoot, she couldn't wait to take her Norfolk terrier, Buster, for a walk.

There weren't too many people in the park, just the occasional mother with her children, or a jogger running in search of immortality. When Mary Lou saw the two men coming toward her, she felt a brief spasm of alarm. There wasn't anyone else on the path. Her immediate, instinctive response, as a woman, was to see two large males as a threat.

She told herself not to be so silly. The men didn't look like any muggers she'd ever heard of. They were executive types in their thirties or forties, respectably dressed. Besides, they were deep in conversation, paying no attention to her: two typical Washingtonians wanting privacy while they plotted.

As she reached the men, they politely stood to one side of the path to let her and Buster go by. One of them smiled pleasantly and touched a finger to the brim of his hat in salute. Mary Lou returned the smile with one of her own. She'd been raised a proper southern lady and liked to see a gentleman respecting proper, courtly conventions.

Distracted for a second, she didn't really notice the other man as he stepped in front of her. She was completely unprepared when he drove his fist, reinforced by steel knuckle, hard into her midriff, forcing the air from her body and doubling her up in pain, exposing her neck and the back of her head to the next blow. The lead-weighted, leather-covered blackjack that the courtly gentleman had concealed in his other hand crashed into her skull, just as a second punch pummeled her temple. As her legs gave way beneath her, the blackjack caught her again.

By now the terrier was scampering around its mistress, challenging her attackers with sharp, high-pitched barks and nipping at their heels with its teeth. It was rewarded by a kick from a steel-capped shoe that sent it skittering across the path until jerked to a halt by the leash. It lay there moaning, barely conscious, while the two men aimed a swift, brutal series of kicks at its mistress's head and torso.

It was forty minutes before the body was found, over an hour before police investigators were on the scene. By then the two men were checking in for the early-evening Austrian Airlines flight from Dulles International to Vienna, connecting there with a flight to Moscow. And they were hundreds of miles into their journey when General Kurt Vermulen got off the plane from San Antonio, glad to be home after his meeting with Waylon McCabe, and discovered that he was going to need another secretary.

27

The gun remained quite still in Olga Zhukovskaya's right hand.

"So," she said, "tell me how my husband died."

Alix stayed silent. She wondered what form the widow's revenge would take. But Zhukovskaya took her by surprise, stretching out her left arm and resting her hand on Alix's forearm. She gave it a gentle, soothing squeeze.

"It's all right. It was hardly your fault. Yuri caused his own trouble. I spoke to him that afternoon. He told me the Englishman was flying over to Switzerland, hoping to rescue you. He thought that was funny. He was looking forward to humiliating him."

She sighed and shook her head. "Men and their stupid egos . . . Why didn't he just shoot him?"

That sounded like a rhetorical question. Certainly, Alix had no explanation.

"I'm just trying to establish what happened," said Zhukovskaya casually. "You know that for Yuri and me it was always more professional than romantic. I would not have encouraged him to take you as his mistress otherwise."

Alix relaxed a fraction and asked a question of her own: "Did he leave a will?"

Zhukovskaya laughed out loud.

"Ah, that's my little Alix! So practical, so direct. I've missed you these past few months."

"Well . . . ?"

"Yes, he did, as a matter of fact. Naturally, I have inherited the bulk of his holdings, but you have not been forgotten. I will give you the details in good time. But first, I need to know: the bomb. How did Carver do it?"

"He was carrying a laptop computer—he said it contained all the files about how Yuri had arranged the death of the princess. He was hoping to trade it for me. But the computer wasn't booby-trapped—Yuri made the men check it. So the bomb must have been in the bag it was carried in."

"And you knew nothing of this?"

"No. The last time I'd spoken to Carver had been in Geneva, two days before. We had an argument . . ."

She paused as a thought struck her. "I guess that was the last time I ever spoke to Carver. Spoke properly, I mean. . . ."

Zhukovskaya nodded sympathetically.

"He touched you deeply, this Carver. After all these years, finally someone got through. . . . And now you blame yourself for his suffering?"

Alix gave an exhausted shrug.

"I don't know what I think anymore."

While they'd been talking, the taxi had headed out of town, along the northern shore of Lake Geneva. Mansions clustered along the shoreline displayed the insignia of nations represented at the United Nations headquarters in the city. One set of gateposts bore the double-headed eagle of the Russian Federation. The gates swung open and the taxi swept into the graveled forecourt of a magnificent waterside villa.

The driver walked around to open the two passenger doors.

"Why don't you go and freshen up?" said Olga Zhukovskaya. "Your room has everything you will need."

Upstairs, a sable-trimmed mink coat had been hung up next to dresses by Chanel, Versace, and Dolce & Gabbana: Alix's coat, her dresses. She ran her fingers through the soft, luxuriant fur, then rippled her hand over a multicolored flutter of silk, sequins, and lace. Below the clothes, shoes were arranged in a line across the cupboard, each higher and flimsier than the last.

Here were the trophies of a Moscow mistress, the pretty little fruits of her labors.

Her underwear, blouses, and tops had been folded away in a mahogany chest of drawers, her makeup arranged on the dressing-table, her soap and body oil left in the bathroom that opened off the bedroom, her favorite photograph of her parents placed on the bedside table. Alix sat on the edge of her bed, still dressed in her absurd Heidi outfit, looking around at all the luxury laid out before her, contemplating this womanly power play.

Yuri and Carver had fought each other like men, in brutal, physical conflict. Olga Zhukovskaya, however, had chosen a very different form of attack. She had entered Alix's Moscow apartment, removed her most intimate possessions, and brought them some fifteen hundred miles to a particular room in Geneva, Switzerland, in the absolute certainty that Alix would also end up there.

And now she was tempting her: Just give in, bend to my will, and all this can be yours once again.

Zhukovskaya must have known that Alix would feel violated by the penetration of her home and the seizure of her property. That effect, too, would have been calculated: Resist me, and I will remove you as easily as I removed those dresses.

Alix undressed and showered. Afterward, she got dressed again in her working uniform. She went barefoot. She didn't put on any makeup.

She left the room and walked down a great baronial staircase. A white-jacketed servant was waiting for her at the foot of the stairs. "Madame Zhukovskaya is waiting," he said, leading her into the main reception room.

The deputy director was sitting in an armchair by a mighty, open fireplace filled with blazing logs. She was wearing reading glasses and examining the contents of a ring-bound folder. An identical chair had been arranged next to hers.

As Alix drew closer, Zhukovskaya closed the file, took off the spectacles, and looked her up and down with a faint grimace of distaste.

"Could you not decide what to wear?"

Alix let her look, without reacting in any way, then sat down in the empty chair.

Zhukovskaya watched her for a few more seconds, then nodded to herself.

"I see. Well, then, let us get down to business."

She reopened the file and put her glasses back on. There was a photograph paper-clipped to the inside cover of the file, a color portrait of a U.S. Army officer in full dress uniform. He looked strong, determined, golden-haired, and square-jawed. She passed the photo to Alix, who looked at it for a few moments, then handed it back.

"A handsome man," she said, without any hint of enthusiasm.

"His name is Lieutenant General Kurt Vermulen," said Zhukovskaya. "This picture was taken three years ago. At the time, he was leading the U.S. Special Forces Operations Command at Fort Bragg, having previously commanded the First Battalion of the seventy-fifth Ranger Regiment and served a tour of duty at the Defense Intelligence Agency."

"An American hero," murmured Alix dryly.

"Oh, yes," Zhukovskaya continued, "he is a true soldier. He began his career as part of the Americans' imperialist adventure in Vietnam. He won a Distinguished Service Cross there, one of the very highest awards for gallantry the American army can bestow. One should respect a man, even an enemy, who possesses such a decoration."

Alix pursued her lips dismissively. Zhukovskaya continued, regardless.

"Vermulen retired from the army in May 1995, age fifty, soon after that picture was taken. His wife was dying of cancer and he wanted to be with her in the final months. After that, like a good American, he began to make himself rich."

"So why are you telling me all this?"

"Because of this."

Zhukovskaya removed another photograph from her file. It was a grainy, long-range shot of Vermulen, now dressed in civilian clothes, talking to a middle-aged man with a mustache.

"That is Pavel Novak, a former officer in Czech military intelligence."

"What is he doing with Vermulen?"

"That is precisely what we want to know. Twenty-five years ago, Novak became a double agent, passing secrets to the Americans. He did not know that we were aware of his treachery, so we used him as a means of passing false, misleading information. He was, in effect, working for us all the time. For part of that period Novak's American handler was this Vermulen. In recent years, Novak, like Vermulen, has become a businessman, but perhaps a less respectable one. Today, he trades our secrets to Arabs, Asians, and Third World countries. And of course, we still know and monitor what he does.

"But never before has he had any business dealings with the Americans. So why is he making contact now? What can he offer them that they could possibly want? Novak may wish Vermulen to be some kind of middleman. Or maybe the Americans are playing another game we don't even know about as yet. This is what you must find out."

Alix frowned.

"Me? How?"

"By doing what you do best, my dear. Since his wife's death, Vermulen has only had one or two casual affairs. It is time he fell in love once again."

"Not with me. I won't do another trap—not with him or anyone else."

The good humor vanished without trace from Zhukovskaya's voice, replaced by a Siberian chill.

"You will do exactly what I order you to do, and I will tell you why."

She started flicking through the pages in the file.

"You currently owe the Montagny-Dumas Clinic a sum of, let me see . . ."

She found the page she was looking for. "Forty-seven thousand, seven hundred and thirty-two francs. That was the total at six o'clock this evening. It will be more by tomorrow morning, once they've added another night to the total."

Alix hissed, "You bitch."

"Come, now. Is that any way to speak to someone who is about to solve all your problems? If you agree to target Vermulen, we will arrange for payments to cover Mr. Carver's medical bills for as long as he requires. Believe me, you will hardly notice the expense. Yuri was very appreciative of your services."

"What if I say no?"

"Then you and your boyfriend will have to accept the consequences of killing my husband. The penalty for murder is death. Maybe you are ready to sacrifice yourself for your principles. But would you sacrifice your man as well?"

"I need to talk to Samuel, to let him know what is happening."

"No," snapped Zhukovskaya. "That will not be possible. You will spend the night here. Your flight to Washington, D.C., leaves at nine in the morning."

"But . . ." Alix began to speak, but was instantly silenced.

"Do not argue. These are your orders. You remember orders, don't you . . . Agent Petrova?"

Alix lowered her eyes submissively.

"Yes, Madam Deputy Director. May I ask how I am supposed to approach General Vermulen?"

"You will be hired as his personal assistant. Your cover, full legend, and job application have already been prepared. By Wednesday, you must be ready for your job interview. You will have excellent references. There are still many powerful men who know that it is in their interest to help us."

"As ever, you have thought of every detail," said Alix. "But there is one thing I do not understand. How do you know that Vermulen needs a new assistant?"

"That is being dealt with. . . ."

Zhukovskaya consulted her watch.

"Correction. It has just been dealt with."

MARCH

28

Ten minutes on the treadmill and already Carver was exhausted. Dr. Geisel was sympathetic, too, which made it even worse.

"Don't worry—this is normal," he said, standing beside the apparatus, as calm and immaculate as ever. "You have been sick for many months. You cannot expect to be fit right away. The main thing is, you are making great progress."

Carver just about managed to speak between gasps for breath.

"How much longer before I'm ready to be discharged? I've got to find out what happened to her."

"I understand, Mr. Carver, but you must appreciate that you are a long way from being cured. When you were admitted, you had suffered a very serious psychological trauma, a rift cutting you off from your own identity. Normally, in a case such as this, I would expect an additional trauma, such as Miss Petrova's departure, to have set you back, maybe worse than ever. And yet now, Mr. Carver, it is as if the shock has dislodged some kind of obstacle. The boulder has rolled away, the cave is open, your consciousness is free. Really, it is a kind of psychic resurrection."

"Well, if I'm so much better," Carver wheezed, "why won't you let me out?"

"Because nothing in psychology is ever that simple. Yes, you are recovering your long-term memory, but chaotically, randomly, and traumatically. Your prognosis is still unclear. You might, indeed, continue this remarkable progress. But, equally likely, the shock of these recovered memories could push you back over the edge, even deeper than ever before."

"So when is it safe for me to leave?"

"When the odds are not so equal. Now enjoy the rest of your workout. I strongly recommend physical fitness as an aid to your mental recovery."

When Geisel had gone, Carver stepped off the treadmill. His thighs were quivering, his legs barely able to support him as he walked across to the weight machines. He managed forty pounds on the lat pull-down and sixty on the bench press, low reps and feeble weights on the leg extensions and curls, sit-ups in sets of six.

Carver could now remember when he possessed the extreme levels of fitness required of an officer in the Special Boat Service. For him to be struggling with a routine like this was like a professional soccer player getting beaten in a kids' scrimmage. But just to sweat, to feel the burn, and to keep driving himself onward, made him feel alive again.

He accepted that his mind was still balanced on a knife edge between recovery and relapse, just as Geisel had warned. He had a feeling some of his mental doors would stay firmly locked for a while yet. But after the terrible nonexistence of the past few months, he refused to countenance the prospect of failure.

"Come on," he panted, stepping back onto the treadmill. "Go faster."

And so he ran, and the memory came to him of another time he had run, a dash down a street in Geneva, late one night. In his mind's eye he saw a white van, painted with the logo of the Swisscom telephone company. He could not see the man at the wheel, but he knew who he was: Kursk, one of the Russians. Carver felt his stomach tighten with tension at the memory of that name. He knew, too, who had been in the back of that van. Alix had been Kursk's prisoner. The Russian had driven her away. But Carver had gone after her, though he still could not recall precisely what had happened.

He knew one thing, though. He'd got her back. How else could she have been sitting by his bedside for all those months?

With his awakening had come a profound conviction of his love for her, and hers for him. Carver was certain that Alix would never willingly have left him without even saying good-bye. Wherever she had gone, it had not been her choice. He would not rest until he had found her and made her his again.

One of the gymnasium staff was walking toward the treadmill, a look of concern on his face as he ran his eyes over Carver's scarlet face, his heaving chest, and his pale-gray T-shirt, darkened with puddles of sweat under his armpits and down the small of his back.

"Maybe you should stop now," he said.

"No," said Carver. "I want to keep running."

Across town a man was steeling himself to make a difficult call. He was way over six feet tall and beanpole-thin. His milk-skinned, freckled face, illuminated by gentle blue eyes, was topped by a starburst of red-blond dreadlocks.

Thor Larsson took a deep breath and started pressing the buttons. He waited a few moments until the clinic's switchboard had answered and then said, "Monsieur Marchand's office, please."

He paced up and down, waiting to be put through to the finance director.

"It's about Monsieur Carver's account . . ." Larsson began. "Please, can you just give me another few days? I think I may be able to get some money. Maybe not all the bill, but a lot of it, I assure you."

To his amazement, the voice on the other end of the line was reassuring, almost obsequious.

"Monsieur, please, do not derange yourself," said Marchand. "There is no need to be concerned. Monsieur Carver's account has been settled in full and instructions have been left for any future expenses. He is welcome to stay as long as he likes."

"What? When did that happen?" asked Larsson.

"Pah! Let me see . . . it must have been two days ago, I suppose."

"Who is paying the bill, then?"

"I am sorry, monsieur, that I cannot say. We have simply received instructions to pass any outstanding invoices to a lawyer acting on behalf of a client. Who that client might be, well . . . this is Switzerland, monsieur. We respect people's privacy here."

29

The moment she walked into his office, Kurt Vermulen knew that Natalia Morley would be his new assistant. He'd already been impressed enough by her résumé. She was thirty years old, born in Russia, but carried a Canadian passport, thanks to her marriage (now dissolved) to an investment banker, Steve Morley. They'd met in Moscow, where they both worked for a Swiss investment bank—she was his boss's assistant and she'd taken another high-level P.A. job when Morley had been posted to the bank's head office in Geneva. They'd moved again to the States, where the marriage had broken up. Now she was looking to start a new life on her own. It didn't look as if she would have too much trouble doing that. Her letters of recommendation were outstanding, and when he called the men listed as her references, they all sang her praises. Then he saw her, and he understood why.

Natalia Morley was a head-turning, jaw-dropping beauty. Over the past few weeks, Vermulen had been on a couple of pleasant, but unexceptional dates with Megan, the lawyer he'd met that night at the Italian restaurant in Georgetown. Megan was a fine-looking woman. Natalia was in a totally different league.

Even so, looks will get you only so far. Kurt Vermulen had the same basic instincts as any other heterosexual male, but he was also an intelligent, thoughtful man. What really hooked him was a deeper quality, something that suggested vulnerability, and even sadness, as though life had wounded her in some way. It could have been the divorce, he guessed, although, in Vermulen's experience, that was more likely to induce anger or even bitterness in a woman. All he knew was that he sensed a personal loss in Natalia Morley that echoed his own bereavement.

At one point in their first meeting he even found himself talking about Amy and her death. It was, he realized, an inappropriate subject for a job interview. But it happened so naturally, and Natalia was so gracious in her response, that he found himself wanting her to be in his life.

The job offer was really just a means, even an excuse, to have her near him. She'd started the following Monday.

Since then, her work had been impeccable. His appointments, correspondence, and travel arrangements were organized with flawless efficiency. The brutal murder of a general's secretary, right in the heart of the capital, had attracted a fair amount of media attention, but Natalia had been adept at keeping even the most persistent reporters at bay. Knowing that there was no one at home to look after him, she saw to his dry cleaning, found contractors for his household chores and garden maintenance, and arranged for deliveries of fresh produce and deli items from the D.C. branch of Dean & DeLuca to his townhouse near Dumbarton Oaks. The rest of the staff at Vermulen Strategic Consulting seemed to like her, too, including the other women. That struck Vermulen as quite an achievement. He'd have expected them to resent her looks and her closeness to their boss.

Then again, she'd never got that close. Natalia Morley was perfectly friendly. She laughed at his jokes, listened to his problems, and charmed any client who set foot in the office. If she ever had a bad mood, Vermulen never saw it. But neither did he see any evidence that she was as interested in him as he was in her. Her manner was always entirely proper. She didn't flirt with him at all, and while her elegant clothes could not help but show off her figure, her skirts were knee-length and her blouses demure. If anything was going to happen, he would have to make the first move.

Meanwhile, he still had a business to run and, most important of all, a false-flag operation to organize. Vermulen had persuaded himself that if he was right about the threat from Islamist terrorism, then it would be inexcusable to sit back and do nothing. Even if his actions were questionable, they were better than the alternative.

His plans were beginning to form now. He was going to take a couple of months off from the business. If anyone asked, he'd tell them he was taking a break by traveling around Europe, combining a spell of R & R with the opportunity to make new contacts. He would not mention, however, that the contacts were those required to procure a nuclear bomb. His itinerary would take him to Amsterdam, Vienna, Venice, and Rome, to start with. After that, he'd see how things panned out. Natalia could book him transportation and hotels as he needed them.

And then a thought struck him. If he was in Europe and she was back in D.C. it would always be tricky keeping in touch and ensuring that everything ran smoothly. It would really be much more efficient if she was with him, right there on the spot, looking after him day to day. Obviously he couldn't tell her who the people he was meeting really were, and he'd have to send her home well before the final phase of the operation. In the meantime, though, they'd be thrown together in some of the world's most romantic cities. If nothing happened then, it never would.

Vermulen could simply have ordered Natalia to accompany him, but that wasn't the best way to go if he wanted her to feel good about him. He'd be asking her to spend several weeks away from home, on call 24/7, with only him for company. If she didn't want to do that voluntarily, he wasn't going to gain anything by forcing her.

When he asked her to come into his office, his heart was pounding. He felt like a nervous kid summoning up the courage to ask for a prom-night date.

As always, Natalia looked poised and imperturbable as she awaited his instructions.

Vermulen reminded himself that he was a decorated combat veteran who had faced enemy fire on three separate continents and had commanded thousands of fighting men. How tough could it be to face one beautiful woman?

"As you know," he said, adopting what he hoped was a relaxed but businesslike air, "I will be spending some time in Europe this spring. I need a break, need to get away—it's been a tough few years."

"Of course," she said. "I quite understand."

"Good . . . good . . . Anyway, as you know, I will be doing some business while I'm away, taking meetings and so forth, so there'll be a fair amount of administration required, which would best be handled on the spot. I was wondering, therefore, whether you would be willing to accompany me on the trip. It would be in a purely professional capacity, of course, and I would compensate you financially for the loss of weekends and free time while you were away. Does that sound, ah . . . agreeable to you?"

She looked at him for a moment, frowning slightly.

"Do you want me to arrange separate tickets for myself, coach class?"

"Oh, no, that wouldn't be right. You can travel first class, like me."

She seemed surprised.

"That's very kind, sir, thank you. And accommodation?"

"We'd stay at the same hotels. So, are you interested?"

She thought for a second.

"I will have to change some personal arrangements. And I would need to arrange for someone to cover for me here while I am away. But that should be possible, so, yes, I would be happy to travel with you, sir."

"Outstanding," said Kurt Vermulen.

That evening, Alix Petrova met the FSB agent who was her Washington handler on the steps of the Lincoln Memorial.

"The assignment is proceeding as planned," she said. "Vermulen is clearly infatuated. He has asked me to go with him on a trip to Europe. He is telling everyone, including me, that he is taking an extended vacation, but I am certain that there is more to it than that."

She handed over a plain white envelope.

"The itinerary for the first three weeks is in there, including flight numbers and hotels. It should not be difficult to arrange meetings and drops at any of the places we will be visiting."

"Excellent," said her handler. "So, what is he like, this General Vermulen?"

"If you want to know," she replied, "he is a very fine man. I like him, which only makes me despise myself even more for what I am doing to him."

The handler raised an eyebrow.

"I think I will leave that last observation out of my report to the deputy director."

"No," said Alix, "please don't. It will make her happy to think that I am suffering."

30

A week later, Kurt Vermulen was in Amsterdam. He'd given the woman he knew as Natalia Morley the day off. Now he was standing on a piece of scrubland down by the docks, where weeds grew between the boats pulled up onto the shore, and an old barge rusted in the water at the end of the plot. He was about to put a face to a name he'd known for a decade or more, an old Defense Intelligence Agency case file transformed into a live human being.

A car turned off the road, drove past him, and pulled up about fifteen yards beyond. A thin man in a black suit, lank hair falling over the collar, emerged, smoking a cigarette. He threw the stub onto the damp, gravelly earth and crushed it with his heel, immediately lit another, then walked toward Vermulen. They didn't bother to shake hands.

"Jonny Koolhaas?" asked Vermulen.

The man shrugged. He angled his head and blew a plume of smoke into the air, away from Vermulen, still looking at him from the corner of his eye.

"So what do you want?"

"A supplier of untraceable weapons and equipment, accessible at short notice. I'll need pistols, submachine guns, grenades, plastique. Nothing fancy. Also vehicles. Untraceable, of course."

"And why would a respectable American officer want all that?"

There was a glint of amusement in Koolhaas's eye. It always pleased him to watch upright, law-abiding citizens having to trade in his criminal world.

"Well, perhaps you will tell me when it is over," he said, when Vermulen had not answered. "But yes, I can arrange for those goods to be available at any time."

"That's good. Does your network cover Eastern Europe?"

"I have associates in the East, yes."

"How about the former Yugoslavia?"

Koolhaas stubbed out the cigarette.

"Possibly, yes."

The following day, Vermulen transferred the first installment of Koolhaas's payment to an account in the Dutch Antilles. Natalia Morley had accompanied him to the bank, where he made the transfer.

He took her arm as they walked away.

She didn't seem to mind. Maybe he was making progress.

Another three days had passed, and they were taking their places in the magnificent white-and-gold horseshoe of boxes that rings the auditorium of the State Opera House, Vienna. The performance that night was Mozart's *Don Giovanni*. Vermulen, however, hadn't come for the music.

Vienna was the city where Pavel Novak conducted his business, trading people, weapons, and information. It was no coincidence at all that Vermulen and Alix happened to bump into Novak and his wife, Ludmilla, in the bar before the performance. After introductions had been made, while the ladies were complimenting each other on their dresses, Novak stepped close to Vermulen and spoke into his ear, the way you do when you're middle-aged and it's getting harder to make out what someone's saying over a background roar of conversation. Or when you're passing on secrets about weapons of mass destruction.

"The sale of documents has been confirmed. The vendor is a Georgian, Bagrat Baladze. He is paranoid, out of his depth. He refuses to put his goods in a bank, insists on having them in his possession at all times. He is also terrified that another, bigger gangster will find out what he has and take it from him. So I have arranged for him to go into hiding at a series of locations while the sale is arranged. In four weeks' time, he will arrive at a converted farmhouse in the South of France. That will be your best opportunity. I will give you exact details nearer the time. . . ."

Novak glanced back at the ladies with a smile on his face and a twinkle in his eye.

"You are a lucky man, Kurt. I love my Ludmilla, of course. But to have a woman like that in my bed, well . . . I envy you."

Vermulen shook his head.

"No need—she's not in my bed."

"You're joking!"

"Kid you not . . ."

He gave Novak a hearty pat on the back.

"But believe me, pal, I'm working on it."

In the first interval, Alix walked to the nearest ladies' room. A line had already formed. In front of Alix stood a silver-haired Viennese matron, plumped up by a lifetime of chocolate cakes and whipped cream. Alix gave her a polite smile, then took up her position, idly looking around at the operagoers in their dinner jackets and evening gowns.

She was wearing a simple, floor-length column of pearl-colored satin, with a matching sequined evening purse in her hand. Suddenly, something or someone caught her eye. Her eyes lit up and she turned to wave, lifting the hand that held the purse, just at the exact moment that a slender brunette in her early forties, her cheeks hollow with dieting and nervous energy, arrived in the line behind her. Alix's arm swept into the woman, whose own bag, a silver metallic-leather clutch, was knocked to the floor. It was a total accident, but Alix was overwhelmed by embarrassment. As the other woman hissed with irritation, she dropped to the red carpet, picked up the clutch, which had fallen open, and, having snapped it shut, returned it to its infuriated owner.

"I'm so sorry," Alix said, her eyes pleading for forgiveness. "I really didn't mean to—"

She was met by a volley of incomprehensible German insults that had the portly matron, her ears burning, barely suppressing a squeal of delighted horror: Here was a story to tell her companions when she got back to her seat! Then the brunette turned on her stiletto heel and stalked off in search of a more civilized place to pee.

But Maria Rostova, whose diplomatic accreditation listed her as a first secretary in the trade and investment section of the Russian Federation Embassy, Vienna, did not stop when she came to the next facility. Instead, she went down the stairs and out through the magnificent arched loggia to the Opernring outside. A car pulled up as she reached the side of the road. Rostova got in and, as the car moved away, opened her bag. She rummaged around inside it and removed a small tube of rolled-up paper, about the size of a cigarette, stuck in place by a small square of adhesive tape. She prized open the tape and unrolled the tube, which revealed a page torn from a onetime code pad, covered in rows of numbers written in three-digit groups.

Rostova put the paper back in her bag, then took out a mobile phone and dialed a Moscow number. When she got through she simply said, "I have this week's delivery."

31

It was shortly before five-thirty in the afternoon and Clément Marchand was about to leave his office at the Montagny-Dumas Clinic when he received a call from a man with a Russian accent. Marchand was informed that his wife was being held hostage. By way of confirmation, the receiver was held up to her face just long enough for him to be certain that the few sobbed words he heard had come from his Marianne.

"Please, don't hurt her," he stammered. And then, "What do you want?"

Marchand was given a very simple set of instructions. First, he was assured that this was not a conventional kidnapping. His wife's captors did not want any money. As a consequence, they had no incentive to keep her alive. If he refused to do as they told him, at exactly the specified time, or made any attempt to contact the authorities, they would kill her.

"Anything!" he pleaded. "Just tell me what I must do."

"Work late," said the voice on the other end of the line. "Invent an excuse. At precisely half past eleven tonight, you will call the duty nurse on the third floor of your clinic. You will tell her that you need to see her. If she protests, you will insist. Say that you have uncovered an irregularity in the records of drugs administered to patients. Say anything you like. All that matters is this: The nurse must be in your office, in your presence, away from her station, between eleven-thirty and eleven forty-five. After that time, she can return to her post. At midnight, you may leave the clinic and drive home. If all goes well, your wife will be waiting for you, unharmed."

"Thank you, thank you." Marchand was almost weeping with relief.

"Do not thank us until you have completed your task," said the voice. "And one more thing. If you should ever decide to tell anyone about this conversation, or what has happened to your wife, we will know. And you will both be killed."

Marchand put down the phone, wiped the sweat off his brow, and told his secretary he would be working late. She, however, was free to go home at the normal hour.

Carver's recovery had not gone unnoticed in Moscow, nor its possible consequences. Deputy Director Olga Zhukovskaya had made it plain to her staff that she wanted the matter dealt with at once. Now they were obeying her orders.

32

C arver awoke and found to his surprise that he had not been asleep for half the night, as he'd imagined. The clock by his bedside read 23:35—he'd been out for less than an hour. He rubbed his eyes and then frowned. Something was wrong, something out of place, but he couldn't work out what it was.

Then it struck him. He couldn't hear the TV. The night nurse on duty this week was a kid called Sandrine, and she always had a late-night movie on in the staff room when she thought the patients were asleep. So why would tonight be any different?

Carver got out of bed and, keeping the light off, padded across his room to the door. He opened it a fraction and paused, listening for any unusual sounds outside. He thought he could hear footsteps down at the far end of the floor. Very slowly, he eased the door open another few degrees, just enough for him to lean around and catch a glimpse down the corridor. He saw the shape of a man, bending over the nurses' reception desk, running his finger down the top sheet on a clipboard. He was checking the list of rooms and their occupants.

He might have been looking for someone else, but Carver wasn't going to take that chance. He closed the door and looked around the room, giving himself no more than a couple of seconds to make his decision. Then he went to the bathroom, switched on the light, and turned on the tap, letting it run in a steady dribble that sounded like a man taking a leak. When he quit the bathroom, he left the light on and the door half open, before going to stand to one side of the bedroom door, his back to the wall between him and the corridor.

Steps came pacing down the corridor. The man's rubber soles squeaked against the vinyl tiled floor. They paused outside the door to Carver's room and he saw the handle move as it was twisted from outside. The door opened. It was now between Carver and the other man, whoever he was, blocking each of them from seeing the other.

Carver's bathrobe was hanging on a hook on the back of the door, a cord strung around its waist. Carver gently slid the cord from the robe, then held it in both hands, forming a loop like a lasso. He knew he had only meager reserves of strength and stamina. Whatever he did, it would have to be fast.

The man closed the door behind him. His attention was focused on the bathroom, unaware of Carver behind him. There was something in his right hand, a thin tube that protruded a few inches from his fist. At first glance Carver thought it might be a small flashlight, but then the man's hand moved and caught the light from the bathroom door. The tube was a plastic injector pen, the kind used by diabetics for their daily doses of insulin.

Now he understood. An overdose of insulin, given to a sleeping patient, would swiftly induce hypoglycemic coma as the neurons in the brain were starved of glucose. Death would follow if the condition was left untreated, and if the injection site itself were not spotted, there'd be no reason to suspect foul play. Insulin was one of the most effective murder weapons a hospital could offer.

Carver had no intention of being its latest victim. He came up behind the intruder, slipped the bathrobe cord over his head, and pulled it tight around the neck.

The man reacted instantly. He brought his left hand up to the cord, trying to pull it away from his throat. At the same time he jerked his head back, hard, hoping to catch Carver on the face.

Carver anticipated the move and swayed back, his own movement adding to the tension on the cord. But now he had another problem to deal with—the man swung his right arm around behind him, jabbing the injector pen at Carver like a deadly snake, with insulin as its venom.

Carver twisted to one side to avoid the pen. The movement shifted his balance and gave his opponent the chance to push backward. Carver was sent crashing into the wall between his room and the one next door. The breath was knocked from him by the impact, but he forced himself to hold on to the cord. Ten or fifteen seconds' pressure on the carotid artery would be enough to bring on unconsciousness, but fifteen seconds was an eternity when two men were fighting to the death.

They lurched around the room, their bodies linked like two drunken dance partners as they collided with a chair, knocking it over; then the bed; then a side table, sending a glass of water flying. And all the while the injector was jabbing at Carver, searching for his flesh and the moment when it could finally release its deadly cargo.

Groggy calls of complaint started coming from the patients on either side of Carver's room. One of them started banging on the wall and calling for a nurse. It would not be long before someone came to see what was happening.

As the seconds passed, the fight was becoming a test of endurance between Carver's enfeebled muscles, desperately hanging on to his improvised noose, and his enemy's oxygen-starved brain. Whoever gave in first would die. And then came a stroke of luck. The assassin's flailing hand struck against the iron frame of Carver's bed and the injector was knocked from his grasp. Desperately, he tried to bend down to pick it up, but that only gave Carver the opportunity to plant his feet and give one last heave of the cord.

He felt the other man slump into unconsciousness and let the cord play out through his hands, lowering the lifeless body to the floor.

Suddenly there was a hammering on the door.

Carver dragged the body into the bathroom, then opened the door. Christophe, the crack-addicted son of a prominent local banker, was standing in the corridor in shorts and an old T-shirt, his usually pallid features inflamed with indignation.

"What the hell have you been doing in there?" he whined, making no attempt to keep his voice down.

Other heads began peering out of doors up and down the corridor.

"It's okay—I'm sorry," said Carver, turning to one side and then the other, holding his hands up in apology and surrender.

"I must have been sleepwalking or something. I had one of my nightmares, then I woke up and I was in the middle of my room and it was all smashed up. I don't know what happened. But I'm really sorry if I woke you guys up, okay?"

He looked around in feigned bewilderment. "Has anyone seen a nurse? I could really use some meds. . . ."

The others shook their heads and retreated back into their rooms, like crabs scuttling back into holes, not wanting to get involved. Carver watched them disappear, then went back into his room. Wherever the nurse had got to, she'd be back at any second. He heard a groan from the bathroom. His assailant was coming to.

Carver's eyes darted around his room until he found the injector lying on the floor by his bed. He picked it up, strode into the bathroom, sat astride the man's body, forced his head down with one hand, then jabbed the injector at his carotid artery with the other. As soon as the plastic tube hit skin, Carver pushed the trigger button, sending a dose of insulin straight into the bloodstream. Then he pressed it again, twice more, just to make sure the maximum possible dose had been administered and the injector was completely empty. The man gave a barely audible moan. He wasn't dead yet. But he was heading that way fast.

Now that the fight was over and his adrenaline levels were plummeting, Carver felt shattered, but he couldn't afford to let up. He righted the bedside table and put the chair back in its place. Somehow, he found the strength to drag the comatose body back out of the bathroom and across the floor to the bed.

The man had been wearing a heavy overcoat. Carver pulled his arms from the sleeves, then heaved him up onto the mattress and covered him with a blanket and top sheet, leaving just the top of his head exposed on the pillow. The subterfuge would survive only the most cursory look into the room. But it might buy Carver time to get out.

He put on some clothes and shoes, followed by the dying man's overcoat. There were car keys in one of the side pockets, along with a phone. The inside pocket held a wallet. Carver opened it. He found money, credit cards, and an I.D. in the name of Dr. Jean Du Cann, consultant psychiatrist. That would have got the would-be killer past the guard at the gate. He must have used it again at the front desk or slipped in through a service entrance. Those doors were all locked, but they wouldn't pose any barrier to a professional. They wouldn't stop Carver getting out, either.

He was about to leave the room when he heard more footsteps: the slightly sharper patter of a nurse's footsteps. Sandrine had returned. There was a distinct, familiar pattern to the noise she was making: a few paces, then a pause as she looked into the patients' rooms, through the windows in the doors, just a routine check to make sure they were all okay.

Carver rolled under the bed as her footsteps drew near. He held his breath and remained perfectly still as she stopped outside his room, then exhaled in blessed relief as she walked on. A couple of minutes later, he heard one last, uninterrupted walk down the corridor, followed by the sound of the TV being turned on again. He waited a few minutes, giving the nurse time to fix herself a cup of coffee, kick off her shoes, and relax in front of the box.

He used the time to sort out the dying man's possessions. Carver kept the coat, the phone, the car keys, and the cash. The wallet, with the doctor's I.D. still inside, he placed on the bedside table, along with the injector. That would give the police plenty of material to go on when they tried to figure out what had happened—material that should make it obvious that the victim was far from innocent. Finally, Carver slipped out through his door, turned away from the nurses' room, crept down the corridor, and made his way to the emergency staircase.

Less than a minute later, he was sitting behind the wheel of his attacker's car. He turned up the collar of his overcoat, then drove toward the barrier, giving the guard a little wave of thanks as he passed. As the barrier closed behind him, he pressed the accelerator to the floor and sped away toward Geneva.

At a quarter past midnight, Clément Marchand came through his front door, an eager, expectant look on his face. "Marianne? *Chérie?*" he called out.

Then blood blossomed on his shirt front and spattered his forehead as he died just as his wife had.

The killer let himself out of the apartment without any fuss. As he drove away he called his boss, reporting the situation at the apartment and requesting his next instructions.

33

C arver kept checking the rearview mirror to see if he was being followed. He found himself getting jittery if he saw the same set of lights for more than a mile or two. Whenever a car behind turned off the main road, or overtook him without incident, his shoulders slumped with relief and gratitude, only to tighten up again when another vehicle pulled into view.

He told himself not to be so stupid. He had almost always worked alone. Why shouldn't the man now lying on his bed have done the same? But his head was filled with fears of pursuit. His body, meanwhile, was exhausted. He'd forgotten how draining a fight could be. It might only have lasted a few seconds, but the fear and tension that preceded it, the intense physical strain of the battle itself, and the release that came with survival had overwhelmed him. His muscles ached. His brain felt sluggish and unfocused. He had reached the outskirts of Geneva when another thought hit him: What if the car had been fitted with a tracking device?

He cursed his sloppiness. It should have been automatic: Check an unknown car for a tracker or booby traps. But that hadn't even crossed his mind until it was far too late. No wonder he wasn't being followed. They didn't need to bother. They already knew where he was.

Then he thought of the killer's phone, still sitting in his coat pocket. As long as it was on, anyone with access to the local networks could use that to locate him, too. He reached inside the coat and switched off the phone. After one last look in the mirror, he pulled over to the side of the road, stopped the car, got out, and looked around. He was somewhere in the ribbon of suburbs and small towns that sprawled northeast from the city and ran right around the northern shore of the lake to Lausanne and on to Montreux. The road he was on ran parallel to a railway line. Up ahead he could see a sign for a station, barely more than a halt on the line, called Creux-de-Genthod. The name rang a bell. He'd been there before.

He started jogging along the road toward the station and had almost reached the entrance when he remembered that there was a restaurant on the far side of the road, down by the lake. He'd taken women for lazy meals by the water. Sometimes he'd hire a boat for the day and sail there, mooring at the jetty just along from the terrace where they put out tables in the summertime. He had a vivid impression of walking up to the place and seeing blue parasols and striped awnings, the girl he was with squeezing his arm, happy to be arriving for a meal by boat. Then he remembered something else, the way he'd felt at times like that: not sharing the other person's pleasure, but cut off, his mind still processing the death he'd just inflicted, or planning the one to come.

Carver thought about going down to the restaurant to use the phone. It was past midnight and they'd be closing up, but he'd say his car had broken down. He wanted to get in touch with Thor Larsson. He felt badly in need of an ally. But then he saw a flash in the corner of his eye, the gleam of a train's headlights coming down the track. If he ran, he could catch it and go all the way into town. The journey would take less than fifteen minutes. He'd call Larsson when he arrived.

On the train, he found a seat at the far end of a carriage, from which he could easily monitor anyone who came in through the sliding door beside him, or moved down the aisle between the rows of seats. This probably was the last train of the night; there weren't too many other people onboard. Still, he couldn't relax. He stared at the other passengers, trying to work out which of them might pose a threat. He told himself to stop—they'd think he was a nutcase. But he kept doing it anyway. It had been months since he'd been out in the world, surrounded by strangers. It was hard to fit back in.

As he left the train at Geneva, he kept darting glances at the other people walking down the platform. A teenage boy, out with his mates, caught his eye.

"What are you looking at?" the kid shouted.

One of his friends, made bold by the presence of his gang, joined in. "You some kind of pervert or something?"

"He's a pedophile," said one of the others, and they broke into a jeering chorus: "Pedo! Pedo!"

Carver turned away from them, his shoulders hunched. By the time he reached the public phones, he was sweaty with embarrassment and shame. He called Larsson.

"Carver?" Larsson sounded like he'd just heard a ghost. "That's not possible. I mean . . . how . . . what happened?"

"I got better. Look, we need to meet. My flat, soon as possible."

"Hold on," said Larsson. "Where are you calling from? How come you're not at the clinic?"

"Had a bit of trouble there. I'm in town now. I need to leave tonight, get right away from here. But there's a couple of things I've got to do first."

"What kind of things?"

"Nothing dramatic. I just need to start looking for Alix. Look, can you get to the flat or not?"

"I guess so."

"Great. And bring the keys. You've still got them, right?"

"Yeah. Alix had the original set, but I've got copies."

"See you there."

Carver took a cab, looking out of the window all the way, getting used to the sights of the city again. He made the cabbie drop him off a couple of blocks away from his apartment, started walking off in the wrong direction, then corrected himself and made his way through the warren of narrow, twisting streets at the heart of the Old Town. He was constantly looking back over his shoulder, checking out the parked cars, twitching with nerves at every unexpected movement or sound.

A few doors down from his destination, Carver stopped for a moment outside a small café whose front door was set a few feet below ground level, just down a short flight of steps. The building looked familiar, but there was something out of place. It was the sign over the café door—he was sure it had been changed. He tried to recall what had been there before, or what the significance of the café had been, but this time the image wouldn't come. He stood there for a second, frowning in concentration, trying to get at the memory that was still so tantalizingly out of reach. He wondered what had happened here that was so bad his brain still refused to acknowledge it. Then he turned away and walked on, cursing himself for standing like that, stock-still, out in the open, where anyone could get at him.

———

On the other side of the city, a Russian FSB field agent named Piotr Korsakov, the man who had just killed Marianne Marchand and her husband, Clément, hailed a taxi. He gave the driver precise directions to
his intended destination: a place to which, his superiors had decided,
Carver would most likely head. His next target was on the move. There
was no time to waste.

34

On the shores of Gull Lake, Minnesota, with the last traces of daylight fading from the iron-gray sky and the trees on the far side of the lake barely visible, Dr. Kathleen Dianne "Kady" Jones got ready to meet her first live nuclear bomb.

A research scientist at the Los Alamos nuclear facility in New Mexico, Kady was one of the volunteers on call to a unit of the U.S. government's Department of Energy known as NEST. The initials stood for Nuclear Emergency Search Team and they precisely described the unit's task, which was to cope with national security's worst nightmare: a bad guy with a nuke.

Since NEST had been founded in 1975 there had been more than one hundred reports of possible threats. Of these, around thirty had been investigated. They were all hoaxes. Homemade portable nukes made great storylines for movies. A team of seventeen government scientists even tried to build a bomb as an experiment, just to see if it could be done. But in actual fact, there had been no unauthorized nuclear weapons of any kind on U.S. soil.

Until now.

The call had come in from the FBI in Minneapolis–St. Paul to the Department of Energy's Emergency Operations Center in Washington, D.C. From there, it was routed to the NEST headquarters at Nellis Air Force Base northeast of Las Vegas. Within minutes, Kady had been assigned to lead a seven-person NEST team. Within the hour, they had taken off from Los Alamos County Airport, on the way to Minneapolis.

The team's destination was a waterside vacation property on the shore of Gull Lake, a popular destination for city dwellers seeking fresh air, good fishing, and fun on the water. The FBI had cordoned off the area with the help of local police. Floodlights had been brought in to light up the modest timber cabin. The special agent in charge was named Tom Mulvagh.

"So what's the story?" Kady asked, as her team began unloading gear from one of the two black Econoline vans that had transported them to the site. She was holding a gloved hand across her brow to keep the rain out of her eyes. A bright-red fleece hat was jammed down over her chestnut hair.

"The owner here, name of Heggarty, bought the place four years ago," said Mulvagh, his face half in shadow beneath his hooded parka. "Now he's looking to convert the loft space, fit in an extra bedroom. Anyway, he's measuring up and he can't figure it right. The interior dimensions of the loft space don't match the exterior dimensions of the building. He keeps coming up three feet short. Then he realizes that the end wall of the loft is really a partition, with space behind it. So he knocks it down and that's when he sees a large, brown leather suitcase—he described it as kind of old-fashioned, not like a modern style. He looks closer and there's an electric cable coming from this sack, connected to a power supply in the wall."

Kady grimaced. "Tell me he didn't open the case."

"Sure he opened the case—human nature. That's when he saw a metal pipe, a black box with a blinking red light, and what he called, and I quote, 'That damn towel-head writing.'"

She frowned. "Arabic?"

"Don't think so. From his description, we concluded it was Cyrillic script—Russian."

"Okay, so now did he keep his hands off the pipe and the box?"

The special agent grinned. "Yeah, he was smart enough to get scared at that point. He called up the PD in Nisswa, and they passed him on to the Crow Wing County sheriff's office in Brainerd. They contacted us, and here we all are."

"Better check it out, then." Kady looked around. "We're going to be wearing protective suits. I guess we can change in the vans."

"Sure," said Mulvagh, "but do it quick. Makes me nervous standing around here, thinking about what's in there."

She gave him a reassuring pat, as if she were his protector, even though Mulvagh looked a decade older than she, and was six inches taller and probably fifty pounds heavier.

"Trust me—it's okay. If that device really is some kind of Soviet bomb, it's almost certainly got a permissive action link—that's a specific code to be entered before it's armed. Without that, nothing's going to happen. My guess is it's been in position for a decade, probably more. And if it hasn't gone off in all that time, why's it going to blow now?"

"Because it doesn't like being disturbed?"

"Don't worry. I'll be extra polite."

35

Larsson's battered Volvo station wagon was already waiting outside Carver's building when he finally arrived. The Norwegian got out and looked Carver up and down appraisingly, looking for any visible signs of trouble.

"You okay?" he asked.

"Get us inside," Carver replied. "I don't like being stuck out on the street—too exposed."

His voice was tense, strung out.

"You all right, man?" asked Larsson. "You don't sound so good."

"I'm fine."

"Whatever you say."

Carver hurried into the apartment building and started making his way up the stairs to his top-floor flat. Larsson let him get ahead a few paces, watching him skeptically, then followed on up the old wooden staircase that wound up through five stories, creaking under his feet with every step. When he got to Carver's flat, the door was already open. Carver was standing in the living room, looking around, aghast at what he saw—or, rather, didn't see.

"Where is everything?" he asked.

The room had been stripped bare of furniture.

"We sold it," said Larsson. "We had to."

Carver calmed down for a moment as he accepted the truth of what Larsson had said. Then a look close to horror crossed his face, and he dashed off into the kitchen.

"Christ, you didn't . . ."

Larsson hurried after him. "Didn't what?"

"It's okay . . ."

Carver was standing by the kitchen island. The wine racks were empty. The low-level built-in fridge had been taken from its housing. All that was left was the carcass. But he didn't seem too bothered by that.

"I suddenly thought you might have sold the kitchen units," he said.

Larsson grinned for the first time that night.

"Who'd buy that shit?"

Now it was Carver's turn to smile, if only for a moment. He leaned down and reached inside the wine rack, in the middle of the second row, three spaces along. He grimaced for a second as his fingers groped blindly, and then his smile reappeared as they found their target.

"Watch," he said.

There was a barely audible humming sound. Larsson looked in amazement as the center of the granite work surface rose from the island. Its smooth ascent revealed a metal frame, within which was fitted a large plastic toolbox, arranged in half a dozen clear plastic-fronted trays of varying depths.

"Unbelievable!" Larsson gasped.

"Looks like my kit is still in one piece then," said Carver. He was calming down, reassured by familiar surroundings and the presence of the toolbox.

"Okay, the top two trays should be filled with regular gear. . . ."

He opened it up to reveal a thick pad of charcoal-gray foam, within which a series of custom-cut openings housed a selection of immaculately shiny wrenches, screwdrivers, saws, and hammers. The second tray was devoted to miniature power tools and soldering irons.

"It's all there," he said. "Next two trays, I think, are gadgets, electronics, that kind of stuff."

Larsson sighed contentedly as a selection of timers, detonators, brake and accelerator overrides, and radio remote controls were presented to view.

"Oh, yeah, I recognize some of these babies. Nice to know you gave them such a good home."

"Okay, next down there should be . . ."

Larsson was confronted with blocks of plastique and thermite.

"And finally . . ."

Carver slid open the last, deepest tray. It contained a Heckler & Koch MP5K short-barreled submachine gun, with a suppressor and three magazines, plus a SIG Sauer P226 with the same essential accessories. Larsson gave a knowing nod. Both weapons were standard equipment for British Special Forces.

"There's something else," said Carver.

He pulled the toolbox out of its housing and placed it on the floor in front of him. Then he got down on his haunches. The lid of the toolbox was a couple of inches deep. He lifted it to reveal another compartment, inside the lid itself, accessed via a hinged plastic hatch. He opened that to reveal a fat, padded brown envelope, roughly twelve by eighteen inches.

"Little did you know . . ." he said.

Carver took out the envelope and shut the hatch again. Then he removed the SIG, the suppressor, and two magazines from the bottom tray. He closed up the toolbox, keeping it on the floor as he pressed the button inside the wine rack again. The empty housing disappeared back down into the island. Carver put the envelope and the gun back on top of the work surface.

"That got money in it?" asked Larsson, nodding at the envelope. Suddenly he didn't feel quite so cheery.

"Yeah."

"Enough to pay the bills?"

"Easily."

"And you remembered about it when, exactly?"

There was a bitter, sarcastic edge to the words.

"A few weeks ago, pretty soon after I started coming around."

"So you didn't need her money at all, then?"

"Sure I did. As long as it was coming through, I knew she was still alive."

Larsson was forced to accept the logic of Carver's argument. But he had a legitimate grievance of his own.

"You owe me, too. More than twenty thousand bucks."

Carver nodded silently. He reached in the envelope and took out an ornately engraved document. It was a fifty-thousand-dollar bearer bond, registered to a Panamanian corporation and signed by him on the reverse. Effectively, it was as good as cash. He gave it to Larsson.

"Thanks, but that's way too much," the Norwegian said.

"It won't be," said Carver dryly. "Not in the long run. Look, I'll pay Alix back, too . . . but first I've got to find her. We should start at the last places she'd have been seen. I know she was working at some late-night place. Do you know where it was?"

"The *bierkeller*? Of course—I used to give her a lift to work some-times."

"Fine—you can give me a lift, too. I just need a couple of minutes to get fixed up."

Carver picked up the envelope, the gun, and the magazines and left the kitchen. Walking through the living room, he saw the picture of Lulworth Cove on the wall, the only one of his most valuable possessions that hadn't yet been sold. He remembered talking to Alix about it. She'd been wearing his old T-shirt, curled up in the chair, her body fresh from the shower. He could happily have stood there, eyes closed, just wallow-ing in the thought of her, but not tonight. He had to keep moving.

In his bedroom, he opened up his closet. His gear was still hanging there, pushed over to one side to make way for Alix's pathetically small collection of clothes. He picked out a jacket from her end of the clothing rod and held it up to his face, catching a faint trace of her scent, savoring it like a dog about to be let loose on a trail. Then, quite unexpectedly, something clicked inside his brain—an automatic, unbidden reflex that switched off the emotional, indulgent, inefficient side of his conscious-ness and left him suddenly cold and clearheaded.

The panic and uncertainty had gone. There was no heavy, sickening ache of fear in the pit of his stomach, just a strong sense of urgency and purpose.

He reached up to a shelf above the rod and pulled down a leather trav-eling bag. Then he strained his arm farther into the shelf and extracted a shoulder holster and a broad money belt. It took him barely thirty seconds to pack the bag with two plain white T-shirts and two pairs of socks and underpants, followed by one pair of jeans and a lightweight fleece, both black. Another minute was spent getting dressed in a set of clothes identical to the ones he had packed, except with a charcoal-gray, V-necked pullover instead of a fleece. He chose a pair of plain black lace-up shoes, with thick cushioned soles.

The money belt went around his waist. From the envelope he took a block of one-hundred-dollar bills and another two bearer bonds, iden-tical to the one he had given Larsson. He also extracted two passports, one Australian, the other Swiss. They were both in different names but bore his photograph. He peeled a few of the bills off the top of the block and stuffed them in a trouser pocket, along with the Swiss cash he'd taken from the hitman at the clinic. Everything else went into the belt. Then he closed the envelope, which was still more than half full, and placed it in his bag.

He strapped on the shoulder holster. When the SIG went in, it felt entirely familiar, the holster already adjusted to fit it and him perfectly. There was a short black wool coat hanging in the closet, and he put that on last. The coat covered the holster without any apparent bulge. The spare magazines slipped right into its pockets. It was elegant enough to get him into any hotel or restaurant, but sturdy enough to keep out the cold. There was another coat exactly like it still hanging there, along with more black jeans and three apparently identical dark-blue suits. The drawers from which he'd taken the T-shirts, underwear, and tops had been equally repetitive. So this was how he had been: methodical, functional, finding something that worked and sticking to it.

Other drawers held watches, dark glasses, mobile phones, again with minimal variations. He took one of each, not needing to waste time choosing between styles, plus a couple of spare SIM cards for the phone. Then he noticed a photograph in a frame by the bed. It showed Alix by his chair in the clinic's dayroom. She had a hopeful smile on her face. He just looked bewildered. He couldn't remember the photo being taken. He spared it no more thought, but removed it from the frame, folded it in two, splitting himself from Alix and stuffed it in his inside coat pocket. If he wanted to find the woman, a picture would come in handy.

Larsson was waiting for him by the door of the apartment, carrying the toolbox. When he saw Carver, he said, "Hey, you look like a guy I used to know."

"Yeah—what was he like?" asked Carver.

Larsson was deadpan. "Total bastard."

36

D r. Geisel had warned Carver he was a long way from being cured. There was always the possibility of a relapse. Short of that, he could expect sudden, violent changes of mood.

He was beginning to understand what the shrink had meant. It was barely a five-minute drive from his flat to the *bierkeller,* but as soon as the Volvo got moving, the glorious sense of confidence and self-assurance began to fade and his uneasiness returned, his guts tightening, shoulder muscles tensing. Carver took a series of long, deep breaths and slowly rotated his head, lifting his chin up, then coming around and down till it was almost resting on his chest, breathing out as his head came down, then back in as it rose again.

"You all right?" asked Larsson from the driver's seat.

"Yeah, just trying to get myself level, you know."

"You'd better tell me what happened at the clinic."

Carver sighed deeply as he lowered his head, eyes shut. He remained like that for a second, screwed his face up in a grimace, then turned his head toward Larsson.

"Someone tried to kill me."

"And . . . ?"

"And someone else will be discovering the body any time now, so just shut up, keep driving, and help me get on with finding Alix."

Larsson brought the car to a sudden halt. He sat quite still as Carver snapped, "What the bloody hell are you doing?"

Without warning, Larsson shot out his right arm and grabbed Carver by the throat, pushing him back until he was forced against the side of the car.

Carver struggled to free himself, his body impeded by the seat belt, his feet stuck in the passenger footwell.

"I don't like people who are rude to me," Larsson sounded like he was explaining a misunderstanding, getting things straight. "So just stay cool, all right?"

He let go his grip and gradually brought his arm back, never taking his eyes off Carver.

"Okay," said Carver. "I apologize. I just want to get Alix back."

"Maybe, but you're not going after her now."

"Why not?"

"Because you're not in shape. Look at yourself—you let me grab you one-handed. Your mood's up and down like a yo-yo. You can't climb the stairs to your apartment without getting out of breath. You're weeks away from being fit."

Carver's eyelids drooped in tacit acknowledgment.

"Okay—maybe you're right . . . maybe. But I can't just sit around on my arse doing nothing. If I can work out what she was doing, where she was before she disappeared, at least that's something. Look, this beer place will be closing any minute and I can't come back tomorrow, because I've got to be out of town. I'll just go in, have a drink, ask a few questions, nice and easy. Trust me—I won't start any fights."

"Thank God for that," said Larsson as he started up the engine again.

37

In that Minnesota loft, Kady Jones felt like an explorer finally about to cast eyes on a mysterious animal species, often written about but never seen. To a scientist from Los Alamos, the suitcase nuke was as potent a myth as Bigfoot or the Loch Ness monster, and just as irresistible a lure.

She climbed up the ladder in her inflatable plastic suit, looking like the mutant spawn of a human being and a bouncy castle, buzzing with anticipation and nervous tension. Despite her confident words to Tom Mulvagh, she was only too aware of all the things that could go wrong. If the device was genuine, it could be booby-trapped. Even if it wasn't, an accidental detonation was not totally out of the question. The likelihood was infinitesimal, but it existed nonetheless, so the protocol was clear: Look but don't touch. And stay as far away from the device as possible.

Her head poked through the hatch. The loft was illuminated by a single, bare bulb, whose harsh light revealed the case, lying by the far end wall, wide open, daring her to come and take a closer look. She clambered up onto the floor, dragging an air hose behind her. Then she leaned back down to grab a video camera, passed to her by one of the team. A tripod followed, and a bright orange metal box, with a black handle extending two thirds of its length. A cable ran from the box back down through the hatch.

She set up the video camera on the tripod, switched it on, and focused on the case. "Are you getting that?" she asked, speaking into the microphone mounted in the headpiece of her suit.

Her deputy, Henry Wong, was sitting in one of the vans outside, facing a rack of electronic equipment, dials, and screens.

"Yeah, and it sure looks real to me."

"Only one way to find out," said Kady.

Leaving the camera, she picked up the orange box. At one end of it were a numeric keypad and a small backlit screen. The box was a handheld gamma-ray spectrometer, an instrument designed to measure and analyze the radiation emitted by whatever objects it was investigating.

The various nuclear materials that can be used in bombs all decay at specific rates, giving off particular quantities of gamma rays. Some of them, like plutonium, emit enough radiation to be detectable over a considerable distance. Others, however, register only at very short range. Standing by the camera, Kady wasn't getting a reading on her spectrometer. That immediately ruled out most of the possible suspects, but not all. That case could contain a dummy weapon, yet another false alarm. Or it could be armed with weapons-grade uranium. Kady had no choice. If she wanted to find out the truth, she was going to have to get up close and personal.

She crept across the floor toward the case, hardly daring to breathe, starting at every creaking board. As a little girl she had loved playing Grandmother's Footsteps, sneaking up on her dad when his back was turned, her heart thumping as she dared herself to take just one more step before he sprang around and caught her. Now there was a bomb where her father had been, and one wrong move could make it spring into action, too. She was perspiring inside her plastic bubble, unable to wipe away the drop of sweat that was trickling down her forehead.

She could feel her pulse racing, her breath coming in short, shallow gasps. The spectrometer was quivering in her hand. The way she was now, she might easily trip on a loose floorboard, or drop her gear. If she knocked into the case, and it was booby-trapped . . . She didn't finish the thought. She knew she had to calm down. She stood still, her eyes half shut, arms down by her side, trying to regulate her breathing and slow her heartbeat. Gradually the frenzied drumming of blood in her ears slowed to a more regular rhythm.

When she got near the case, she spoke to Henry Wong once again.

"Okay, here we go."

"Be careful, Kady."

"You think?"

She stepped right up to the open case, which was maybe thirty inches long, rectangular, with reinforced corners. The contents were nestled within a thick polystyrene base. The main unit was a metal pipe, which ran for most of the length of the case. One end was thicker than the other, as if ringed by an additional reinforcing band of metal. A wire extended from the other end, and ran to a black control unit, with a series of switches, a keypad, and a digital timer. There were no numbers showing on the timer, no dramatic countdown, just a bunch of controls with Russian markings. A single, small red bulb glowed, to indicate that the unit was receiving power from its electric cable.

Kady pointed the spectrometer at the unit. A series of digits and letters appeared on its display, and, via the cable, on a screen in front of Henry Wong. There was a low, awestruck whistle in her ear.

"Weapons-grade uranium—two thirty-five. You just found a genuine suitcase nuke, Kady. Man, that is cool."

She smiled, the tension momentarily broken. "That's not the word I'd have chosen. It looks to me like Alexander Lebed was telling the truth. The Soviets really did cache portable nukes all over the Western world. But if this is one of them, where are the rest?"

"Not our problem," said Wong. "And nothing we can do till this one's deactivated. Why don't you get on down here, we can recheck those readings?"

"Sure. But not till I get a close-up of this thing on video. We need to have a record of exactly what we're dealing with."

She made her way back to the camera, still taking care over every step, but feeling a fraction more secure now, having faced the weapon once and survived. Now that she knew what she was dealing with, she felt as if she were more in control of the process. As she unscrewed the video from its tripod and carried it back toward the case, she told herself she'd worked on far more powerful warheads, both Russian and American, and never come to any harm. Why should this be any different?

She didn't notice the loose nail protruding from the floor till the boots of her suit snagged against it. Her hands were gripping the camera, so she had no way of using her arms to regain her balance or break her fall as she tripped.

"Kady!" shouted Wong, as she fell on top of the case, becoming hopelessly entangled in her air tube as the light on the control unit began flashing and the bomb emitted a rapid series of high-pitched beeps.

Like a warning.

A booby trap activated.

The tension she had felt since she clambered up into the loft was blown away in an instant by a nauseating, heart-pounding, flop-sweating rush of pure terror. The fear seemed to blur her vision her as she thrashed her limbs, frantically trying to scramble away, as though that would do any good.

In her ears she could hear Wong's voice, "Oh, shit . . ."

The beeping stopped.

There were no more words in her headphones.

She lay stock-still, unmoving, unable to breathe in the absolute silence of the loft.

From somewhere inside the case there came the noise of a feeble detonation, no louder or more powerful than a Christmas cracker. Then silence once again.

Kady scrambled back onto the floor, trying to get her breath back. Then she noticed the electric plug, sitting at the end of the cable that led from the case. It had been jerked from its socket by the impact of her fall. The flashing and beeping were simply a warning to the bomb's users that its power had been cut. There was no booby trap.

But there were Soviet suitcase nukes loose in the world. And neither Kady nor anyone else in America had any idea where they were.

38

The staff of the *bierkeller* weren't too anxious to let Carver and Larsson in. A waitress tried to tell them the place was about to close. Carver took out a hundred bucks.

"We'll only be a few minutes," he said.

The waitress took the banknote and nodded toward the empty tables. "Help yourself."

They ordered a couple of wheat beers, an authentic taste of Germany, right in the heart of French Switzerland. Carver looked around. There was only one other customer in the place, a bland-looking man in his thirties or forties, sitting in a corner of the room, nursing a glass of whiskey. He was thinning on top, wearing a mass-produced gray suit, just one more lonely salesmen on another solitary night.

Carver turned his attention to the phony Bavarian decor and the two waitresses in their wigs and costumes, both tired and short-tempered at the end of a long shift. He felt ashamed to think of Alix working in this dump, into the early hours every night. She'd always been at the hospital first thing in the morning—she must have been exhausted. Maybe that's why she'd run away. She needed a decent night's sleep.

He finished his drink and went up to the bar.

"How much for two beers?"

"Ten francs," said the barman.

Carver paid with a fifty and told him to keep the change.

The barman thanked him, then regarded Carver, an eyebrow raised, lips pursed, as if to say, "There has to be a catch."

Carver caught the look. "You're right," he said, slipping into French without a second thought. "I do want something."

He slipped his photo of Alix across the table.

"Do you know this woman? Her name is Alexandra Petrova. She used to work here."

The barman said nothing.

"Look," said Carver, "I'm not a cop. I'm just a friend of hers. She's disappeared and I'm trying to find out what happened to her, that's all."

Finally the barman spoke. "You English?"

"Uh-huh."

"Been in the hospital lately?"

Carver unfolded the photograph and showed him the other half.

"Okay," said the barman. "I heard about you. But I don't know where Alix went. One night she was here, the next . . . poof!"

He shrugged and lifted up his hands to emphasize his bafflement, then pulled out a cloth from behind the bar and started wiping the countertop in front of Carver.

"But maybe Trudi can help you. She was a friend of Alix's."

The barman gestured at one of the waitresses—the one Carver had met at the door.

"Hey, Trudi! He wants to buy you a drink."

The waitress made a show of looking Carver up and down.

"Do I get another hundred dollars?" she asked and sauntered over.

The balding man in the corner, attracted by the sound of conversation, watched her as she walked toward the bar. Carver saw him and just for a second thought he caught something in the man's eye, a way of looking that suggested intense concentration, a kind of professional curiosity. But then Trudi was standing next to him, cheerful, busty, the classic barmaid—her costume laced extra-tight to make her cleavage all the deeper—and the thought vanished.

"So, are you going to get me that drink?" she said.

"Sure," said Carver. "What are you having?"

"Double vodka and tonic."

The drink appeared. Trudi downed half of it in one gulp and gave a contented sigh.

"I needed that. So, what can I do for you?"

"It's Alix. I'm trying to find her."

Trudi looked at him for a moment, then a sly smile crossed her face.

"So you're her mystery man, huh? She talked about you a few times. Not often, though—it upset her to say too much. I thought you were sick in the hospital."

"I was. Now I'm not. What happened to Alix?"

"I don't know—she just . . . well, she just vanished."

"When? The last time she came to visit me was around the middle of February."

Trudi considered for a moment. "Yes, that sounds right. She walked out just before our big Valentine's Day party. I was cross with her, leaving the rest of us to fill in. It never occurred to me she wasn't coming back."

"Had she been worried about anything?"

"Sure," said Trudi. "Paying your hospital bills. She really loved you."

"Tell me about the bills. What did she say about them?"

"Just that she didn't know where she was going to find twenty thousand francs. It was really on her mind."

"And the last time you saw her, the night you say she walked out: Do you remember what happened?"

Trudi took another sip of her drink.

"Okay, I remember. I'd been working a couple of hours before Alix arrived, and I was waiting for her to start work, so that I could take a break. I saw her come out from the dressing room, just over there . . ."

Trudi pointed toward a door set into the wall not far from where they were talking. There was a sign on it forbidding entry to customers.

"Then what happened?" asked Carver. "How did Alix seem to you?"

Trudi gave a quizzical little pout. "I don't know, normal, I suppose—at first, anyway. But then suddenly she stopped completely still, right in the middle of the floor. She was staring at one of the tables, like she'd seen a ghost, you know? Then she turned and walked really fast, right out of the bar, toward our dressing room. I thought it was kind of odd, but I didn't have time to think about it because I was serving customers. There was a problem because two men got up and left without paying and Pierre, the barman, was giving me shit for letting them do that, but in the end it didn't matter because a woman paid their bill. Weird, huh?"

"Yeah, maybe," said Carver impatiently. "But concentrate on Alix. When did you know she'd left the building?"

"About ten minutes later. She hadn't come back and I still hadn't had my break and I just thought she was being a selfish cow, so I went to look for her. But when I got to the dressing room, she wasn't there, and her bag and coat were both gone. And that was the last time I saw her."

"Go back to when you last saw Alix. She came out of the door. She saw something. What did she see?"

Trudi thought for a moment. Then she got up and said, "Come with me."

She led Carver across the room till they were standing in front of the door from which Alix had emerged. Behind them, the man in the cheap suit had come to the bar and was settling his account with Pierre. From time to time, he glanced up to check out the pantomime being acted out by Trudi.

"Right," she said. "Alix was looking over . . . there!"

She pointed across the room. Directly in her sight line there was a single small table.

"Who was sitting there?" asked Carver.

Trudi puffed her cheeks. "Oh, monsieur, it was many weeks ago—how can I remember one customer?"

"Start with the basics: Was it a man or a woman?"

"I don't know!"

Carver could feel frustration rising inside him. He was close to losing his temper, but that would serve no purpose at all. As much to calm himself as Trudi, he spoke as gently as possible, coaxing her like a stage hypnotist.

"Take your time. Just close your eyes, relax, and try to go back to that night. There's someone sitting at the table. Tell me about them."

Trudi did as she was told. Her eyes had been shut only for a few seconds when her face suddenly came alive again.

"Of course!" she cried. "I remember now. It was the woman, the one who paid the bill for the two men I was talking about, the ones who ran out without paying."

"That's great," said Carver. "Well done. Now, this woman, what did she look like?"

"Well, she had very dark hair, cut short, in a bob."

Trudi framed her face with her hands to illustrate what she meant.

"How old was she?"

"Oh, quite old, maybe fifty. But quite chic . . . you know, for a Russian."

"Hold on—this woman was Russian?"

"Yes, I think so. Her accent, it was a bit like Alix's, and she is Russian, right?"

Carver nodded distractedly, no longer paying attention to Trudi. His mind was fully occupied trying to make sense of the Russians: the woman and the two men. Who had they been? What did they want from Alix? He had a strong sense that the answer was in him somewhere. He had the information he needed to solve the problem if only he could retrieve it. Like Trudi, he needed to close his eyes, relax, and think. He couldn't do that now.

"Is that all?" Trudi asked, sounding disappointed that her information had not been met with more enthusiasm.

"Yeah," said Carver. "Thanks. You've been great. But you'd better clear up."

The other waitress was placing chairs upside down on top of the tables, banging them down hard, just to let the world know she wasn't getting any help. Larsson had got up from their table and was standing by the main exit, waiting to go. The barman was trying to disentangle himself from the solitary drinker's attempts at conversation. Carver heard him say, "You've got to leave now, my friend."

Carver nodded farewell at the barman and gave Trudi a short, brisk wave as he started to walk out.

She called out, "If you find Alix, send her my love," and he forced a smile to show that he'd heard.

He was feeling edgy again, just as he had on the train. It was the drinker, who was now turning away from the bar and following Larsson and Carver as they walked out. Carver didn't like the look of him. Ever since he'd walked into the *bierkeller,* he'd felt that the man had been looking at him and trying to listen in on his conversations. He was being kept under surveillance—he was sure of it. He had to take action before it was too late.

As he walked through the main exit to the street, Carver slowed his pace, waiting for the sound of the door swinging open again behind him. He heard the footsteps of the man in the suit. Then, without any warning, he turned around, swiveling on his toes, then he took one strong, quick stride back the way he had come and punched the man full in the face.

He caught him right on the bridge of the nose, which crumpled under his fist.

The man gave a muffled cry of pain, held his hand up to his face, and staggered back through the door. Carver followed him, grabbing him by the collar and throwing him to the ground.

"What are you looking at?" he snarled.

The man's eyes widened. He had been caught totally unawares. He was in pain. He was frightened, and he was baffled.

"Why did you hit me?" His voice was as plaintive as a bullied child. "What have I done?"

Carver could not answer him. He did not know what to say. He had attacked an innocent man for no reason other than his own paranoia. He looked up and saw Pierre running toward him, the waitresses looking on in horror.

Pierre stopped beside the wounded man, uncertain what to do next. He turned his head toward the women and said, "One of you, call the police." Then he reached into his trouser pocket and pulled out the handle of a knife. He pressed a button and the blade flicked open.

He looked at Carver. "I know how to use this," he said.

The man at Carver's feet moaned in pain. Blood was seeping through his fingers and spattering his clothes.

Now the door crashed open again and Larsson was there, grabbing Carver and dragging him away from the scene.

"Get out!" he shouted and Carver's legs started pumping, his feet scrabbling on the floor until he got some purchase, and he dashed out of the *bierkeller* after Larsson.

Pierre hesitated, not knowing whether to follow the two fleeing men or attend to the wounded victim. Then he hurried to the man on the floor, who was making a groggy, disoriented effort to get to his feet. The man let himself be led away from the exit, under a low stone arch, into a small, deserted office.

"Wait here," said Pierre, lowering him onto a chair.

The man groaned. He wasn't going anywhere.

Seconds later, the door opened and Trudi walked toward him. "You poor thing," she said.

He winced as she dabbed some cotton soaked in disinfectant over his face, gasping in pain when she touched his broken nose.

"Look at what that bastard did to you," she said. "I'm not surprised Alix ran away if that's what he's like."

She paused, the cotton dripping in midair, as she suddenly realized what she'd done.

"Oh, my God. I've helped him find her! I just hope the police—"

The man gripped her arm with surprising force. "No police," he mumbled. "Don't want police. No time. Too busy."

"But, m'sieur, we must . . ." Trudi pleaded. "I mean, they're already on the way."

"No!" the man exclaimed, spitting blood.

He got up, pushing Trudi out of his way, as he half ran, half stumbled from the room, through the *bierkeller*, and out onto the street.

"My God, what a night," muttered Trudi, ripping off her wig and heading for the dressing room.

39

In the Volvo, Carver was racking his brain, trying to make the connection between Alix and the woman. "That waitress, Trudi, said she was Russian, age about fifty. I'm sure I know who she is. I just can't get at it...."

"I think I know," said Larsson. "Alix and I used to talk a lot, when you were sick. She told me a lot about her past, what happened between you two..."

He paused. "She told me what happened in Gstaad that night."

"And?"

"The woman in the *bierkeller*, I don't know her name—not her first name. But I think I know who she was: the woman who first found Alix, when she was just a kid, and trained her to... umm..."

Larsson's face twisted in embarrassment.

"Yeah, I know what she trained her to do," said Carver.

"Right," said Larsson, visibly relieved. "And this woman's husband was another KGB officer. He ran Alix's operations and then when that all ended, Alix was ... look, I'm sorry, man ... she was his mistress. Until she went to Paris and met you, right? The guy was called Yuri Zhukovski. He was the one you killed in Gstaad...."

"Jesus," said Carver. "Alix slept with this woman's husband and I killed him. Well, that explains why Alix got the shits when she saw her at the *bierkeller*."

"It probably explains why someone tried to kill you tonight, too," agreed Larsson.

"Okay, but what about the bit in the middle? Alix does a runner. The woman sends two guys after her. The next thing we know, Alix has money and is paying my bills. How does that add up?"

"I don't know," admitted Larsson. "But we've got a couple of weeks to work it out."

"What do you mean?"

They'd crossed the river and were driving through the residential areas between the lake and the international airport on the edge of town, passing smart, modern apartment blocks.

"That's how long it's going to take to get you into shape. I'd like twice as long, but I know you won't wait. Hold on . . ."

He pulled up outside one of the blocks. Carver looked around. This was where Larsson lived. He'd been here before. He'd been surprised—just as he was now—to find a guy like Larsson living in such a bourgeois location. With his wild hair, torn jeans, and vintage rock-band T-shirts, the Norwegian looked as though he should be sitting in some funky warehouse, surrounded by computer parts and empty pizza boxes. But Geneva didn't do funky warehouses.

Larsson patted him on the shoulder. "Wait here, okay? I'm just going to get some cold-weather gear and my laptop."

"Why? Where are we going?"

Larsson grinned. "The end of the world, Carver. My world. I'm going to make your life hell. And you just paid me a lot of money for the privilege."

40

B arely a mile away, Piotr Korsakov was sitting in an FSB safe house, while a doctor tended to his nose. His cell phone rang. He checked the number—Moscow, calling on a secure line—and motioned to the doctor to leave the room.

"You had a bad night, Korsakov." The voice was cool, female, authoritative.

"Yes, Madam Deputy Director."

"You lost a partner and a target."

"Yes."

"Matov paid the price for his incompetence. What happened to you?"

"I was taken unawares. I did not believe that the target, Carver, had spotted me as a potential threat. I was wrong. He assaulted me. I could have retaliated, of course. Doubtless I would have killed him. But there were several witnesses. I felt it more prudent to play the innocent victim."

"That may have been the correct judgment. We will have a hard enough time covering up the deaths of Matov and the couple you terminated. We do not need any further complications. Did you see where Carver went?"

"No, ma'am. He left the building while I was still inside and I was unable to follow him. But he was not alone. There was another man, very distinctive, almost six and a half feet tall, with long hair. He would be easy to identify again."

"That will not be necessary. I am already aware of his identity."

"So what would you like me to do now?"

"Return to Moscow. I will decide what we shall do about Mr. Carver... and his hairy friend."

She hung up the phone.

And in the meantime, we must get a message to Alix, she thought. The assassination has failed, for now, but there is no reason she should know that. Let's see how well she does her job when she's not distracted by thoughts of another man. . . .

Thirteen hundred miles away, alone in her hotel room, Alix was look-ing across the waters of the Canale della Giudecca toward the lights of Venice. Here she stood, in one of the most romantic cities in the world, and right there in the next-door room was a man who yearned to be her lover. For weeks she had been keeping him at bay, but all her train-ing and professional expertise told her these stalling tactics were rapidly outliving their usefulness. Denying a man what he most desired was an excellent way of keeping him on tenterhooks, but beyond a certain point even the most lovesick male would eventually decide that the effort wasn't worth it.

If Olga Zhukovskaya could see what was happening now, her orders would be simple: "Sleep with Vermulen, immediately."

So what was stopping her?

Loyalty to Carver, and a refusal any longer to whore in the service of the state: Those were the obvious answers, but she knew they were just phony self-justifications. The real reason Alix was not in Vermulen's room right now was precisely the fact that part of her wanted to be there just as much as he did.

She did not love Vermulen the way she loved Carver, or had loved the man he once was. But the general was present in her life, and Carver was now just a memory that seemed to fade a little more into the distance with every passing day. Vermulen was a good, kind man, whose feelings for her were unmistakably real. Just as important, he had money, influ-ence, and a degree of power. He offered her the possibility of protection, some refuge at least if she should ever defy Zhukovskaya, and walk away from the FSB.

Sooner or later, that promise of security would be impossible to resist.

41

There were eight men sitting at the mahogany table in one of the meeting rooms that form part of the five-thousand-square-foot complex known to its users as the Woodshed, but to the rest of the world as the White House Situation Room. One of them was the President's national security adviser, Leo Horabin. The other seven were senior representatives of federal agencies, including the FBI and CIA. These were men who had made it to the commanding heights of the establishment. They exuded a common aura of power. But they had all come to listen to Dr. Kady Jones.

She began the meeting by describing the discovery and analysis of the device found in Minnesota. A photograph of the inside of the case filled a screen on one of the Situation Room walls.

"The best way to describe this bomb is to say that it's a classic piece of Russian military design: basic, but effective. What they did was essentially the same concept as Little Boy, the bomb we dropped on Hiroshima more than forty years ago. It's what's known as a gun-type design. This here"—she pointed at the metal pipe filling most of the case—"is the gun barrel. It's fired by a signal sent from the control box, here, in the form of an electric charge. It passes down this wire into one end of the barrel and ignites a conventional explosive charge. Right next to the charge is a fifteen-kilogram mass of weapons-grade uranium."

She brought up another slide. One side of the barrel had been cut away, revealing the contents.

"Exactly like a charge of gunpowder propelling a cannonball, the explosive fires the uranium down the barrel, where it hits a second fifteen-kilo slug of uranium, at the far end. Now, a total of sixty pounds would not normally be enough to create a critical mass of uranium–two thirty-five—that's the amount needed to create a nuclear chain reaction. But the Russians were smart. They put a ring of beryllium around the end of the barrel—see how it thickens there, at the end? That beryllium acts as a reflector, concentrating the forces released by the impact, so that the reaction takes place at a lower mass. That creates a nuclear explosion, which we'd estimate in the range of one to five kilotons. That's nothing compared to a strategic nuclear-missile warhead, but it's still enough to devastate the heart of a major city, take out a military base, or flatten an oil refinery."

"Dear God . . ." Horabin's sagging, downcast face—all drooping jowls, double chins, and baggy eyes—was ashen. "And you're sure this thing is Russian?"

"Well, it was certainly manufactured from Russian components, using their uranium. And we believe it's at least a decade old, dating back to Soviet days, when the state still had total control of all its stocks of weapons-grade nuclear materials. So it was made either by a Soviet government agency or by someone with very, very high-level access."

"And it's still in working order?"

"Well, thankfully it didn't detonate when . . . ah"—she hesitated for a moment, hoping that no one could see the blood she felt flushing her cheeks—"when struck by a heavy falling object. But we couldn't find anything wrong with the basic bomb. Anyone with the correct arming code could have set it off."

"Excuse me, Dr. Jones . . ." The speaker was Ted Jaworski, the CIA representative. "When we investigated the Lebed claims at Langley, our analysts told us that if the bombs really did exist, they would most likely be inactive by now. But you're saying that's not the case. How come?"

Kady felt the atmosphere in the room crackle with anticipation. Jaworski was making a play, pitching his agency against hers. The people around the table were Washington veterans. They seemed to lean forward a fraction, anxious to see if the newcomer could defend herself.

"That's simple," she said, letting the room know that the question hadn't fazed her. "Your people would have made the same assumption we did at Los Alamos before we'd actually seen this thing. We all figured the Soviets would use plutonium for any small-scale weapon, because that's what we would have done. Plutonium is far more efficient than uranium. You get a much bigger bang per kilo. But it also decays a lot faster. Much beyond a decade, it's lost its explosive power, so the whole unit needs servicing and updating. But uranium lasts for hundreds of thousands of years. It's crude. It's inefficient. But it keeps right on working."

Kady saw Jaworski give her a slight nod of the head, an acknowledgment that she'd passed his test.

"All right," said Horabin. "I get it."

He looked at the agency representatives around him. "I have to brief the President on this, and I don't want to walk into the Oval Office with nothing but bad news. We know there are bombs out there. Now we've got to get to them—all of them—before our enemies get there first. I need a strategy. What have you got for me?"

The agencies had all received preliminary briefings prior to the meeting. As a matter of institutional pride they had already drafted action plans. Five of the men reached for their cases and withdrew their documents. Only Jaworski remained motionless, indifferent to the activity around him.

"Don't you have anything, Ted?" asked Horabin.

"Yes, I have one very strong piece of advice."

"Great. Let's hear it."

"Do nothing."

There was a murmur of disapproval around the table.

Horabin glared at him: "Is that all you have to offer?"

The CIA man seemed unruffled. "It's all I recommend right now, in public, at least. The only thing we have going for us is that no one knows what we've found. If we start mounting search operations, people will want to know what we're looking for. And, believe me, they will find out. So then we'll have a major diplomatic incident with the Russians. We'll have the TV news telling folks there could be nukes in their backyards. And we'll have every terrorist leader in the world trying to figure out how he can get one of these things for himself.

"That means we've got to be discreet. I suggest a small, dedicated team, backed by the full resources of all our agencies. This team must be tasked to search for any clues to who's got these bombs, where they are, and who still knows how to make them explode. But they've got to do this quietly—and I mean really, really quietly."

42

The first morning, Carver stumbled over the finish line of his three-mile course like a newborn foal on an ice rink, unable to control the skis and poles on the end of his thrashing, twitching, uncoordinated limbs. He lay facedown in the snow, his chest heaving, his throat gagging until Thor Larsson reached down, grabbed the collar of his windproof jacket, and dragged him, coughing and wheezing, to his feet.

"Keep moving," growled Larsson. He hit Carver hard across the backside with a ski pole, just to underline the order.

"I said move," he repeated.

Carver raised his goggles onto his forehead and stared at Larsson with an expression that combined exhaustion and loathing in equal proportions.

"Thought this was the end," he finally croaked, dragging icy air into his lungs between each word.

Larsson shook his head.

"Move," he said for a third time, wielding his stick again. "Now!"

Carver spat emphatically into the snow, just inches from Larsson's skis. He yanked his goggles back down and set off again along the municipal trail that snaked through the countryside around Beisfjord, a small town near Narvik on the northwest coast of Norway, inside the Arctic Circle. Spring might be blooming across the rest of Europe, but up here winter had yet to relax its deep-frozen grip.

They barely hit walking pace past stands of stunted, bedraggled birch trees. Carver struggled for rhythm as he lifted his heels and slid his metal-edged, military-specification Asnes mountain skis forward, all the while driving his poles into the hard-packed snow.

Larsson had been cross-country skiing since he was in kindergarten. He'd received winter training during his national service as an intelligence officer in the Norwegian Army. He effortlessly glided ahead, always ensuring that no matter how hard Carver tried to catch up, he was always tantalizingly out of his reach.

They'd gone about another half-mile when they came to a rifle range, located by the trail so that biathletes could practice their shooting and skiing in competition conditions. Carver followed Larsson into the range, pulled off the Anschütz Fortner target rifle strapped across his back, and flopped down on his belly by one of the firing positions.

"Five shots, quick-fire," said Larsson. "You have twenty-five seconds."

Carver tried to aim his gun at the target: five white discs set against a black background. His muscles were overloaded with lactic acid, making his aching arms shake in protest as they tried to hold the weapon still and straight. Sweat was pouring into his eyes. It took him forty seconds to get his shots away. By the last one, he barely had the strength to pull the bolt back to load the next round. And the only target he hit was next to the one he was aiming at.

"Not good enough," said Larsson. "Fire another clip."

There were three more five-shot magazines in a holder on the right-hand side of the gun, a few inches in front of the trigger. Carver reloaded, fumbling like a new recruit.

"Twenty seconds," said Larsson. "And this time, get your shots away inside the limit or you do another course."

Larsson's voice made it plain that he was utterly indifferent to the prospect of Carver's suffering if he had to go around again. It reminded Carver of other voices, at another time and place. He remembered the twenty-mile runs he'd endured at Lympstone Commando Training Centre, on the way to his marines beret, and the ferocious workouts amounting to institutional sadism that were handed out by the instructors who supervised his selection for the SBS.

They'd not broken him, and he wasn't going to let this overgrown computer geek make him look like a noddy now.

He got off the next five shots in a fraction over nineteen seconds. He hit two more targets.

Carver rolled over onto his back to take the weight off the elbows and biceps that had been supporting his upper body and the gun.

Larssson looked down at him with a contemptuous curl of the lip. "You have another twenty seconds to get back into position, reload, and hit the remaining two targets. Same deal. You fail, you ski."

Ten years earlier he could have done it in five seconds. Throughout the Cold War the Royal Marines had been the U.K. armed forces' Arctic-warfare specialists. As a young lieutenant, Carver had been up to Beisfjord for winter training with 45 Commando. Even now, he was wearing his old leather ski march boots, as unyielding as iron when they'd first been issued, but gradually worn in to fit the exact contours of his feet and ankles. Carver had even tried out for the marines' Olympic-standard biathlon squad before the SBS came calling. But now . . .

"Go!" shouted Larsson, looking at his watch.

Carver heaved himself back onto his front, grabbed the gun, ripped out the empty magazine, and groped for its replacement. Actions that had once been second nature now seemed entirely foreign. It all used to be automatic. Now he had to think everything through, one agonized motion at a time. His hands were quivering with cold as well as exhaustion. He could barely focus his aching, sweat-stung eyes on the target.

"Fifteen seconds left," Larsson intoned.

Not one shot fired.

Carver gathered himself and aimed at the first standing target. He fired as he was breathing out, to help steady his aim.

And missed.

"Come on!" he muttered to himself as he pulled back the bolt.

"Ten seconds."

Carver felt his stomach tense. That was good. Somewhere his body had found a last shot of adrenaline-fueled energy. There was no time left to think. He just had to go for it.

Pull . . . aim . . . breathe . . . fire.

A hit. One left.

"Five seconds."

He shot again. Another miss.

Shit!

Pull . . . aim . . . breathe . . .

"Two."

You bastard!

Fire.

Carver blinked, trying to clear his vision. He couldn't see what had happened. He rolled over again in despair.

"Get up," said Larsson. "Move it out."

Carver was muttering under his breath, repeating like a mantra, "Don't let him beat you . . . don't let him beat you . . ."

Larsson looked at him as he slowly got to his feet. And this time there was a smile playing around the corner of his mouth.

"You hit the target," he said. "So we'd better get back to the farm. Ebba will have lunch ready by now. And, Carver?"

"Uh?"

"Stop talking to yourself. She'll think you're totally crazy."

"She won't be wrong," wheezed Carver, following Larsson as he skied away down the track.

43

Carver's recovery had caused almost as much discomfort in MI6's London headquarters on the south bank of the Thames as it had in Moscow. The thought of a renegade assassin alive, well, and in full command of his senses gave Jack Grantham cold sweats. This new situation could easily turn into a disaster. Somehow he had to make it work for him.

"What's the news from this bloody clinic?" he asked, not bothering to disguise his irritation.

His deputy, Bill Selsey, was unruffled by Grantham's bad temper. He'd long since learned to let it wash over him. He asked nothing more from life than a secure job, a modest home in the south London suburbs, and a guaranteed pension at the end of his career. He knew the pressure his boss was under and he didn't envy it one bit.

"Carver's done a runner, leaving a body behind," Selsey replied. "The corpse in question had a fake I.D., some bogus psychiatrist, but I'm pretty sure he is, or was, Vladimir Matov, known to his chums as Vlad the Impaler. He's an experienced FSB hitman, used to work for the KGB back in the good old days. Bulgarian by origin, like a lot of their best killers."

"So friend Matov was sent to sanction Carver, only to find himself on the wrong end of the operation?"

"Looks like it."

"And there's no one else who could have sent him—he doesn't freelance for anyone?"

Selsey shook his head. "Not as far as we know. He's a state employee, no moonlighting."

"So why does Moscow want Carver dead? Specifically, why do they want him dead now? He's been a sitting duck for months for anyone who wanted revenge for Zhukovski's death."

"Like his dear wife," Selsey interjected.

"Right. But Mrs. Z. doesn't do anything for six months until suddenly she, or someone equally high up, feels the need to take action. And then, how the hell did Carver beat this man? I thought he was supposed to be bonkers, no bloody use to anyone. What's he doing taking out a pro like Matov?"

"Apparently, he got better."

"You don't say." Grantham's voice was drenched with acid sarcasm. "I managed to work that out for myself, thanks, Bill. But when did this miracle cure happen, and why?"

"I've got people looking into that, talking to doctors and nurses at the clinic. Should have the answers later today. But I think I may have a lead on why the Russians want him dead."

"Do tell."

"There's a Romanian in Venice, name of Radinescu, does some low-level work for the FSB, basic courier stuff, nothing fancy. We've been tossing him a few bob to copy us in on anything he gets."

"And?"

"And he just passed on a message to Moscow from an agent who happened to be passing through Venice, a female agent. The woman in question was a bit of a looker, so Radinescu followed her for a while . . ."

"Bloody perv."

"Maybe, but while he was stalking this woman, he took a couple of photos and when he sent us a copy of her message, he chucked in a picture of the girl, hoping we might pay him a bonus for uncovering a Russian spy."

"He's got a nerve."

"Don't be so sure. You might think this is worth standing Radinescu a drink."

A plasma screen at one end of the room sprang into life. A series of color images appeared, showing two women—one black, the other white—wandering the crowded Venice streets.

"Good Lord, that's the Petrova girl," said Grantham. "But what's she doing in Italy?"

"Well, she's staying at the Cipriani with a man called Kurt Vermulen—separate rooms, before you ask."

Grantham frowned.

"Vermulen? That name's familiar . . ."

"American, ex-army, did some time in the DIA, and spent a couple of years in Grosvenor Square as their defense attaché. You probably bumped into him then. Anyway, Moscow seems to have taken an interest in him. Presumably Petrova's been told to get as close to him as possible."

"Who's the woman with her?"

"Her name is Alisha Reddin. She and her husband, Marcus Reddin, are staying at the same hotel as Vermulen and Petrova. And here's an interesting thing: Reddin served under Vermulen in the U.S. Army Rangers."

"Could just be a couple of old comrades meeting up," Grantham observed.

"Could be, yes," agreed Selsey. "But presumably the Russians think there's more to it than that. Why else have they inserted Petrova?"

For the first time, Grantham's mood seemed to lift a fraction. The merest hint of amusement crossed his face.

"So she's gone back to her old trade, for her old employers. Dear, oh dear... Carver won't like that. He's convinced she's a good girl, really."

"He may not know what she's up to," Selsey suggested.

"I'm sure he doesn't have a clue. And you're right: That explains what Matov was doing—making sure Carver died in blissful ignorance. After all, if there's one thing we know about Carver, it's that he'll do anything to get his bird back. The Russians know that, too; they learned it the hard way. So the last thing they want is Carver setting off after his one true love and blundering into Petrova's mission, whatever that is."

"Which means they'll have another go at killing him."

"If they can find him, yes. Meanwhile, we need to know what was in that message Petrova sent Moscow."

"We're working on it," Selsey assured him. "Should have it decrypted by close of play today."

Grantham looked a lot more cheerful than he had at the start of the meeting.

"See if you can hurry it up—there's no time to waste. We need to find out everything there is to know about Vermulen. Where else has he been, with whom, and why? Keep tabs on him. And find Carver. We have to get to him before the Russians do. Then we'll suggest that he find out what his blessed Alix is doing, tell her to stop it, and cause the maximum havoc to all concerned while he's about it."

"The Russians won't like that."

"I certainly hope not."

"What about our cousins across the water? Should we keep Langley informed?"

"I don't see why—not yet, at any rate."

"Really? They are supposed to be our colleagues."

"And so they are, Bill," said Grantham. "But only up to a point."

44

In the corps they'd have called it an "up-homer"; bunking with a local family, instead of roughing it with the rest of the company in one of the disused caravan sites hired by the Ministry of Defense. Carver and Larsson were staying with one of the Norwegian's cousins, Ebba Roll, who was married to a local farmer. Six feet tall and strappingly built, Ebba was the kind of woman who could just as easily stick a child under her arm as a sack of animal feed. She had powerful maternal instincts, but she didn't show them through gushing affection or teary-eyed concern. Instead they were expressed by the no-nonsense efficiency with which she made sure that her menfolk and offspring (all of whom she treated as lovable but essentially hopeless) were kept clean, warmly dressed, and well fed at all times.

The two men had developed a routine. They got up no later than five-thirty and ate a breakfast that set them up for the day: porridge and fruit, boiled or scrambled eggs, cold meats and cheese, toast and jam—sometimes all of them—washed down with gallons of orange juice, coffee, and (Carver insisted) strong, sweet tea.

While the food was digested, Larsson worked on Carver's mental fitness: memory tests, spot-the-difference puzzles, anything that boosted his ability to take in information fast, notice patterns or anomalies, and recall what he had just seen. Next time he checked out his surroundings, or walked into a new environment, he'd have his wits about him.

Midmornings were spent on the ski trails and rifle range. In northern Norway, the winters are dark, with only a few hours a day of gloomy blue light before the sun finally rises over the mountains at the end of January. But by the last week in March the sun rises at 5 A.M. and doesn't set until 7 P.M., and the light on the snow can be dazzlingly clear and intense. The landscape is raw, but spectacular: the white snow, blue skies, gray-black rocks, and deep-green sea all colliding as the mountains plunge into the fjords, where the waters of the North Atlantic mount their eternal, erosive assault.

As time went by, Carver realized that although there was never a ski session that did not involve a steadily escalating quantity of pain, inevitably building up to a grand finale of tortured muscles and burning lungs, it took longer every day for the agony to kick in. Little by little he actually began to enjoy the process. He took pleasure in his increasing fitness and pride in his rediscovered proficiency on the rifle range. He was able to appreciate the majesty of his surroundings. Some days, he even managed to complete an entire course without once wishing to kill Thor Larsson.

That, though, was never a good sign. Larsson always noticed any lessening of Carver's hatred. The next day, he would go that little bit further, pressing harder and faster, just to crank the pain and the fury back up to the proper level.

Lunchtimes, they replaced lost energy with pasta, potatoes, or brown bread. Protein came from chicken, fish, or, if Ebba was feeling indulgent, lean, intensely flavored cuts of moose and reindeer. His stomach full and his body shattered, Carver collapsed into bed for a couple of hours' rest, only to be raised again for an afternoon of weights, weapons training, and unarmed combat in one of the farm's outbuildings. Guns are legal and relatively easy to come by in Norway, compared with much of Europe. Within ten days, Carver was stripping and reassembling a rifle and pistol as fast as Larsson, and easily outsparring him. His body was gradually returning to its natural shape: 175 pounds of muscle and bone, a balance of endurance and strength. He felt like a fighting man once again.

Three weeks in, the temperature was regularly several degrees above freezing, and down on the lower ground the snow had started to melt. Finally, at the end of an eighteen-mile ski, Larsson told him, "Okay, now you are ready. Tomorrow we prepare our equipment. The day after, we leave."

"Leave for where?" Carver asked.

Larsson turned to his right and pointed up into the mountains. "Up there, four nights. We'll carry everything we need. Now we find out just how fit you really are."

45

The customer-relations executive could barely contain his enthusiasm as they walked toward the aircraft. A fortnight beforehand, Waylon McCabe had asked for some unusual modifications to be made to one of his executive jets, for a charitable project he had in mind. The corporation's Special Missions Department thought about it for a couple of days, just to see if his requests were technically feasible, but there was only ever going to be one answer. For the past five years, having switched his supplier after the Canadian disaster, McCabe had bought all his jets from their range. They keenly appreciated his business. They had no intention of losing it.

"I just want to say, on behalf of our whole team, that we think what Mr. McCabe is doing is just great," said the suit, pausing at the foot of the stairs that led up to the cabin. "Airlifting medical supplies to the starving people of Africa—you know, it's a privilege to be able to contribute to something like that. It sure is a pity we couldn't tell Mr. McCabe in person."

McCabe had sent his lawyer to take care of the handover.

"Sadly, he's a little indisposed at this time, but I'll pass on your good wishes," said the lawyer, who didn't know what his boss planned to use the plane for, exactly, but it certainly wasn't Africa.

He glowered at the executive, who didn't seem to be moving.

"So, can we take a look at the plane?"

"Sure, sure, of course, my pleasure. Our chief engineer will show you around."

The executive stepped aside, and the engineer led the way up the stairs, bending his neck as he stepped into the cabin. Take out the fancy decorations and the high-tech accessories, and the main body of the plane was nothing but a metal tube with an internal diameter of less than six feet. There wasn't a lot of room. The men formed a single line, the engineer leading, as they made their ungainly way through the cabin.

"You gentlemen are all familiar with one of these, right?" asked the engineer rhetorically. "Okay then, up ahead of us, at the rear of the cabin, there's a closet and a restroom, and aft of that a small baggage hold. The regular bulkhead at the back of that hold offers structural support to the rear of the aircraft. Well, we took that bulkhead out and moved it forward, right up against the side of the restroom. That opened up the whole of the rear section of the fuselage, so's to make more space for loading up whatever it is you're going to be dropping. As you can see, we've put a hatch, kind of like on a submarine, right there in the bulkhead."

He stood by the crude undecorated wall that now blocked off the end of the cabin, with the oval hatch beside him.

"We didn't want to compromise the strength of the bulkhead, so we had to make the hatch kinda snug, but there's just about room to step through into the new, bigger hold we made there."

The engineer opened up the hatch. Through it, the empty rear end of the aircraft was dimly visible.

"It's pretty tight, so you gents might want to take a look one at a time. You'll see, in back, on the floor of the new hold, there's a door. It's hinged at the front, so that it opens downward, like a ramp, with the open side at the rear. It's hydraulically operated from the pilot's cockpit, or you can see a handle, like a pump, right there on the floor next to it. That's the manual option. We fixed up a rig you can put your load in, so's it can be dropped when the door is opened. Or there's just room for one person to be in there, do the job himself. We fixed up a safety line there, so he won't fall out."

"Glad to hear about that," said the lawyer. "Wouldn't want a lawsuit from a grieving window."

There was a peal of sycophantic laughter from the executive, more of a grunt from the engineer.

"Hope that's what you were looking for, anyway," the engineer concluded. "Mr. McCabe gave specific instructions. I believe we were able to follow them pretty much to the letter."

"Yes," said the lawyer. "I believe you did."

Back home in Texas, McCabe now knew that he had a plane capable of dropping a bomb over Jerusalem. Even now, despite everything, when he thought about what he had in mind, McCabe still asked himself if he was really doing the Lord's will. He wasn't too sure how you could be certain about a thing like that, but he decided it would soon be clear enough. The doctors had told him the tumors were getting worse. They were begging him to undergo chemotherapy, but McCabe had said no. He knew what those chemicals did and he didn't see the point in buying a few extra weeks if it meant puking like a dog after every treatment and watching his hair fall out. He'd rather be his real self when he came to face his maker. If he lived to see Armageddon, he'd know that God had been on his side. If he died before then, he'd expect a warm welcome in hell.

Either way, it was going to be soon.

46

Carver was feeling like a normal human being again. He wanted to act like one, too. The night before their four-day trek, he and Larsson skipped the training diet and went into Narvik for a few cold beers, hefty portions of steak and chips, and some flirtatious banter with the waitresses.

Driving home, Larsson asked, "What if she doesn't want you back?"

Carver laughed. "She'd have me back, all right. Not sure about yours, though."

"Not her," said Larsson. "Alix. What if you go to all this trouble, and you find her, and it turns out she didn't want to be found?"

Carver frowned. The possibility hadn't occurred to him. But maybe Larsson was right. Maybe Alix had left because she couldn't stand being around him anymore.

"Christ, that's a depressing thought," he said, his good humor suddenly vanishing. "I don't want to think about that. Anyway, you're wrong. She'd want me to come after her. She did last time. Why would it be any different now?"

"I don't know," Larsson admitted. "I mean, she was definitely still crazy about you the last time I spoke to her."

"Right—so why do you think she'd change her mind?"

"I don't. I was just asking a question. Hypothetically."

"Well, don't," said Carver. "I'll assume she wants me to come get her, until she tells me otherwise. And bollocks to hypothetical."

"Oh, shit!"

Larsson was looking in the rearview mirror. He shook his head in disgust and pulled over to the side of the road. Only then did Carver notice the white Volvo with the flashing lights pulling in behind them and the cop getting out of the driver's door.

Larsson wound down his window and started talking to the policeman in Norwegian. Carver couldn't understand a word they were saying, but it didn't sound good. He knew from his Royal Marines days that Norwegian cops could be tough, unforgiving buggers, a million miles removed from the British image of Scandinavians as laid-back, liberal types.

Larsson was asked to leave the car and escorted around to its rear, where another brief exchange took place. Then he was made to take a Breathalyzer test. The policeman entered Larsson's details in a handheld terminal, then finally waved them on their way with an irritated look on his face.

"What got him so pissed off?" Carver asked.

"I was under the limit," Larsson replied. "He couldn't bust me for drunk driving, so I'll keep my license. But he got me on a broken rear light; I'll have to pay a fine."

They drove back to Ebba's farm. And as they did, a computer trawling ceaselessly through the world's network systems came across a name to which it had been programmed to respond, and flagged the data to which that name was attached. And a few hours later, at the start of the working day, a man walked into his boss's office and said, "Guess who just turned up in Norway."

APRIL

47

Arriving with Alix at the Excelsior Hotel in Rome, Vermulen found a postcard waiting for him: a picture of a hill village in the South of France with the words *Tourrettes-sur-Loup* written over it in fancy script.

On the back there was a message. It read, *I told you I'd find somewhere great! You MUST try this place: Bon Repos, Chemin du Dauphin. It needs work. For a good contractor try Kenny Wynter . . .* A phone number followed and then a signature, *Pavel.*

"Novak again," said Vermulen with a grin, when Alix asked him about it. "That man, he never stops trying to sell stuff."

That had been two days ago. Now Alix was in the hotel steam room, letting the heat and humidity relax her muscles and sweat the toxins from her body.

There was one other woman in the room. She caught Alix's eye.

"Just like home, enjoying a Turkish bath!"

The words were spoken in Russian.

Alix smiled. "Except in Moscow we wouldn't have to wear bathing suits. We could be naked—so much more comfortable."

"What do you expect? This is an American hotel." The woman shook her head in mock sorrow. "Crazy people."

"Careful," said Alix. "My boyfriend is American."

"Maybe he is an exception!"

The woman looked around, confirming that they were still alone. Then she spoke again, not so chatty anymore.

"So, your boyfriend, what has he been doing?"

"He had a meeting yesterday, with an Italian, he would not say who. But I know they met in a park, on the Aventine Hill. He said it had a magnificent view of St. Peter's. Maybe there are cameras nearby that you can check. Also, he had a message from Novak. I do not know the significance, but it concerned a particular house, in France."

She passed over the details. The woman did not seem impressed.

"This is not enough—a meeting, but you do not know who with; a house, but you do not know its significance. Moscow will expect more than this."

"I'm sorry. I'm doing my best."

"In any event, I have a message from the deputy director. She regrets to inform you that your friend in Geneva passed away. As a consequence, payments to the clinic have been stopped."

Alix gasped. She looked wide-eyed at the other woman before bending over, her head in her hands, the sobs shallow at first, then convulsing her whole body.

The other woman made no attempt to comfort her.

"You must understand," she said eventually, "this makes no difference to your mission. You are to continue as before. That is an order."

She got up to go.

"Enjoy the rest of your bath."

"What's the matter?" asked Vermulen when Alix got back to their suite.

Now there was a good question. Alix was distraught, unable to hide the pain from her eyes. But when she asked herself why, the answer was more complicated than a simple matter of loss.

Of course, she was devastated by the news of Carver's death. She thought of the man he had been, their time together, the time they might have had. For months she had clung to the hope that somehow he might recover, maybe not completely, but enough that they could have some kind of future together. Now that hope had been dashed forever, and the constant, dull ache of watching him eke out a half-life in the clinic was replaced by the absolute desolation of grief.

And yet, though she could barely admit it, even to herself, she felt another emotion: relief. The burden of responsibility Carver's incapacity had created had weighed on her, and poisoned her feelings for him. Deep down, she resented him for deserting her, disappearing into his madness and leaving her to cope, forcing her to take the job with Vermulen. Then she'd felt guilty for harboring such terrible, unfair thoughts. And that had made her resent him even more.

Now he was gone, and the weight was lifted. She could remember Carver as the man he had been when they first met. And she could try to rebuild her life, free of the creature he had become. Somewhere on the edge of her consciousness, there was even a sense of excitement, the possibility of being free for something new.

"Oh, nothing, really," she said. "I just met someone in the lobby, someone I knew from home. She told me about a friend of ours. He'd not been well for a long time and she just heard . . . he's died."

Vermulen had been sitting at a writing desk. Now he got to his feet and held out his arms. His eyes conveyed profound understanding, as though a question had been answered, a problem solved.

She went to him at last, and it wasn't because she was doing her job, but because he was a living, breathing man and she needed the shelter of his arms. She laid her head on his chest and he stroked her hair as she cried. He lifted her head and dried the tears from her cheeks. They kissed, tentatively at first and then with rising intensity until, without another word, he took her arm and led her into the bedroom.

48

Three days out, one more to go. It was early evening, still a while to go before sunset, and they were traversing a southeastern slope, taking shelter from the wind that had been blowing in from the sea, away to the north and west. The mountains were no more than five or six thousand feet high, but topped by razor-sharp shark's tooth peaks that made them seem much more imposing. Carver and Larsson were back on equal terms now as they tacked from side to side up the slope, using kick turns to change the angle of their ascent. They weren't talking much. With the amount of effort they were expending every day, breath was too precious to waste on conversation.

There was a long, exposed ridge up ahead, a spine of rock a few yards wide, which jutted from the main body of the mountain, dropping away almost sheer on either side before it fanned out again into a less precipitous slope that fell, like one side of a pyramid, to the valley floor a thousand feet below. The two men planned to cross the ridge, then ski back down to lower, sheltered ground, where they could pitch their two-man tunnel tent, brew up some water on their gas stove, and mix it with their dried rations. Carver was looking forward to beef curry and rice for supper, a classic piece of dehydrated cuisine from the Royal Marines cookbook—a taste of the old days.

The higher they climbed, the less cover there was around them. They began to feel the wind picking up, snatching at their clothes, pushing against their backpacks, beating the hoods of their parkas against their ears. For the past hour or so, the slope that rose ahead of them and to the left had filled most of their field of vision. Carver had become aware of a gradual darkening of the heavens as the blue sky gave way to thickening gray clouds. But now, as they approached the ridge, the view opened up and they could look out toward the Atlantic.

A few strides up ahead, Larsson was jabbing his arm back and forth, pointing at the horizon, and calling out a single word, "Storm!"

Carver didn't need telling. Away to the northwest a solid wall of charcoal-colored clouds was bearing down upon them and blocking out the waning sunlight like a giant blackout curtain drawing closed.

The wind was picking up speed with every minute that passed, and flurries of snow were whipping through the air, blowing almost horizontally into their faces. As the temperature dropped, windchill would become an ever-greater threat. Exposed skin could suffer frostbite within minutes.

Carver looked past Larsson at the ridge, then glanced back toward the onrushing weather. There was no way they could make it across the ridge before the storm hit them. If they got caught out there, with no shelter on any side, they would be blown off the mountainside like seeds from a dandelion. Even if they survived the wind, they would have to cope with a whiteout. The windblown snow and diffused, cloudy light would remove all definition from their surroundings, leaving them lost and disoriented. On flat ground a whiteout was dangerous enough. On a narrow ridge, with deadly drops on either side, it meant certain death.

Carver pointed up ahead, then gave a single, decisive shake of the head and drew a finger across his throat. Larsson nodded in response and pointed back toward the main bulk of the mountain. "Make camp—now!" he shouted, barely able to make himself heard over the battering clamor of the wind.

They turned around and skied back a dozen strides to a short, flat shelf in the lee of the mountainside that gave some meager protection from the elements. They took their skis off and jabbed them vertically into the snow along with their ski poles, then slung their packs down next to them. Both men had snow shovels strapped to the outside of their backpacks. They freed them and wordlessly began digging a rectangular hole, shaped like a section of a shallow trench, fighting the wind and snow that seemed as determined to cancel out every effort they made.

When the hole was about knee-deep, Carver stepped over to Larsson's pack and untied the nylon bag that contained their tent. If they could just erect it inside the trench, then shovel snow back over the flaps along either side, that should provide enough shelter to enable them to ride out the storm.

Working quickly, methodically, Carver sorted out the pegs, guyropes, and poles: far better to spend a minute doing that now than waste five panicking if anything went missing. He and Larsson drove the pegs into the snow, ready to take the cords. The tent was brand-new, designed for easy assembly. Under normal circumstances it just took a few minutes to erect, but the storm had other ideas. The gale was rising to a murderous intensity, the snow thickening. Carver and Larsson were both strong, fit men. They knew what they were doing. Their equipment was top of the line. They threw every ounce of their strength and energy into the task of securing the ultralightweight material. Yet the two men could no more resist the might of the elements than King Canute could hold back the oncoming tide.

The blizzard now reached a new crescendo, whipping the bright-red nylon tent into the air like a kite, its flight visible for no more than a second or two before it disappeared into the all-enveloping whiteness.

Carver watched it disappear. He allowed himself a quick, sharp spasm of frustration, then turned his mind to the problem of survival. Visibility was getting worse by the second. Already he could barely see the outlines of the packs and skis just a few feet away, and Larsson was little more than a shadow, half hidden by the driving snow.

"This way!" Carver shouted.

He reached out and grabbed Larsson's arm, then dragged him along as he fought against the buffeting wind toward their equipment, lying by the rising mountain face.

There were deep drifts of snow piled between the mountainside and the wide ledge on which they were standing. In a perfect world, they'd burrow into them to create a proper snow hole, protected from the elements like an underground igloo. But that would take two or three hours. Carver estimated they had no more than fifteen minutes before the freezing wind and snow completely overwhelmed them. Their only hope was to hack out a rudimentary cave. It would be partially open to the elements, but at least it might provide some degree of shelter.

Carver set to work, stabbing at the snow and removing it in chunks like icy white bricks. By now, he'd been on the go for the better part of nine hours. The last food he had consumed had been a midday snack of energy bars and chocolate, eaten on the march. He was cold and dehydrated, shivering and sweating at one and the same time. He was wearing several layers of specialist mountain clothing, designed to expel moisture from his skin, keeping him as dry and warm as possible. But as his energy and liquid levels dropped, the clothes became less effective. He had to complete the hole as fast as possible, but the very weakness that made rest and shelter so vital was slowing him down, making every strike of the shovel an effort.

Even through the blizzard, he could see that Larsson was faring no better. His movements were slow and ineffective. He turned and looked at Carver, and though the Norwegian's eyes were hidden by his goggles, the way his head was lowered and his shoulders slumped told Carver that his friend was close to admitting defeat.

Carver pumped his fist and screamed, "Come on!" He had no idea whether his words could be heard but the sense of them seemed to get through to Larsson. He drew himself up for a second, then turned back to the hole, attacking the snowdrift with one last, desperate spasm of energy.

By any rational standards, Carver had gone beyond the limits of human endurance. The exhaustion of his muscles, the desperate shortage of oxygen in his lungs, the relentless battery of the wind, and the insidious tentacles of cold worming into his body had fused into one all-encompassing agony. And all he had to do to make it go away was give in to the temptation to stop: to lie down in the snow, go to sleep, and surrender his life to that ghost-white embrace. But there's a reason Special Forces selection and training involve the infliction of pain at a level that would be considered a criminal breach of human rights, amounting in any other context to virtual torture. It's not just a matter of physical toughening. There's a psychological, almost spiritual, element, too: accepting agony and exhaustion and—because you can always, at any time, admit failure and drop out—choosing to make them part of your life. It's the same talent for self-mortification, or perhaps the same madness, that makes a gold-medal marathon runner or a world-champion boxer. Carver hurt. He wanted to stop. And yet, relentlessly, he chose to keep digging.

Beside him, however, Larsson was faltering again. He had given all that any man could reasonably expect. But he could not go beyond that and make the unreasonable effort on which his survival depended. He was barely able to lift his shovel, scraping at the snow, rather than attacking it. Carver could see that Larsson was past the point where encouragement would be of any use. He would have to finish the job by himself.

He hollowed out a space about waist-high, stretching back a little over a yard or so into the drift and just wide enough for the two of them to huddle, side by side, facing the open air, with their gear piled beside them. Larsson fell to the ground before summoning up enough energy to drag himself into a sitting position against the back wall with his arms folded over his knees, which were drawn up to his chest. His head was lolling forward as if his neck no longer had the strength to support it. A spasm of shivers shook him as violently as a fit.

Carver dragged Larsson's sleeping bag from his pack and unfurled it. "Get into this," he ordered.

Larsson grunted incoherently and did nothing. Carver lifted up Larsson's goggles. His eyes were bleary and unfocused. Hypothermia was setting in.

Lifting up Larsson's boots with his left arm, Carver used his right to drag the sleeping bag over Larsson's feet and halfway up his legs. Next he grabbed Larsson around the back and heaved him off the ground in a sort of fireman's lift, slipping the rest of the sleeping bag under his raised backside and then, once Larsson had been lowered to the ground again, pulling it up his body. Now, at least, the sleeping bag was insulating Larsson from the chill of the shelter's icy walls and floor. But there was still much more to be done.

It was vital to get a hot drink into Larsson's system. Carver unpacked the gas stove, set it up, and pumped the fuel reservoir to create the pressure needed before the burner could be lit, the old-fashioned way, with a naked flame. Carver had a packet of matches, but he couldn't hope to light them with his hands encased in thick ski gloves. He ripped off his right glove, exposing his hand to the cold. It started to shake. He tried to strike a match against the box, scrabbled feebly across the surface, overcompensated when he tried again, and snapped the end off the match, unlit.

Three more attempts followed. On each occasion, he got the match alight, only for the flame to be snuffed out by the gusts of air eddying around the snow cave.

Larsson gave another convulsive shiver.

This wasn't going to work. They needed more shelter. Carver pulled his glove back on, crawled out of the hole, and reached out for one of the blocks of snow he'd cut from the drift. He hauled it back toward him and positioned it at the opening of the cave. It took five precious minutes to build a low wall, shin-high, across the entrance: five minutes in which Larsson's spasms became progressively more feeble. But now, at least, there was a pocket of still air and Carver could finally ignite his stove, cram a pot full of snow, and brew up some strong tea, sweetened with sugar and condensed milk.

He poured half of it into a cup and held it to Larsson's lips, gently pouring it into his mouth. At first, Larsson gagged, unable even to swallow. But then he relaxed and drank. A flicker of life returned to his eyes.

Carver gulped down a few mouthfuls of tea for himself. Then he opened one of the outside pockets of his backpack and pulled out a bar of Kendal mint cake, a white, creamy block of sugar, glucose, and water, flavored with mint oil. It contained virtually no protein, vitamins, essential minerals, or anything else that would please a health-conscious nutritionist. But as a means of providing an exhausted body with a shot of raw fuel, it was pretty hard to beat.

They split the bar. Larsson didn't eat the cake so much as let it melt in his mouth and trickle down his throat. Carver took a good look at him, checking out the lower half of his face, the area that had been exposed to the wind, for any sign of white, waxy patches that would indicate frostbite.

"Looks clear," he said. "But you could still have frostbite on the way. Is your face prickly, itchy?"

"Nuh." Larsson shook his head. It wasn't exactly sparkling repartee, but at least he was responding.

"I'll get you some food," Carver said, and went away to boil up some rice and mix hot water with the freeze-dried curry.

By the time they had eaten, darkness had fallen. Carver climbed into his own sleeping bag. Over the next few hours, he made more drinks. Larsson seemed to stabilize. The shivering subsided, and when he finally fell asleep, his breathing was shallow but reasonably even. Carver knew, though, that even though the immediate crisis had passed, the fundamental threat had not. Unless Larsson could be rescued from the mountain and given expert medical care, he had only hours to live.

49

Kady Jones was reading e-mails, an affectionate smile on her face. A few days ago, two of her favorite people at Los Alamos, Henry Wong and Mae Lee, had got married. They'd gone on a honeymoon to Rome and, being techies, they hadn't sent postcards home by snail mail. They'd found an Internet café instead. Mae's message to Kady was chatty, detailed, and intimate: one close girlfriend to another. Henry's had consisted of a couple of lines, assuring her that Rome was pretty cool, plus a bunch of digital holiday photos, with captions attached.

His favorite was a shot of Mae posing in a park on the Aventine Hill, with a view across the Tiber to the dome of St. Peter's Basilica. She looked great, her face suffused with a happiness that seemed to light up the whole shot.

"Man, am I one lucky bomb-geek!" he'd written on the caption.

Kady was looking at the shot on her lab computer, whose screen was far larger, with much better resolution than the one in the Roman café. So she noticed what Henry hadn't, that there were two guys talking in the background of his shot, and the perspective made them look like weird midgets growing out of Mae's armpit. Out of idle curiosity she zoomed in on them to take a closer look.

And then she gasped. "Holy shit!"

The man on the right was only vaguely recognizable, but his companion was all too familiar. If the two of them were having anything other than a casual, social conversation, this innocent holiday photograph had suddenly acquired a whole new level of significance.

She dialed a number in Washington. FBI Special Agent Tom Mulvagh, the man who'd supervised the operation at Gull Lake, had been transferred to D.C. to work on the secret team searching for the Russian bombs. They'd built up a good working relationship. She told him to expect an e-mail and waited a few seconds.

"Do you have the picture on your screen?"

"Yeah, thanks for sending me that, though e-mailing shots of hot broads is most often a guy kind of thing."

Kady could picture Mulvagh's grin. He liked to kid around a little when the situation allowed. She didn't have any problem with that.

"Very funny, Tom. That 'broad,' as you call her, is Mae Wong, the beautiful, sensitive, and highly intelligent wife of my associate Henry Wong. And she's not what I want you to look at. Go in on the two guys . . ."

"What, the ones in her armpit?"

"Exactly. . . . Recognize them?"

There was silence on the line while Mulvagh thought, then: "The one on the right looks familiar."

"That's what I thought," agreed Kady. "I'm pretty sure I saw his picture in a magazine. He's that general. His assistant got killed in the park in D.C."

"Vermulen," said Mulvagh. "Right, I remember. But what's the significance to you or me?"

"Well, it's not him that caught my attention. It's the other one, with the darker hair. He's Dr. Francesco Riva. He's Italian, came over here in the late seventies, got a masters at MIT, and worked at Lawrence Livermore National Lab for more than a decade. That's where I got to know him, and you can take it from me, Mulvagh, Frankie Riva is really a fantastic nuclear physicist."

"And I should care about this because . . . ?"

"Because, for one, Frankie's specialty was the miniaturization of nuclear weapons; and for two, he quit the lab five years ago and disappeared right off the map. You've got to understand, pretty much everyone in our business knows everyone else, by reputation or in person. We know who's doing what, and where. But for the last few years, Frankie Riva hasn't been doing anything. Not in public, anyway."

"And now you're going to tell me what he's been doing in private." said Mulvagh.

"Well, I don't know. Not for sure. But the thing about him was he didn't live like a nerd. He wasn't at home with his PC and his pizza boxes. He liked European sports cars, pretty girls, and dinners for two at the kind of place where the maître d' had to translate the menu."

"So he needed money."

"Exactly," Kady continued. "That's why he quit Livermore. He said he wanted a private-sector salary. That's not unusual. Plenty of guys go to commercial research labs. But Frankie's not at any lab I know. The word on Nuke Street is he's been selling his skills to people who want bombs, and who'll pay whatever it takes to get them."

"How come we've never heard of this guy?"

"If he's gone back home to Italy, he's not in your jurisdiction."

"But no one from the Agency's mentioned him to me at any of our briefings."

"Well, you know, Tom, I don't want to sound disloyal or unpatriotic, but the Agency's not always as well informed as it could be . . ."

Mulvagh laughed. "I hear that!"

"Okay, so now ask yourself, What would Frankie Riva be doing with General Vermulen? I checked out the general's clippings on Lexis. There are claims he's a middleman in international arms deals. His old assistant gets murdered in a park where no one's been killed in years. He takes a sabbatical from his job to travel in Europe, and a couple of the gossip columns say he's taken his hot new assistant along for the ride. And now he's in Rome, having a private conversation in a secluded park with a nuclear scientist who knows everything there is to know about the kinds of bombs we're looking for. I mean, doesn't that strike you as . . . I don't know . . . interesting?"

"I don't know how it strikes me, Kady," said Mulvagh. "I don't exactly understand what you're telling me here."

"I'm telling you that a man who has high-level contacts all over the world, who deals in weapons for a living, and who is supposed to be on holiday screwing his secretary, is having secret meetings with a guy who could make a basic gun-design suitcase nuke with his eyes closed, and upgrade an existing one even easier. I'm telling you that we may not be the only ones who know that Lebed was telling the truth."

"I get that," said Mulvagh. "But I don't know that I buy it. And even if I did, I'd want to be damn sure of my evidence before I took this any further. Vermulen has friends, the kind that could end my career and yours if we start making false accusations—"

"We don't have to accuse him of anything," Kady interrupted. "Not yet. . . . But you could check him out, you know, discreetly. I mean, if Vermulen met Frankie Riva in Rome, maybe he had other meetings in other cities. And if we knew who he talked to, that might give us a picture. Plus, and you can put this down to feminine intuition if you want to be sexist about it, I just think it's kinda convenient that secretary number one—a woman in her fifties, by the way—gets knocked on the head, and five minutes later, in comes a hottie who just happens to be hanging on the general's arm as he tours the romantic hotspots."

"Maybe you're just jealous," suggested Mulvagh.

"Now why would I be jealous of a woman younger than me who hooks up with a great-looking, unmarried general? Seriously, Tom, this could be worth looking into. It's not like we've got a million other leads to distract us. Just run a few checks through a few databases. I'll buy you a drink next time you're out west. . . ."

"Well, in that case, Dr. Jones, how could I say no?"

50

At some point in the night, Carver must have given way to his exhaustion, because he suddenly found himself waking up and realizing that the rising sun was shining in his face. As he screwed up his eyes, adjusting to the light, he noticed something else: the silence. The storm had passed.

Now he had to get help for Larsson. Up in the mountains, cell-phone signals were patchy, at best. The only way to be sure of getting through was to get to one of the hikers' huts the local tourist authorities had scattered around the countryside and use the emergency telephone there. Carver consulted the map. The nearest hut was about three miles back the way they had come the day before. The journey was mostly downhill. He heated up bowls of porridge for himself and Larsson, promised his friend that help would soon be on its way, and set off back down the trail.

As he skied through the fine powder of freshly fallen snow, which dazzled in the sunlight from a cloudless sky, Carver realized that he was overcome by an entirely new and unexpected sensation. He felt great. He had faced and passed a supreme physical and mental test, and that knowledge filled him with confidence. Now he was ready to set off on his quest and find the woman he loved. In the meantime, he had no fear for Larsson. When he reached the hut and contacted the rescue team, he had absolute confidence that they would get to the cave in time. It came as no surprise to Carver, when he in turn was picked up by a cheerful figure on a snowmobile, that Larsson had been admitted to the hospital in Narvik, still badly sick, but with every prospect of making a full recovery.

Carver was also taken to the Sykehus, as the hospital was called, just to be checked for signs of frostbite or hypothermia. After he'd been cleared on both counts he visited Larsson, made sure he was doing all right, and promised to be back in the morning.

"Don't worry—I'll be fine," Larsson said, summoning up an exhausted smile.

A nurse had come over to check his pulse and temperature. She was a classic Norwegian beauty: tall, blond, and blue-eyed.

"I'll bet you will be," Carver said.

He wandered out of the hospital, thinking he'd grab a beer and something to eat before finding a cab back to Beisfjord. Then something caught his eye.

There was a man standing a few steps away, just by the front door, reading an English newspaper. He looked up, saw Carver, and smiled.

It took a couple of seconds before Carver registered who it was.

"What are you doing here?" he said, his good mood vanishing as instantly as it had arrived.

"I got bored waiting for you to turn up on my doorstep," said Jack Grantham. "Thought I might as well turn up on yours."

He grinned and slapped Carver on the shoulder like a long-lost pal. "Come on. My hotel's not far away and I've got a car waiting. I think you're going to be interested when you hear what I've got to say."

51

Grantham had one of his men waiting by the door of the car. Another was behind the wheel. They drove only a few hundred yards to a little old-fashioned hotel. There was a small lounge off the main reception area: a sofa and a couple of armchairs, ringing a fireplace; an ornate chandelier hanging from the ceiling; a tapestry on the wall; a coffee table in front of the chairs.

One of Grantham's men handed him a laptop, which he placed on the table. Then the man joined his colleague standing a few yards away, keeping an eye on their boss and, by their very presence, discouraging anyone else from coming into the room.

"Pull up a chair—make yourself comfortable," said Grantham, beckoning Carver closer.

"So what's your big news?" Carver asked.

Grantham opened his laptop and clicked on a PowerPoint file. The screen was filled with a formal photograph of a U.S. Army officer in full dress uniform.

"His name is Kurt Vermulen," said Grantham. "Until a few years ago, he was a three-star general in the U.S. Army."

He gave a quick rundown of the general's military career.

"Captain America," said Carver.

"Something like that."

"So why do you want me to kill him?"

"I didn't say we did."

"Why else would you come all this way?"

"Depends," said Grantham.

"On what?"

"On what he's really up to. . . ."

Grantham opened a new page. It showed a series of grainy color photographs of Vermulen, now dressed in civilian clothes. Some were lifted from closed-circuit TV footage, others had been shot by photographers. He was in the crowd at a fancy theater, walking by a Venetian canal, standing by a crossing on a busy city street.

Carver looked at them all with equal indifference.

"Well, good luck with that," he said. "I've got other business to take care of."

"I know," Grantham said. "Just like old times, isn't it? But before you go, there's something else you should see."

"I don't think so." Carver got up to leave.

Grantham remained unruffled. "I'd stay if I were you. You'll want to see this."

Carver looked at him. Grantham had the calm of a man who was absolutely sure of his hand. The only way to see what he had was to call him on it.

"Okay," said Carver, still standing. "Show me."

"Take another look at these," said Grantham, flicking through the shots of Vermulen once again.

"I told you already—I'm not interested."

Grantham smiled. "Now watch," he said.

He opened a new file. Up popped the same set of photographs, but this time the frames of the pictures were wider. They revealed the figure who had been cropped from the first set, the woman who was standing next to Vermulen in a satin evening dress at the Vienna opera, who was with him, and a black couple, outside the Hotel Gritti in Venice, who was sightseeing with him in Rome. And then, in a final sequence of new pictures, they showed Vermulen and the woman on a yacht; him in white Bermudas and a polo shirt, her in a bikini, sunglasses pushed up into her blond hair. The shots were grainy, extreme long distance. The couple was standing under an awning near the stern of the boat. In the first shot they were talking. Then she put her hand on his chest. Carver couldn't work out if she was playing, or trying to ward the man off. By the third frame his hands were on her upper arms. In the fourth he was leading—or was it dragging?—her into one of the yacht's staterooms. And they were gone.

"You shit," hissed Samuel Carver.

"Yes," said Jack Grantham. "Thought that would do the trick."

52

Ever since he'd started putting himself back together, Carver had been wondering what he really felt about Alix. As his recovery progressed he began to piece together images of the few short days and nights they had spent together. A woman brushed past him in a store in Beisfjord, and as he caught a waft of her perfume in the air he knew at once, without thinking, that Alix had worn the same scent, and suddenly it was as if she were lying next to him again. And of course, he and Thor Larsson had talked about her, Larsson telling stories of the months in Geneva before her disappearance, or joking about his own first sight of Alix, dressed in La Perla lingerie and a brunette wig. She'd been getting ready to seduce a Swiss bank official who was their only link to the hidden men who had bought Carver's deadly services, betrayed him, and then tried to have him killed.

"Man, she looked good," Larsson had said wistfully. "I was seriously jealous of you. I mean, I could tell what you'd been doing!"

Larsson had laughed out loud and Carver had laughed along with him. But though he could recall a vague image of Alix in that hotel room, and though he knew, as a historical fact, that they had made love that afternoon, the memories were fleeting and insubstantial, unreal ghosts of a time that had vanished beyond recovery.

And then he saw the picture of Alix on the yacht, being grabbed by another man's hands, and all the emotions that had been hidden out of his reach burst through, and the pain he felt was like a branding iron on his heart.

"Sit down," said Grantham. "I'll get you a drink. You look like you could use it."

He flicked a finger at one of his men, as if summoning a waiter. "Whiskey, chop-chop."

Carver looked at Grantham's smug features.

"You don't give a toss, do you?"

Grantham let the anger wash over him.

"On the contrary—I certainly give a toss about the job I do, and the country I do it for. That's why I'm here. Someone assigned Alexandra Petrova to do a honeytrap on Kurt Vermulen. And I'm sure you've worked out, same as I have, that she's gone back to her roots, working for the Russians. I don't know why. Maybe she got bored sitting around, waiting for you to wake up—"

"She was paying my bills," said Carver.

"How admirable. Sacrificing her somewhat tarnished virtue for the man she loves."

Carver looked at Grantham, glanced across at his men, then leaned forward.

"It's a funny thing, the way my memory comes back. You talking like that reminds me of the last time we met. You made another one of your smart-arsed remarks, and I pointed out that I could kill you with your own pen. Do you remember that?"

"Point taken," said Grantham. "It was a cheap shot. So let's get down to business. Do you know how they got to Petrova, put her up to this escapade?"

"It was Yuri Zhukovski's widow. She went to the place where Alix was working. Alix tried to escape. Obviously, she didn't make it."

"Ah, yes," murmured Grantham appreciatively. "We thought this had the touch of Deputy Director Zhukovskaya—a very powerful, impressive lady, that one. Call me a cynic, but it strikes me Miss Petrova may well have been working for her all along."

"I doubt it. Alix was screwing her husband."

"Exactly. Zhukovskaya was controlling her husband's mistress. That's the kind of woman she is. Brilliant. . . ."

For a moment Grantham seemed lost in admiration. Then he recovered himself.

"Anyway, let me tell you what Petrova has been doing since you last saw her. We think she got her hooks into Vermulen in Washington—that's his normal base—but they've been in Europe the past few weeks, charging about like demented honeymooners. I can see why the Russians are curious, because Vermulen is certainly on some kind of a mission. He had a meeting in Amsterdam, though we don't yet know who with. Next he went to Vienna to see a chap called Novak, who makes a murky living trading arms and information. His Venice contact was a former U.S. Army colleague, name of Reddin. As you can see from the picture, Mrs. Reddin came along, too, so it's conceivable that was just a social encounter, though I doubt it. After that was Rome. We tracked him to another meet there, but the pictures were hopeless and we couldn't identify the other party. Now they're on a yacht that Vermulen has rented, ostensibly for a Mediterranean holiday.

"Those last shots I showed you were taken a couple of days ago, off the Corsican coast. My interpretation is that they're having some kind of an argument. Or maybe she's getting cozy, calming him down. Look, she's operating alone, without backup. She has to do whatever it takes to keep him sweet. But the closer she gets, the more pissed off he'll be if he ever discovers she's been deceiving him. She can't try to run for it, because then he'll know for sure. She's in the shit, Carver. And it's all because of you."

"So what do you want me to do?"

"I thought you'd never ask."

Grantham opened up a new file on his laptop. This time the photographs showed a U.K. passport photo of a man in his mid-thirties, with sandy hair and a defiant, uncompromising expression.

"That," said Grantham, "is Kenny Wynter. And two days from now, he's due to meet Kurt Vermulen for lunch at the Hotel du Cap, on the coast between Nice and Cannes, down in the South of France."

"Sounds very civilized."

"I doubt it. Vermulen has a job for Wynter. We intercepted a call. It's a blind date. The men have never met before, but evidently Wynter has been recommended."

"What's the job?"

"Vermulen wouldn't tell him. Said he'd give him the details in person. But there's only one reason you call Kenny Wynter, and that's to steal something. The man's spent the past fifteen years doing jobs to order: confidential documents, industrial plans and prototypes, financial papers, the occasional safe-deposit box. And he's not fussy about his clients. He's stolen military secrets for the Russians, the Chinese, the Iraqis, and the IRA, and we've lost good men and women because of it. The man is an unscrupulous shit, with blood on his hands. But he's never once been caught. Arrested, of course, countless times, but there's never been enough evidence to convict. Kenny Wynter has bought himself a flashy house up in Totteridge and a box at the Arsenal. He drives fast cars, screws gorgeous women—"

"Now him I could kill," said Carver, sarcastically.

"Good," said Grantham, dead serious. "Because you're going to."

53

"**H**ave we heard from Petrova yet?" asked Olga Zhukovskaya.

The FSB colonel standing before her shook his head.

"Not since that meeting in Rome, Madam Deputy Director. I have ensured that the standard notice is placed in the classified advertisement section of the *International Herald Tribune,* but she has not responded."

"Do we even know where she is?"

Another shake of the head, almost sorrowful this time.

"No. We have reason to believe that Vermulen might have chartered a yacht, but we have been unable to confirm that, and we would not be able to track it, even if we had. As you know, ma'am, our resources are not what they used to be. We have not launched a single reconnaissance satellite since September 1995. We have been completely blind since it ceased to function a year later."

He sighed, somewhat theatrically.

"We used to impose our will across the globe; now the best we can hope for is to steal pictures off Western commercial satellites. . . ."

Zhukovskaya was not in a mood for self-pity. It was not an emotion for which she'd ever seen any need.

"That may be. The fact remains: We need to find them. Vermulen is planning something. I can feel it."

The colonel stayed silent, letting his boss think in peace. It did not take long for her to come to a decision. Olga Zhukovskaya was a woman who knew what she wanted. It was one of the qualities that made her such an effective leader.

"Whatever Vermulen is doing, it involves Pavel Novak. He will know what is happening. And very soon we will know, too."

54

Kenny Wynter worked hard at being respectable. He belonged to his local Conservative Association, donated money to the church restoration fund, and had memberships at the golf and tennis clubs. A lot of women were seen coming and going from his house, which irritated his female neighbors, but also increased their interest in him. Their real annoyance, however, was reserved for their husbands' obvious admiration and envy of Wynter's harem, and the eagerness with which they attended his swimming-pool parties every summer, eyes on stalks at all the young things in their bikinis twittering around their host.

So it was that Kenny Wynter both obeyed the social rules and gave everyone plenty to gossip about. In this leafy north London suburb of detached houses, large gardens, and expensively filled garages, he was the perfect citizen.

Thursday evenings, Wynter headed for the tennis club. He was part of a regular men's foursome. They'd play the best of three sets, work up a gentle sweat, then grab a drink and a bite to eat at the Orange Tree pub in Totteridge Village. By eight o'clock, his brand-new Porsche 911 Carrera S was sitting in the parking lot behind the pub. It was slate gray, with a black leather interior. Wynter was already in the pub, getting in the first round of beers.

A car pulled up next to the Porsche. It was a ten-year-old Honda Accord with faded blue paintwork. Just about any passerby with a minimal knowledge of cars would be able to identify the 911. But to any but the most dedicated Honda-lover, the old Accord was just another drab, anonymous, totally unmemorable sedan. That was why Carver had bought it for £450, cash, from a small ad in *Auto Trader,* just that afternoon.

He got out of the car. He was wearing a gray polyester suit and a white polyester shirt. His blue tie, with paler blue and white stripes, was made of rayon. His shoes were shiny pale-gray slip-ons, decorated with snaffles across the instep, whose gold coloring had flaked away in places to reveal the bare metal underneath. The briefcase beside him was old and scuffed. His tinted, wire-framed glasses were a drone's pathetic attempt at individuality and cool.

Carver was unshaven. A mousy wig straggled over his ears and hung down the back of his neck. It added to the general impression of a white-collar nonentity, and it concealed his actual hair, which had been cut and dyed to match Wynter's. In the morning, he would put in contact lenses the color of Wynter's eyes. By the time he stepped onto the plane to France, he would be Kenny Wynter.

Now he got out of the Honda. The driver's door was next to the passenger side of Wynter's Porsche. Carver stepped onto the pavement, then turned back to grab his briefcase from the seat. As he pulled it out, the clasp gave way, the case fell open, and its contents—a half-eaten sandwich in a cardboard and cellophane box, a cheap pocket calculator, a heavily chewed Biro pen, and a copy of the *Daily Express*—fell to the ground between the two cars.

Cursing to himself, Carver got down on his haunches and started gathering up his belongings. He looked up for a second and scanned the parking lot. He was the only person in it. He ducked back down and removed a small, clear, Ziploc bag from his inside jacket pocket. From it he took a small tool, just a few inches long. At one end, a flat black plastic disc enabled the tool to be placed upright on the ground. From the disc protruded a cylindrical shaft, like that of a miniature screwdriver. The far end, however, was not flattened into a blade. Instead, a notch was cut across its circumference.

Carver unscrewed the cap of the Porsche's front near-side tire valve and placed it on the pavement. Then he inserted the tool into the top of the valve, which nestled in the notch, and turned it counter-clockwise. The valve unscrewed from its rubber housing and slipped out, still attached to the tool. Air began to hiss out of the open tube. Carver stuck his left thumb across the tube to prevent any more escaping. The last thing he wanted was any noticeable loss of tire pressure. With his right hand, he put the tool down on the ground, the tire valve pointing upward. He removed the valve from the tool and slipped it into his trouser pocket.

Next he slipped his fingers back into the Ziploc bag and extracted what appeared to be an identical valve. He stuck it on the end of the tool, then removed his thumb and screwed the new valve back into the tire, replacing the screw-on cap when he had finished. The entire operation had taken no more than thirty seconds.

A car pulled into the lot and parked about twenty yards away. A man and a woman got out. Carver started picking up the junk that had fallen from his case. He needn't have bothered. The couple were far too interested in each other to notice his presence. They wandered arm in arm into the pub.

Carver gave them a few seconds' start while he put all his crap away in the briefcase. Then he went for a pint of his own.

No one paid the slightest attention to Carver as he sat nursing his lager and reading his paper. Wynter and his tennis-playing pals were sitting at the next table. Carver watched out of the corner of his eye and listened. Wynter, as always, looked the part: faded jeans, a dark-blue V-necked cashmere pullover worn over a plain white T-shirt, a top-of-the-line TAG Heuer watch. He didn't attempt to impose himself on the conversation, but when he spoke he exuded a sense of relaxed good humor. His voice was neutral, with just a trace of his working-class London roots. Every so often he went a bit more Cockney, just for comic effect. But if he mocked something one of the other men had said, there was always a friendly smile, just to let them know that he was bantering, not seeking to cause offense. None was ever taken. It was a masterful performance.

Carver had spent the past few days studying every aspect of Kenny Wynter's life. Grantham had given him the basic biography while they were still in Norway.

"Our Kenny was born in Kensal Rise, north London, May 15, 1961. His father, Reginald 'Nutter' Wynter, was a villain, robbed banks and security vans, didn't mind who got hurt when he did it. Got sent down for twenty years soon after Kenny was born and died inside after fifteen. Kenny was brought up by his mother, Noreen. He was a bright lad, passed his eleven-plus exam, went to grammar school, and got into Oxford University. He graduated in 1982 with a first-class degree, a nice new middle-class accent, and a love of fine wines. And then he went into the family business. Our Kenny became a thief, just like his dear old dad. Except, being brainy, he did it very differently."

Oh, yes, Wynter was a cold, calculating bastard underneath that cozy cashmere. No matter how friendly he might seem, there would always be a part of him sitting to one side, observing, emotionally detached. He would be perfectly happy using women for sex and decoration, without the slightest need for any greater emotional connection. The last thing he needed was any complication that would interfere with his working life. And when he received an assignment, he would carry it out without compunction, irrespective of its consequences, untouched by moral consideration.

Carver knew just how that felt.

55

FBI Special Agent Tom Mulvagh liked Kady Jones a lot. He thought she was pretty hot for a scientist, which helped. But mostly he just appreciated the way she got on with the job. She didn't put on any airs. She'd laugh at a joke, instead of acting offended. Basically, she was cool.

That being the case, he'd been happy to put in a few hours following up her crazy theory about the general and the physicist. At first it seemed straightforward. Vermulen had made no secret of his initial movements. He and his assistant, Ms. Natalia Morley, had taken scheduled flights, first class, to Amsterdam, Vienna, Venice, and then Rome. They had stayed at the best hotels, but in separate rooms every time. Vermulen's credit cards showed the kind of charges you'd expect from a man trying to get a woman into bed: restaurants, fancy stores, opera tickets. Some people would say it was pathetic, going to those lengths, but it was hardly a crime.

Next Mulvagh moved on to Vermulen's phone logs, only to draw a blank. The general had a couple of cell phones registered in his name, but neither of them had been used for several weeks. At the hotels where he stayed, the phone charges were minimal. That made sense in one respect: Who paid hotel call charges if he could avoid it? But unless Vermulen had decided to avoid all telecommunications, he had to be using a phone of some kind.

Mulvagh tracked down all the corporations that listed him as a director, then checked all the phones registered to those corporations, then tracked their usage over the period Vermulen was in Europe. There was no correlation at all. Now Mulvagh was getting interested. He went back to the credit cards. They showed no record of any handset being purchased, nor of any call charges or time charges. That meant Vermulen had bought a prepaid phone, using either cash or a card that he didn't want anyone to know about. He was meant to be a guy on an extended holiday, but these were the security precautions of an experienced professional on a mission.

It was time to bring in some help. Mulvagh had built up a pretty good working relationship with Ted Jaworski, over at Langley, and Bob Lassiter, the NSA's man on the bomb team. He gave them the gist of Kady's story, plus his own findings. They both told him he had to be out of his mind even thinking about this investigation, but he just about persuaded them to take a look, off the record. Then he went to the police.

The D.C. police were as defensive as any other cops when it came to liaising with the FBI, but once Mulvagh had persuaded the detective in charge of the Mary Lou Stoller case that he wasn't trying to muscle in on anyone else's investigation, they were able to have a useful conversation.

"This is just you and me talking, deep background, yeah?" asked the detective.

"Sure," said Mulvagh. "I just need to know what you think went down. I don't need proof. I want what your instinct is telling you."

"Okay. Officially, this was a mugging gone bad. But what my instinct says is, That's bullshit. Whoever killed Mrs. Stoller was a pro."

"How come?"

"The job was too good. I mean, sure, they made it look like a mugging, but the area was clean. No trace evidence anywhere: no prints, no DNA, and the only footprints came from a new pair of standard Florsheim dress shoes, size ten. Totally untraceable—they sell thousands of those things. But it tells me something, anyhow. I mean, when did you ever know a mugger to wear Florsheims? And plus, your average street punk has less intelligence than the yucca plant my lieutenant keeps in her office—you know what I'm saying? Not forgetting that he's most likely out of his mind on meth. So he's going to make mistakes, leave evidence. Christ, you know what these bozos are like. But whoever did this job, trust me—they were not stupid. They knew what they were doing. And we ain't ever going to catch them. That's what my instinct tells me, Agent Mulvagh."

"Thank you, Detective, I appreciate your honesty."

"So, if you don't mind me asking, what are the Feds doing making personal calls to check up on this particular investigation? God rest her soul, but Mrs. Stoller wasn't anyone important."

"No," said Mulvagh, "but her boss is."

"Aw, shit—I shoulda seen that one coming . . ."

"Don't worry, Detective. I gave you my word our conversation was private. None of this will rebound on you."

Mulvagh hung up, deep in thought. He'd started this investigation as a favor, but it was now impossible to ignore the fact that something very strange was going on around Kurt Vermulen. The general's trip to Europe was obviously far more than an extended vacation. But had he also planned his secretary's death? If he wanted to get rid of her and bring in a younger model, all he had to do was fire her. So who stood to gain by Mary Lou Stoller's death? The only candidate was the new secretary, this Morley woman. But she sure as hell didn't beat a woman to death in Glover-Archbold Park. Had someone done it for her? And if so, why?

He put in another call to Ted Jaworski.

"I've got to be honest," he said. "I still can't be sure that this directly relates to our unit's terms of reference. But Kady Jones thinks it might— she's the expert on nuclear scientists—and everything I've found out so far has backed up her first hunch. We need to take a look at this Natalia Morley, find out everything there is on her, in this country and overseas. Someone wanted to get her that job with Vermulen. We should find out who they were."

56

Kenny Wynter left home at half past five in the morning, aiming to catch the early-morning British Airways flight to Nice from Heathrow. It was forty-five minutes to the airport, maybe less—at this hour of the day the Porsche would eat it up. Drop the car off at the valet parking, check into British Airways business class, hand baggage only: no worries.

He wondered what Vermulen would be like. His handler, communicating, as always, via his personal message box on an Arsenal FC fansite, had given him the bare outline. Vermulen was ex–U.S. Army, a brass hat who'd gone into business on civvy street. He wanted something stolen from a house in the South of France: a small, high-value package. That could mean anything from a diamond necklace to a computer disc filled with industrial secrets. Whatever, this Vermulen character was a serious player, with impeccable connections and a deep pocket. The least Wynter could do was hear what the man had to offer. And the worst he would get was a nice trip. He planned to stay the night, treat himself to some fun on the Riviera.

He swung onto the M25, the orbital highway that described a ragged 117-mile circle around the outer edges of London. For much of the day it was little more than a gigantic traffic jam, but right now, with the road still swathed in dawn mist, there was barely a car in sight. Wynter swung over to the outside lane and settled into a steady eighty-five-mile-per-hour cruise. He was tempted to go much faster—plenty of people did. But that would be tempting fate. If there were any cops on the road, they'd ignore a car in the eighties, but once you got over ninety, you were asking to be stopped.

He looked in his rearview mirror. There was a clapped-out old heap behind him. The driver was thrashing the engine hard, coming up fast on his tail. He looked like a right idiot, wearing dark glasses and a baseball cap when the sun was barely up. Wynter gave a quick squirt on the accelerator and the Porsche eased forward, opening up the gap again. But the old banger just kept coming, getting closer and closer until it was practically touching the 911's rear bumper.

Then the other car flashed him, three long glares from the head-lights.

Wynter had to laugh. This bloke was really taking the piss.

So now he had a choice. He could floor it and get the hell out, but it was Sod's Law that there would be a cop around the next bend, and he had to be on that plane. So he pulled into the inside lane and slowed down to let the heap past.

As the cars drew level Wynter shook his head in wonderment. He was actually being overtaken by a Honda bloody Accord. He looked at the lunatic behind the wheel and gave him a gentle, condescending shake of the head, just to let him know what a sorry twat he was. Then he turned back to the road.

As he did so, he heard the sound of a revving engine and squealing tires to his right and the Accord veered across the lines into his lane and smashed into the side of his Porsche. The cars were locked together for a second, like wrestlers, sparks showering past their windows. Wynter could hear as well as feel the side panels of his car crumpling—his beau-tiful, brand-new car.

Wynter's first reaction was disbelief. He'd heard all about road-rage attacks. The M25 was famous for them; its traffic problems could turn the Dalai Lama psychotic. But his incredulity soon turned to outrage. What kind of a moron attacked a Porsche with an Accord? It was the dis-respect as much as the violence that shocked him. Wynter had strength, weight, and speed on his side. He was going to get away, but first he wanted to teach this numpty a lesson. He pulled the wheel hard to the right, intending to shove the other car right into the central barrier.

But the car wasn't there anymore. The driver had anticipated Wyn-ter's move, braked hard, and effectively ducked under the Porsche, end-ing up directly behind it. The Honda's lights came on again, full beam in Wynter's rearview mirror. Then the Honda rammed him from behind.

Wynter's concentration was all focused behind his car. He didn't notice the tractor-trailer pulling into the middle lane up ahead, as it passed a cement mixer lumbering along an uphill stretch of the highway. He didn't spot the Range Rover that had to swing into the outside lane to avoid the overtaking truck. By the time he looked up and saw that there was a line of vehicles right across the road, he was on top of them.

Wynter slammed on the brakes. The Porsche slowed instantly from more than ninety to less than sixty. The Honda hit him again, clipping the rear passenger-side corner of his car before sliding alongside him again, this time on the inside. Then he rammed him a second time, wrecking yet more panels.

Wynter had had enough. Up ahead, the Range Rover had passed the trucks and returned to the center lane. The outside lane was open again. Wynter moved into it and pressed the accelerator to the floor.

"Exploding nipples."

That's what Jerzy Garlinski, the lunatic expatriate Pole who'd taught Carver all about sabotage, used to say. Year after year, the faces and uniforms in his audience might change, but the routine was always the same.

"Question: how to take out a moving car so we leave no trace? Answer . . . exploding nipples."

Every year, the SBS trainees would laugh, even though they knew the line was coming. They'd all heard it a hundred times before, because every man who did the course felt obliged to perform his own Garlinski impersonation to any poor sod who would listen. But you couldn't knock the guy's teaching methods. No one ever forgot how to take out a moving car.

By "nipples" Garlinski meant tire valves. A tiny, remote-controlled explosive device, replacing the normal valve, was a discreet alternative to a conventional car bomb. It could not be spotted by a regular security sweep, nor did it leave any trace when detonated. The only problem was getting to the target vehicle ahead of the assignment—and the moment Wynter was picked up by the Government Communications Headquarters, booking his valet parking and giving the registration number of the car he'd be leaving at the airport, that problem was solved.

All Carver had to do then was find a way of provoking Wynter to drive at a speed that would prove fatal in the event of an accident. He'd been curious how he'd cope under pressure. He didn't know for sure that he'd have the balls for it when the moment actually came. But he'd felt completely calm as he taunted Wynter and smashed into his fancy car. He remembered the satisfaction that lay in dealing retribution to men who saw themselves as above the law, putting them on the receiving end. An old soccer hooligans' chant, no more than a childish taunt, came to his mind like a mantra.

"Come and get it," he thought, the words going around in his head as he drove the Honda into the side of the Porsche.

"Come and get it," watching the rage on Wynter's face as he accelerated away.

"Come and get it," picking up the remote detonator and pressing the button.

"If you think you're hard enough," as the Porsche's front tire blew out, the blast propelling the rigged valve out of the tire like a bullet from a gun, leaving it invisible in the shoulder by the side of the road, while the Porsche spun across the highway, as helpless as a leaf in a whirlpool, smashing into the central barrier and rebounding back into the road, past the desperately swerving Range Rover, straight into the path of the tractor-trailer.

The truck driver swung left, trying to dodge the Porsche, but the tail of his trailer lost its grip on the road and started swinging around counterclockwise, into the middle of the road, colliding with the out-of-control sports car.

The Porsche hit the side of the trailer head on. There was just enough clearance for the hood to slide underneath it, but the passenger compartment was sliced from the rest of the car body like the top off a boiled egg, ripping Wynter's head and shoulders from his body.

The trailer and the ruins of the Porsche came to a rest, lying across the highway, right in the path of the cement mixer, which braked, skidded, and slammed sideways into the wreckage.

By the time the two truck drivers had stopped shaking and clambered down from their cabs, Carver was a mile up the road. He left the highway at the next exit and pulled into a service station. A car was waiting for him, a black Rover 800. Carver parked the Honda and walked across to the Rover, passing a leather-jacketed, crew-cut man coming the other way. He got into the back of the Rover.

Grantham was waiting for him in the front passenger seat. He glanced up as Carver got in, looking at him in the mirror.

"Bit messy, weren't you? Blood all over the carriageway, heads knocked off? Not exactly discreet."

Carver shrugged. "I'm out of practice."

Grantham twisted around to face him, holding out an envelope.

"Here are your tickets," he said. "That fancy leather bag on the seat next to you is your hand luggage. Your suit is hanging up on the hook behind me. There's a wallet in the jacket pocket, litter in the trousers. You can change at the airport. And there'll be a gun waiting for you in Nice: your usual make and model . . . What's the matter?"

"Thinking about the job just now. You're right—it wasn't good enough."

"You got it done—that's the main thing. And don't worry—we'll have a quiet word with the police. No one's going to be announcing Kenny Wynter's passing any time soon."

"I hope not," said Carver. "Otherwise, how's he going to have lunch?"

57

Carver was met at the airport by a courier bearing a sign that read WYNTER. He was given a brown padded envelope, for which he signed. As the courier disappeared into the milling crowd, Carver worked the envelope with his fingers, feeling the outline of the SIG and the spare magazines. Reassured by the possession of a weapon, he acquired the kind of underpowered, midmarket sedan that constituted a luxury vehicle in the eyes of the airport's car-rental companies and set off along the coast to Antibes and the legendary Hotel du Cap. The Grill was located in a waterfront pavilion known as Eden Roc. He got there ten minutes early.

The restaurant was perched on the edge of a cliff, the customers protected from the drop by a ship's railing made of glossy white-painted metal, topped by a polished wooden handrail. The whole place had a nautical feel to it. The floors were decked in pale wood, the tables and chairs were all white and shaded by a white canvas awning, the waiters had crisply pressed trousers and polo shirts, also dazzling white, the better to set off their permanent tans.

The maître d' led Carver to a rectangular table, set for three, right next to the railing. He had an uninterrupted view out across the bay, past Juan-les-Pins, toward Cannes. Underneath the railing, a narrow strip of vegetation, the bright blue and yellow flowers bobbing about in the breeze, clung to the rock above the clear turquoise water. After the freezing blizzards of Norway and the drab grayness of England, the bright sunlight that sparkled across the sea and warmed the air filled him with energy and good cheer.

Turning his attention back to the restaurant, Carver sipped a glass of iced mineral water and casually scanned the other tables, just like any other lone male checking out the talent. On a weekday in April, the hotel had only just reopened for the season and the Grill wasn't too busy, just a smattering of rich, middle-aged customers taking a spring vacation.

Carver looked away. He wasn't going to stop checking, but he was pretty sure the place was clean. Now he could concentrate on the yacht, at least a hundred feet long, that was cruising slowly across the bay, moving so gently through the water that it barely left a ripple in its wake. It had a dark-blue hull and dazzling white superstructure designed like the outline of a giant paper dart raking down toward the dagger point of the bow: The cabins and staterooms massed at the stern.

As the yacht came to a halt about one hundred yards offshore, Carver could see two figures, a man and a woman, leaning against the stern rail of the open upper deck and looking toward shore. The man had his arm around the woman's waist, holding her body close. She was going with it, leaning into him, molding her body to his.

Carver recognized Vermulen because he'd instantly matched the man and his boat to Grantham's photo file. But he knew that the woman was Alix on a far deeper level, that animal instinct that makes one instantly aware of a lover's presence with an intensity that burns with excitement and pain in equal measure.

She was wearing a simple summer dress. Every so often the wind would catch it, fluttering the skirt, or pressing the fabric to her body, outlining the lines of her thighs and the curves of her hips and breasts. Carver felt the stirrings of sexual desire reawaken in him, like an old friend returning after a long journey to a faraway destination. Finally, Alix was real, there in the flesh, and this mission wasn't just a challenge thrown down to him by Grantham. It was a compulsion. He had to get her back.

Down at water level, a door slid open at the stern of the vessel and two crewmen appeared, maneuvering a speedboat, maybe fifteen feet long, that was lowered into the sea at the end of a line. Vermulen pointed this out to Alix and the two of them went back inside before reappearing a minute or so later beside the crewmen, down by the water.

The general was carrying a black leather briefcase. He was about to get into the speedboat when Alix stopped him and adjusted the collar of his pale-blue shirt, fiddling with it for a moment until it was exactly to her satisfaction. It was a very feminine, proprietorial gesture: a woman taking possession of her man before she kissed him good-bye and let him loose in the world.

Carver felt an acid stab of jealousy, then told himself, Get a grip.

That's what she does—she makes men believe that she cares. But with you it's real.

As Alix waved him off, Vermulen jumped into the speedboat, which brought him to a jetty at the foot of the cliffs. He came ashore, then made his way up a steep set of stone steps from the jetty to the restaurant.

Carver got to his feet to greet him. He wanted to be eye to eye with the man who had been sleeping with his woman, the man he might soon have to kill. He wanted to know exactly what kind of competition he faced.

Close up, Vermulen's face was a little fuller than it was in his army photograph, the jawline less cleanly defined. His full head of hair, swept back from his forehead, was as much silver as gold, and he was carrying a very slight paunch. But none of these flaws detracted from the aura of purpose and energy that seemed to charge the atmosphere around him. In fact, they added to the effect, giving him the imperious air of a man who was living life to the utmost, taking everything the world had to offer, certain of his ability to master any circumstance or individual he might encounter.

The general stuck out a tanned forearm and gave Carver a crushing handshake. "Hi. Kurt Vermulen," he said. "Pleased to meet you."

"Kenny Wynter," said Carver. "Likewise."

Vermulen gave Carver his own once-over, looking him up and down as if he were a soldier at a parade-ground inspection. The two men sat down, the briefcase on the floor between them. The general summoned a waiter.

"Just get us a nice selection of seafood—lobster, oysters, whatever's fresh and good today. We'll take some green salad with that, some bread and butter." He looked around the table. "You okay with that?"

It was strictly a rhetorical question. The officer was taking command. Carver shrugged his assent.

"Good," said Vermulen. "I don't consume alcohol at lunchtime. We'll take a large bottle of still water, please. Unless you want some wine, Mr. Wynter..."

"No worries," Carver replied, thinking his way into the character: the north London street kid whose brains had got him into Oxbridge, and whose criminal instincts had bought him a life of confident, classless wealth. "I'm here for business, not booze."

"And your business is taking things that are not your own?"

Wynter wouldn't have let that one go, so Carver didn't, either.

"I thought the U.S. Army was in that business, too."

Vermulen laughed. "Touché, Mr. Wynter."

They talked some more, sparring, each seeing what the other was made of. Then the food arrived, a great plate heaped with half-lobsters, langoustines, oysters, squid, and fillets of the Mediterranean sea bass the French call *loup de mer,* the wolf of the sea. Once plates were filled and glasses of iced water poured, Vermulen became more serious.

"You are an educated man, Mr. Wynter, so you will appreciate my meaning when I say that I feel that we are living in a time akin to Ancient Rome at the end of the fourth century A.D. Our civilization is still intact. Our comforts are greater than ever. But our will is crumbling. We lack the guts and determination to defend ourselves. And all around us, a dark age is drawing on. Enemies are prowling; populations are on the move. They sense our weakness and they await the moment to strike."

The rhetoric sounded grand enough, but to Carver it seemed hypocritical, coming from a man in a luxury restaurant, not a warrior on the front line.

"You're the one who left a military career," he retorted. "You stopped fighting. How can you blame the rest of us for not doing our bit?"

For a second, Carver could sense Vermulen prickling at this assault on his self-regard. But then he recovered his composure.

"On the contrary, I left the U.S. Army precisely because our defense and foreign-policy establishment was not prepared to fight the necessary battle, the one that I believe will determine the fate of the West: the battle against radical Islam."

That took Carver by surprise.

"What are you, some kind of Crusader?"

"Absolutely not: I don't want any war at all. But I fear it's coming anyway. It began in Afghanistan. It's being fought in Chechnya right now, and in the former Yugoslavia. Islamic terrorists are aiming to create a radical Muslim state in Kosovo, able to stab a knife right into Europe's guts. And the States will be next."

"You reckon?" said Carver. "What's that got to do with why I'm here?"

"Because you are going to acquire something I need very badly for our struggle. And by getting it, you're also going to deny it to our enemy.

Now, you come to me highly recommended, so let me make you a serious offer. You bring me what I want, in pristine condition, and I will pay you five hundred thousand dollars, half in advance, in any form you want, into any account you name."

"What is it you want?"

"A document. Don't ask me about its contents, because I will not reveal them. All I can say is that they could be vital to the future peace of the world."

Carver looked as indifferent as Wynter would have.

"You say that as if I should care. So where is this document?"

Vermulen leaned forward and lowered his voice.

"Sitting in a plain brown file, secured by a wax seal. This seal must be intact when you return it to me, or I will refuse to pay the rest of your money. The file is currently being kept inside a safe, located in a house about a dozen miles from here, in the hills above a village called Tourrettes-sur-Loup, due west of the town of Vence. It is guarded by armed men and trained attack dogs, as well as motion detectors, inside and out. There are alarms on the ground-level doors and windows. I have no information as to the model of the safe, or the exact nature of its lock. The combination, if there is one, is also unknown. You'd better assume, though, that it is protected by palm- or eye-scanners, in addition to that combination.

"The occupants of the house are ethnic Georgian gang members, based in Russia. Their leader is a man named Bagrat Baladze. He doesn't like to stay too long anywhere, so his people and his document will only be at this location for the next ninety-six hours maximum, maybe less. I do not know where they plan to go next and cannot be certain of tracking them. That means it has to be done now. Are you interested?"

Carver didn't look too impressed. "I'm not sure about that. See, I like to plan my work thoroughly. It can take weeks, even months. But thorough planning prevents stupid mistakes. That's why I'm sitting here with you, not rotting in a cell."

"The exact same principle applies in the military," Vermulen agreed, speaking normally again. "But equally, there are times when speed is of the essence. This is one of them. So can you do it, or do I need to consider other options?"

"Depends. Tell me about the building where these muppets are staying."

"There are detailed plans in the case."

"Maybe, but give me the gist of it, all the same."

"The layout is typical of vacation properties in this area. It's an old farmhouse, newly renovated. It hasn't even gone on the rental market yet, not officially anyway."

"So the builders have only just moved out?"

"I imagine so."

"Okay, that could be useful. Now tell me about the setting—what's the size of the grounds? Are there a lot of other properties close by? How about topography and cover—trees, bushes, rocks, that kind of thing."

"The property is right at the northern edge of the village. It has been chosen for its seclusion and privacy. There are no other houses within five hundred feet in any direction. The lot covers about two and a half acres. It's on the lower slopes of a four-thousand-foot hill—"

"In Britain, four thousand feet is a mountain," Carver interrupted.

"Well, it's just a damn hill to me," Vermulen replied. "Called the Puy de Tourrettes, faces south, toward the sea. The house is at the highest point of the property, to maximize the views, with a pool directly below the house and an access road that leads downhill to the nearest road. There are trees in front of the house and around the pool; otherwise the ground is virtually bare, denying cover to intruders and providing clear fields of fire. But above the house, on the hillside, you've got light woodland and undergrowth. That's where I'd put my observation post, if I were you."

That's where Carver was planning to put it, too.

"Sounds about right," he said.

Carver's plate was empty. He pushed it away from him. Then, to Vermulen's evident surprise, he got to his feet.

"Okay, give me ten minutes," he said. "I'm going for a walk—helps me think. When I come back, I'll tell you if I can do the job, what I'll need, and how much it'll cost."

"I already named the fee."

"But I didn't agree to it. See you in ten."

58

Carver had walked past the swimming pool, ringed by deserted lounge chairs, and up through the hotel's wooded grounds. He was gone a shade over eleven minutes.

"Well?" said Vermulen, as Carver returned to his seat.

"You're on. But the price is a million, sterling, same half-and-half split, now and on delivery of the item. Take it or leave it."

Before Vermulen could answer, Carver went on. "And there's one other thing. I came out here on a commercial flight, expecting to take a meeting. So I wasn't carrying the gear for the job. Some I can get myself. But some you're going to have to supply."

Vermulen looked to either side, to check that he could not be overheard.

"What are we talking about: weapons, specialist equipment?"

"That kind of thing," agreed Carver. "I need nonfatal weapons, specifically a multiple-shot forty-millimeter grenade launcher, preferably an MGL Mark One. I want six rounds of CS gas for the launcher plus three M-eighty-four stun grenades, a collapsible twenty-one-inch baton, a lightweight ballistic-grade protective vest, a combat-level gas mask, and twenty-five-milligram Valium tablets . . ."

"You don't look like the nervous kind," Vermulen observed.

"Yeah, well, looks can be deceptive. Now, I want every item within forty-eight hours. Leave it as *poste restante* in the post office at Vence. And, finally, I'm going to be spending a lot of time over the next few days keeping out of people's way, nice and quiet. So all communications will be via text-messaging—no calls unless I decide otherwise. I'll give you a number to use, and I'll need you to give me one, too."

Vermulen's jaw tightened. His face darkened with anger, like the shadow of a cloud scudding across the ground.

"You know, Mr. Wynter, you have quite an attitude for a hired hand. I don't know that I like being given orders by a man who's working on my dollar."

"I'm not giving you orders, General. I'm explaining the way things have to be if you're going to get the item you've ordered, and I'm going to walk away unscathed."

"I could determine another way of doing the job. I have men of my own."

"The matelots on your boat? Bunch of sailor boys in shorts? I don't think so."

"That wasn't who I was thinking of," said Vermulen. He looked at Carver, his eyes narrowed. "You know, that's an interesting word, 'matelot.'"

"It's French," said Carver, knowing he'd just made a stupid, careless, amateur mistake, still a few percent off his best.

"That it is. Also happens to be the slang that British marines use for regular naval personnel. I've heard them say it myself. So I'm wondering how come you know that word, and also seem to be so familiar with the designations for military ordnance: MGL grenade launchers, M-eighty-four grenades. If I recall correctly, you have no military experience. So perhaps you could tell me how a civilian came to be so familiar with all that soldier talk?"

Carver shrugged. "I get around."

Vermulen said nothing. He wasn't convinced. Carver went all out.

"All these years, doing what I do, you think I don't know the tools of my trade? And 'matelots'—that's what my dad always used to call sailors. Dunno where he got it from. National Service, maybe? Or more likely down the nick, doing porridge with some old bootneck. See, that's more slang. I can do some Cockney rhyming for you, if you like."

A wry smile crossed Vermulen face. "Okay, you win. So, assuming you get the goods, when and where will you make the delivery?"

"It'll be right here, at the hotel bar, just off the front hall, either three or four nights from now—I'll text the exact time once the mission has been accomplished. There was a bird on your boat—sorry, a woman . . ."

"Yes, my secretary." There was a hint of suspicion in Vermulen's voice.

"You trust her?" asked Carver.

"Of course."

"Good—then she can do the pickup. You and I can't meet again— we've taken enough of a risk as it is. So what's going to happen is a nice, respectable woman is going to meet an old friend in the bar of a hotel. What's her name, by the way?"

"Natalia Morley."

"Natalia . . . very nice. Anyway, Natalia and Kenneth will say hello, how are you, all that stuff. They'll have a nice little drink. She'll ask him what he's been up to, he'll take out the file, and she'll cast an eye over it politely. At some point, she'll take a call from her 'husband'—that's you, obviously—and she'll tell him that she's just bumped into good old Kenny. Then, when you've asked her if I've got the goods, she'll hand the phone over to me, like you're just dying to have a word with your old mate. You'll tell me that you've wired the outstanding payment into my account. When I've got confirmation from my bank, I'll pass Natalia the document, nice and discreet, and she'll put it in her handbag. Then we finish our drinkies, say good night, and go our separate ways. All right?"

"I don't want Miss Morley placed in any danger."

"Nor do I, General. If she's in danger, so am I."

"Okay, but I need to make sure she's comfortable with this. Let me speak with her."

Over the past half-minute, Carver had taken out a black Moleskine notebook from his jacket pocket and written something on one of its pages.

"You do that," he said, tearing the page out of the book and handing it to Vermulen. "But before you do, this is the sort code for my bank and the number of my account. I'd appreciate it if you transferred the first installment now. Neither of us is leaving this table till I've got my half-million."

Vermulen did not even glance at the torn page.

"Once again, Mr. Wynter, your attitude won't make you any friends."

"It's not personal, General. I've just learned the hard way not to deliver my side of a deal until I know for certain that the other side is delivering his."

Vermulen made the call. Carver got his confirmation. He immediately transferred the money to another account before Vermulen could attempt to cancel the transaction: That was another lesson that had cost him millions.

There wasn't much left to do. Vermulen handed Carver an envelope containing plans to the house and a detailed map of the surrounding area. He called "Miss Morley" and obtained her agreement to pick up the document. Carver could just make out Alix's voice on the other end of the line. The sound of her tore at his heart. When he heard her call Vermulen "darling," he had to grab a glass of water and look out to sea, so as not to give himself away.

When everything had been sorted out, Carver got up from the table. He reckoned this was about the time that Wynter, having got what he wanted, would turn the charm back on. So he held out his hand with a smarmy smile.

"Thank you, General—that was an excellent meal. It's been a pleasure doing business with you."

Vermulen got up and shook hands, but he wasn't going to get carried away.

"Good-bye to you, Mr. Wynter. If you don't mind, I'd rather reserve my judgment until our business is complete."

"You do that, General. And send my regards to Miss Morley. . . ."

59

On the way to Tourrettes-sur-Loup, Carver made a detour to Cannes. He dumped the piece of junk he'd hired at the airport and went to one of the specialist luxury car-rental companies that cater to the assorted stars, producers, and account-toting executives from the entertainment industry who flock to the town's festivals and sales conventions. There he hired an Audi S6 sedan, his personal transport of choice. He loved it for looking as dull as a Ford Mondeo but driving as fast as a Ferrari—faster, in fact, on many roads, thanks to the grip produced by its four-wheel drive: the perfect getaway vehicle.

He stopped at a Géant big-box store outside town to buy basic provisions, outdoor clothing, and camping gear, including binoculars and some heavy-duty hiking boots. Then he drove up into the hills. These Georgian gangsters had certainly picked a spectacular location for their hideout in the foothills of the Maritime Alps, a landscape of jagged slopes scattered with pines and oaks, and scoured by spectacular gorges, where switchback roads and absurdly picturesque villages clung to the sides of precipitous cliffs.

The most direct way to the house was off the main road between Vence and Grasse, and up through the village of Tourrettes itself. But Carver went the scenic route, skirting the side of the Puy de Tourrettes, until the pavement gave way to a dirt road, and then a track impassable even by a car with four-wheel-drive. He parked the Audi, put on his knapsack, and started hiking toward a point on the mountain directly above the house, making the final approach on his belly until he found the ideal spot for his observation post.

Down below him, he could see the people he had come to rob. Their voices drifted up to him on the breeze, along with the barking of their dogs. They had not spotted him.

Carver got out his binoculars. Now all he had to do was watch, and wait.

That, and work out how the hell he was going to steal Kurt Vermulen's precious document.

60

"**M**an, that's a sight to behold now, ain't it?"

Early morning, East River Park, and a steady stream of joggers was taking the path down from Twenty-third Street to the South Street Seaport and back, under the Williamsburg, Manhattan, and Brooklyn bridges, past the Fulton Fish Market. This was New York City and people were too bound up in themselves to spare a glance for the three men standing by the railings, ignoring the views across the river, watching the girls go by.

"Makes me wish I were thirty years younger," Waylon McCabe went on as a hot young blonde trotted by, her taut thighs and peachy backside sheathed in black running tights. "Hell, even ten years'd do me."

He turned to one of the other men, who was balding, his over-developed muscles now melting into fat, a brown leather jacket open to reveal a spreading paunch. His name was Clinton Tulane and he had been a military instructor back in the days when McCabe was providing assistance to West African guerrillas. Tulane had helped him out then, just as he'd helped out a whole lot of other people, from Sarajevo to El Salvador. That was how he knew Dusan Darko, though that was not the name under which the man in the black overcoat with the lank, greasy hair had entered the United States. When you were a Serbian warlord, wanted across the Western world for crimes against humanity, it paid to travel incognito.

"You can leave us now, Clint," said McCabe. "It's been real good of you to make this introduction. But me 'n' Mr. Darko here gotta talk business, and it's kinda private."

"Yes, sir," said Tulane, any resentment at his exclusion more than covered by the wad of hundred-dollar bills now nestled in his jacket pocket.

McCabe waited long enough to let Tulane get out of earshot, then fixed his attention on the other man.

"So, Mr. Darko, Clint tells me you're a man of some influence in your country—is that so?"

Darko shrugged as if to suggest that he was, indeed, influential, but too modest to say so out loud.

"So supposing I wanted to enter your country by air, find a place to land and refuel, pick up a package, and leave without anyone hasslin' me—you could make that happen?"

"But of course . . . for a price. You understand, people would need to be paid. But it is possible, certainly."

"Uh-huh, I get it. And you got men under your command, fightin' men?"

Darko stood a little straighter.

"My men have fought alongside me for seven years. Against Croats. Against Bosnians. Now against Albanian scum. These men are lions—like the partisans who fought against the Nazis, they cannot be defeated."

McCabe did his best to keep a straight face. He didn't need any lessons on fighting from some greasy wop who was second cousin to a Gypsy.

"Well, that's just fine, Mr. Darko. Let me tell you what I have in mind. . . ."

61

Carver didn't know what any of the wildflowers covering the hillside were, but he was glad of their rich, herbal scent. He'd been watching the house for forty-eight hours. During that time he'd drunk water, eaten chocolate, nuts, and dried fruit, and crapped into a sandwich bag before burying it in the earth behind his hideout. He'd also refined his plans for getting the document out of the house.

The property was arranged so that all the social areas were on the southern, downhill side, to maximize the views across the hazy, gray-green hills of Provence to the glittering waters of the Riviera. Everything practical was hidden away out of sight. So the driveway up to the house was over by the right-hand perimeter of the grounds, from Carver's perspective, looking down from above. There was a small drop-off area by the front door to the house, but the actual parking was to the rear, so that cars would be kept out of sight. There was no garage, but a massive seven-seater Mitsubishi Shogun was sitting under a metal-framed, plastic-roofed awning.

Up against the back wall of the house, a lean-to was filled with logs for the fireplace, which was, according to the architect's plans, the dominant feature of the main living room. Farther along, on the far side of a rear door that led into the kitchen, two red one-hundred-pound canisters of propane, as high as a man's shoulder, supplied gas for the stove.

There was still work to do on the area between the house and the rear perimeter. The low brick wall enclosing the parking area was unfinished and much of the ground was still covered with builders' debris: rubble, discarded bits of woodwork, empty cans, even a small cement mixer. Someone, however, had cleared a space for the high chain-link fences that kept the two dogs caged until they were let loose for the night.

The place had six human inhabitants: four male and two female. The weather had stayed warm, and around about midday the men had staggered outside for a busy day of drinking, smoking, and leering at the bimbos lying by the pool, trying to turn their fake tans into the real thing. It hadn't taken Carver long to work out which one was Baladze. The cock-of-the-walk way he carried himself, the fawning obedience of the men, and the shrieks of female laughter made it obvious who was the alpha male.

Carver had passed the time working out names for the people who would soon come under his attack. He toyed with soap-opera characters, historical figures, even Jesus and his apostles. In the end he went with Beatles. Baladze he code-named John, the original leader of the band. The man who looked like his second-in-command, a pot-bellied greaser with dirty-blond hair, was therefore Paul. A younger, skinny underling with long dark hair was a natural for George. That left Ringo for the fourth gang member. He had the grossly overdeveloped muscles, the furious expression, and the Pizza Hut complexion of a man who sprinkles steroids on his breakfast cereal and spends too much time alone with his dumbbells. The pelt of wiry black hair across his shoulders wasn't too pleasant, either.

The women were easy. One was a brunette, the other a blonde, Yoko and Linda, all the way.

During daylight hours, either George or Ringo was on duty as a guard down by the gate to the property. Whoever had the first morning shift had to get up early and put the dogs back in their cage before he went down to his post. The only visitor seemed to be the local baker, whose van turned up midmorning. Judging by the quantities of food and drink that the driver carried in through the back door to the kitchen, along with his loaves of breads, pizzas, cakes, and pies, he'd got some kind of deal to keep the place fully provisioned.

There was a barbecue on the terrace and Paul had been given the job of grilling steaks and kebabs every evening. Aside from that, the domestic chores were left for the women, who were multitasking as the men's housemaids, cooks, eye candy, and sex toys. Carver could imagine describing the scene to Alix. He didn't know exactly how she'd respond, but whatever she said, it would be knowing, cynical, and spiked with bone-dry black humor. He wondered how often she'd been treated like one of those women, but didn't dwell on that, preferring to concentrate on the future. Not long now, and he'd see her again. Just kiss Vermulen good-bye and they could both give the life up for good.

On the afternoon of the second day, Carver decided he'd seen enough. He'd do the job tomorrow. Tonight he'd find a hotel room and get a decent night's sleep, a hot shower, and a square meal. But before that he had to pick up Vermulen's package from the *poste restante* in Vence, then go shopping. He'd written another list of what he needed: sugar, linseed oil, food coloring, wax earplugs, and a bunch of other stuff, from paint brushes to meat pâté. It would mean visiting a few different shops.

And there was one final item: fish-tank oxygenating tablets. He made a mental note to himself: Don't forget the pet shop.

62

"Please, Mr. Novak, have as much as you want. I am a woman, I must watch my figure. But I like to see a man enjoying his food."

Olga Zhukovskaya looked encouragingly at the legendary hors d'oeuvres trolley of Vienna's Drei Husaren restaurant. The trolley held more than thirty seasonal dishes, from calves' brains to caviar.

Sadly for the waiter in his striped waistcoat, standing attentively beside the trolley, Pavel Novak did not have much of an appetite. Nor was he in any mood to appreciate the homely luxury of the Library, the smaller of the sixty-five-year-old restaurant's two dining rooms. Under normal circumstances, he would have felt soothed and contented among its shelves filled with ancient hardbacks, its baskets of spring daffodils, the stone statues in niches on the wall, and the restful tones of the wooden paneling and dark-green dining chairs. But not when his worst nightmares were coming to life before him.

The very fact that he and Zhukovskaya were speaking Russian was enough to bring back his darkest memories. For almost fifteen years he had worked to overthrow the rule of the Soviet Union, passing secret information to the West. In all that time, he felt sure he had escaped detection. And now, more than eight years after the Velvet Revolution that had brought freedom to his Czech homeland, the Russians had finally caught up with him.

When he had received the phone call inviting him to dinner, he had known exactly who Zhukovskaya was, and what she represented. He had accepted because there seemed no point in refusing or trying to escape. If they were after him, they would catch him. If they were not, he had nothing to lose from meeting one of the legends of the Soviet spy trade. His fatalism, however, did not make him any less nervous.

Zhukovskaya, of course, was fully aware of Novak's unease. She had enjoyed it, even toyed with it for a while, before deciding to put him out of his misery. She, too, would lose her appetite if she had to watch this miserable weasel with his pathetically drooping mustache sweating with fear before her eyes. There was no point coming to one of the finest restaurants in Vienna, where food is taken as seriously as in any French or Italian city, and then being unable to enjoy the menu.

"Are you worried, or fearful of what might happen to you? Please, these are not the old days. We are not Stalinists anymore."

Novak relaxed a fraction. He managed to order some chicken in jelly.

"Good," said Zhukovskaya, "and for the main course I recommend the *tafelspitz*—boiled beef, hashed potatoes, creamed spinach, and apple sauce—they say it is the best in Vienna. But of course, you know that, being a local. So, let us not talk business while we eat. Let's tell stories about the good old days . . . when you worked for the Americans."

It was all Novak could do not to spit his mouthful of chicken all over the table. He chewed and swallowed his food, trying all the while to think of a reply.

Zhukovskaya continued.

"Come on—how incompetent did you think we were? Of course we knew. But it suited our purposes to let you live. You were a trusted source because you truly believed that the information you were passing on was genuine. But I'm afraid that much of it was not. We made sure of that. So, far from harming us, as you must have hoped, you were actually doing the Soviet Union a great service by misleading our enemies. . . . Oh, look, your wineglass is empty. Perhaps the sommelier will get you some more."

Finally, Novak was able to speak.

"When did you know?"

"Well, I was just a junior officer back then, so I was not informed until much later. But my superiors were aware of your treachery from the moment you made your first, nervous approach to the Americans."

"My God . . . how deeply did you penetrate the DIA?"

"We were able to blackmail a few officers; we paid others. One or two worked for us for ideological reasons. But the total was not great, fewer than a dozen. Your handler, Vermulen, was always completely loyal to his country. Both you and he were absolutely sincere in what you were doing. That was important to us."

"So why do you want to see me now?"

Zhukovskaya pushed away her half-eaten portion of caviar.

"All right, then, if you prefer, we can do business and then eat.

Perhaps that is better, after all. So . . . what were you discussing with Vermulen at the opera?"

"Nothing. I have not seen Vermulen in years. And I do not particularly like opera."

A pained expression crossed Zhukovskaya's face.

"Once again, Mr. Novak, I must make the same request: Please do not underestimate us. You attended a performance of *Don Giovanni* at the opera house here in Vienna. You spoke to Vermulen in the bar before the performance. So I will ask you now, why did you meet? What did you discuss? What communication have you had since? And I will repeat, if you are open with me, we can all behave like civilized people. If you are not . . . well, let's not spoil our dinner thinking about that."

Novak was indifferent to her threat. So far as he was concerned, he was already a dead man. The one noble act he had undertaken in his life, his personal campaign against the Communist occupation of his country, had been exposed as a sham. Far from helping the cause of freedom, he had probably harmed it. Now his feeble attempt to prevent the list of bombs from falling into the wrong hands was unraveling in front of his eyes.

He supposed he could make a grand, sacrificial gesture. He could refuse to say anything, and let this Russian witch try to beat the truth out of him. Perhaps he could hold out for long enough to enable Vermulen to do what he had to. But that resistance would require effort and mental energy to sustain and he was suddenly and painfully aware that he had no further capacity for that kind of effort. Why bother to maintain the pretense any longer?

Novak summoned the sommelier.

"I would like a bottle of red Bordeaux, something to remember for a lifetime. The price is irrelevant."

The sommelier, well aware who was paying for this meal, glanced at Zhukovskaya. She gave a fractional nod of assent before he answered Novak's request.

"In that case, *mein herr,* I would suggest the 1982 La Mission Haut-Brion. A magnificent vintage from one of the great châteaus. I think you will find it an almost spiritual experience."

A tired smile played briefly over Novak's face.

"Spiritual, eh? Then the Haut-Brion will be perfect."

Zhukovskaya did not hurry him as he tasted the wine, signaled his approval, savored the intensity and complexity of its aroma, then took his first few sips. She understood as well as he did what was happening.

When he had finished his first glass, Novak began to talk. He described how he had been approached by Bagrat Baladze, who was trying to sell the list of missing bombs; how he had gone in turn to Vermulen, hoping to get the list to the Americans; how he had provided him with the location of the list and the means to obtain it.

When he had finished, Zhukovskaya reached across the table and gave his hand a gentle squeeze.

"Thank you," she said with quiet sincerity. "Now enjoy the rest of your meal."

Her smile was unexpectedly charming, so feminine, almost flirtatious as she added, "And your spiritual wine!"

Somehow, perhaps because the burden of his secret had been lifted, or simply because the Bordeaux was a magical elixir, Novak was able to enjoy his dinner. He and Zhukovskaya made the conversation of two middle-aged people who had shared similar experiences over many years and observed the same absurdities. He was a man with a gift for a funny anecdote; she was a woman who was happy to laugh at his humor.

At the end of the meal, Zhukovskaya was as civilized, as *kulturny,* to use the Russian phrase, as she had promised. With great politeness, she asked him to hand over his cell phone. She also told him that there was about to be a problem with the telephone lines running in and out of his apartment building. He could not, in other words, alert anyone to what he had just told her. She informed him that he would be given a lift back to his home, and his wife.

"Please," she said, "make this easy for both of us."

Fifteen minutes later, Pavel Novak let himself in through his front door, crossed the hall, and stepped into the elevator, an ornate metal cage that had run up through the middle of the building's spiral staircase for the better part of a century. He stopped on the fifth floor and went into his apartment. His wife was asleep in their bedroom. He kissed her face and whispered, "I love you," in her ear.

She gave a sleepy little murmur of reply.

Novak looked at her with the love that a man has for a woman who has shared his life for almost three decades, a love in which youthful passion has given way to a far deeper blend of affection, knowledge, and mutual forgiveness. He laid his hand briefly on her shoulder, then he left the room.

He walked up to the top of the building and out through the door that led to the roof. He walked to the edge, looked around him at the lights and rooftops of Vienna, took one last, deep breath, and stepped out into the void.

63

Last thing at night, Carver called Grantham in London.

"It's going down tomorrow," he said. "Sometime in the afternoon."

"Do you have any idea yet what you're after?"

"Not yet. All the client told me was he was hoping to retrieve some kind of document in a sealed envelope. He didn't tell me what was in the document that was so valuable. He just said, and I quote, that it was 'vital to the future peace of the world.'"

"He what . . . ?"

Whatever Grantham was expecting, it wasn't that.

"Yeah, I know," said Carver. "I thought it sounded pretty crazy, too. And that wasn't the half of it. He's got this obsession that we're like the Romans, just as the empire was collapsing, with barbarians at the gate. Only the barbarians aren't Huns and Vandals; they're Islamic terrorists, trying to take over the world."

"You're joking." Grantham gave a short, irritable sigh.

"Well, you can argue that out with him. All I know is, I'll be aiming to make the handover sometime in the early evening. The location is the Hotel du Cap, same as our lunch. I'll give you the precise time tomorrow. Within fifteen minutes of that time, I aim to be walking out of the hotel with the woman and, if possible, the document. I told Vermulen I didn't want any of his men there when the deal went down, but I can't believe he'll keep to that. He'll want to protect his investment. So I'm going to need extraction—a car, maybe even a driver, someone good—and a safe house for the night."

Grantham gave a snort of disbelief. "Would you like me to lay on a private jet as well? You seemed to like those, as I recall."

"Or I could just give Vermulen's goons the document in exchange for Alix . . ."

"I'll see what I can do."

64

E ven the powerful have bosses. And just as Olga Zhukovskaya could make her subordinates quake, so even she felt twinges of anxiety when calling her agency's director in his bed to tell him bad news. She reported everything Novak had told her, stressing the urgency of the matter. In her view, the list of nuclear weapons and their precise whereabouts had to be recovered within twenty-four hours. After that, it could be lost forever.

"We know the whereabouts of a document that is of enormous military and political significance to the Motherland," she concluded. "We should make immediate plans to seize it."

The director had not survived a life of secrecy, infighting, and continual, often deadly regime changes by being rash or lacking in calculation. His immediate response was cautious.

"Can we be sure that this list really exists, or has the significance Novak claimed? The deployment of those weapons was under KGB control, their locations are still known to us alone, and I am not aware of any documents missing from our files. I suppose, theoretically, that Defense Ministry operatives might have found a way of copying or stealing our documentation . . ." He paused to contemplate the disturbing possibility that another agency might have outwitted his own, however temporarily. "In any case, Novak was a traitor who became a profiteer. All good reasons to disbelieve anything he says."

"Quite so, Director. In any other circumstance I would agree with you on all counts. But I sat one meter from Novak when he was talking. I am certain that he was telling the truth."

"Feminine intuition?" sneered the director.

"No, sir—twenty-five years of experience in the conduct of interrogations."

"Very well, let us assume, hypothetically, that this list is as dangerous as you claim. Another problem arises. It is located in a foreign, sovereign

nation and we do not wish to provoke a diplomatic incident by under-
taking a violent action against armed criminals, who would have the
advantage of a defensible position."

Zhukovskaya countered that.

"But, Director, we undertake violent actions on foreign countries all
the time—"

"So you proved—with regrettable lack of success—in Geneva
recently," her boss snapped. "Our coverup may have fooled local
police and media, but do not suppose that our enemies were deceived.
The operatives chosen were far too easily identifiable as our assets. In
any case, we have a further difficulty. As you know, all government
agencies are facing severe financial restrictions at the moment. We are
no exception. . . ."

"It is very sad, Director," Zhukovskaya murmured, keen to get him
off his hobbyhorse and back to the matter in hand. "But I do not see the
relevance here—"

"The relevance, *Deputy* Director, is that I have no money to pay for
the operation you propose. I have already funded an undercover operation on your behalf."

"Which has led to our discovery of Novak and his document—"

"At the cost of sending men to America and Switzerland, arranging
contacts across the whole of Europe, not to mention the American dollars spent on Miss Petrova's cover, which apparently involved buying
clothes no good Russian woman could afford, and primping herself in
beauty parlors. . . ."

As the old man ranted, a smile slowly spread across Zhukovskaya's
face. She had just seen a way in which she could carry out the operation, recover the document, save the state money, create total deniability
in the event of anything going wrong, and cause maximum embarrassment to the outmoded dinosaur who stood between her and the top job
she craved.

"Are your official instructions that I should not expend any agency
resources on this matter?" she asked dutifully.

"Indeed they are," said the director. "And as for Miss Petrova, I must
say that I am amazed that you are prepared to have anything to do with
her, given her role in your husband's death. If I were in your place, I
should have taken great pleasure in killing her."

"Perhaps, in due course, I will. For now, though, I am happy to use her talents to advance our interests."

For the first time the director's voice was laden with genuine admiration.

"I must say, my dear, that is admirably cold-blooded, even for you."

GOOD FRIDAY

65

I t was another perfect spring morning in Provence. Carver met the baker's decrepit old van on the street, half a mile from the house, and thumbed a lift. Now it was chugging and clattering up to the gate. The gang member he had christened Ringo appeared in the driveway, signaling for them to stop. Up close, where the tufts of hair on his back and chest sprouted over the neck of his T-shirt, he looked even less appealing. But he was carrying a combat shotgun, and from the way he carried it, angled across his body—the stock nestled in the crook of his right arm, right hand on the trigger, the barrel pointing down—someone had trained him to use it properly.

Ringo glared at the baker, ignoring the tradesman's polite *"Bonjour, m'sieur,"* offering not even a grunt by way of acknowledgment that he recognized his face. He just pointed at the keys in the ignition and flicked his fingers, indicating that they should be handed over.

Once the van had been immobilized, he walked around the vehicle and opened the rear doors. With an air of infinite suspicion, he examined the rows of baguettes, round loaves, cakes, tarts, and croissants arranged in the back of the van, seemingly immune to the temptation posed by their crisp brown crusts, succulent fillings, and mouthwatering aromas. So far as he was concerned, every *pain au chocolat* was a potential booby trap, every quiche a hidden hand grenade. He looked inside the plastic bags filled with meat, vegetables, and booze. Finally, he satisfied himself that the contents of the van posed no danger to anything other than the arteries and brain cells of the people who consumed them.

The bull-necked gangster closed the doors, then resumed his circuit of the van. He came to a halt by the passenger door. He signaled for the window to be wound down. When it had been, he pointed the gun through the opening, bent his head, looked along the barrel, and stared Carver full in the face.

Ringo's single eyebrow knitted even more tightly as he considered the threat posed by this unfamiliar individual wearing white housepainter's overalls. He took a step back, positioning himself just to the rear of the door, making sure his field of fire was unimpeded, then motioned with the gun barrel, telling Carver to get out of the van.

Carver stepped out into the warm, scented sunshine, putting his hands up as he did so, the natural reaction of an innocent, inexperienced civilian confronted by a man with a gun. The Georgian pointed his gun at the worn, khaki canvas shoulder bag on the floor of the passenger compartment. He wanted Carver to retrieve it. Once again, Carver did as he was told. He carried out the apparently simple task in slow, distinct stages, making it clear at every point that he was doing nothing untoward.

Once he was standing upright again, with the bag in his hand, he opened it up for inspection. There were two cans of paint inside: one white gloss, brand-new and unopened, the other empty and stuffed with old rags. Alongside the cans lay three brushes of varying widths, a large can of paint thinner, a packet of potato chips, a glass one-liter bottle filled with orange juice, and a small, greaseproof-paper package.

"Sandwiches, for my lunch," said Carver in French, holding it up. He strongly doubted that the guard spoke the language, but he kept going anyway.

"I just came to do some painting. My *patron* said the woodwork in the kitchen and lounge needs touching up. Told me he'd spoken to the man that's renting the place . . . *comprenez?*"

Ringo glowered some more before he got out a phone and, still keeping one hand on his gun, hit the speed dial. He had a brief conversation in a language Carver had never heard before, but assumed must be Georgian. Then he signaled to Carver to get back in the van, and jerked his head in the direction of the house.

The baker started up the rackety engine once again and they headed up the hill, around the building to the parking area at the rear. There, the baker got out and walked toward the kitchen door, carrying a couple of shopping bags filled with provisions. He glanced nervously at the two dogs, standing by the wire cage, growling and barking at his approach as he knocked on the door. It opened and the brunette woman, Yoko, stuck her head out. She shouted at the dogs, who lowered their barking to a mean, resentful grumbling and backed away a few paces from the wire. Then she let the baker into the building.

Carver hung back, as if waiting his turn to say his piece. He was standing about fifteen feet away from the kitchen door, by the pile of firewood, under its wooden shelter. He looked around. There was no one watching him. He crouched down at the back of the log pile by the wall of the house and opened up his bag.

Over the next few seconds, he carried out a series of quick, precise actions. First, he took out the small packet of sandwiches and placed them in his pocket. Then he gently slid out a small log at the back of the pile, as if he were removing a brick from a Jenga tower, and shoved the bag of chips and the bottle of orange juice into the gap where the log had been. The canvas bag was tucked out of sight on the ground, in the shade of the shelter, right by the wall of the house. Carver left the bag open, with the can of paint placed across the top of the used paint can stuffed with rags.

Then he walked past the kitchen door. Inside, the baker was holding out a tray of pastries for Yoko to inspect. Again making sure that no one could see him, Carver opened his packet and lobbed the two sandwiches into the dogs' cage, where they were instantly devoured. He turned back again and hovered outside the kitchen door while the woman made her selection and the baker noted it down on a pad before picking up his tray again and going back to his van.

When it was his turn to speak, Carver stepped into the doorway and launched into the same garbled explanation of his presence that he had given the guard at the gate. Yoko looked puzzled at first, then anxious. She looked behind her, into the house, clearly trying to decide whether it was worth waking her boss. To Carver's relief, she concluded that it was not and started shooing him away, gabbling indignantly as she did so.

He took the hint and walked back to the van, where the baker was waiting with a grin plastered all over his face—the delighted smile of a man who has just seen another male getting it in the neck from an angry woman. As he got into the passenger seat, Carver shook his head ruefully and blew out his cheeks.

"*Les femmes, hein?*" he sighed.

The baker laughed, then started up the van, and they rattled away down the hill.

66

Ivan Sergeyevich Platonov, commonly known as Platon, was the man entrusted with expanding the Podolskaya crime clan's activities in Western Europe. He had been in bed in his Paris apartment with one of the women whose bodies provided so much of his gang's revenues when Olga Zhukovskaya called.

"How are you, Ivan Sergeyevich?" asked Olga Zhukovskaya.

"Very well, thank you, and you?"

"Also well. You know, my husband always spoke very warmly of you. . . ."

"He was a great man. My condolences. You received my wreath, I hope."

"Yes, thank you, very impressive. I'm not disturbing you?"

The girl had woken up, yawned, and then dutifully started running her fingers down Platon's stomach. He shooed her away.

"Of course not. What can I do for you?"

"I need something collected, or perhaps *retrieved* would be a better word. . . ."

While Platon listened, occasionally breaking in with specific, practical questions, the deputy director explained about a missing document, the property of the Russian people, that was currently sitting in a safe in a house in the South of France, about 550 miles from where he now lay. It was currently guarded by four Georgians, led by a low-rank gang leader named Bagrat Baladze. Within the next twenty-four hours, it would be either sold to a filthy Arab terrorist or stolen by the agents of an even more despicable American, unless Platon and his men could get to it first.

"You have fought for the Motherland in the past," said Zhukovskaya. "Now she calls you for one more mission."

There was something almost seductive in her voice; it was less the command of a senior officer than the request of a vulnerable woman made to a mighty warrior.

Platon wasn't falling for it.

"Naturally, I am a patriot," he said. "Even now, when I live as a peaceful businessman, I am willing to do my duty. But there will be costs. Men may die. Their families must be considered."

He had never paid a single ruble to a widow or orphan in his life, a fact of which Zhukovskaya was fully aware.

"Of course, you must be compensated," she agreed. "I was thinking, you may be aware that my late husband was involved in the production and sale of certain munitions, on behalf of the state."

Platon knew that, all right. Zhukovski had made a fortune flogging land mines until that English princess had stuck her interfering nose in his business. That had been the death of her . . . and of him, too. Since then, as political pressure against them grew, the mines had been rotting in warehouses all over Russia. But the illicit demand for them was unabated. Mines sold by the tens of thousands, and each one was worth three hundred U.S. dollars in pure profit. If he could secure the concession, there was a massive fortune to be made.

"I would be proud to assist my country, but it will not be easy," he said. "I must take my best men away from their current assignments. They will need equipment. And of course we must all get to the property as fast as possible. A helicopter will be the fastest method. The French make one called a Dauphin. It will easily seat six men and take us all the way there, right to the front door, with just one refueling stop. If I can charter one this morning, I can be at this place by early afternoon."

As it turned out, Platon's takeoff was delayed. The chopper he hired had technical problems. It was not until lunchtime that the Eurocopter Dauphin left the Paris heliport and began the three-hour flight south.

67

There had been a number of problems confronting Carver as he tried to work out how to get the document Vermulen wanted from the house where Bagrat Baladze was keeping it. For a start, he was not a professional thief, unlike Kenny Wynter, the man he was impersonating. He did not know where in the building the document was hidden, and the only method he knew of opening a safe was blowing it up: not such a smart idea if you wanted to preserve a flimsy cardboard folder filled with bits of paper. And, of course, there were six potential opponents— because he couldn't assume that the women would be useless in combat—and only one of him.

Of these considerations, the last was the least significant. Given the element of surprise and a properly planned assault, he could soon even the odds. He'd done it often enough before. But he wasn't there to kill people. He was there to steal. So he worked through the problem logically, considering all the possible permutations, until he came to a solution that made sense. Which was why he needed his shopping list. That, and a working knowledge of basic chemistry as it applied to the art of sabotage.

The logic was simple. The simplest way of getting the document out of the house was to make Bagrat Baladze do the work for him. Pondering that led Craver inexorably to the chemical properties of the substances on his list.

Linseed oil, for example, is prone to spontaneous combustion, as painters and decorators—not to mention their clients—sometimes learn, at their own cost. When the oil is exposed to air, it oxidizes and releases heat. The greater the exposure, the greater the heat generated. If the linseed is spread thinly across a relatively large area of cotton rag, that maximizes exposure, and so the heat rises. Over a period of approximately six hours, the rags can reach a temperature of more than 430 degrees Centigrade, some 800 degrees Fahrenheit, which is enough to produce a flame.

But there's a catch. If there's too little ventilation, the oxidation process is greatly reduced. If there's too much, the flow of air around the rags simply disperses any heat it creates. It's just like blowing on a fire. Stifle it and it dies. Blow too hard and you blow it right out. You've got to get the balance just right.

The ideal between too much and too little air is to place linseed-soaked rags in an open container. An empty paint can is perfect.

Aquarium pellets have equally potent chemical properties. Their job is to freshen up water by producing oxygen, and their active ingredient is potassium chlorate, an extremely efficient oxidizing agent. Just as with linseed oil, this oxidization produces energy in the form of heat. If the release of energy is sufficiently powerful, it creates an explosion. Potassium chlorate is a very effective oxidizer, which explains why it is also an active ingredient in many homemade explosives, whether formulated by fireworks hobbyists or homicidal terrorists. Carver had ground down the tablets using a pestle and mortar and then mixed the resulting powder with sugar, which would burn to produce a bigger, brighter bang.

He had poured the mix into the bottom of an opened, emptied bag of potato chips, replaced the chips, and glued the bag back together. Then he prepared the bottle of "orange juice," which actually consisted of acetone—bought from the same hardware store where he'd found the rest of the painter's supplies—orange food dye, and, once again, sugar. Acetone is an extremely highly flammable liquid whose vapors can explode on exposure to a spark. Among sugar's properties is that it caramelizes under heat, becoming extremely sticky. So the addition of sugar to this sort of bottle bomb, or Molotov cocktail, causes the flame to adhere to its target, much like napalm.

Carver didn't have to add anything to the paint thinner or the oil paint. They would be fine just as they were.

His painter's bag and its contents were, essentially, a self-detonating incendiary bomb. Once they were in place, Carver had ridden back to the village in the baker's van, checked out of his hotel, and driven back up the mountain, this time by the scenic route. He made a second trek across the mountainside to his observation post, now carrying the equipment that Vermulen's people had delivered to the *poste restante*, as per instructions. After that, he'd just waited.

By midday, the air temperature had risen into the high seventies. The women sunned themselves with the gratitude of northern Europeans released at the end of a cold, dark winter. The men went shirtless, revealing torsos covered in the tattoos that are an essential mark of status in Russian gangland culture. The dogs lazed in their cage, their laid-back demeanor caused less by the hot sun on their fur than the large quantities of Valium—fifty milligrams crushed and mixed with the pâté in each of their sandwiches—coursing through their bloodstreams.

The humans lunched late, at around two in the afternoon. They drank heavily with their meal. By half past three, George had taken over sentry duty by the gate. Bagrat and Linda had gone back indoors for sex and a snooze. Everyone else was flopped semicomatose by the pool. That was when Carver saw the first wisps of smoke coming from his canvas bag.

He texted Vermulen's number: "Delivery 19:00 in bar as planned." Carver spelled the words in full. He regarded text-speak as infantile twaddle and presumed a retired general would feel the same way. Thinking about it, he doubted whether Vermulen had ever before in his life been obliged to use text at all.

By the time he'd finished, a flame was clearly visible. He'd painted the inside of his bag with linseed, too, just to add to the effect. Once the spark caught, it would quickly spread.

There was a sudden, sharp crack, a shattering of glass, and a whoosh of flame as the bottle of cleanser cracked open and its contents ignited. From there it was a chain reaction. The flame from the cleanser lit the bag of chips, which then went off with an explosive fizz, like a Roman candle. That shattered the drink bottle, releasing a fireball of acetone and sugar, which in turn set the bone-dry logs aflame.

Carver was already wearing his bulletproof vest, with his pistol holstered below it. The loaded grenade launcher was slung around his back. The baton was in his hip pocket. The wax plugs had been stuffed deep into his ears. His hands, encased in tight leather gloves, were holding his gas mask. It would be the last thing to go on.

By now the woodshed was completely ablaze, the flames dancing up the side of the house. A first-floor window was open, and the fire caught on the wooden shutters and window frames and the nylon net curtains rippling in the hot currents of air generated by the fire. The flames slipped into the room beyond as stealthily as a cat burglar. Above them, the massive oak beams under the eaves of the tile roof began to smolder. It would not be long before they, too, added to the conflagration.

68

I t was the sentry, down by the gate, who realized what was happening first. Carver watched George's reaction as he saw the smoke rising over the top of the house and dashed back up the hill, shouting at the top of his voice. By the pool, Paul slowly raised himself to one elbow to see what had caused the commotion, took a few seconds to process what he was seeing, then sprang to his feet and screamed at Ringo to wake up. Yoko started shrieking. The three men raced around the side of the house. They disappeared from Carver's view for a few seconds, then reappeared on the ground behind the house, where they stood, pointing at the fire, backing away from the flames and shouting at one another.

A window was flung open above the kitchen and Bagrat stuck out his head. Carver could see the look of horror on his face as he saw the blaze and then watched the expression turn to panic as the Georgian looked down at the propane-gas cylinders beneath him. If they exploded, they could take half the building with him. He screamed a series of orders at the three men, threw a set of keys out of the house onto the ground in front of the men, then ducked back inside.

Carver's entire plan hinged on what Bagrat did next, but he didn't have time to wait and see what would happen. He had to get moving and hope that his enemy's logic was the same as his own.

Down below, the men had split into two groups. George and Ringo were frantically trying to disconnect the propane cylinders and drag them away from the fire. This wasn't good. Carver wanted the men well out of the way. He'd assumed they'd make a dash for the front of the house, away from the threat of the fire. Paul had picked up the keys from the dirt and was moving toward the Shogun. Carver had planned to hit the Georgians when they gathered together in a group in front of the burning house. As any normal people would do.

Time for an instant rethink.

He pulled on his gas mask and scrambled down the hillside, charging through the undergrowth as fast as he could, heedless of the noise he was making. He knew the men's attention would be fully focused on the fire.

He was making for a point on the boundary wall halfway between the gas tanks and the carport, almost exactly opposite the fire. The wall was about seven feet tall. It felt just like being back on the marines' assault course as Carver leapt up, grabbed the top of the wall, scrambled for purchase with his feet, then propelled himself, rolling over the top and down the other side.

The moment his feet touched the ground, he reached for the grenade launcher and fired twice: the first round toward the car, the second at the canisters. Two plumes of white gas belched from the grenades, trapping the three men in thick clouds that burned their eyes and rasped their throats. The Georgians staggered, dizzy, disoriented, and retching, as Carver came at them out of the smoke, swinging his steel riot baton at their defenseless skulls and necks with ruthless brutality.

The men by the canisters were his first targets. When they were downed and unconscious, he went for the one by the car, beating him to his knees, where he doubled over with coughs and dry vomits until Carver laid him out on the ground with a vicious kick to the side of the head.

But where were the car keys? They weren't in the hands of the unconscious gang member, nor the lock of the car. Now Carver had to fall to the ground and fumble around in the smoke, staring through the clear plastic bubble of his gas mask as his hands scrabbled across the dust and debris on the ground. It seemed an age before his fingers closed around the plastic key ring and he could get back up to his feet and make for the Shogun.

He turned on the ignition and gunned it, accelerating down the drive and then slewing left into the small graveled forecourt in front of the house. Bagrat was waiting there, with the two women. Yoko was still in her bikini, while Linda had fled the bedroom in nothing more than a pair of panties and a blanket, which was draped over her shoulders and clutched tight in front of her breasts. Bagrat was only marginally less exposed. Bare-chested and shoeless, he had nothing on but a pair of jeans. His right hand was clutching a gun. But the good news for Carver was the briefcase chained to Bagrat's left wrist.

He saw it as he came around the corner and knew at once what had to be done. With his right hand on the wheel, he brought the Shogun to a skidding halt in a shower of gravel. At the same time, his left hand ripped one of the stun grenades from his vest. He pulled out the pin with his teeth and threw the hexagonal perforated-steel tube out of the car window, ducking his head, and closing his eyes tight shut as he did so.

The British Special Forces, for whom stun grenades were originally designed as means of overcoming hostage takers, always called them "flashbangs," a name that means exactly what it says. The grenade detonated in front of the three Georgians with a scorching dazzle of light, equivalent to the glow from more than 100,000 standard sixty-watt domestic lightbulbs, just a few feet from their unprotected eyeballs. At the same time it emitted a sound blast eight times as loud as a fighter plane's jet engine. Carver was expecting it and had taken precautions, but even he was stunned for a few seconds. Bagrat and the two women were poleaxed.

The two women were sitting on the ground with vacant, zombielike expressions on their sightless, deaf faces. Linda's blanket had fallen from her body, but she was completely indifferent to or simply unaware of her exposure.

Bagrat was barely any better. He was on his knees and trying to get to his feet, though his limbs seemed unwilling to obey his instructions. His gun was weaving to and fro in his hand as he swung his torso around from one side to the other, blindly trying to seek out his attacker. Suddenly, the gun went off and a bullet smashed through the Shogun's rear windows. Carver came to his senses fast, kicking open the door and falling to the ground. He scrambled across the gravel toward Bagrat, keeping as low as he could as the gun fired three more random, aimless shots. One fizzed over Carver's head. Another ricocheted off the steps that led from the house down to the pool. The third caught Linda full in the throat, ripping through her windpipe and lodging in her spinal cord. She was thrown onto her back by the impact and lay there helplessly as the blood spurted from her gaping, gurgling wound.

She was going to take a while to die, but there was nothing that Carver or anyone else could do to save her. He concentrated on Bagrat, feeling enraged that his attempts to avoid any fatalities had been frustrated, a fury that emerged in the venom with which he whipped the baton back and forth across his head three times in quick succession. Once he'd knocked him out, Carver picked up Bagrat's gun hand, pointed the pistol at the dying woman, and, keeping the other man's finger on the trigger, squeezed it once more. The shot hit her in the skull, killing her instantly and putting her out of her misery.

Carver was tempted to turn the gun on Bagrat himself. But he had been sickened enough by the woman's unnecessary death. He had no desire for more cold-blooded slaughter. Instead he held the gun, still in Bagrat's right hand, against the chain that connected the briefcase to his left wrist. He fired one last time, breaking the chain, then grabbed the barrel of the gun and threw it into a clump of weeds and scraggly shrubs over by the pool. If the police ever turned up, they would find it there, with Bagrat's prints all over it, gunshot residue on his hands, and two matching bullets in the dead woman's corpse.

He reached for the case and got up. Roughly fifteen seconds had passed since the flashbang's detonation. The grenade's effects would persist for about a minute more. The other three men would be impaired by the CS gas for up to twenty minutes. But when they all got to their senses, they would be four angry Georgians. In the meantime, there would soon be police cars and fire engines coming up the road from Tourrettes-sur-Loup, attracted by the flames that were now tearing through the whole house, sending dirty black smoke high into the clear blue sky. It was time to get out.

Carver grabbed the grenade launcher from the Shogun and slung it around his back again. He collected the used flashbang casing and ran back around the burning house. The CS gas had cleared, but the three men were still incapable of stopping Carver as he dashed past them. He managed to pick up the grenade that had gone off by the carport, but the other one, by the propane canisters, was too close to the flames, which were now beginning to lick around the two red metal tubes. It would be only seconds before they blew, and that realization hit Carver with a surge of adrenaline that sent him flying up and over the wall and hurtling across the mountainside, away from the house.

He had got about a hundred yards through the trees when the canisters exploded. The deafening blast seemed to turn the air itself into a solid, unstoppable force that hit Carver in the back, picking him up off his feet and throwing him into the trunk of a nearby tree, where he lay, bruised and winded, while a flurry of twigs and leaves blew at him. Then the blast reached the outer extent of its radius and imploded back in again, rushing back over him, sucking the air from his lungs until finally the storm had passed.

Every inch of his body hurt. His brain felt as bruised and battered in his skull as if he'd just fought ten heavyweight rounds. As he got to his feet, watching a fireball that dwarfed all the previous flames ascending over the scorched ruins of the house, he tested his limbs for broken bones and was amazed to find he could still walk and even run, tentatively at first and then with growing confidence.

Carver was just about okay, but he didn't like to think what had happened to the helpless, incapacitated men who had been caught just a few feet from the explosion, or the dogs lying drugged in their wire cage. There would be no trace of them left upon the earth.

69

Kurt Vermulen had been talking to the mayor of Antibes when his cell phone bleeped loudly and a message appeared on its screen, telling him that he had a text. He apologized to the mayor, who indicated that he was not in the slightest bit offended, certainly not by such a distinguished guest as *monsieur le général*.

Vermulen jabbed helplessly at the telephone keypad before giving up, with a sigh that conveyed the absolute impossibility for a civilized man of keeping up with all the latest gadgets. The mayor chuckled sympathetically.

Alix took the phone from Vermulen's hand, with a look of womanly amusement at the failings of helpless men.

"Here, let me," she said. Her fingers moved expertly over the phone and a message flashed up.

"It's Wynter," she said. "He says he'll be ready for drinks at the hotel at seven."

Vermulen looked at his watch.

"Well, that's not a problem for time," he said. "But I'm still not happy about it. Are you sure you want to go through with it? He can't complain if I meet him instead. Today, of all days . . ."

He looked out of the window of the mayor's office. The town hall, with its sandy pink walls and white shutters, looked down on the Cours Masséna, right in the heart of the oldest part of town. Every day, the square was filled with market stalls selling freshly caught fish, or fruit and vegetables that had come direct from the farms up in the Provençal hills. The Cathedral of Notre Dame stood across the way. The sea was just a skipping stone's flight away.

Alix slipped her arm through his and gave a reassuring squeeze.

"It's all right," she said. "I can cope. That's why I'm here, after all . . ."

Vermulen's smile lit up his eyes with genuine affection. The mayor, seeing its sincerity, smiled, too.

"Yeah," said Vermulen, holding Alix to his side, "I know. You can cope with just about anything."

Then he looked at his watch again.

"Well," he said, "I guess we better get going . . ."

"*Bien sûr, mon général,*" agreed the mayor.

70

The view from the Dauphin helicopter toward Tourrettes-sur-Loup, three miles away, was spectacular: a jumble of rough stone walls and tiled roofs jammed on to a V-shaped promontory. The buildings clung to the very edge of the cliffs like a herd of lemmings, daring one another to make the jump. But sitting in the copilot's seat, Platon had no interest in the aesthetic appeal of the place. His only concern was correlating the landmarks ahead of him with the map in his hands. He'd been given coordinates for the house where the Georgians were hiding out. Now he just had to find the place.

Then he saw the plume of black smoke halfway up the mountainside, looked down at the map, and that problem was solved. The fire was a beacon, exactly where he'd expected to find their destination. But they'd arrived too late. Unless those peasant scum had somehow set their own house on fire, the American's hired thief had got there first.

"Aim for the smoke," he told the pilot. "Fast!"

They'd been flying parallel to the valley at the foot of the Puy de Tourrettes. Now the helicopter banked hard to the right as the pilot changed course and began his descent. They were heading directly for the smoke when it was obliterated by an explosion that launched a fireball into the sky in an eruption of twisting, bubbling, rocketing flame.

Platon spat a string of Russian expletives into his headset microphone, then twisted in his seat so that he was facing the five men in the passenger compartment behind him. They were all wearing bulletproof vests and carrying automatic weapons equipped with bulbous silencers. These were Platon's best men, hardened veterans who had fought with him in Afghanistan, or served in the savage campaigns against the guerrillas of Chechnya.

"We'll be there in thirty seconds. You two, out first, find cover, and be ready to lay down covering fire. The rest of you, come with me."

The pilot slowed down as he approached the house, looking for somewhere to land his machine, nervously skirting the fire and smoke that had engulfed the house. Close up, Platon could see that a gigantic bite had been taken from the rear of the building, where the explosion must have taken place. He could see only three people, two women and a man, scattered across the ground at the front of the house, not far from a four-wheel-drive SUV.

The man was crouched over one of the women, shaking her shoulders. He seemed completely unaware of the helicopter's approach. Finally, when it was barely two yards above the ground and thirty yards away from him, he turned his head, screwing up his eyes, and jerking his mustachioed face from side to side. He got to his feet, but made no attempt to run away. He looked bemused by everything going on around him.

The Dauphin had come in with its cockpit pointing toward the building and the nose wheel touching the ground. Because the land fell away so steeply, the pilot had kept the rotors turning, half hovering, so that his craft remained completely horizontal, with the rear wheels off the ground.

The first two men jumped down from the sliding passenger door and ran across the ground at a crouch before flinging themselves flat, their guns pointing toward the man. Their three comrades followed, moving forward up the hill to the nose of the helicopter, covering Platon as he got out of the copilot's door. Then all four walked forward toward the man, the front three holding their guns at their shoulders, ready to fire.

The man up ahead wasn't carrying a weapon. Yet they could see now that the woman beside him was dead, shot in the throat and head. She was naked but for a pair of panties. The other woman, who seemed as oblivious to their arrival as the man had been, was wearing a bikini. The man had on nothing but a pair of jeans. He looked at them for a few seconds, blearily, as if he could barely focus, and then, quite unexpectedly, he bent forward, put his head in his hands, and began to sob.

"Mother of God . . ." muttered Platon, whose years of exposure to the effects of combat had not made him any less disgusted by those who fell apart under pressure. Now that he was close to the blubbering wreck he could see that he answered to Bagrat Baladze's description. So this sniveling wretch was supposed to be a gang leader. No wonder he'd been such an easy target. He'd given up easily, too. Someone had given his head a good beating, but aside from that, there wasn't a scratch on him.

Platon grabbed him by the throat.

"Are you Baladze?" he asked.

The Georgian gave him a blank stare, then frowned and tried to shrug his shoulders.

Platon slapped him across the face.

"Are . . . you . . . Baladze?" he repeated, his voice tensing with anger.

Panic returned to his captive's eyes. He raised his forefingers to his ears and shook his head.

"Can't hear . . ." he whimpered, and then, "I think I killed her. But I don't know how . . . I don't know . . . oh, God . . ."

He began weeping again, his face crumpled in Platon's hands, as tearful and snot-ridden as a little child's.

When Baladze had raised his hands, Platon had noticed the cuff still attached to his left wrist, with its chain hanging loosely down his arm. He grabbed the chain and yanked it upward, bringing the wrist with it. He had to get it within inches of Baladze's nose before the Georgian could see it.

Platon gave the chain a shake. His unspoken question was obvious.

"It's gone," said Baladze. "Someone took it. Didn't see him. Couldn't see . . . couldn't hear . . . so loud . . ."

Platon gave an order to one of his men.

"Ask the bitch. Maybe she saw what happened."

The brown-haired woman was no more use than her boss: just as deaf, just as blind. When she realized her blond friend was dead, she started wailing, too.

Next, Platon turned his attention to the four-by-four. It had left a clear trail behind it, showing that it had come downhill at speed, turned hard, and then slewed to a standstill. Whoever had driven it must have taken Baladze by surprise: He would not have expected an attack from uphill, inside his own property.

Platon realized that the attacker must have used a stun grenade to disable Baladze and the two women while he took whatever had been attached to that handcuff: a case of some kind, presumably. If Baladze had cared about it enough to chain it to his body, its contents must have been valuable. That document Zhukovskaya wanted had to have been in there. Platon would get to that in a moment, but not before he had secured the rest of the property. The first two men out of the helicopter were still in position. Platon signaled to them with quick hand movements, indicating that he wanted them to flank around the side of the house and report back what they found. Then he focused on Baladze again.

The effects of the grenade should be wearing off by now. He put his mouth close to the Georgian's ear and then shouted: "Can you hear me?"

Baladze tried to look blank and uncomprehending, but a flicker in his eyes, an involuntary admission that he'd understood Platon's words, gave him away.

"Thought so," said Platon. "So . . . what was in the case?"

"What case?"

Platon punched him, very hard, in the stomach. Then he pulled his head up by the hair.

"The case on the other end of that chain," he said.

Baladze was still winded, wheezing and gasping for breath. Platon had not let go of his hair. He gave it another hard tug, jerking Baladze's head up and back.

"Well?"

For the first time, Baladze showed some defiance. He spat at Platon, leaving a dribble of spittle and phlegm on his chest. Platon smiled.

Then he kneed Baladze in the crotch.

Platon had retained his hold on the other man's head. When Baladze automatically doubled up, his head was held, agonizingly, in place.

The pain was about to get worse. Platon whipped a two-fingered jab into Baladze's eyes. Three of the most sensitive areas of his body were now all in agony, simultaneously. Baladze howled and writhed, which only increased the tugging on his scalp. His knees gave way, but Platon yanked him back up. He screamed again.

When the noise had died away, Platon repeated his question. "What was in the case?"

"A list . . ." Baladze whined.

"What kind of list?"

"List of bombs."

Platon's eyes narrowed. He leaned forward, pulling Baladze's head toward him until their faces were barely a hand's breadth apart.

"What kind of bombs?"

Baladze's shoulders slumped.

"Nuclear bombs, old Soviet ones . . . all over the world . . . a hundred of them."

Platon let go of his grip in sheer astonishment. No wonder that dried-up old witch had been so secretive. They must be shitting on themselves in Moscow. The former rulers of a mighty empire, so humbled that they had to call on gangsters to rescue their dirty secrets: If ever you wanted a sign of how things had changed, that was it. Still, it gave him an opportunity. If he could get the briefcase back, or even destroy it and then bluff that he had it, he would be in a very powerful position.

But where had the thief disappeared to?

Ignoring Baladze, who was now lying in a fetal position on the ground at his feet, Platon put himself in the attacker's position. He had come from the back of the house: Why? Because he'd been watching from up on the hill—that was obvious. So where had he gone? Platon looked down the drive to the front of the property. The gates were still closed. So he hadn't gone out that way. That made sense: Why head toward any oncoming cops? The obvious way out was back the way he'd come. Judging by Baladze's condition, it can't have been long since he'd been attacked. And barely three minutes had passed since he'd seen that explosion rip through the sky.

Platon stared up at the slope of the Puy de Tourrettes. The man was up there somewhere, or running like hell to get off there, more likely. He could still be caught.

"Kill her," he said to his soldier, standing over the brunette.

There were three quick pops as the silenced burst of nine-millimeter bullets ended her life.

Platon put two shots of his own into Baladze.

By now, all his men had gathered alongside him in the forecourt.

"Nothing there," said one of the men who'd been sent to scout around the back.

"We're out of here," said Platon. "Get back to the chopper. Fast!"

He ran back to the helicopter, yanked open the door, pulled himself back up into the copilot's seat, and put on the headset.

"Go!" he shouted. "Up the mountain. We're going hunting!"

71

C arver did not hear the helicopter until it was almost on top of him, just a couple of hundred yards away. Those bloody earplugs! He pulled the lumps of wax from his ears and was almost deafened by the clattering rotors. He dashed for the shelter of the nearest tree, pressing himself against the trunk and standing stock-still as the chopper flew overhead and disappeared again from view.

As it had passed him, Carver had seen the open copilot and passenger doors and the men leaning out, scanning the ground beneath them. They were looking for him. But who were they? The helicopter had civilian markings, not police or military.

It had to be Vermulen. That slimy Yank bastard had reneged on the deal. He wanted to save himself half a mil and remove any security risk by getting rid of a hired hand he couldn't trust. Well, Carver had been there before.

Ahead of him, the sound of the helicopter diminished, then grew in volume again as it turned and came back again over the tree-strewn slope, slightly farther uphill this time. It was traversing the ground, to and fro, like a gardener mowing a lawn.

Whoever was up there, they knew he was down here. As soon as they spotted him, the hunters would be dropped and come after him on foot. Vermulen had commanded a U.S. Army Rangers regiment, so he'd hire only the best, and then equip them with the finest equipment. Carver had been very, very good in his day, but he was still short of full fighting fitness. Unless he was extremely fortunate, or they suddenly forgot everything they'd ever learned, they would get him in the end.

He did, however, have one advantage. Vermulen could not afford to lose the document that was, he fervently hoped, tucked away in Bagrat's case. So he was, effectively, holding a precious paper hostage. He had to put himself in a situation where he could not be attacked without the safety of that hostage being threatened. Somewhere like his car.

He waited, motionless, as the noise of the helicopter diminished again, then sprinted, flat out, toward where the Audi was waiting for him, parked just off the path, facing back toward the base of the mountain.

Twice he had to stop and wait again as the helicopter patrolled above him. But then he was there, chucking the bulky grenade launcher onto the passenger seat and getting behind the wheel.

When he floored the pedal, the 4.2-liter engine roared into life. The four wheels spun on the soft earth for a fraction of a second, then found their grip and shot the car forward, rocketing onto the trail that sloped across and down the hillside before reaching the level where it became a proper road.

Carver had arrived at his car just as the helicopter was at the farthest reach of its patrol area. He'd barely gone four hundred yards before it turned, facing in his direction once again. Seconds later he was seen. The helicopter dashed forward like a predatory bird, spotting its prey. Carver saw it looming in his mirrors as it swooped low over the tree line and felt a surge of adrenaline as he forced his rally-bred machine even faster over the rutted, crumbling surface of the path.

Even with his belt on, he rattled around like a dried pea in a whistle as the Audi crashed into potholes, slewed from side to side, and leaped into the air as it hit exposed boulders and tree roots or raced over sudden dips in the road. The hammering impacts of compacted earth, stone, and wood against the bottom of the car created a deafening percussive clamor that almost drowned the howl of the engine, the agonized grind from the overworked transmission, and the whomping of rotor blades just a few feet above his head.

But not the sharp crack of gunfire, or the sound of bullets smashing glass and ripping through the bodywork: Carver heard that, all right.

The pilot was swooping over and around the car, trying to find the best firing position. His guns were all concentrated on one side of the chopper, firing broadside like an old-fashioned battleship. But as long as he flew alongside Carver's car, parallel to the path, the trees on either side denied the shooters a clear line of fire. But there was another way. The pilot put on speed, racing a few hundred feet ahead of the car, before turning his helicopter ninety degrees and bringing it to a dead stop, hovering directly above, and across the line of the path, directly ahead of the onrushing car.

The windshield seemed to fill with the sight of the helicopter, its open doors, and the men lining up a volley that would hit Carver head-on. He was doing over eighty miles per hour, closing on the hovering chopper at almost 120 feet per second. The mouths of the submachine gun barrels ahead of him lit up like a barrage of paparazzi flashlights. The earth in front of the car was torn apart by the impact of gunshots. He heard and felt the impacts as other rounds ripped out a headlight, demolished a sideview mirror, and ricocheted off the Audi's flanks.

Miraculously, Carver had not been hit, but his good fortune would not endure much longer. As a futile dash toward certain death, this was right up there with the Charge of the Light Brigade. So Carver did what the Light Brigade could not. He stopped charging.

As he yanked the steering wheel hard left, he slammed on the brakes, but kept the power full on as the rear end of the car fishtailed around, skidding on the trail for a fraction of a second before the rear wheels recovered their grip. In an instant, the car had turned ninety degrees and was now pointing straight downhill, into the trees.

Carver released the brakes and sent the car racing away again. For now the helicopter could not get him. But the trees that gave him shelter were a deadly threat of their own. Forcing himself not to take his foot off the gas, overriding every instinct that told him to slow down and take care, he plunged into an automotive slalom down the face of the mountain, slewing one way and then the other as he zigzagged between the trunks that offered certain death as the price for any miscalculation. Now the ground beneath him was even rougher and less secure, offering precious little traction for his wheels to cling to. His steering wheel was all but useless. He had to navigate with his brakes and gears alone, ignoring the low branches that whipped across the windshield and roof and praying that none of the bushes and saplings through which he drove could offer any serious resistance.

And then ahead of him he saw that the trees were thinning and clear sunlight was shining beyond them, and he knew that his problems had only just begun.

It would have been bad enough if this were the light from a clearing, an open glade in which he would be a sitting target for the helicopter, still pursuing him above. But what lay before him was not a woodland glade, but the near-vertical drop of a deep mountain gorge. A hang glider could swoop from the lip of the cliff and descend in graceful spirals to the river valley below. For a car, the plunge would be fatal.

Carver gave himself one chance of survival. The road up the mountain clung to the side of the gorge, twisting up the rockface in a concertina sequence of hairpin turns. But the road was only a few yards wide and offered no hope of a safe landing for a car traveling across its path at high speed. Carver slewed the Audi left again, changing the angle of approach, so that he came at the road diagonally.

There were just a few more trees to negotiate, a last tangle of brushwood to charge through, and then the afternoon sun burst through the windshield and Carver was flying through the air, less like a driver than an airman trying to land his plane on the safety of an aircraft carrier's deck, with an ocean of death all around it.

Beneath Carver's wheels, the road plunged downhill toward a 180-degree bend. He had to get down onto the pavement in time to be able to brake and turn, but he had too much momentum through the air, and the car would not fall fast enough.

He could see over the corner now, to the drop beyond.

Still the car refused to obey the laws of gravity.

The steel safety barriers guarding the curve were getting closer and closer. They seemed only inches away.

And then the wheels hit the road surface.

Carver turned hard right, hit the brakes, heard the rear wheels scream in protest again as they slewed around the bend, and offered up a prayer of thanks to the inventor of four-wheel drive as the car responded to his commands and clung to the oh-so-welcome pavement. He had made it onto solid ground. He could drive hard and fast down a proper road.

But the helicopter was waiting for him.

It was hanging in the air, perhaps fifty yards from the mountainside. And to judge from the blazing guns, the men inside it still had plenty of ammunition.

Once again, however, the trees came to Carver's rescue. They ran along both sides of the road, uphill and down, giving him cover. And this time, the chopper could not come in close enough to cut off his path. If it did, the rotors would hit the rock face. For about half a minute, the two machines were locked in a stalemate, as Carver negotiated four more dizzying turns. But both sides knew that it would soon end. For the mountain was flattening out and soon Carver would be spat out into more open country, where the pursuit would begin in earnest again.

He knew now that whoever was in the helicopter, they had nothing to do with Kurt Vermulen. They did not want to retrieve a stolen document. They wanted to destroy it, and him, too.

Carver asked himself who had an interest in destroying valuable papers originally stolen from the Russian government. He thought about the only known traitor in Vermulen's organization, and the agency she had worked for—was most likely working for now. Then he gave a wry smile at the irony of it all. Here he was, risking his neck to get to Alix, and she was, unknowingly, helping to kill him.

72

I n the cockpit of the Dauphin helicopter, Platon was beating his left hand against the top of the control panel as he vented his anger and frustration. This whole mission had been a screwup from start to finish. It had all been done in too much of a hurry, with too little information. No one, including him, had thought anything through, and now it was turning to shit in front of his eyes.

Whoever was driving that car was a maniac, whose appetite for taking risks was equaled only by his will to live. By now he should have been blasted to pieces by bullets, pulverized by a tree, or obliterated by a two-hundred-yard fall, yet there he was, racing between the villas and farmhouses dotting the lower slopes of the mountainside like a man possessed. But where was he racing to? Surely he must know that he could not hope to outpace a helicopter.

As the road down from the mountain hit the main route from Vence to Grasse, the Audi had turned right, westward. Now there was plenty of other traffic on the road, passing in both directions. Platon was tempted to blast away regardless, reckoning the loss of the other drivers' lives would be worthwhile if he could take out the target vehicle as well. In Russia, he might have acted on that logic. Gang warfare was so much a part of life there, the police so hamstrung by lack of resources, and his clan's connections with the state so powerful that he could probably have got away with it. But this was France, where the forces of law and order were strong and his political influence weak. Up on the mountain, with no one around, he and his men had been able to blaze away. Down here it was different. He could not afford collateral damage.

And the man they were after was being canny, too. Instead of racing flat out along the road, risking an accident and exposing himself to fire, he was using other vehicles as shields. He would hide behind a car or truck going in the same direction until a line of traffic approached, coming the other way. Then he would dash ahead at top speed, using the oncoming vehicles as his shield.

Sooner or later, however, he would find himself out in the open. For Platon, it was just a matter of holding his patience until the moment came, and the road builders of Provence had conspired to make his life easier. For now the road formed a massive hairpin. It swung north along one side of a valley before crossing the river that ran along the valley floor and then turning back on itself and proceeding south along the far side of the valley. If the helicopter hovered in the middle of the hairpin, it could cover the car all the way around.

Half a dozen times, Platon's men opened fire as the Audi bobbed and weaved along the road. Each time, the car kept going, hit but not mortally wounded. And then, just as Platon's frustration was mounting again, a miracle happened.

The road was approaching another absurdly picturesque little town, crowded onto a cliffside promontory. Platon looked at his map. The place was called Le Bar-sur-Loup. Just outside the village, there was a viaduct that cut across a spur of the river valley in a rhythmic, marching line of stone arches. There were no cars on the viaduct, but a handful were scattered about a parking lot at one end. Platon could see a few people strolling out over the valley to admire the view.

He also saw the Audi pull into the parking lot. He saw the driver get out, carrying something close to his chest, something bulky. His head looked misshapen, covered in some way. The man started running, turning his shoulders, so that the package in his arms was half hidden and impossible to identify from the helicopter. Platon reckoned it must be the missing case.

For a few seconds the running man was masked by a clump of trees, but then he reappeared, right out in the open, racing toward the very middle of the viaduct.

The man stood right by the stone parapet. Now it was evident that he was wearing a gas mask. Platon assumed he did not want to be identified by the people around him. The Russian smiled: Well, they'd leave identification to the pathologist.

The man placed whatever he had been carrying on the ground, behind the parapet, then raised a gun in the air. Platon could not hear any shots over the sound of the helicopter, but he assumed some must have been fired, because the other people out there on the viaduct started running away to either side.

Platon tried to work out what the man thought he was doing. Did he think he could bring down a helicopter full of armed men with a mere pistol? Or was he hoping to cut some kind of deal? If he really did have the case that had been attached to Bagrat Baladze, maybe he'd threaten to throw it off the side of the viaduct, hoping that might save him.

Either way, he could go screw himself. Platon was sick of playing games. He intended to wipe this infuriating thief off the face of the earth.

"Go down," he said to the pilot. "Get us as close as you can."

73

Standing on the viaduct, Carver saw the helicopter turn toward him and smiled. He stood tall as it approached, knowing that he was not in any danger until it turned its side to face him.

He was counting on that.

He also reasoned that the helicopter was a lot bigger target than he was. And he was the one standing on the solid surface of an earthbound structure, while his enemies were being jerked around in an airborne craft that was never perfectly still, even when hovering.

He hoped that would count for something. If it didn't, he was screwed. At best, he'd get only one shot.

So he stood, and he waited, as still and straight as a prisoner in front of a firing quad. The helicopter was barely a hundred yards away now and still nosing toward him. As it came ever closer, the sound of the rotors slicing through the air was deafening and the downdraft beat on him like a man-made gale.

They thought they had him—that was obvious.

Finally, the chopper's forward movement ceased. In the moment of stillness that followed, Carver thought he recognized the man in the copilot's seat, but then the thought vanished from his mind as the tail of the predator swung around, bringing the guns in the open doors to bear on him.

And as it did so, he picked up the grenade launcher that was lying at his feet and, in the same movement, brought it to bear on the helicopter. Then, with the ice-cold patience of the well-trained soldier, he waited the extra fraction of a second needed to present the biggest possible target. The helicopter finished its rotation and, just as the first bullets shot past him, with that terrible, insect whine, the full width of the door was opened to him and he pulled the trigger.

The very instant that the grenade left the barrel, Carver was hit in the chest by two rounds, knocked off his feet, and thrown across the full width of the viaduct, crashing into the opposite parapet. The impact of the stone against the back of his head dazed him for a couple of seconds, so that by the time he was able to focus on his target, the gas had already formed an impenetrable cloud inside the Dauphin's cabin and the machine was lurching and pitching in the air as the pilot was overcome.

Carver saw one of the men who had been firing at him emerge from the billowing smoke, blindly walking right out of the open door and tumbling to his death, his throat too scarred by gas to scream as he fell.

Then the helicopter started moving and Carver realized to his horror that it was heading right for him. Fear swept the dizziness from his head and he scrambled to his feet and ran for his life as the helicopter collided with the side of the viaduct in a cacophony of roaring engines, screaming metal, and blunt stone, its rotor blades gouging into the parapet and sending projectiles of stone flying through the air in every direction. One hit Carver on the back, and once again he thanked the sheer chance that had spared him any time since he'd left the burning house in which to take off his bulletproof vest.

Behind him, the helicopter had lost its grip on the viaduct, first sliding off its stonework and then plunging down to the valley floor, where it landed with a final, metallic crunch, a moment's silence, and an explosion of flames.

Carver walked back to where he had been standing, picked up the grenade launcher, and threw it into the inferno below. He checked to see that there was no one nearby, and then pitched the gas mask over, too. Then he looked at his watch. It was half past five. That gave him an hour and a half to drive to Cap d'Antibes, check into the Hotel du Cap, grab a shower, change into whatever clean clothes he could find, and get ready to see Alix again.

That sounded just about perfect.

74

I t was half past eleven in the morning in Washington, D.C., and they were back at the White House, in the Woodshed meeting room. Leo Horabin wanted an update on the investigation. The story was told from the beginning, with Kady Jones screening Henry Wong's photograph of Vermulen and Francesco Riva, and explaining the potential significance of their meeting. Tom Mulvagh then described his investigation into Vermulen's movements in Europe and the death of his personal assistant Mary Lou Stoller.

"I began a detailed analysis of Mrs. Stoller's replacement as the general's assistant, Ms. Natalia Morley, in conjunction with Ted Jaworski. Ted, perhaps you'd like to present the findings of that analysis."

The CIA man took over.

"Certainly. The bottom line is, Natalia Morley does not exist. It's a false identity, prepared well enough to stand up to the level of investigation an employer makes into a secretarial hiring. There was a birth certificate, marriage license, and divorce papers, references from prior employers, credit-card records, and so forth. But the moment I started looking deeper and wider, it all fell apart. I could find no trace of her supposed husband, Steve Morley. The couple's home addresses in both Russia and Switzerland were phony. Ms. Morley had given a name and number for the human-resources department of the Swiss-based bank that had employed her, but when I called that number it had been disconnected and no one at the bank had ever heard of her.

"So if this woman isn't Natalia Morley, who is she? Since she claimed to be Russian, that was the first place to look. I had my people secure security footage from Dulles International the day she and Vermulen left for Amsterdam, and compare it with known KGB and FSB operatives."

He called up a picture, covering half the screen at the far end of the room.

"Okay, then, this is 'Natalia Morley' a month ago at Dulles. And this . . ."

The other half of the screen was filled by a second shot. The two faces on the screen had been taken many years apart, but they unmistakably showed the same woman.

". . . is former KGB agent Alexandra Petrova. She is age thirty. She was born in the city of Perm, several hundred miles east of Moscow, and began work in Moscow about nine years ago. The KGB used her in honeytraps. Her specialty was seducing powerful, middle-aged Western males. She's not been involved in any intelligence activity that we know of in the past five years. But it looks like she's gone back to work."

"You'd think a man as experienced as Kurt Vermulen might know better," Horabin said. "Do we warn him he's been compromised?"

"No, sir," retorted Jaworski. "On the contrary, I propose we find out why the Russians have gone to so much trouble to compromise him. They think General Vermulen justifies their attention. We think he may be involved in some kind of project that involves miniaturized nuclear weapons. Put those two things together and what you get looks very much like Russian suitcase nukes. We've been tasked to find those nukes. I think this is the lead we've been waiting for."

"Dear Lord," muttered Horabin. "What's Vermulen doing now?"

Jaworski grimaced.

"That's the problem. We don't know. We don't believe he's still in Rome. He left his rental car at Leonardo da Vinci International Airport, but he hasn't taken a commercial flight out that we know of, and there's no record of him chartering any private aviation. There is one other possibility, though. Da Vinci's located at a place called Fiumicino, about eighteen miles out of town. It's right by the coast and there's also a harbor there, with a yacht marina. It's possible he could have departed Italy by sea."

"What do you mean 'it's possible'?" rasped Horabin. "Are you telling me you don't know?"

"'Fraid so," said Jaworski. "I haven't had the resources to uncover that information. For security reasons, and frankly for political reasons, too, our investigation of this matter has been limited to a very small number of people. General Vermulen is a decorated war hero who has never been suspected of wrongdoing, let alone arrested or indicted."

"I'm well aware of that," snapped Horabin.

Jaworski kept going.

"My view, and I think I speak for Tom, too, is that if we're going to commit ourselves fully to this investigation, with the resource allocation that would entail, and the strong possibility of political fallout, we need authorization . . . from the top."

Horabin was about to speak, but was interrupted by a cough from halfway down the table. It came from the uniformed colonel representing the Defense Intelligence Agency.

"Excuse me, sir . . . but before anyone makes that determination, there's something else you should know. It's a matter whose relevance only became apparent once I'd heard today's briefing."

"Go ahead."

"Thank you. It concerns a former Czech military intelligence officer named Pavel Novak. Back in the day, Novak was a double, worked as an agent for us. Late last night, Novak fell to his death from the roof of his apartment building in Vienna. Now, Tom mentioned General Vermulen had been in Vienna recently. I don't know—maybe it's just coincidence. But when the general was attached to the DIA, he was Novak's handler."

Tom Mulvagh muttered, "Holy shit," under his breath. There were similar murmurings right around the table. Leo Horabin brought the meeting back to order.

"Thank you, Colonel," he said. "I will take all this under advisement. And yes, Ted, it will go right to the top."

75

S amuel Carver got out of Le Bar-sur-Loup and drove the car down a zigzag succession of country lanes to the southeast of town before finding a field where he could park without being observed. A quick change of clothes—ironically, back into the suit he'd worn for Kenny Wynter's lunch with Vermulen—a pair of shades, and suddenly he looked a lot less like the madman who'd just shot down a helicopter from the old viaduct.

He took the bag with Wynter's remaining clothes and toilet kit out of the trunk of the car. That, and the jerry can that held all the acetone that had been left over after he'd finished his homemade bomb. He left the can open on the driver's seat. On top of it, he placed the car's red-hot cigarette lighter. Then he closed the door and started running. He got about two hundred yards down the road when the can exploded, followed, shortly afterward, by the gas tank, still three quarters full. There was no one else on the lane to watch as he dusted himself off, wiped a trace of sweat from his brow, then strolled about half a mile back up to the main road. Not long after that, he found a Bar Tabac, where he ordered a well-earned glass of ice-cold beer and called for a cab. He took his time over his drink, finishing it just as the cab pulled up. Half an hour later, he was standing in the shower of his junior suite at the Hotel du Cap.

It was only after he'd washed that he finally prized open Bagrat Baladze's briefcase to discover what he'd gone to so much trouble to steal. There it was, a brown file folder, just like countless others. It had the tired, flimsy look that comes with passing time, and the Russian script written across it had faded. The seal was still intact. Vermulen would be happy with that. Though what it was that he hoped to find inside this sad bureaucratic relic, Carver couldn't imagine.

Not that he gave a damn at this point. His mind had turned to Alix. He examined himself in the mirror. Considering what he'd just been through, he didn't look too bad. A hell of a lot better than the last time she'd seen him—that was for sure. As he put on his jacket and straightened his shirt collar, he felt as excited as a kid on Christmas morning, and he couldn't wait to open his present.

He looked at his watch. Seven o'clock precisely.

Showtime.

76

The bar opened right off the hotel lobby, in one continuous, airy, white-painted space. Carver spotted two men sitting in the lobby, another leaning oh-so-casually against the paneled-wood bar counter, a black dude the size of a wardrobe. He realized it was Reddin, the man from the Venice photograph. Vermulen had ignored Carver's instructions and sent some muscle to watch over his courier and the package she was collecting, just as Carver had anticipated.

And then there was Alix, sitting in a soft white armchair at a table for two, a posy of yellow flowers in a small glass vase in front of her, waiting for him.

He had a couple of seconds to pause in the doorway and look at her before she spotted him. She looked fantastic: not wearing anything fancy, just being the woman he loved.

There was something that nagged at him, something out of place. But the thought vanished as she heard him coming across the marble floor, looked up, and for a fraction of a second the expression on her face was . . . absolute horror. Shock. As if she'd seen a ghost. As if she weren't just surprised to see him, but appalled.

She forced a smile across her face.

Carver had seen Alix play a part before. He'd seen her pretend and dissimulate. But he'd never seen anything as phony as that smile.

He didn't have any time to think about it, because she'd got to her feet and put her arms around him, like one old friend meeting another, air-kissing either side of his face and whispering two words. "I'm wired."

They sat down. Carver hadn't been sure how it would be when the two of them finally met, but he hadn't expected this terrible discomfort, almost embarrassment, a tension filling the air between them.

"So . . . Natalia." He put a heavy emphasis on the name, thinking himself back into the part of Kenny Wynter, remembering Vermulen would be listening somewhere. "How's life with the general? Hope he doesn't work you too hard . . ."

"No, he doesn't. . . . In fact, I don't really work for Kurt at all anymore."

"Really? Has he fired you?"

He didn't have to fake the sly grin on his face as he said the words, or the gently teasing note in his voice.

"No," she said, and the next words were so quiet that Carver thought for a second that he hadn't heard them properly. "He's married me."

"I'm sorry . . . ?"

"My name is now Natalia Vermulen," she said, in a voice whose cheerful intonation was utterly contradicted by the devastation in her eyes. "We were married this afternoon . . . by the mayor of Antibes."

Carver wanted to be sick. He felt as though someone had stuck a fork in his guts and was twisting his intestines like strands of pasta. Still, he had to be Kenny Wynter, the callous thief who couldn't care less if a Yank general was daft enough to marry his sexy secretary just to get into her knickers.

"Congratulations, love," he said, and then glanced at the ring—the one he'd refused to acknowledge when he first set eyes on her. "Nice rock."

"Thank you . . . Kenny."

"Don't thank me, darling. Keep flashing that around much longer, I might be tempted to nick it."

She giggled politely.

"I'm sure you're not really like that."

Her voice had the sound of casual conversation, but her eyes were pleading. For what? Understanding? Forgiveness? As if Carver should be considering her problems, putting himself in her position.

She was still talking.

"We only decided to get married on the spur of the moment."

"Good of you to waste your wedding day on me."

"Well, I'd promised Kurt . . ."

"And you didn't want to let him down. He's an impressive bloke, your general, got a bit about him. Special, right?"

"Yes he is, very special."

Carver assumed that was for Vermulen's benefit, and now she was trying to explain what had happened.

"Spending so much time together, over the past few weeks, I've got to know Kurt very deeply. He's a remarkable man, and he was so kind to me. You see, I was told that someone close to me, someone I loved, had died. Kurt was there for me. He made me feel life was worth living."

Suddenly Carver realized that he'd only half understood. She was trying to explain, all right. But she wasn't explaining a terrible mistake they could find a way to put right. What he heard now was: You're history.

He felt humiliated, stripped of all pride. The anger and hurt were filling his skull, building up pressure that must surely crack him open, till he just lashed out at something, anything—smashed the glasses from the table and threw the bottles at the bar; took out his gun and started firing at everyone around him, going for body shots, so they'd all hurt as much as he did. He wanted to kill Alix. He wanted her back. He didn't know what he wanted. . . . Somehow he summoned up a faint trace of professionalism.

"Yeah, that must mean a lot, a bloke doing that for you . . ." he said, responding the way he always did to emotional pain, by forcing himself to detach, shutting down his emotions.

"Tell you what—why don't I tell you what I've been up to while you've been busy getting married. I've found a property that's well worth investing in. I reckon your old man'd be interested."

She could play that game just as well as him. In an instant she was Natalia Vermulen, the untroubled new wife of a wealthy, powerful man.

"Really? That sounds fascinating. Do you have anything you could show me?"

"Here, check it out . . ."

He handed over the file and she examined the Russian script on the cover and the seal keeping it closed, the design a simple cross of Saint George: the symbol and the saint shared by Georgia and England alike.

"That certainly looks like something that Kurt would want to get involved in," she said. "Let me call him."

She took out her phone and pressed the speed dial. "Hello, darling . . ."

She smiled, and stifled a giggle at something Vermulen said.

"Yes, I'm looking forward to that, too, darling. . . . Anyway, Mr. Wynter is right here. He has something to show me that I think you'd like to see. Why don't I hand you over to him?"

"Evening, Wynter."

It was obvious from Vermulen's tone that he'd not picked up the undertones of Alix and Carver's conversation. He gave no sign of the arrogance of a man talking to his defeated rival, nor the insecurity of a lover under challenge. He was just doing business.

"Good evening, General," Carver replied. "And congratulations—your new missus is certainly an extraordinary woman . . . full of surprises."

Now it helped to be Wynter. He'd not bother to be polite for long.

"You got the money? Let's just get it done so we can all get out of here."

The money was transferred. Carver's bank confirmed receipt of half a million pounds sterling, then immediately moved the money to another account. Carver had made a million pounds in less than a week. He'd have happily lost it all, and every penny deposited in every one of his accounts around the world, just to have arrived back at the hotel a couple of hours earlier, before Alix had walked into that mayor's office, when there was still a chance to change her mind.

Maybe even now it wasn't too late? He took her face in his hands, gazed longingly into those intoxicating blue eyes, and put his lips to her ear.

"Come with me—please, I'm begging you . . ."

She pulled her face away from his, and when she looked at him again it was as though a transparent barrier had descended between them, as if he were a prisoner and she his visitor, separated by bulletproof glass.

"It's been a pleasure seeing you, Kenny," she said.

The worst moment of his life, his heart being broken, and he couldn't even be himself.

She was looking him right in the eye, without a trace of emotion.

"I must go now. Good-bye. . . ."

At some point in their conversation, more of Vermulen's men must have slipped into the bar, because now they were forming a protective group around her as she walked from the room. When Carver tried to follow her, Reddin blocked the door and prevented his getting out.

"Wherever you think you're going, man, you ain't," he said.

Reddin was big, he had a voice like Barry White, and he looked as if he could handle himself. Even so, Carver felt sure he could take him down, and chase after Alix as she left the hotel. But what was the point? He could beat up as many bodyguards as he liked, shoot them if he had to, but they weren't the problem. She was. And she was gone for good.

As he sat down, Carver thought of the car that was waiting for him and Alix outside. His mission for MI6 had failed; the document had not been secured. Jack Grantham would not be a happy camper. Right now, that was the least of his worries.

77

Many months ago, overwhelmed by guilt at her part in a murder, and shocked by Carver's apparently callous indifference to what he had done, Alix had cried out, "Don't you think at all about what you've just done?"

He replied, "Not if I can help it, no."

Carver saw no point in worrying about things that had already happened and couldn't be changed. He believed that sort of thing could drive you crazy—far better to deal with the here and now. As one of Reddin's men drove her away from the Hotel du Cap, Alix thought about that conversation and realized Carver had been wrong. Sometimes you could change the past. Sometimes you had no choice.

The knowledge that Carver was alive and well, that Olga Zhukovskaya's claim he had died was nothing but a vicious lie, had all but overwhelmed her. She had found herself telling lies of her own, leading Carver to believe that she no longer loved him. Her mind had been reeling: confused, uncertain, barely conscious of what she was saying, torn apart by the pain she was so cruelly inflicting upon him. And it had to be that way.

She knew that if she had given Carver any reason to hope, he would have tried to take her there and then. She also knew, because she had been present when Vermulen gave his orders, that her bodyguards would not have hesitated to use lethal force against the man they knew as Kenny Wynter. There were four of them against one of him. Carver would always favor himself against those odds, but she could not afford to take the risk that he would lose. She had suffered the pain of his death once. She could not bear it again, nor the guilt of knowing that she had been its cause.

Somehow she had to find a way of letting Carver know the truth: She was his, she always would be, and she would find a way of getting back to him, no matter how long it took. If he knew that, he would wait for her—she was sure of it.

Meanwhile, she had another, more immediate problem to resolve. As of this afternoon, she was committed to Vermulen. She had sworn a vow of her own free will. Now she had to be seen to keep it.

"You all right, Mrs. V.?" the driver said, looking at her in the rear-view mirror. "You don't mind me saying, you look a bit shook up. Don't blame you, doing a pickup like that. Must be kinda stressful if you're not used to it."

"Yes, it was," she said, without thinking. All she'd really heard was the name "Mrs V.," and it came as such a shock, the reality of it, that the rest of his words had been little more than an indistinct blur.

She forced a smile and added, "I'm all right now, thank you."

"Don't you worry, ma'am. We'll get you back to the general safe and sound, so you can enjoy the rest of your wedding night. You know what I'm saying?"

The driver's name was Maroni. He'd given her a saucy smile and a wink with that last remark. Then he looked more serious, almost embarrassed by what he was about to say.

"Just want you to know, I served under the general, and it's great to see him looking good again, y'know, like the old days. That's because of you, ma'am. All of us guys, we appreciate what you've done for him. Anything you need, you name it—you only have to ask."

"Thank you, Mr. Maroni," she said. "That's very kind of you."

He gave her a little nod of the head, as if it were nothing, but she could see he was delighted by the fact that she'd acknowledged him, remembered his name. She was suddenly struck by the bitter irony that her new husband did not even know her real name. He had fallen in love with a woman named Natalia, and so, for the time being, she would have to become Natalia Vermulen for him.

In a way that made it easier. Natalia didn't know Samuel Carver.

78

The MI6 agent in the car behind Alix had finally got through to headquarters. His boss didn't bother with pleasantries.

"Have you got the document?" Grantham asked.

"'Fraid not. Carver never left the hotel. The woman, Petrova, came out with a group of men. She didn't appear to be under any duress. She was holding a sealed file. I presume that was what we were after."

"Sod it . . . where are you now?"

"Trailing Petrova. She's in a car with one of Vermulen's men. The rest are in a van, immediately ahead of her. Hang on . . . they're turning off the road, entering Cannes Mandelieu Airport. Most of the traffic here is private, or charter aviation. Do you want me to follow them in?"

"Absolutely. If she's flying out, I want the registration number of the plane. We'll track it from here."

The agent ended the call and drove into the airport complex.

In London, Grantham put a call through to the assistant cultural attaché at the Russian Federation Embassy. Regular diplomatic and consular business ended at 4:30 P.M. on weekdays, but the assistant attaché wasn't a regular diplomat. As the FSB resident in London, his country's most senior agent in the United Kingdom, he was open all hours.

"Koyla," said Grantham, "I need you to do me a favor. Get me a number for Deputy Director Zhukovskaya. Tell her we need to speak personally. It's a matter of extreme importance for our two services. And it requires immediate action."

79

Vermulen's yacht had left Antibes thirty-six hours before, bound for southern Italy, but he was waiting for her by the plane that would take them to meet it. Alix ran to him, wrapped her arms around him, and pulled their bodies tight, crushing her breasts against his chest, feeling him hard against her. She looked up at him, eyes half closed, lips fractionally parted, and he kissed her with a fierceness that filled her senses with the smell, the taste, the feel of him.

Vermulen let go of her, and looked for the nearest one of his men.

"Maroni."

"Yes, sir!"

"Tell Mr. Reddin that the men can stand easy for the next fifteen minutes. Then come back here and assume sentry duty at the foot of these steps. No one gets in the plane till I say so. You got that?"

Maroni grinned. "Yes, sir!"

Vermulen led Alix up into the plane. In the cramped cabin, he gave a crooked, apologetic smile.

"Not very romantic, I'm afraid. I've got champagne and flowers waiting on the yacht."

She leaned forward, brushed his cheek with her lips, and whispered in his ear, "I don't care."

He had no idea she was faking.

80

The first sensation that hit Carver once Alix had left the hotel was one of vast, aching emptiness, an absolute loneliness, a chasm in his life where her love for him had been. The second was a sharp spasm of fear. He thought of Dr. Geisel's warning that a traumatic event could send him back to the hellish limbo of madness. The shock of losing Alix once had jolted him into recovery. If he now had lost her again, would that reverse the effect?

Carver was a brave man. He had faced death more times than he could count. But the prospect of insanity, a lifetime trapped in an unending cycle of forgetting, was far, far worse.

Screw that. He needed a drink.

He headed up to the bar and ordered a double Johnnie Walker Blue Label. Then he remembered the last time he'd drunk it, with Alix, the night of the killing. Christ, why did everything have to remind him of her?

"So it didn't work out, huh?"

It was a woman's voice, American. She was sitting a few feet down the bar. Her long, glossy hair, as rich and dark as bitter chocolate, fell to her shoulders and swept across her forehead, almost covering one of her pure brown eyes. She had high cheekbones and her lips were painted with a sparkling pink gloss that made them look as though she'd just licked them. Her dress was draped over one shoulder and then swooped low enough to show off a spectacular pair of breasts. The skirt was slit up the thigh, and she was perched on a bar stool with her legs crossed, leaving plenty on display.

His look was a frank appraisal, the calculation every man makes, balancing the desirability of what's on offer against the chances of success. As if reading his mind, she held up her left hand to display the diamond on her fourth finger. Then she shrugged in a what-the-hell way.

Carver had to laugh. Every woman he met tonight seemed to be showing off a ring. This one didn't seem quite so married as the last one, though. He took his drink over to her, absorbing every detail of the way she looked. She smelled pretty good, too, a rich, spicy, super-female scent that made him realize just how long it had been since he'd been laid. Maybe he should remedy that. They could have a few drinks, take dinner in the restaurant down by the sea, and screw each other's brains out all night—see if that made his pain go away. It wasn't the most mature response to a broken heart, but it certainly beat going crazy.

"Hi," he said. "My name's Samuel Carver."

She held out a slender hand with long scarlet nails.

"Madeleine Cross—pleased to meet you."

"And you, Madeleine. So, are you going to introduce me to Mr. Cross?"

"I sure as hell hope not."

"Don't tell me he's left you all alone, in a strange hotel, in a foreign country. That sounds risky."

She laughed. "Who for?"

"All three of us, quite possibly."

She looked Carver up and down. "No, I reckon you could handle him."

"I don't doubt that," he said. "But can I handle you? That's the question."

It was bullshit; he knew it, and so did she. But it was what he needed, and maybe she did, too. She was a big girl; she could make her own decisions.

He ordered them both another drink and Madeleine told him her story.

Her husband made a fortune selling medical supplies. She'd been a clerk at a hospital that was one of his biggest clients, a girl from Boise, Idaho, ten years in Chicago, still single, struggling to make ends meet. He took her away from all that and stuck her in a fancy house in Winnetka to shop, decorate, and bitch with other bored suburban women. Now here they were on this fancy European vacation and he'd gone off to the casino in Cannes, leaving her behind, all dressed up with nothing to do but get drunk.

"The casino sounds pretty exciting. Why didn't you go, too?" Carver asked.

"Believe me, it's not so good. He spends all night at the blackjack table, playing three hands at a time, cursing every time he doesn't get the right card. He doesn't pay a bit of attention to anything else. Or anyone else, either."

Carver looked suitably appalled.

"Any man who'd rather spend a night looking at playing cards when he could be looking at you needs his head examined."

"Well, you know what? I think so, too," she said. They laughed and leaned a little closer together. Carver felt her hand on his knee, that lightness of a woman's touch that feels so good to a man.

"You want to get something to eat?" he said.

She looked him right in the eye.

"I'd rather work up an appetite first."

Carver woke with the sun streaming in through the windows and the bedside clock reading 9:17.

There was a note on the bedside table, with a telephone number and the message *If you're ever in Chicago . . . Maddy xox.*

Then he noticed the red light flashing on his phone—he must have been woken by the ringing. Carver picked up the handset and pressed the button. He screwed up his face when he heard that familiar, angry voice.

"Carver, you useless sod, it's Grantham. I'm downstairs in the foyer. Get your lazy arse down here, now, before I come up there and kick the bloody door down."

"Shit," said Carver, and heaved himself out of bed.

EASTER SATURDAY

81

Carver couldn't see any good reason he should come running, just because Grantham had called. He spent fifteen minutes getting washed and dressed before heading down to the hotel lobby. It was worth the wait, simply to see the irritation on Grantham's face. There was something else there, too, Carver realized as he got closer: The MI6 man's normal self-assurance, arrogance, even, had given way to a nervy edginess that he'd never seen before.

"Where's my document?" snapped Grantham.

"The same place as my girlfriend, cuddling up to Kurt Vermulen," Carver said, as if it didn't bother him one bit. "She married him—did you know that?"

That news had been meant to knock Grantham off his stride, but it had the opposite effect. A smug smile crossed Grantham's face, a look of sheer pleasure that Carver had been dumped in even deeper shit than he had.

"That must have come as a shock."

"Just a bit," said Carver.

"Still, you don't look very heartbroken."

"What would you prefer, drunk and tearstained?"

"Something like that."

Carver shrugged. "I thought about it. But I found a better alternative. Nice girl."

"And you accuse me of not giving a toss?"

"Listen, I loved Alix. That was real; probably still is. But it won't do me any good now, moping around. I'm just going to forget her, move on, put as much distance between us as I can."

Carver wondered if he sounded any more convincing than he felt. Evidently not—Grantham looked at him with an expression of profound skepticism before his face cleared, a new thought striking him.

"You got time to grab a late breakfast before you go? There's someone I want you to meet."

Carver groaned. What now?

"Come on," Grantham insisted. "They do a splendid buffet down by the sea. Great food, fantastic view . . . I'm paying. And I think you'll be interested when you find out who's flown in to see you."

Carver followed Grantham across the lobby and out through the doors that opened onto the hotel's magnificent wooded gardens. As he walked down the path that stretched down to the sea, one tiny hope flickered at the back of his mind and kept him moving toward an appointment he otherwise would have refused. And then he realized it was ridiculous even to consider such a notion. It was another Russian woman sitting at the table, with a bob of black hair framing eyes that were assessing him with cold, impersonal objectivity as Grantham gestured in her direction.

"May I introduce Deputy Director Zhukovskaya, of the Federal Security Service?"

She held out her hand with a smile that was even chillier than her eyes.

"Hello, Mr. Carver. You killed my husband."

"I was provoked," he replied, before letting go of her hand.

Grantham ordered coffee, orange juice, and a selection of pastries.

"I think I'll have a proper cooked breakfast, actually," said Carver, gesturing toward the buffet. "Feeling quite peckish this morning."

He took his time getting scrambled eggs and smoked salmon, crisp white rolls and dewy chunks of unsalted Normandy butter. He made a point of tucking in, knowing the other two wanted to talk. But in the end, it was he who cracked first. He couldn't help himself.

"Did you tell her I was dead?" he asked Zhukovskaya.

"Yes, I gave the order for her to receive that information," she said, without any hint of embarrassment or apology.

"Why?"

Carver was uncomfortably aware that there was more emotion, even desperation, in that single syllable than he'd intended.

"It was a practical necessity," Zhukovskaya replied, still quite unruffled. "You killed the man I sent to eliminate you, and then you left the hospital. You were no longer a patient; therefore the payments to cover your bills would have to stop. It was possible Petrova might find out about that, if she checked her financial records. She would naturally want to know what had happened. I simply anticipated that moment."

"But she only did the job to keep me alive. Why would she stay with Vermulen if I was gone?"

"Self-preservation," said Zhukovskaya, as if the answer were obvious. "Alexandra Petrova is an agent of the Federal Security Service, under my command. She knows that any agent who leaves an assignment without orders from a superior officer is guilty of desertion, and she also knows the penalty for that offense. In any case, I preferred to look on the positive side. Without you to think about, Petrova was free to concentrate on General Vermulen."

"Well, you got that wrong. She concentrated on him so much, she married him. She's not yours anymore, or mine. She's his."

Zhukovskaya sipped at her coffee.

"You think?" she asked. "Of course, I have considered that proposition, but I myself am not so certain. Many agents regard marriage as a useful adjunct to their cover; Petrova may well be one of them. That, however, is not my main concern at the moment, and it should not be yours."

She put the coffee cup down on the table, and when she looked at him again there was finally a sign of real emotion. Zhukovskya was angry.

"You have caused a great deal of trouble, Mr. Carver. The document you stole was the property of the Russian state. It was removed from a state facility approximately ten weeks ago. It would have been recovered yesterday by elements acting on behalf of the state, had you not interfered. They had orders to destroy it, rather than let it fall into the wrong hands."

"For heaven's sake, what is this thing?" asked Grantham.

"A list of small-scale nuclear weapons, also property of the Russian state, currently positioned in Europe and North America, a few in South America, Asia, and Australia, their locations and arming codes," recited Zhukovskaya in a flat voice.

The color drained from Grantham's face.

"How many weapons?"

"Around one hundred."

"My God . . . and what about the U.K.?"

She looked at him blankly.

"But they're all on this list . . ." said Grantham.

"Yes, and thanks to Mr. Carver, it is now in Vermulen's hands."

Carver grimaced, uncomfortably aware that his priorities needed a radical reordering.

"Where's Vermulen gone now?" he asked.

Grantham seemed relieved to be able to answer this question, at least.

"Back to his yacht. It spent the night moored off the Italian coast, right down south, near Reggio di Calabria, slipped anchor shortly before dawn, heading east. We lost it soon afterward, between satellite sweeps."

"At least you have satellites," remarked Zhukovskaya wryly.

"So find the boat again," said Carver. "Send in a few of my old mates from the SBS, or some of your Spetsnaz boys, to board the boat. Seize the document, and Bob's your uncle."

Grantham was not impressed.

"No, Carver—in that scenario Bob would actually be a major diplomatic incident in which the Americans went ballistic about the unauthorized hostile seizure of a boat owned by one respected, powerful U.S. citizen and used by another, while the Italian government tried to decide whether this constituted an act of war within their territorial waters."

Carver tried again.

"All right, then, who's the other citizen?"

"Sorry?"

"Who's the other U.S. citizen, the one who owns the boat? See, there's something odd about all this money Vermulen's got to splash around. Unless he's made a shitload since he left the armed forces, someone's bankrolling him. And if it isn't the U.S. government, maybe it's the bloke who owns the boat. So who's that?"

"Some good ol' boy from Texas called McCabe," replied Grantham impatiently, not seeing the value of the question. "Made a fortune in oil and mining. The boat belongs to one of his many corporations. But I don't see him being interested in bombs. The man's a born-again Christian, had a dramatic conversion a few years back, devotes his time to philanthropy and good deeds."

Carver gave a clipped, disbelieving laugh.

"McCabe . . . Waylon McCabe?"

"Yes. Why—do you know him?"

"Our paths crossed."

"And he lived to tell the tale? That's unusual."

"Unique, as it happens. And I'll tell you one thing about Waylon McCabe—I don't care how much of a conversion he had; he's a bastard, pure and simple. Whatever he's doing with Vermulen, I guarantee it's not a good deed."

Carver frowned: The pieces were starting to come together in his mind.

"Hang on—you said that boat was going east . . . which would take it into the Ionian Sea, and then the Adriatic, towards Yugoslavia. When we talked, Vermulen mentioned Yugoslavia. He said that was one of the places the Islamic radicals he was going on about were fighting, trying to open up a back route into the West."

He turned to look at Zhukovskaya.

"Did you put bombs in Yugoslavia?"

"I cannot possibly answer that question," she said, needled by the impertinence of such a direct inquiry.

Carver smiled, feeling the balance of power around the table start to tilt in his direction.

"I think you can, Deputy Director. You're in the crapper, too. Not just your organization, or your country, but you, personally. You sent those idiots in the chopper to get the document, and now they're crispy bacon at the bottom of a gorge. You've got to put that right—that's why you're here. And you . . ." He turned his gaze on Grantham. "Well, it wouldn't go down too well in Whitehall if anyone found out who you'd been using to do your dirty work, or how we first happened to meet. As for me, I got Vermulen this list. Plus, something tells me you'll be able to date McCabe's religious conversion to the day he miraculously escaped an air crash in the wilds of the Yukon. That was down to me, too. We're all in this together, like it or not, so answer the question: Yugoslavia?"

He was pushing his luck, but she seemed disinclined to object. He'd been right: The mighty deputy director was in no position to complain.

"Two," said Zhukovskaya. "One in central Belgrade, the other near the Trepca mining complex. It is the single most valuable natural resource in Yugoslavia, producing lead, zinc, copper, gold, and silver—a natural target for economic sabotage."

Grantham nodded to himself, as if agreeing that the locations made sense. He did not bother to ask her how the KGB knew the location of weapons that were lost to the rest of the Russian military and government establishment. He, of all people, needed no lessons in the keeping of secrets from a security service's political masters.

"Where is this place?" asked Carver.

"Kosovo," said Grantham, before Zhukovskaya could reply.

"Where Vermulen's supposed Islamist terrorists are busy starting a civil war. Christ, is that mad bugger going to nuke them? That would get a war going, all right."

"Personally, I would not do anything so obvious. . . ." said Zhukovskaya.

Grantham looked at her inquisitively.

"A false-flag operation?"

"Yes," she agreed. "I like that better, I think. Much more effective to make the world think that the terrorists had the bomb. We think alike . . . but would Vermulen? He has intelligence experience . . . it is possible. But how to stop him? That is the problem."

"Get me to Trepca," said Carver. "That's the one lead we have. I'll see what I can do."

"Just you?" asked Zhukovskaya.

"You got anyone else you can call?"

82

Her cover had worked too well. Alix Petrova was a trained field agent who had seduced, deceived, and even killed dangerous men. But Natalia Vermulen was an innocent personal assistant who'd just married the boss, and as far as her new husband was concerned, his duty was to keep her safe, not lead her into harm's way. So she had no argument when, as they lay in bed—her head on his chest, her hand on his shoulder, the early-morning light, reflected from the ocean, playing on the walls of the yacht's master bedroom—he told her, "You can't come with us tonight."

"I understand," she said. "It's just . . . I want to be with you. I can't help it."

There were tears welling in her eyes. As she blinked them away, she realized that they, at least, were genuine. She truly felt like crying, even if she was lying about why.

He felt the flutter of her eyelashes against his skin.

"It's okay," he said, wrapping his arm around her and holding her tight against his body. "I've been thinking a lot about what I have to do. I had some crazy notions, but what I'm planning is going to be a lot simpler, and a lot safer now."

She could sense him gathering his thoughts, almost working up the courage to speak again, the way men did when they were about to say something personal, a revelation that would leave them exposed and vulnerable.

His voice was thick with emotion as he said, "Now that I've found you, I have something to live for again. I think I lost that for a while. It affected the way I thought, even made me a little crazy. Not now. There's still something I have to do, something that matters. But I love you too much to take dumb risks. . . ."

He smiled, lightening the mood, catching her eye as she looked up at his face.

"Just really smart risks, ones worth taking."

"It makes me scared, not knowing what's happening to you," she said.

"That's what you get for marrying a soldier, even an ex-soldier. It's really tough, having to stay at home, not knowing whether the person you love is dead or alive."

"How did Amy manage it?"

"I don't know. When I went to 'Nam, we were just kids. She'd only recently turned twenty-one, had the party just before I shipped out. All those years, left on her own so many times. You know, she never once complained . . . Oh, God, I didn't mean . . . I wasn't comparing you . . ."

She squeezed his shoulder in reassurance.

"Don't worry—I was the one who mentioned Amy. I like it that you remember her with love. It proves that you are a good man."

Vermulen shifted his weight. The arm that had been wrapped so protectively around her pulled on her shoulder, so that she was rolled off his chest and onto her back. Now he was on top of her, his mouth pressing on hers and his legs forcing her thighs apart with a strength that she could not have resisted, even had she wanted to. So she wrapped her legs around his waist and pulled their bodies together.

As they began to make love, she was smiling. Her happiness was as real as her tears had been, but once again, the reason was not the one that Kurt Vermulen might imagine.

He was leaving her alone on the yacht for the night. Then, perhaps, she might have the chance to escape.

83

C arver had been wrong. There were people Grantham could call. Had to call, in fact. He could not hope to keep this operation completely private anymore; there was far too much at stake. But if he was going to spread the word, he had to do it discreetly. Like all senior MI6 officers, he had close contacts with his counterparts in the CIA. While Carver was upstairs, clearing out of his room, Grantham stepped outside and considered his options. He needed someone he could trust enough to call on a personal, off-the-record basis.

Ted Jaworski was dragged from sleep by the ringing of his bedside phone. His hand reached out from beneath the blankets and scrabbled for his handset. He screwed up his eyes, trying to make out the caller ID, then mumbled, "Jack, hi . . . do you know what the friggin' time is here?"

"A little after four. But this can't wait. Is your line secure?"

"Sure—what the hell is this about?"

"We've obtained information—stumbled across it, really—about one of your people, an ex–army general, Kurt Vermulen."

Jaworski was getting out of bed now, figuring he'd better take the call somewhere more private. He put a hand over the mouthpiece and whispered, "It's okay—go back to sleep," to his wife as she looked up at him blearily.

"Uh-huh—what kind of information?" he asked Grantham.

"It's complicated. But the bottom line is, last night Vermulen obtained a document which contains the precise locations and arming codes of more than one hundred Soviet nuclear weapons."

"What did you say?"

"You know those legendary missing suitcase nukes? Turns out it wasn't a legend. They really are out there. Vermulen knows where to find them, and we think that's what he's going to do, probably within the next twenty-four hours."

Jaworski stopped dead in the corridor and gave a low whistle.

"My God, she was right . . ."

"Sorry?"

"Something someone over here said . . ." Jaworski replied, moving again. "Put it this way—this doesn't come as a total surprise."

Grantham sounded mildly irritated. "So you know about McCabe as well?"

"Okay—now there you got me."

"Waylon McCabe. He's some bigshot from Texas, fundamentalist Christian."

"Oh, sure, know the name . . . what about him?"

Jaworski had made it to his home office. He slumped into the chair behind his desk as Grantham replied.

"I don't know, exactly. But whatever Vermulen is up to, McCabe is backing him. Right now, Vermulen is somewhere in the Adriatic Sea, on McCabe's yacht, and we think he's headed for Kosovo. One of the bombs is planted there."

"How do you know?"

"Friends in Moscow. Turns out this was a KGB operation. Some of their people knew where the damn things were all along. I'll bet they've got their own copy of this list, just haven't seen fit to pass on the information, even to their own government. You'd better have a word with the White House about that. Someone should call the Kremlin, tell them to force the top brass in the FSB to hand over the list. Suggest it's their last chance to do this hush-hush, or else you're going public. You need to see it. So do we, come to that. I get the distinct impression both our countries are littered with bloody bombs."

"Yeah . . ." said Jaworski distractedly, squeezing a rubber ball in his spare hand.

"You sound remarkably unconcerned by what I've just told you."

"Oh, no, I'm concerned, all right, Jack. You can trust me on that. But what you just said, that wasn't exactly a surprise, either."

"What? You knew about these things all along?"

"Kind of . . ."

"And when, exactly, were you planning to inform your closest ally of the dangers we both face?"

"When we knew exactly what that danger was."

"Well you know now."

"Sure do, and we're going to do something about it, too."

"Do keep me posted on that," said Grantham sarcastically.

"Don't worry, Jack. The day is young. But you and I are going to be talking a lot, a helluva lot, before it's through."

Jaworski ended the call. Then he started dialing. And suddenly his attitude wasn't half so casual.

Dawn was still more than an hour away when Kady Jones arrived at Andrews Air Force Base. She'd been woken by a series of firm, insistent taps on the door of her Washington hotel room. She stumbled out of bed and made her way to the door. Through the peephole she could see a man in military uniform. Without undoing the chain, she opened the door a fraction.

"What is this?" she mumbled.

"Dr. Kathleen Dianne Jones?"

"Uh-huh . . . who are you?"

The man held up an I.D. card, which named him as a captain in the Marine Corps.

"May I come in, please, ma'am?"

Kady hesitated, her hand hovering over the chain, uncertain whether to trust a stranger, even one in uniform. Yet the I.D. looked genuine enough. She opened up and stepped back into the room, her suspicions now giving way to the embarrassment of being seen with no proper clothes, her hair unbrushed, her face un-made-up, and her room a mess.

"Thank you, ma'am," said the captain. "You need to get ready to leave here at once. There is a car outside, waiting to take you to Andrews. You will be boarding a flight there. I cannot tell you the precise destination of that flight, but I have been authorized to inform you that it is somewhere in Europe, and you are advised to pack for a trip of two to three days' duration, some of which may involve work in the field."

"But . . ." Kady just stopped herself from saying, "I haven't got a thing to wear." Instead she managed, "My field equipment is all back in New Mexico."

"I'm sure whatever you need will be provided, ma'am. But you've really got to hurry. I'll leave you now. I'll be waiting outside the front entrance. Five minutes, okay?"

The captain did not wait for her reply before he left the room. He simply assumed she could wash, dress, fix her appearance, and pack, all within the space of five minutes.

Only a man could be that dumb.

Jaworski told Tom Mulvagh to cancel his plans for the weekend.

"Does Horabin know about this?" asked Mulvagh, once he'd been told the news about Vermulen and the link to Waylon McCabe.

"He will. But you know Horabin, Tom. He doesn't wipe his ass without figuring out how it'll impact the President's poll ratings. We can't wait for him to make up his mind how to respond to this. We have to find out what McCabe's been doing. Now."

"I'm on it."

The FBI is no different from any other organization: At half past four on a Saturday morning it's not at its most dynamic. So agents weren't leaping from their beds and making for their cars within minutes of Mulvagh getting the call. People had to be found, woken, and briefed— both FBI staff and the people they needed to interview. A couple of hours went by before the first information started getting back to Mulvagh.

In Europe and the Middle East, however, the day was already well under way. Even if the Pentagon brass were groggy when they got the call from Jaworski, their men and women in the field were wide awake and ready to go.

84

I t was midday in the Adriatic. For the past three hours, Vermulen
had been locked in consultation with Marcus Reddin, his second-in-
command, transforming the information from the bomb list into a
workable mission. The yacht's communications systems had been used
to download maps and plans. Calls had been made to the contacts supplied by Pavel Novak and the Dutchman Jonny Koolhaas.

Now there were nine of them in the main saloon: Vermulen, Alix, the
Italian scientist Frankie Riva, Marcus Reddin, and the five men under
his command. The room had been swept for bugs and a screen had been
set up at one end, where Vermulen was standing, with a remote control
in his hand. He was about to start when there was a respectful knock
and a steward poked his head around the door.

"Sorry to disturb you, General, but the captain thought you might
like some refreshments. I have coffee, juices, some pastries, if you'd like
them."

Vermulen was about to refuse the offer, but then he saw the faces of
Reddin's men light up with the soldier's instinctive willingness to accept
any offer of food and drink, whenever it may come.

"Sure—come on in," he said, and the steward pushed in a cart laden
with enticing snacks, from which the aroma of fresh coffee wafted. The
next few minutes vanished in the filling of cups and loading of plates.

"Everybody ready?" Vermulen finally asked. "Okay, then, gentlemen,
let me brief you on your mission.

"What we are going to do tonight has the potential to change the course
of history. We have the chance to strike a mighty blow against not one, but
two of the greatest threats currently facing the world: rogue nuclear weapons and international terrorism. And this is how we're going to do it."

He pressed the remote and the screen filled with a map of a land-
locked territory shaped like a roughly drawn, irregular diamond, one
hundred miles across at its widest point.

"This is the province of Kosovo, which is currently part of the Federal Republic of Yugoslavia. It lies inland, roughly eighty miles from the coast of the Adriatic Sea to the west. Kosovo is currently entering the early stages of a civil war between the majority of the population, who are ethnic Albanians—that's Albania, down there on the southwest border of Kosovo—and the minority, who are Serbs—that's Serbia, to the north and east. Long story short, the Serbs have been ruling the Albanians, and the Albanians don't like it. They want Kosovo to be an independent state. The Serbs don't want to let them go.

"So what's it got to do with us? Simple. The Albanian cause is being hijacked by Islamic terrorists, just like the cause of freedom was hijacked in Afghanistan. These terrorists, operating all over the world, pose a clear and present danger to the United States, and our government is choosing to ignore it. And that danger is all the greater because there is a small-scale nuclear bomb, right here in Kosovo, planted by the Russians ten years ago or more. It is unguarded, sitting in a suitcase, just waiting for someone to come along and find it. We cannot allow that bomb to fall into terrorist hands. So that someone is going to have to be us."

"Holy shit," muttered Maroni. "Now I know why the pay's so good."

Vermulen outlined the mission. Late that afternoon they would rendezvous at sea with a fishing boat carrying the weapons they would need. The yacht would then sail into Croatian waters and moor in a secluded bay near the village of Molunat in southern Croatia, right by the border with the Yugoslav province of Montenegro. At dusk, around seven-thirty, they would go ashore and be met by a guide. He would have the vehicles needed to take them the 125 miles overland to their destination, the main administration building of the Zvečan lead smelter, part of the sprawling Trepca mining complex in northern Kosovo, where the bomb was located. Reddin and his team would stand guard while Riva used his spectrometer to uncover the bomb's hiding place.

Once it was found, Vermulen would record a brief statement on video, describing what he had found, and where. He'd stress the dangers posed to global security by the lethal combination of international terrorism and unsecured, small-scale nuclear weapons. That done, the bomb would be moved, under Riva's close supervision, to their vehicles. They would then drive southeast a farther sixty miles to the border with the neighboring republic of Macedonia, where NATO forces were stationed. The last few miles might have to be undertaken on foot, to avoid detection by border guards. Once the video statement had been released to the media, preventing a coverup, the bomb would be handed over, as would additional information, which would be retained aboard the yacht for safekeeping until that point.

Vermulen swept his gaze around the room, looking each man in the eye.

"I believe that once we have released our statement to the world media, and provided proof to the U.S. government, two things are bound to follow. First, a major effort will be made to retrieve all the missing weapons. And second, the reaction from the media, and the American people—hell, people all over the world—will force our politicians to wake up and take action to protect us from the threat of global terror. If we can stop Islamic extremism now, we can make the world a safer place for our families, our neighbors, for people everywhere. If we do not, then I truly fear what the future may hold.

"Gentlemen," he concluded, "this mission is fundamentally very simple. It involves covering a distance shorter than the drive from Boston to New York City. We've got to be on the lookout for Serbian or KLA units, and avoid police or military roadblocks. But if we take due care, there is no reason to anticipate the need for violent action. The bomb itself is perfectly safe. Absent its detonation code, it will not explode. Nor will it give off dangerous levels of radiation.

"So rest up, get some sleep if you can. It's going to be a long night."

Up on the bridge, the captain was in radio contact with a private plane, currently flying northwest, two hours out of San Antonio.

"Did you get that, sir?" he asked.

"Certainly did, Captain, every word. So how did you fix it? I figured Vermulen would be smart enough to check for bugs."

"He was, sir. Swept the room before the meeting. So we offered him some refreshments, and stuck a listening device inside the lid of a carafe of coffee. Worked out fine."

"That it did, Captain. I'll be calling you with more instructions later, regarding one other little job I need you to do for me."

"Yes sir—I'll look forward to that."

——

Waylon McCabe sat back with a feeling of satisfaction so deep it almost dulled the pain of the tumors eating away at his body from within. In a few minutes he would call Dusan Darko in Belgrade and pass on the information he would need to intercept Vermulen and seize the bomb. The assault would have to be expertly handled. McCabe wanted the weapon intact and Vermulen alive. He also needed Dr. Francesco Riva in one piece. From the moment Vermulen had told him about the meeting in Rome, McCabe had realized that the Italian's expertise would be vital to his plans.

So now it was Easter Saturday: Just one day to go before Armageddon would be unleashed, the warrior Christ would descend from heaven, and he would be led to eternal life. True, there would be suffering. But McCabe didn't care. He had killed a lot of people for a lot worse causes than that.

85

When agents from the FBI's San Antonio field office called at McCabe's Kerr County ranch, they were told that he wasn't home: He'd left for Europe, on business. It didn't take too long after that to establish that his private jet had taken off from Stinson Municipal Airport, six miles south of San Antonio, shortly after 3 A.M., local time.

"Can you describe the aircraft?" asked the special agent who'd made the call.

"I don't know the exact model, just a regular executive jet, eight-seater . . ." replied the airport official.

The agent was barely paying attention and about to hang up when the official interrupted himself and said, "No, wait—that's wrong. . . ."

"What is?" The agent didn't even bother to disguise her lack of interest.

"Well, Mr. McCabe just had that plane adapted, only got it back no more'n ten days ago. So now it's got kind of a bulge in its belly and, you know, a door that opens up, I guess like a bomber, or something. . . ."

Now she was a lot more interested.

Nine in the morning, Eastern Standard Time, and the pace was picking up. A bunch of aeronautical engineers and corporate executives were trying to explain how they had been pleased to work on Waylon McCabe's aircraft for free, believing the modifications were going to be used to drop supplies to starving Africans.

By now the plane had left U.S. airspace. McCabe's pilot had filed a flight plan to Shannon, Ireland, right at the limit of the plane's range. The tracking data, however, suggested he was actually heading farther north, toward Reykjavik, Iceland.

"Can't we get someone at State to call the Icelandic authorities, get them to impound the plane, arrest McCabe?" asked Mulvagh when Jaworski passed on the information.

"On what grounds?" came the reply. "Waylon McCabe is not a fugitive from justice, has committed no crime, and we have no reason to believe he's carrying any contraband, drugs, or weapons."

"Yeah, but he's just about to . . ."

"About to what, exactly?" Jaworski interrupted. "We don't know what he's going to do—that's the problem."

By now, McCabe's telephone, travel, and financial records were undergoing extensive investigation and analysis. McCabe's doctors refused to discuss their patient's health in any detail, citing their absolute duty of confidentiality. But trips to cancer-treatment centers in Houston and New York told their own story. It didn't take long, either, to spot the million-dollar donation to the Reverend Ezekiel Ray, and the calls between the two men.

Mulvagh handled that interview personally.

"Can I ask you what you discussed, Reverend?"

Ray hesitated.

"I'm afraid I can't talk about that. It's a personal matter between me and one of my congregation."

"I understand, but it's not like the confession booth, right? I mean, you aren't obliged to keep your conversation secret."

"That's correct, but even so . . ."

"Reverend, I appreciate your position. But I have to tell you, this is a matter of national security. We need to know what's been on McCabe's mind. Could you at least tell me what kinds of things you talked about, in general, even if you don't go into specifics?"

Several seconds' silence were followed by a thoughtful sigh.

"Yes, I suppose I could do that."

"And. . . ."

"Well, as you probably know, my ministry is centered on the concept of the rapture, the ascension into heaven of the chosen, at the end of time, as prophesied in the Book of Revelation. Mr. McCabe was deeply moved by the prospect of rapture, as are many, many of the decent Christian men and women who attend my services."

The preacher was hiding something. Even down a telephone line, unable to see the other man's face, Mulvagh could sense it: Something to do with the rapture had put Ray on his guard.

"I'm sure they are, Reverend," Mulvagh persisted. "And when McCabe talked about the rapture, what was it, exactly, that moved him? What made him want to talk to you in person? He must have wanted to know something—something he couldn't find out just by listening to your sermons, or watching you on TV."

"He wanted to know . . ."

Again Ray paused.

"Yes?" asked Mulvagh.

"He wanted to know about the final battle against the Antichrist. That's the conflict that Saint John prophesies that will bring about the coming of Christ."

"What about that battle?"

"Oh, my . . . I just don't know if I should tell you this. But what Mr. McCabe wanted to know was, What would God think if he—that's McCabe—started the battle himself?"

Hour by hour, the investigation picked up pace. By lunchtime agents had made the connection to Clinton Tulane and established a further link between McCabe and Dusan Darko. It was clear now how McCabe planned to get hold of the bomb, and in what country. All that remained was its ultimate destination.

A brainstorming meeting was convened at the White House; all the agencies involved in the case were invited.

"We've got to consider every possibility, no matter how crazy it sounds," said Leo Horabin, the national security adviser. "So whatever you've got on your mind, don't be afraid to say it."

Tom Mulvagh waited his turn, letting others air their ideas before he said his piece.

"I think you have to consider the religious aspect," he said. "We've been thinking about this subject for a while at the Bureau—you know, religious crazies trying to bring about Armageddon. In fact, we're planning a research paper on the subject. We're thinking of calling it Project Megiddo, because that's the hill, in Israel, where the Book of Revelation says the final battle will occur. So if I were looking for flashpoints, places where a crazy with a bomb might be heading, that would be where I'd start."

"I hear you, Tom," said Jaworski, "but it could be just about anywhere. A lot of these guys really hate the Arabs. Maybe he wants to take out Mecca, or Jerusalem. . . ."

"How about St. Peter's Basilica in Rome?" said an officer from the DIA. "Hundreds of thousands of people gathered to hear the Pope—helluva target."

Horabin looked around the room, then came to his conclusion.

"I think you're right, Tom. The target will have some kind of religious significance. And it would make sense if it was within easy reach of Kosovo, within Europe or the Middle East. I want a complete list of all possible targets that fall within those parameters. And I want contingency plans for all of them."

86

Night had fallen in Macedonia, and Carver had just taken possession of the quintessential Balkan car, one of the countless battered old Mercedes sedans that are shipped south from Germany to poorer, less discerning markets. This was an eight-year-old C-class diesel, with a creamy-beige paint job that made it look like a motorized crème caramel, and a broken exhaust that spewed thick, gray-blue smoke into the atmosphere. An MI6 agent in Macedonia's capital, Skopje, name of Ronan Biddle, had given it to Carver when he flew in that evening, along with the passport, visas, and accreditation papers that identified him as a BBC radio news reporter. The pockets of a scuffed leather fisherman's bag held the tape recorder, laptop, phone, map, and notebooks that backed up his cover. He'd also been provided with the standard equipment he required as an assassin and saboteur: a selection of tools, plastic explosives, knife, gun, and ammunition. Underneath his clothes, he wore, as ever, the money belt containing the cash, bonds, and passports that were his constant companions. His hair had been clipped short, a basic barbershop crew cut, just before he left France. He was fed up with seeing Kenny Wynter every time he looked in a mirror.

"It isn't a SIG, I'm afraid," said Biddle, sounding more pleased than apologetic about this inability to deliver the weapon Carver wanted. "Grantham said you liked them, but you'll have to make do with a Beretta Ninety-two—best we could drum up at short notice. It's good enough for the U.S. Army, so it can't be too bad. We got you a silencer, too."

Biddle looked at Carver resentfully.

"Don't know why London had to send someone," he continued. "We've got plenty of first-rate people here, and there are special forces chaps hanging around the place who know Kosovo like the back of their hand. But they never trust the men on the ground, do they?"

Carver just shrugged and opened up the trunk of the car, looking for the best place to hide the plastique. He had no interest in starting a conversation. Minutes later he was on the road out of the airport, on the way to the Kacanik Defile, the gorge that provides one of the few passes between Macedonia and southern Kosovo.

The line at the border was ninety minutes long, a motley gaggle of trucks, vans, and family cars, their roof racks piled high with goods from Macedonia that had become unavailable as violence and anarchy descended on Kosovo—everything and anything, from fresh fruit to video recorders. The people in the line were standing around by their vehicles, smoking, drinking, and talking to the other drivers. Carver couldn't tell which ones were ethnic Albanians and which were Serbs. There was no sign of any tension or polarization. Everyone was getting on just fine, grumbling about the delay, sharing their bottles and cigarette packets, good-naturedly joshing the kids who ran about between the cars. But as soon as they crossed the line into Kosovo, they'd be divided into warring tribes, each out to obliterate the other.

Carver had seen plenty of communal violence in his time. He'd served in Northern Ireland and Iraq. And no matter where or when it happened, it never made any more sense.

The border guards were shaven-headed thugs in blue paramilitary uniforms. One of them took Carver's passport and papers and disappeared into a low-slung building decorated with the crest of the Federal Republic of Yugoslavia, which stood beside the checkpoint. A few minutes later, he reemerged and signaled to Carver to move his car out of the way and park it to one side so that other travelers could come through the checkpoint: This was going to take some time.

It was getting late, but there was still a duty-free store and café open in the no-man's-land between the Macedonian and Kosovan sides of the border post. Carver went in to take a leak and get a double espresso. Four more guards were sitting at a table, their submachine guns propped against their chairs. They were sharing a bottle of plum brandy. It was standing on the table next to a couple of empties. The guards simmered with the brooding tension of drunks who were a long way down the road that leads from cheerful inebriation to unrestrained violence. As Carver passed by on the way to the men's room, they looked at him with a malevolence that sought out any excuse—a single, inadvertent glance or gesture would do—that would allow them to attack.

When his coffee arrived, he took it outside. He wanted to be able to think in peace. The truth was, he was so angry himself, that if the border guards even looked like they would give him a fight, he might take them up on the offer. And that would just be one more entry on his long list of stupid mistakes.

It went against all his principles, but he couldn't help thinking of the past, wishing he'd done things differently. If he'd done a better job back at the Inuvik airport . . . if he'd just told the Consortium to screw their assignment when they'd ordered him onto the plane to Paris . . . if he'd never let himself become involved with Alix . . . if he'd put his business before his balls and just handed that bloody list over to Grantham . . . so many ifs, and nothing he could do about any of them.

Alix wasn't coming back to him, not now. She'd made her decision and she wasn't going to change it. He didn't blame her for what she'd done. When she'd left him at the clinic, he'd been a vegetable. Then she'd been told he was dead. It was hardly surprising she'd fallen for the healthy, successful, powerful guy standing right next to her. He hoped he'd have the chance to tell her that, let her know he understood and bore her no ill will, no matter how much he was hurting. But when were they going to meet again? He couldn't believe Vermulen would involve her in whatever he was planning to do with the bomb, so she wouldn't be anywhere near Trepca. And by the end of the night, the chances were that either he or Vermulen would be dead, maybe both. Even if he survived, what then?

Presumably she'd been kept on the boat. He imagined coming aboard: "Hello, darling—sorry I topped your old man. No hard feelings."

That wasn't going to go down too well, however he tried to play it.

He could just turn back, of course. If he didn't get Vermulen, someone else would, and sooner rather than later. Too many people had reasons to want the man dead. If Alix was back on the market again, he could try to win her over.

But that wasn't exactly a classy idea, hitting on the grieving widow. And it wasn't going to happen, anyway. The only way to atone for all his mistakes was to clear up the mess he'd made. That meant tracking

Vermulen down and taking him, and his bomb, out of commission, whatever the cost. But what about the list? Did Vermulen have it with him? The answer came to Carver in a moment of absolute certainty. No, he'd have kept it safe on the yacht, with Alix.

A sardonic, humorless smile twisted the corners of his mouth. Maybe they would meet again, like it or not.

Across the floodlit no-man's-land, he could see an official waving at him. His papers had been accepted. He was into Kosovo.

87

E arlier that afternoon, when everyone onboard was fully occupied preparing for Vermulen's expedition, Alix had slipped into the ship's galley and found a large plastic garbage bag, a number of smaller food bags, and a couple of yards of twine. Now the men were all gone and she was alone in the master bedroom, preparing her getaway.

She was wearing a bathrobe, and beneath that a swimsuit. The yacht was moored less than two hundred yards from the shore. Alix was a strong swimmer—she felt sure she could cover the distance without any trouble, even allowing for the bag she'd have tied around her waist. She was taking the absolute minimum she would need: her wallet, passport, and phone; a sweatshirt; a pair of jeans; and her lightest pair of flat, slip-on shoes. Aside from the jeans and sweatshirt, each item was individually wrapped in a food bag, and then everything went inside the garbage bag, which she'd sealed with packing tape. She planned to leave around one in the morning, when there'd be only one man keeping watch from the bridge. If she could make it to shore, she'd be long gone by the time the sun came up.

There was a knock on the door and the steward's voice. "Mrs. Vermulen?"

She shoved the bag under her pillows and called back, "Yes?"

"Message from your husband, ma'am. Captain asked me to hand it to you in person."

"Just coming . . ."

She walked to the door and opened it. The steward was standing there. But he held no message in his hand. Instead, he was pointing a gun at her, and there was not a trace of his former servility in his voice as he said, "Put some clothes on. You're going on a trip."

She stepped back into the room, opening the door wider to let him in. As far as the steward was concerned, she was just the little blond wifey. He was taken completely by surprise when she slammed the door back in his face, flung it open again and kicked him hard in the crotch. As he bent double in agony, Alix stepped forward and drove her knee into his face. She had no idea why the crew had suddenly turned on her, but there was no time to worry about that now. She ran back to her bed, grabbed the garbage bag, and hurried out into the passageway.

The master bedroom was on the main deck. Alix raced through the saloon where Vermulen had held his briefing and out into the open air. She had got as far as the stern rail, and was just about to leap over the side when a burst of gunfire exploded just a few feet above her, and a line of bullets tore through the planking at her feet.

She looked up and saw the captain standing by the rail of the upper deck, looking down at her over the top of an automatic rifle.

"You better stop right there, Mrs. Vermulen," he said. "Or the next burst goes through you."

88

Fifteen years earlier, the Zvečan lead smelter had been part of a thriving enterprise that had employed twenty thousand workers and provided wealth for a nation. Now it was just another ramshackle old Communist enterprise, brought even lower by the combined effects of corrupt mismanagement and social anarchy. The whole place, nestled at the floor of a valley between thickly wooded, mineral-laden hills, purveyed an air of irreversible decline: rusting pipes, stationary conveyor belts, office windows broken and unrepaired. A few desultory puffs of bitter smoke emerged from the giant red-and-white-striped chimney that towered over the plant, in feeble acknowledgment that this was, in theory, a round-the-clock operation. Occasional lights overhead shone a weak orange glow over their surroundings. But there was no one to check Vermulen's team as their Land Cruisers rolled through the main gates, no sign of workers on the roadways between the giant processing sheds.

The bomb was behind another false wall, this one in the basement office of the maintenance worker in charge of the central-heating boilers. Vermulen was struck by the contrast between the drab banality of the leather case and the astonishing power of its contents. He was accustomed to systems whose capacity was evident in their appearance, be they mighty battle tanks or thunderous artillery pieces. But this was the ultimate stealth weapon. It gave no clue as to its powers of destruction.

The feeble bulbs in the office lights and the gray-green paint on the walls combined to create a grim, ghostly atmosphere, but Vermulen could see that Frankie Riva's eyes were glittering with the fever of a treasure-hunting archaeologist who had stumbled into a pharaoh's tomb.

"*Ammazza!*" he muttered, opening the case and seeing the metal gun barrel. "After all these years . . . incredible!"

"So it is a nuclear weapon?" Vermulen asked.

"Oh yes, General, most certainly it is that."

"In working order?"

Riva raised his hands in a classic Italian shrug.

"Who can say? There is only one way to know for sure, and that is to set a detonator and see what happens. But, just looking at it, I can see no reason why it should not work. Fundamentally, this is a very simple device. One piece of uranium is smashed into another . . ."

He spread his arms wide. "Boom!"

Don Maroni had been a staff sergeant in the U.S. Army Rangers, a member of one of the finest light-infantry forces in the world, trained to the highest levels of fitness and competence. But the operative word was "had." He'd been out of the service five years, working for a civilian security corporation, wearing a suit instead of a uniform. He still went to the boxing gym three times a week and kept his shooting up to standard. By any normal measure, he was not a man you'd want to mess with. But he wasn't as sharp as he'd once been. He certainly wasn't as battle-fit as the men who were slipping through the great, rusting hulks of the smelting works all around him, men who had spent a decade fighting hand to hand in conflicts of vile, unfettered ferocity.

Dusan Darko's most trusted killers had confronted conventional armies, desperate civilians, and fanatical mujahideen flown in from Pakistan, Afghanistan, and Saudi Arabia, whose total absence of scruple equaled their own. They had battled knowing that death was a mercy, far preferable to the torture and mutilation that inevitably followed capture, and they had dealt out as much agony as they had received. More than that, they came from mountain villages where the culture of knife and gun had ruled for centuries. Murder was in their blood.

So as good as he was, Donny Maroni was taken by surprise as he patrolled the perimeter of the office block in which the bomb had been hidden. He caught a brief scent of tobacco and garlic from the hand that clamped across his mouth to stifle his screams, and then the knife was drawn across his throat and blood spurted from the gaping mortal wound.

Reddin's men were scattered around the immediate vicinity of the office building. They were all well armed, all equipped with radios with which they could summon immediate support. And they all died without a word being spoken.

The video camera had been set up in the basement office, with a light that shone on Kurt Vermulen and the opened bomb case that he and Frankie Riva had lifted onto the maintenance man's desk.

"You ready?" he asked Riva, who was standing behind the camera.

"Sure," the Italian replied. "We're running now. Just speak whenever you want."

Vermulen cleared his throat, gave a sharp sniff, then looked directly at the camera.

"My name is Lieutenant General Kurt Vermulen. I retired from the U.S. Army after twenty-eight years' service as a commissioned officer, during which I was proud, and honored, to serve the country I love. I am now in the province of Kosovo, Yugoslavia, in the Zvečan industrial plant. Within a few miles of here, units of the Kosovo Liberation Army are operating, assisted by fighters, weapons, and money provided by the forces of international Islamist terrorism. And this"—he pointed to the case on the desk—"is their ultimate weapon. It is a—"

From the corridor outside there came the crackle of small-arms fire, immediately answered by a blast of firing from the far side of the office door, through which could be heard an animal howl of pain. The door burst open and Marcus Reddin backed into the room. He was unsteady on his feet and his left arm was hanging uselessly beside him, blood pouring from the through-and-through bullet wound that had ripped open his shoulder.

"Red!" shouted Vermulen. Drawing the pistol that was holstered around his waist, he ran to his friend's aid.

"Sorry, man . . . screwed up," Reddin gasped.

Vermulen could hear footsteps scurrying down the basement corridor. Without looking back at Riva, he shouted, "Take cover!" Then he grasped his pistol in both hands, held it up to his face, and stood in the shelter of the door frame, steeling himself for the moment when he would have to step into the corridor and start firing.

But Vermulen never took that step. Not when there was a gun in his back and an Italian voice in his ear saying, "Drop your weapon, General."

One hundred and twenty miles to the west, a helicopter landed on a patch of open ground near the Croatian village of Molunat. A small group of people was waiting for it. While the engines still ran, they hurried toward the chopper, instinctively bending over, even though the rotor blades were well above their heads. In the midst of the men there was a smaller, slighter figure, a woman whose blond hair was whipped around her face by the wind from the rotors. She was in the grip of two men, who had grabbed her upper arms. Her hands had been tied behind her back, and she stumbled as they dragged her up to the helicopter and bundled her through the open side door. After she was in, one of the men reached up toward the open door, holding a thin cardboard file. An unseen figure from within the cabin took the file and slid the door closed, and the helicopter rose again into the cloudy night sky.

89

"Welcome to Rock City, ma'am."

Kady Jones had been flown directly from Washington to Ramstein Air Base in southern Germany. She'd been briefed on the way. There was reason to believe that another one of the Russian bombs had been uncovered in Kosovo. She would be making a determination as to whether it was genuine or not. The tone of the briefings had been urgent, but routine: nothing to worry about. After they were over, she'd received another message, requesting details on her height, body measurements, and shoe size. The moment the cabin door had opened, she'd been led straight to a military transport, already laden with a full army explosive-ordnance-disposal team and its equipment. Another dozen men sat silently and impassively in futuristic black uniforms. Before she'd even strapped on her belt, the wheels were already rolling. Once they were in the air, one of the men in black came over.

"Major Dave Gretsch," he said. "Just wanted to introduce myself, let you know my men and I will be securing the area for you tonight. There's a chance we may be seeing some action, but just do what we ask, and we'll make sure you're fine. Meantime, anything you need to know, just ask."

"Who are you guys?" Kady asked.

Gretsch gave an apologetic smile.

"I'm afraid I can't tell you. But we're the best, is all you need to know."

"Oh. . . . Well, where are we going, exactly?"

"Can't say that, either. They haven't told me yet. Fact, I was kinda hoping you might know."

"So I can ask, but you can't answer . . ."

"Sure looks that way, but that's the army for you."

Now it was ten at night and she'd just arrived at the Tuzla Air Base in Bosnia. As the soldiers got to work unloading their weapons and equipment, she'd been greeted by an air-force corporal, a woman, who was leading her toward a waiting Humvee.

"We call it Rock City 'cause of all the crushed rock everywhere—place was like a sea of mud till they laid that down," she explained. "Anyways, they got a room set aside for you in the officers' quarters, though I don't guess you'll be getting much sleep."

Kady was led to her room, little more than a cubicle with a camp bed, inside a basic, prefabricated structure. The corporal politely instructed her to get changed and wait for further instructions. On the bed were arranged a set of combat fatigues, a T-shirt, a flak jacket, a pair of boots, and a helmet. Now she knew why they'd wanted to check her size.

But what kind of battlefield was she heading into?

90

I n the rest of Yugoslavia, the civil wars had been fought on a large scale: a conflict of armies, air forces, and artillery barrages, with towns besieged, territories conquered, populations deported, raped, and slaughtered. So far, Kosovo had been different. Resistance to the Serbs had been peaceful for so long that most people, on both sides, were taken by surprise when hostilities began. The attacks were random and sporadic: guerrilla assaults on one-off targets, rather than organized military campaigns. As he drove northward, deeper into Kosovo, Carver saw occasional signs of fighting—a burning building in the distance, a truck filled with soldiers almost knocking him off the narrow two-lane road as it thundered by.

He was miles from anywhere, in open countryside, when the phone rang. It was Grantham.

"Change of plan," he said. "Forget Trepca. You're being rerouted to Pristina airport, which is actually located at a place called Slatina, about twenty kilometers east of Pristina city. We have new information. I'm just going to hand you over to Ted Jaworski. He's an American colleague, heading up a task force looking at this issue from the Washington end."

"Good evening, Mr. Carver . . ."

Carver did not reply. His headlights had just picked out a roadblock a few hundred yards down the road. A couple of armed Serbian para-militaries, in the same blue uniforms as the men at the border post, were standing by a crude barrier made of planks and oil drums, lit by spotlights shining down into the road. Their truck was parked behind the barrier, across the road, just to underline the idea that no one was getting by.

"Mr. Carver . . . ?"

"Yeah, I can hear you."

"Okay, you need to know the way this situation is developing. We believe that Vermulen's backer, a man named Waylon McCabe—"

"I know who he is."

The men by the roadblock were waving at Carver, indicating that he should stop.

"Well, McCabe may be planning a double cross."

"Sounds about right."

"I'm sorry?"

"I'm saying I agree—that's what I'd expect him to do. Hold on, I've got company. . . ."

Carver put the phone down on the passenger seat as one of the paramilitaries appeared at his window, rotating his finger in the air to indicate that he should wind it down. As Jaworski's disembodied voice crackled from the phone, "Carver? Are you there?" and Grantham barked, "Stop pissing around," the paramilitary started jabbering in Serbian.

"Sorry," said Carver, playing the dumb foreigner. "Don't understand."

He was wearing a hunting vest, with external pockets at chest and hip level. Slowly, he reached into one of the chest pockets and pulled out his BBC press card.

"Journalist," he said, pointing at himself. "BBC . . . British, yes?"

The man turned back toward his mate and waved at him to come over. That gave Carver the opportunity to pick up the phone.

"Sorry about that. I'm at a roadblock. Be right with you."

He put the phone down again as the second paramilitary came up and in heavily accented English said, "Road close. You no go. Close. Yes?"

"I understand, yes," Carver said. "But I must go. BBC."

Before the argument could go any further, the Serbs were distracted by the arrival of another car, a decrepit Škoda, which pulled up behind Carver. It had a big bundle on its roof wrapped in plastic, which made him think it must have crossed the border just behind him.

One of the Serbs pointed at the pennant fluttering from the radio aerial. It bore a black double-headed eagle against a red background, the national symbol of Albania. He walked up to the car, ripped off the pennant, threw it to the ground, and spat on it before grinding it into the dirt with his boot heel. Then, while his partner pointed his gun at the car, the paramilitary ripped open the driver's door and dragged out an unshaven black-haired man in his thirties, wearing an Adidas tracksuit over a red-and-black-striped AC Milan soccer shirt. The man was pleading, pointing back to the car as he staggered forward a few paces before being thrown to the ground.

While the first paramilitary aimed a couple of halfhearted kicks at the Albanian, the other peered into the car. He gestured at the passengers to get out. A woman emerged from one side, a second, much older female from the other. Carver assumed they were family: the man's wife and mother, maybe. The missus was hugging an absurdly big pink teddy bear that looked like a prize from a tatty fairground stall. Ma was wrapped in a fringed, woven shawl. The man guarding them lined them up by the side of the road, then half turned to watch his partner kicking the man curled up in the dirt. Neither of the paramilitaries saw what happened next. As Carver looked on, the younger woman flung her teddy bear to the ground as the older one threw back her shawl. Both were carrying guns. Neither hesitated for a second before firing at the paramilitaries.

One went down immediately, clutching his belly and screaming out in pain. The other tried to flee the blast of gunfire, but managed only a few strides before a bullet hit the side of his head, splitting his skull like a teaspoon cracking a boiled egg, and throwing him dead to the ground. Several of the shots had missed, the bullets flying straight past the paramilitaries toward Carver's car, smashing his rear window and punching into the bodywork.

A voice over the phone cried, "What the hell was that?" but Carver wasn't around to hear it. He'd already kicked open the car door and rolled out onto the pavement, drawing the Beretta as he went and scrambling into a ditch by the opposite side of the road. A knife had appeared from nowhere in the Albanian's hand and he was standing over the wounded Serb, grinning at his screams with a look that suggested he was going to enjoy the job of giving him a long, slow, agonizing death. But that could wait. He'd spotted Carver's dash across the road. As the screams of the wounded man filled the night air, he picked up one of the paramilitaries' submachine guns and walked toward Carver, peering into the darkness.

The women followed him, the wife crouching low, her pistol held in both hands in front of her, the old woman stomping forward in absolute defiance of any danger.

With a shock of disgust, Carver realized that he was going to have to kill all three of them, the women as well as the man.

He didn't hesitate.

———

Kneel, in the firing position. Two shots into the man's head. Roll left. Kneel again. Two each for the women. Three kills.

The whole thing was over in less than five seconds. Afterward, the only sound came from the wounded Serb, whose howls of fear and pain were gradually subsiding to whimpers. Unconsciousness and death would not be far away.

Carver walked back to his car, sickened by the pointlessness of it all. He wondered how many other scenes like this there had been across this benighted country over the past few years and how many more would follow in the years to come.

Ninety minutes ago the people in that car had most likely been standing around in the line by the border crossing, talking and joking like everyone else. They were alive. They had prospects. Now look at them.

He picked up the phone again. The first voice he heard was Jaworski. "Where the hell have you been?"

"Shut it," snapped Carver. "Five people just died."

"Okay, let's start again, nice and polite," said Jaworski, in a patronizing tone of exaggerated conciliation. "Here's the situation. Waylon McCabe flew into Pristina a couple of hours back. His plane has been adapted to drop a bomb. He's also made some kind of alliance with a Serbian warlord, Dusan Darko. We think Darko's going to seize the weapon Vermulen has located—may have done so already—then hand it over to McCabe. And then we believe McCabe wants to use it to trigger Armageddon."

Carver gave a snort of disbelief.

"He thinks he's fulfilling the prophecies of the Book of Revelation," said Jaworski, with absolute seriousness.

"Jesus wept."

"That's kind of an unfortunate choice of words," said Jaworski.

"So what do you want me to do?"

"Get to the airport, obviously, then locate the plane. We tracked it all the way to Slatina and we know it landed. We're certain it hasn't taken off—it's not on any radar. But the last satellite pass we did, there was no sign of it."

"Okay—I find the plane. Then what?"

"Just observe. Keep us informed. Believe me, you will be playing a major role in resolving this situation by providing the intelligence we need. But I want you to understand, so far as my government is concerned, this is a domestic matter involving U.S. citizens. It will be settled by U.S. agencies, and no one else. Frankly, Mr. Carver, it is none of your business. Your place is in the audience, not on the stage. So do not interfere, and do not, on any account, do anything more than observe and inform."

"You got that, Carver?" Grantham cut in. "Observe and inform. None of your fireworks displays this time."

"Oh, I got that, all right," said Carver before he hung up.

He took his gear out of the shot-up Mercedes and dumped it in the dead Serbs' truck. Then he went back to the man who'd been killed by the shot to the head. He was still illuminated by the headlights of the Albanians' car. Carver looked at the back of the man's uniform, then rolled the body over with his foot and checked the front. Both sides were clear of bloodstains. It was too good a chance to waste. He stripped the body and pulled the Serbian uniform over his own trousers and shirt. The fit wasn't too bad, though the boots were a size too small: He'd have to put up with aching feet for a night. The dead man didn't look too much like Carver, and his I.D. card revealed he was more than a decade younger. Carver went to the other body. This one was older and the likeness was better, so Carver took his wallet and papers instead. So now he was Nico Krasnic, age thirty-two.

He picked up Krasnic's submachine gun and went back to the truck. As he got in, shoving his discarded vest and fisherman's bag out of sight in the footwell in front of the passenger seat, he saw a portable CD player perched above the dashboard. Out of curiosity, Carver pressed play and picked up the earphones. A percussive, machine-gun blast of hardcore rap hammered around his brain. Carver turned it off. If that was the last thing the Serb had been listening to, then death must have come as a blessed relief.

As he started up the truck and set off again on the road to the airport, Carver was already formulating his plan. And it had very little indeed to do with observing and informing.

EASTER SUNDAY

91

In the Church of the Holy Sepulchre, Jerusalem, midnight had arrived and with it the start of the magnificent Easter celebrations of the Greek Orthodox faith. The building was thronged with worshippers of all Christian denominations as the Patriarch of Jerusalem celebrated Christ's resurrection, on the very spot of the tomb He so triumphantly vacated. Amid shouts of "Christ is risen . . . He is risen indeed," the glory of the resurrection and the conquest of death were celebrated in a service of matins that echoed around the 950-year-old building in an act of worship that embodied both the awesome power of faith and the glorious joy of life.

92

Kurt Vermulen bore no physical wounds. To his shame, he had been taken without firing a shot. So now he sat in the back of what had been his Land Cruiser, appropriated by the man who had so expertly defeated him, a man who introduced himself as Dusan Darko.

"We have a meeting," Darko said, looking up from the front passenger seat and watching Vermulen in the rearview mirror as he spoke. "A friend of yours, Mr. McCabe. He is paying me twenty million, U.S., to deliver the suitcase to him. Perhaps you can pay me more. I am always interested in making a better deal. It is not too late."

Vermulen said nothing.

"I guess not," said Darko. "In that case, I will have to deliver you to Mr. McCabe. He will decide what to do with you then. I am sorry about your men, that they had to die. Please understand—it is just business. I have no bad feelings against you. I love America, great country. You do not want to talk—I understand. You have much to think about. Cigarette?"

Darko lit up. His driver was already smoking. Vermulen could see the orange glow of burning cigarettes in the truck ahead of him. No one in Serbia seemed too bothered by the risk of lung cancer or heart attacks. But then, men at war rarely did. They assumed they wouldn't live long enough to catch a disease.

Vermulen was trying to work out how he had allowed himself to fall for the trap McCabe had set for him. The old man had played him right from the start, drawing him into plans that seemed insane to him now. Spending months chasing after nuclear bombs, hiring thieves, leading men into mortal danger—what had he been thinking? Maybe they'd been right, back in Washington, the people who'd tried to tell him, as politely as they could, that the grief of losing Amy had driven him off the rails.

Yet he hadn't been wrong about the things that really mattered. He still believed, as passionately now as ever before, that his country and its allies were ignoring a terrible danger, refusing to recognize enemies who worshipped death, hated freedom, and happily sacrificed their own lives for the sake of killing others. Next to that malignant insanity, his own actions had seemed entirely rational. He had at least tried to raise the alarm.

And he'd been right about Natalia, too. Part of him, the old intelligence agent, had always wondered whether her arrival had been too good to be true. Poor Mary Lou had died, then this vision had appeared on his doorstep: Looking back, he knew it was too pat, too convenient. But even accepting that, he had no doubt that Natalia's love for him was genuine. Countless times he'd asked himself whether he was just an old fool, letting himself be seduced by a beautiful young woman. Perhaps it had been that way at the start. Perhaps she had been pretending then. But not now. With every day that had passed, his certainty had grown. He was, at the very least, right to trust in her.

Only one aspect of the whole disaster still remained a mystery to him. He couldn't see why McCabe had double-crossed him. He must have had something in mind all along, a purpose for his treachery. But Vermulen could not comprehend what that might be. And if he found out, what difference did it make? He'd been a professional soldier long enough to know defeat when he tasted it.

93

So that was how the plane had disappeared.

Carver was crouched in the long grass beside the runway at Pristina airport. It ran north–south, along a narrow valley, with mountains on either side. At the north end all the regular airport buildings were clustered: the control tower, terminal, aircraft hangars, and oil bunkers. But Carver, driving with his lights off, had followed a service road to the very southern end of the runway. There, a taxiway left the main runway and ran due west to a broad tarmac apron at the base of a peak that rose thousands of feet into the darkness. It was only when Carver left his truck parked away from the road, and crawled through the grass to the high wire-mesh fence topped with razor wire that lined the taxiway, that he saw that the mountain's rock face was actually pierced by a pair of massive, camouflaged steel blast doors. As he watched, a helicopter came in to land on the apron, waited while the doors rolled open to reveal a giant hangar, dug into the hillside, and taxied into the cavernous opening. Once it was inside, the doors rolled shut again, but not before Carver had caught sight of an executive jet, its belly distended by a slight bulge just aft of the wings. That was McCabe's plane, and it either had its deadly cargo, already sitting like a malignant fetus in its metal womb, or was waiting to receive it.

He needed to get inside. But before he could even think about breaching the doors, he had to penetrate the perimeter fence. The service road curved around toward the hidden air base, but access was only possible through a guarded checkpoint, manned by two sentries. The fence even ran across the taxiway, with a wheeled section that could roll back whenever a plane was cleared for landing or takeoff. Signs at regular intervals indicated that the perimeter was patrolled by dogs.

The only way in was through the main gate. Carver was steeling himself to make a frontal attack, knowing that he would have to kill the sentries, when he saw headlights, away in the distance, coming in his direction. He dashed back to his truck and watched as three vehicles went by: two open trucks, with men sitting in the cargo areas at the back, and one Land Cruiser. He let them get a ways down the road, then swung his truck in behind them, the lights still off.

As the first of the trucks pulled up by the checkpoint, Carver turned on his lights and pulled up at the end of the line. One of the sentries walked up to the driver's door of the first truck. Carver took out his gun, screwed the silencer onto the barrel, and put it within easy reach on the seat to his right. Then he put on the CD player headphones, gritted his teeth, and pressed play again.

Rap had turned Carver into an old man. To him the music sounded like a tuneless, incoherent cacophony and the only words he could understand were the obscenities. He'd spent too long on parade grounds and assault courses, being shouted at by rabid sergeant-majors whose capacity for verbal abuse and physical violence would put any street braggart to shame, to be impressed. But duty called.

Finally the sentry came up to his window. Keeping his face in the shadow inside the cabin, Carver stuck his hand out of the window and handed over Krasnic's I.D.

The sentry asked him something. Carver did not reply.

The sentry tried again. Carver leaned toward him, pointing at his ears and jerking his head in time to the beat. He grinned like an idiot and shouted, "Straight Outta Compton, yeah!!" in what he hoped was a vaguely Serbian accent.

The sentry looked at him blankly for a second, and then he saved his own life. He grinned and started jerking his head, too, in time to the sibilant beats hissing from Carver's earphones. Then he handed back the I.D. card and waved him in.

The other vehicles were already halfway across the tarmac apron, and the blast doors were rolling apart to greet them. Carver hit the gas and took his place in the line, turning off the music with a sigh of relief and a loosening of shoulders that, he suddenly realized, were hunched up with tension. Something about the blaring in his ears, the sensation of inescapable noise, had really disturbed him. His teeth were grinding, his body sweating, and he felt weirdly disturbed, as though that noise had triggered a reaction to some dark, shapeless memory lurking below the surface of his mind.

And then he drove into the hangar, and all thoughts of his own issues were forgotten as he looked around in wonder.

A vast space had been hollowed out from the living rock of the mountain. In the foreground, McCabe's jet was parked by the newly arrived helicopter: two splendid machines, worth millions and capable of extraordinary feats, yet in these surroundings they looked no bigger or more significant than toys. The hangar stretched back as far as Carver could see. In the distance, more jets were lined up in neat rows, at least two squadrons' worth of Yugoslav Air Force fighters: old-fashioned MiG-21s, their nose cones poking out of stubby, stocky bodies, and much newer MiG-29s—sleek, hungry twin-tailed raptors.

A man in ground-crew overalls directed Carver to park his truck in an area to the left of the entrance, next to the other three newly arrived vehicles. As Carver drove up, he saw men springing down from the backs of the trucks, dressed in a motley assortment of combat fatigues, denim, leather jackets, and even sportswear, but all carrying weapons. Most of the men stayed by the trucks, leaning against them and lighting up cigarettes in blithe disregard for the vast amounts of aviation fuel that must be stored nearby. But one of them, responding to an order shouted from the Land Cruiser, walked across, his gun slung around his shoulders, opened one of the rear doors, and dragged out a bedraggled, blond-headed figure by his cuffed hands. It was Vermulen. So McCabe really had double-crossed him. Carver didn't feel much sympathy. A man as astute and experienced as Vermulen should have seen it coming. But he was alone, so at least he'd been smart enough to leave Alix somewhere safe. That was something.

A second man emerged from the other rear door of the Land Cruiser. He had swept-back black hair and the sort of Italianate looks whose impeccable grooming suggests that the owner will never see a face he loves as much as his own. The man wore his smugness like expensive aftershave as he walked around to the back of the vehicle, a shockproof aluminum case in his hand, and watched while a battered brown leather suitcase was removed with extreme caution by two more armed men. They placed it on a long-handled, two-wheeled cart and pushed it away, still supervised by the Latin loverboy, toward a line of offices ranged against the far wall of the hangar, at least fifty yards away.

The Land Cruiser produced one last passenger, with a phone clamped to his ear. He concluded his conversation and strode briskly toward the man pushing the trolley, giving instructions as he went. This, thought Carver, must be Darko. He was certainly the man in charge. Vermulen, meanwhile, brought up the rear, doing his best to maintain an upright, dignified posture as he walked with his captor's gun pressed into the small of his back.

Carver watched as two shaven-headed men emerged from one of the offices to meet the little procession. They were wearing shades, with earpieces in their ears, the unmistakable look of private security goons who want to pretend they're U.S. Secret Service. Their jackets bulged with the clear presence of weapons. The goons watched as the line of men, plus the cart, made their way in. Then they closed the door and stood outside it, arms folded like nightclub bouncers, doing their best to look menacing.

Wankers, thought Carver to himself. But the men had given him an idea. From the moment that Jaworski told him to stay out of this "domestic matter," he had assumed that the Americans were planning some kind of stunt to recover the bomb and take out McCabe, Vermulen, and anyone else who got in the way. But he wasn't going to sit around with his thumb up his arse, waiting for the Seventh Cavalry to ride to the rescue. He'd let McCabe get away from him once, and it wouldn't happen again. That much he'd decided back at the roadblock. He'd also known, in principle, what he wanted to do.

Now he'd worked out precisely how he was going to do it.

94

The three Black Hawk helicopters flew due south from Tuzla, the pilots pushing their performance to the limit, covering seventy-five miles in a little over twenty minutes, before they turned southeast toward the border. They crossed from Bosnia into Montenegro just south of Foča and followed the Tara River southeast toward the airport at Slatina. The helicopters hugged the valley floors, skimming the treetops, hurdling power lines, and skirting the edge of the hills and mountains of that craggy terrain, avoiding towns and villages like night creatures shying from human contact. Kady Jones was in the third aircraft, with the explosive-ordnance-disposal team. She'd been talking to the team leader, agreeing on the protocols under which they would examine and, if necessary, deal with any bomb they found, when their pilot cut in.

"Okay, folks—we're into hostile territory. This is where it gets interesting."

In the White House Situation Room, Ted Jaworski let out a cry of triumph: "Gotcha, you bastard!"

Within the past quarter-hour, an MQ-1 Predator drone from the Tuzla Air Base had arrived over Slatina and begun broadcasting real-time infrared imagery, via the ground-control station at Tuzla, back to the United States. It had spotted the helicopter's arrival, and then the vivid flare of light as the hangar blast doors opened to admit it. Now that they knew where McCabe was hidden, the mission had become a lot simpler. Within minutes, an army general was in contact with Dave Gretsch, in the lead Black Hawk, updating his orders. Meanwhile, U.S. Air Force officers were readying fighter squadrons across the Balkan theater of operations and the Middle East to intercept and destroy McCabe's plane, in the event that it took off before the Black Hawks reached Pristina, no matter where in the region it was heading.

When the general had finished with Gretsch, Jaworski got on the line.

"Major, this is Ted Jaworski, from the Agency. Just wanted to inform you that the Brits may have a man inside the airport facility where you will be deploying. He was tasked to get inside, but we don't know if he made it. The man's name is Carver. He's kind of unofficial, not on any list. So don't hurt him if you can manage it. But it's no big deal if you do. Take it from me—he won't be missed."

95

C arver walked across the underground hangar thinking, At last, I'm doing my job. After all that had happened, he was back to what he understood: drifting imperceptibly into the lives of very bad people, removing them from the planet, then slipping away again.

The different groups of people scattered about the hangar played right into his hands. Darko's militiamen mingled with Yugoslav Air Force personnel, while McCabe's bodyguards looked on, and mechanics and air crew went about their business. No one noticed, still less cared about, Carver.

He'd ripped the two CD player earphones apart and stuck one of them in his ear, letting the wire run down inside his shirt. He was back in his civilian clothes, shades on his face, his gun stuck in the waistband of his trousers, the fisherman's bag slung over a shoulder. He could be anyone.

His luck just kept getting better. There was a mechanic standing on a ladder at the rear of McCabe's plane, with his head and shoulders inside the rear equipment bay, pouring hydraulic fluid from a plastic jerry can. Carver stood at the bottom of the ladder and called up, "Hey you!"

The mechanic turned and looked down at him with a puzzled frown.

Carver held up a hand.

"Hold on there," he said, making the other man wait while he held a finger up to his earpiece, as if trying to hear over the noise in the hangar, then spoke into the wristband of his shirt. "Uh-huh, yeah, I'm on it. . . . I'm there right now. . . . Yeah, I'll do that. Out."

He looked back up the ladder.

"Okay now—you speak English?"

The man shook his head.

"Right, well, see if you understand this. . . . You"—He pointed at the mechanic—"off the plane." He jerked his finger down toward the hangar floor, then repeated the motion, clearly indicating the man should get off the ladder.

The mechanic stayed where he was, uncertain how to respond.

Carver gave a theatrical sigh of irritation.

"All right, then. . . . Plane . . ." Now he gestured at the aircraft. "American. Me"—he tapped his own chest—"American."

Could a Serb who couldn't speak English tell the difference between a real American accent and a bad English fake? Carver would have to hope not.

He repeated his little mantra: "Plane American, me American," then added, "Me go into plane. You . . . off the plane."

The mechanic looked at him, puffed his cheeks, exhaled heavily, then shrugged. He didn't need to say a word to convey his message: He thought Carver was a jerk, but he couldn't be bothered even to attempt to argue with him. He climbed down off the ladder.

"Here, I'll take that," said Carver, taking the jerry can from the man's hand.

He went up the ladder into the bay. Laying his bag on the fuselage floor, he finished topping off the hydraulic accumulator. Then he got out his tools: a wrench to loosen the connections of the hot-air pipes, and a wire cutter to strip as much plastic insulation as possible off the wiring bundles in the same. He wasn't going to hand McCabe another lifeline. This plane was going down hard. And just to underline the point, he left the jerry can, still half filled with inflammable fluid, its top unscrewed, in the equipment bay when he closed up and left.

He made his way back to the truck, sorely tempted just to put that Serb uniform back on and drive out the way he had come, get out before anyone even knew he'd been there. The urge to stay, though, was stronger. He wanted to see McCabe get on the plane, watch it as it roared down the runway, follow its path into the sky. This time he had absolute confidence in the work he'd done. The aircraft was a death trap. The moment the pilot switched on the jets, its fate was assured. He just needed to know that his prey was aboard.

A movement caught his attention. The over-handsome, Italianate man Carver thought of as Loverboy was emerging from the office at the side of the hangar. Behind him came one of Darko's men, pushing the cart on which the brown suitcase was resting. They walked over to the aircraft, and as they did so, the door in the underside of the fuselage opened to meet them, swinging down until it hung vertically from the aircraft. A metal frame, like a cradle, was lowered though the doorway, coming to a halt about four feet above the ground. There was already a military-green bundle filling the top half of the cradle, which looked to Carver like a parachute in its sack. It took two men to lift the case from the cart and put it into the cradle, while Loverboy supervised the operation. He checked that the case was secure and had been strapped onto the parachute, then signaled to someone inside the plane, and the cradle disappeared back up into the fuselage again, followed by the closing door.

The bomb was loaded.

96

Francesco Riva returned to the office where Waylon McCabe was waiting. On his way, he passed the Serbian, Darko, who was leaving with a contented smile on his face, like a hyena who has fed well. Riva opened the office door and went in, followed by the two armed guards who'd been standing outside.

"You done?" rasped McCabe.

It was apparent to Riva that this was a very sick man, one close to death. His face, always lean, now seemed little more than a skull, barely covered by skin stretched so tightly over the bone that it seemed it might split open at any moment. From time to time an involuntary grimace would cross his face as another spasm of pain shot through him. His shoulders were hunched, his fists clenched. Yet his eyes burned with wild conviction and the men under his command, any one of whom could have killed him with a single blow, were still held completely in his sway.

"Yes," said Riva. "The weapon is securely loaded in the bomb bay at the rear of the aircraft. It is not yet armed, but the radio control has been set with the correct code sequence. Once the plane has taken off, simply press the control switch and it will arm the bomb. When you reach your target, open the door and release the weapon. It will fall to a height of five thousand feet, at which point the parachute will deploy. As you saw, I fitted an air-pressure sensor to the device earlier, before it was loaded. At three thousand feet, this will send an electrical charge that will begin the detonation process. Your target, you said, was just below twenty-five hundred feet. It will, I assure you, be devastated by the air burst from this weapon.

"Now, if you will excuse me, I will depart. You have been very generous, Mr. McCabe. I would like to start enjoying my money."

McCabe nodded at one of his guards, who stepped across the door, blocking Riva's way.

"I can't allow that," said McCabe. "My conscience would not permit me to deny you the chance of salvation and everlasting life, in the company of Christ and all His angels. You know where we're headed today? To heaven itself."

McCabe's guards murmured, "Amen," as Riva looked on, too shocked to respond. The next thing he knew, one of the guards was twisting his right arm behind his back with one hand, and pointing a gun at him with the other.

"But you let Darko go!" Riva protested, his voice rising almost to a squeal as his arm was gripped even more fiercely.

"I sure did," replied McCabe. "The man is facin' damnation in the fires of hell for his sins of violence, theft, and fornication committed here on earth. His only hope of redemption is to stay here and fight the forces of the Antichrist in the battle that is to come."

"You're mad!" Riva cried, twisting his head this way and that in search of anything or anyone that could save him.

Lieutenant General Vermulen had been dumped in one corner of the room. He seemed defeated and demoralized. His wife was sitting right next to him, her body almost touching his, and yet she was a world apart, looking away, her eyes anguished and unfocused, lost in her private thoughts.

"Let's go, folks," said McCabe. "Dr. Riva, I want you to know that I'll be prayin' for your soul, despite your grievous lack of faith. And, General, I want you to think real hard, in case you got any plans to try to fight. I know you're a brave man. I guess you ain't scared of takin' a bullet. But take a good look at your pretty little wife. 'Cause if you try anything, my boys are under orders to shoot her first, off the aircraft or on it. And believe me, these boys don't miss."

Twelve miles out from Slatina, the Black Hawks were preparing for their final approach into Pristina airport. The fighting troops were getting ready to lock and load. The bomb-disposal experts were checking their gear one last time. Kady Jones's stomach had been doing backflips since they crossed the border from Bosnia. Now she concentrated on steadying her breathing and relaxing her muscles, just as she had done that afternoon on Gull Lake. She had gone head-to-head with a nuclear bomb. After that, she could surely cope with anything.

arver watched Dusan Darko stride toward his men with a look that suggested he'd just made a very sweet deal. Darko shouted a few words at the men hanging around the parked trucks and the Land Cruiser and they started gathering their gear and loading up their vehicles with a barrage of whoops, cheers, shouts, and backslaps that suggested the bars and brothels of Pristina were in for a busy, but profitable night.

Carver wasn't one for celebrating once a job was done. He liked to get as far away as possible, find some peace, try to come to terms with what he did: earned his living by making other people die.

Nothing more happened for a minute or so, then the door of the office opened, maybe eighty feet away. A cadaverous, twisted figure emerged and made his way with a pained, shuffling gait right across the hangar toward the airplane. It took Carver a couple of seconds to realize this was Waylon McCabe. The last time he'd set eyes on him, at another airport, on the far side of the world, McCabe had exuded the tough, bullying, loudmouthed power of a malevolent alpha male. Now he looked like a dead man walking. Whether Carver killed him or not, he wouldn't last till the end of the month. For a moment, Carver felt a twinge of disappointment, almost as if he'd been cheated. He had to tell himself that McCabe wasn't the issue: What mattered was the bomb hidden inside that suitcase. That was what had to be stopped.

The jets started up, filling the hangar with their high-pitched roar. Carver thought of the air pipes heating up, the temperature slowly starting to rise. The aircraft had become a ticking bomb, counting down to disaster.

And then his world fell apart.

Immediately behind McCabe came Loverboy, held in the grasp of one of the bodyguards. The next pair consisted of Vermulen and his guard. But Carver gave none of them more than a fleeting glance. His entire attention was focused at the end of the line, on Alix.

He whispered to himself, "You're not supposed to be here." And then he repeated himself, banging both hands against the steering wheel. "You're not . . . supposed . . . to be here!"

So now what was he going to do?

He could rescue her. If he moved quickly and quietly enough, he could close on the man who was holding her, double-tap to the head. Use a silencer, so the other guards took a fraction longer to react. Hit them, too. Maybe he'd hit the other two prisoners—that couldn't be helped. With any luck he'd have time to take out McCabe as well.

If no one spotted him running across the hangar with a gun in his hand . . .

If none of the three armed guards were alert enough to react to his attack . . .

If McCabe didn't make it onto the plane and simply fly away alone . . .

If Darko didn't object to him blowing away a valued client . . . And if Darko didn't take this as the ideal opportunity to take McCabe's money and his bomb . . .

Well, then, his plan might just work.

But if any of those possibilities occurred, then he would certainly die, Alix would probably die alongside him, and, far more important than that, the bomb would still be loose in the world.

The American, Jaworski, had told him what was at stake. McCabe was planning to start a war that would lead to Armageddon. Carver did not believe, for a fraction of a second, that the heavens were going to open and Christ would descend to earth just because a religious maniac like Waylon McCabe asked Him to. But he was absolutely certain that thousands, maybe millions of people might die in the chaos McCabe could cause.

Without making any conscious choice, he found himself getting out of the truck, walking around it to where there was a clear line of sight between him and the group following McCabe. They had almost reached the steps to the aircraft. For a second, Carver thought he might have a clear shot as McCabe walked up them. But then one of the air crew emerged from the door of the plane and came down to meet McCabe, taking him by the arm, blocking the line of fire.

Carver could still make the run, though. There was time, just, to reach Alix before the plane doors closed behind her. It tore him up to see her face contorted with pain, the guard leering at her, enjoying the thrill of domination over a beautiful, helpless woman. Screw the odds, screw the bomb, screw everything: Carver wanted to go over and beat the crap out of the ape. He wanted his girl back. He longed for the feel and scent of her body in his arms, her hair slipping between his fingers, her wonderful eyes looking into his, the kiss of her lips. He needed to tell her how much he loved her, how deeply he appreciated the months she'd spent by his bedside, how bad he felt about all the things she'd been through on his account.

He wanted to say how sorry he was that he was killing her.

She was walking up into the plane now. He was staring at her, his eyes boring into her back. She must have felt it because she turned her head and looked in his direction. Just for a second their eyes met. He saw the look of amazement on her face, and then something deeper, a yearning desperation that cut straight to his heart as she cried out, "Carver!"

His reaction was unthinking. He couldn't help it—he took a step toward her and gave himself away.

It was a pathetic, amateur move. But Carver's incompetence saved him. He hadn't even bothered to reach for his gun. So neither McCabe's bodyguards, nor Darko's fighters, milling around behind him, started firing. Not that it would make much difference in the long run, the amount of weaponry now pointing in his direction.

Darko nodded at one of his men, who came up to Carver and patted him down. He found the Beretta, removed it, and threw it clattering onto the floor of the hangar.

McCabe had stopped on the aircraft steps. He looked at Carver.

"Bring him here," he barked, stepping back down to the ground.

Darko snapped out a series of instructions. Carver's arms were grabbed, a man on either side, and he was hauled across the open space toward the aircraft. Darko was strolling alongside, cradling a gun. His face bore an expression of amusement, rather than hostility, as if he were motivated as much by curiosity as by needing to secure his captive.

McCabe glanced at Alix as the four men got closer.

"So you know this man?"

She said nothing. McCabe grunted dismissively then turned his attention back to Carver, peering at him as he came closer. The look became a stare, then the death's head face creased into a savage grin.

"Forget it . . . I know you, don't I, boy? You're the reason I'm here."

Carver stared back at him impassively.

"Don't know what you're talking about."

"You're Lundin . . . the mechanic."

"You heard the woman. She called me Carver."

McCabe coughed violently, then spat a stream of bloodstained phlegm onto the ground between them.

"You fixed this plane, too, boy?" he rasped.

"Like I said, you've lost me."

McCabe ignored Carver's words. He took another shuffling step, leaning forward so that his face was right up by Carver's, as close as a lover, whispering in his ear.

"You care to show me what you done?"

"I haven't done anything," said Carver.

There was only one way now to save Alix, and he went for it.

"If you don't believe me, put me on the aircraft."

Before McCabe could reply there was a shout from the hangar entrance and the guard from the main gate ran in, yelling in Serbian, a desperate edge to his voice.

Darko listened to the frantic jumble of words, then spoke to McCabe.

"He says helicopters are coming, just a few kilometers away. They will be here in two minutes, maybe less."

McCabe considered this new information. He switched his attention back to Carver.

"We don't have time to debate this. Guess you'd better just step onboard."

"No problem," Carver said.

Then he led the way up the steps, into the booby-trapped plane.

98

The Black Hawks came in from the northeast, through a gap in the hills, reaching the airport at the terminal end, a mile and a half from the hangar. McCabe's plane was already on the runway, moving toward them, picking up speed for takeoff.

Major Dave Gretsch ordered the pilots to form up in line abreast, just over the runway, blocking the plane's way. But the jet kept coming.

One of the choppers was a Direct Action Penetrator model, armed with a Gatling gun. Gretsch ordered it to fire a warning burst over the plane. It had no effect. Now the gap between the plane and the choppers was closing at over two hundred feet per second.

"Shoot to kill!" Gretsch commanded.

The Gatling's rotating barrels spewed an unrelenting hail of bullets at the onrushing machine, but it hurtled onward, taking on the helicopters in an airborne game of chicken as its nose lifted up off the ground and arrowed toward the night sky.

"Break! Break!" screamed the pilot in the command helicopter, and the three choppers threw themselves sideways, scattering before the roaring plane, not like predatory black hawks, but panic-stricken, fat gray pigeons, their rotors clawing for purchase in air torn asunder by the jet engines' wake.

The bomb-disposal team was hurled from side to side and buffeted up and down before the pilot was able to regain control.

One of the men shouted, "What the hell was that?"

Kady Jones was still trying to stop her stomach from turning cartwheels.

"I guess that was our bomb," she gasped. "And I think it was saying good-bye."

99

C arver waited until the engines had been turned off, and there was nothing to hear but the rushing of the air outside and the passengers screaming in fear or calling out to their God. The plane was descending fast and it was going to keep going down until it hit the rocky, mountainous earth of northeastern Macedonia. There would be no airstrip to welcome them, no miracle landing. They all knew that. And yet the people around him still strapped themselves into their seats as the pilot instructed, and when the first soft tendrils of smoke wormed their way into the compartment, they reached for the oxygen masks.

As if any of that would make the slightest difference in the end.

Carver had been placed on one end of a three-seat divan that ran along the wall, toward the rear of the cabin. Alix was next to him, Vermulen at the far end. Two of McCabe's men sat opposite them. The third was guarding his boss and keeping an eye on Francesco Riva. They were up front, in club seats the size of armchairs.

For the first few minutes of the flight, the goons in suits had sat there, pointing their guns at the trio on the divan, scowls on their faces, trying to look mean and intimidating. But any threat they posed had evaporated the moment the pilot announced that they had a problem. Then they just became two terrified passengers in a metal tube dropping out of the sky, each of them thinking about nothing but himself.

It was Carver's hand that Alix reached for.

"Don't worry," he said, giving it a reassuring squeeze. "This isn't over." He helped put her mask on.

"Deep breaths," he told her. "Get plenty of oxygen into your blood."

Carver could see Vermulen, looking past Alix at him.

"Who are you?" the general asked, shaking his head in bemusement, as if he were trying to work out how his judgment of people could have gone so wrong. He reached out to Alix, got no response, and sank back into his seat, lost in his own disillusionment.

Carver had no interest in Vermulen's problems. He was more inter-ested in McCabe, who was staring at a control unit in his hand. Carver saw a grin flicker over the old man's face as he pressed the switch. Had he just armed the bomb in one last shot at Armageddon? Carver held a mask to his face, his breathing strong and steady, as he now looked across the cabin, through the steadily thickening smoke, toward the two men on the far side. One of them was having problems with his oxygen supply, yanking on his mask, trying to get his partner's attention. But the other guy was having none of it. He was keeping all his fresh air for himself, one hand on his mask, the other—holding his gun—hanging loosely beside him.

The men were lost in their own dying world. They didn't even notice Carver as he rose from his seat, crossed the aisle with a single stride, wrenched the gun from the limp, dangling hand, and smashed it twice—backhand, forehand—against the pair of naked pink scalps. One of the two slumped forward, unconscious. The other groaned and turned unfocused eyes in Carver's direction. Carver hit him again, knocking him cold.

He turned back to the divan, now barely visible, even a couple of feet away, reached for his mask, grabbed Alix's hand, and gave it a sharp tug. She got the message, unclipped her belt, and got to her feet. Carver could see a dark shadow that must be Vermulen looming beyond her. He lashed out with the handle of the gun, felt it hit something, he wasn't sure what, and the shadow collapsed back toward the chair. Carver gave another pull on Alix's hand, leading her back to the very rear of the cabin.

As they staggered through the acrid fumes, Carver felt the trem-ors running through Alix's body, She was beginning to choke. He was coughing, too, his eyes watering, his nose and throat burning.

Three paces took him to the lavatory door, and then he was gulping down oxygen from the mask dangling over the toilet bowl.

Carver handed the mask over to Alix, pausing for a second to make sure she could still hold it steady over her mouth and nose. Then he left the lavatory and stood by the bulkhead that divided the passenger compartment from the bomb bay, desperately turning the wheel that opened the hatch. There was an audible click as the lock disengaged and a moment of truth as the door was flung open and a blast of thin, freez-ing air roared into the cabin, instantly condensing all the moisture in the atmosphere and turning it into an impenetrable fog.

The aircraft's dive became even deeper and the fuselage swayed one way and the other, like the weight at the end of a pendulum, as the pilots struggled to maintain control.

Carver reached out and grabbed Alix, dragging her after him as he squeezed through the cramped, steel-ringed hatch, both of them banging heads, shins, and elbows, almost forcing exclamations of pain and wasting precious oxygen. Agonizing seconds stretched by as the hatch was closed and locked again to slow down anyone else who realized that their only hope lay in the bomb bay.

Now Carver was kneeling, hands reaching out through the freezing, poisonous fog, fingers stretching, searching, because there had to be a way of opening the doors manually, a fail-safe in case the electrical control in the cockpit didn't work. And there it was, a handle, on top of a metal rod, waiting to be pumped up and down. Desperately he set to work.

For a moment, the doors remained shut. Carver pumped the lever two or three more times steadily, then frantically again and again as he felt his lungs begin to burn, eyes flare and then water, his muscles giving way.

Then doors were opening, letting in a gale that drove the smog from the bomb bay; air that was bitterly cold, but rich and clean enough to breathe in desperate inhalations between hacking, retching coughs. But the pumping never stopped, up and down, pain shooting through arms, shoulders, and back with every motion of the handle, until the bay doors were wide open and the earth was dimly visible down below.

Above it sat the bomb, a drab brown case, crudely strapped to a parachute, cradled in its metal frame. A lever on the frame disengaged the bomb from the cradle—just as well that those blind, grasping hands had clutched the pump handle first.

Carver's eyes darted around the bay, settling on bungee cords looped around hooks on the wall, there to secure the legitimate cargo that the engineers who adapted the aircraft naïvely assumed would be in the plane. He grabbed a cord and looped one end around one of the straps that linked the bomb and parachute, knotting it tight. Then he held Alix close to him, her arms wrapped around his waist. She gave him a little squeeze back as he passed the cord around them in a figure eight, before tying that off, too, forming an umbilical link with the bomb.

The whole aircraft was shaking more and more as it failed to respond to the crew's commands. There couldn't be long before they lost control completely and the descent turned into a freefall.

Suddenly there came a motion from the front end of the bay, the turning of the small metal wheel. Someone was there, on the other side of the bulkhead, trying to get into the bay, and the hatch was opening to reveal Vermulen. He must have recovered and grabbed the other bodyguard's gun. Now he had it out and was firing, the barrel jerking randomly with every convulsion of the doomed plane, bullets ricocheting off the bomb cradle and the aircraft's own metallic ribs.

There was one last, great spasm as the cables snapped. Carver heard Alix give a muffled cry of surprise and felt her body give a sudden jerk. The plane lurched into its death dive, Vermulen was flung back against the bulkhead, and now there was nothing to do but wrench the lever and then put his arms around her head to protect it as gravity took over and the bomb, the parachute, and the two entwined lovers were hurled out, crashing through the cradle into the yawning void, hurtling toward the ground at two hundred miles an hour.

The parachute was set to open at five thousand feet, slowing the descent of the bomb before its detonation over Jerusalem's Temple Mount. But the hills and mountains of northern Macedonia rise as high as fifty-five hundred feet. The earth was rushing ever closer and suddenly Carver heard himself shouting wordlessly in frustration and fear as he realized that nothing that had happened in the past few minutes had made any difference.

The hard, unyielding mountainside was just seconds away now. Carver held Alix's body even closer to him, unable to see her eyes in the darkness. But as the final moment of impact drew near, and his mind refused to shut down, he screwed his own eyes tight shut, so that the explosive impact of the plane, maybe eight hundred feet away, was only heard, rather than seen.

Closer, closer still . . . And then there was a sudden jolt, enough almost to tear clinging arms from their shoulder sockets, as the parachute finally opened, no more than three hundred feet above the ground, barely enough to decelerate the bomb and the two people tied to it as they struck the ground and went tumbling over and over, striking rocks and plowing through undergrowth, down a narrow ravine until they finally came to a halt in the soft, damp earth beside a mountain stream.

Carver had suffered a hairline fracture in one ankle and badly sprained the other. The pain that stabbed through him with every breath told him that several of his ribs were cracked.

He reached over and untied the rope that connected them to the parachute harness and the bomb. As he loosened the loop around his waist, Alix rolled away from him. She came to a halt on the ground next to him, lying on her front, her head tilted away from him, motionless. He spoke her name, but there was no reply.

At first he assumed she'd been knocked cold by their fall down the hillside. And then he realized that his hands were covered with something wet and dark. For a second he thought it might be mud. He prayed it was mud. But then he realized that his chest was covered with it, too, and he knew that it must be blood.

"Oh, God, no . . ." he moaned, and he patted his hands over his body, desperately hoping that they might find the wound that had produced the bleeding. That could happen. You got cuts sometimes, deep ones, and just didn't feel them.

But Carver had not been cut. He knew that.

So then he looked across at Alix and the moonlight cast a gray wash over the ragged, purple-black hole, high up by her shoulder blade, that could have been made only by Vermulen's gun. Carver placed a finger to her throat, feeling for a pulse . . . and it was there, not a steady beat, but a delicate, barely perceptible flutter. He listened for the bubbling, sucking sound of a lung wound and heard nothing. That was some relief at least, but not much.

The entry wound was much bigger and messier than Carver would have expected, as if someone had punched a fist right into her. The bullet must have already been deformed by the time it hit her, maybe by a ricochet off a metal surface. That would explain why it had lodged inside her, instead of going straight through and hitting Carver as well. He tried not to think about the internal havoc the misshapen slug had caused. Even if it hadn't hit any vital organs, she'd lost a lot of blood and more was still pouring from her.

Carver pulled off his shirt, ignoring the stabs of pain from his battered rib cage, and ripped it into strips. Then he gently lifted Alix into a sitting position, wincing as she gave a soft, semiconscious moan, and took off her shirt, exposing the shredded skin, splintered bone, and gaping flesh torn from her back. He crumpled one of the fabric strips into a wad and pressed it against the wound, trying to stanch the flow of blood. He used the other strips to improvise a bandage around her shoulder to hold the wad in place.

It was, at best, a temporary measure. If Alix did not receive proper medical attention soon, she would die. All he could do now was take her body in his arms and hold her. He spoke to her quietly, telling her all the things that had gone unsaid for so many months. There were occasional moments when he thought she might have heard some of what he said, as she blinked or twitched her lips, but that wasn't the point of his words.

He was still sitting there when the Black Hawk found him. It landed on a patch of flat ground not far away, and he saw the beams from the flashlights slicing through the darkness as the people walked toward him. Then there was a figure standing in front of him and a hand on his shoulder.

"You okay?"

It was a woman's voice. He glanced up and saw a slim, petite civilian, looking ill at ease in army combats.

"Yeah," said Samuel Carver, though the word was sighed as much as spoken. "We're just fine."

Then he rose to his feet, with Alix still cradled in his arms, and started limping down the ravine toward the waiting helicopter.

POSTSCRIPT:

This Much Is Also True

The U.S. government was shown advance tapes of General Alexander Lebed's claims that Russia had lost one hundred suitcase nukes and had a response prepared before the interview aired on *60 Minutes.* State Department spokesman James Foley stated, "The government of Russia has assured us that it retains adequate command and control of its nuclear arsenal . . . appropriate physical security arrangements exist for these weapons and facilities . . . there is no cause for concern."

Lebed, however, repeated his claims at a hearing of the Congressional Military Research and Development Subcommittee on October 1, 1997. The following day, he was backed by a senior Russian scientist, environmentalist, and member of the Russian National Security Council, Alexei Yablokov, who testified to the committee that he was "absolutely sure" that the KGB had produced miniature bombs, intended as terrorist weapons, in the 1970s.

The subject was debated in Congress in the autumn of 1999, when Republican congressman Kurt Weldon, a specialist in Russian affairs, stated that 132 suitcase nukes had been manufactured by the Russians. Weldon also claimed to have had a conversation with then FBI Director Louis Freeh in which Freeh "acknowledged the possibility that hidden weapons caches exist in the United States." Weldon maintained, "There is no doubt that the Soviets stored material in this country. The question is what and where."

There have been no public reports of any of the missing bombs being found anywhere in the world. The FBI, however, is believed to have searched an area near Brainerd, Minnesota, looking for possible weapons. Brainerd is close to Gull Lake.

Alexander Lebed died on April 28, 2002, in a helicopter crash in Russia's Sayan Mountains. The official cause of the accident was given as a collision with power cables in foggy weather.

On October 20, 1999, the FBI published its Project Megiddo report. Numerous extremist Christian groups and ideologies were examined, but the report concluded that while the Project Megiddo intelligence initiative "has revealed indicators of potential violent activity on the part of extremists in this country," there were "very few indications of specific threats to domestic security."

Subsequent events have shown this assessment to be well founded. There have been no real-life Waylon McCabes.

In June, July, and August 1998, CIA agents in Tiranë, the capital of Albania, carried out the forcible captures and extraditions of five senior members of Egyptian Islamic Jihad, an organization with extremely close, long-standing ties to al-Qaeda. The men were flown to Egypt, where they were tortured, tried, and found guilty of terrorist offenses. Two were executed, one sentenced to life imprisonment, and the others given lengthy jail terms.

Despite the presence of these known terrorists in Albania, ethnic homeland of the Kosovo Liberation Army, and despite the certain presence of jihadist fighters in Bosnia, U.S. and U.K. policy remained—and still remains—predicated on the conviction that there were, and are, no links between the Kosovo Albanians and Islamic terrorism. This view is hotly disputed by the Serbs and their traditional allies in Russia and Bulgaria. There is, however, considerable evidence that the KLA received both weapons and training from U.S. sources—civilian, corporate, and official— and had similar links to the German BND intelligence service. It would be embarrassing, to say the least, if Western governments had, yet again, been assisting the very forces that were most bent on their destruction.

But what of the terrorist threat, so feared by Kurt Vermulen?

In July 1998, the U.S. Commission on National Security issued the first of three wide-ranging reports analyzing expected global developments up to 2025, the threats they posed to U.S. national security, and the measures that should be taken to make the United States and its allies better able to deal with the threats facing it. None of these reports, whose later editions appeared in 1999 and 2001, included any specific suggestion that Islamic terrorism might be a danger to the United States or its allies, let alone strike directly at their territories and citizens.

———

On August 7, 1998, terrorists acting on behalf of the World Islamic Front for Jihad Against the Jews and Crusaders—a coalition of groups spearheaded by al-Qaeda and Osama bin Laden—drove trucks laden with explosives into the U.S. embassies in Nairobi, Kenya, and Dar es Salaam, Tanzania. More than two hundred people were killed and over four thousand wounded, the vast majority of them local civilians.

On October 12, 2000, during the last months of the Clinton administration, the U.S.S. *Cole* guided-missile destroyer was attacked by a boat manned by al-Qaeda suicide bombers, during a goodwill visit to Yemen. Seventeen U.S. Navy personnel were killed, along with the two bombers, Ibrahim al-Thawr and Abdullah al-Misawa. The *Cole*'s sailors were prevented from firing on their attackers by their rules of engagement, which only allowed them to shoot if shot at first. There was no defensive perimeter around the boat because government policy demanded "a small footprint" so as not to antagonize Arab opinion. The navy's own investigation concluded, "The commanding officer of *Cole* did not have the specific intelligence, focused training, appropriate equipment or on-scene security support to effectively prevent or deter such a determined, preplanned assault on his ship."

On September 11, 2001 . . .

Acknowledgments

Samuel Carver's continuing survival is only possible thanks to the people who so carefully tend to him in London, New York, and L.A. They include (but are by no means limited to) . . . Aislinn Casey, Andrew Duncan, Ben Petrone, Bill Scott-Kerr, Clare Ferraro, Gavin Hilzbrich, Giles Milburn, Josh Kendall, Julian Alexander, Lucinda Bettridge, Mark Lucas, Martin Higgins, Michelle DeCoux, Nick Harris, Patsy Irwin, Peta Nightingale, Sally Gaminara, and Selina Walker.

As always, I was blessed by the kindness and generosity of people who shared their professional expertise. I thank them all. It goes without saying that any mistakes, or deliberate distortions caused by the process of turning fact into fiction, are entirely my responsibility. Specifically . . . Andy Missen attempted to teach this aeronautic ignoramus about the finer points of flying and aircraft technology. Duncan Falconer's book *First into Action* told the true story of the SBS raid into Iraq, with a U.S. SEAL as a passenger, that inspired Carver's nightmare. The SBS and SAS books of Don Camsell and John "Lofty" Wiseman were also great sources of information on Special Forces and their procedures. Professor Cary Cooper OBE spared the time to discuss Samuel Carver's psychological traumas, and his possible recovery, while Danielle Nay's personal experience of a similar case aided my understanding of the effects of a victim's personality changes on loved ones. Craig Unger's December 2005 *Vanity Fair* magazine article, "American Rapture," opened my eyes to the apocalyptic side of Christian evangelism and its political influence. *The Secret History of al-Qa'ida* by Abdel Bari Atwan was both a gripping first-person account of a journey into the heart of international terrorism, and an invaluable aid to understanding Osama bin Laden, his history, and his ideas. Nick Gaskell and Tony Turnbull, of Nordic Challenge U.K., gave me the benefit of decades of experience skiing around Narvik. Pal Hansen not only allowed me (for the second time) to steal his appearance and good nature for the character of Thor Larsson, but also discussed the behavior of

Norwegian traffic cops. Charlie Brocket loaned the villa near Nice that got me thinking about the South of France, and enabled me, like Carver, to lunch at Eden Roc. Radenko Popovic provided me with a whole new insight into Kosovo (and, yes, those underground aircraft hangars really exist), while Tim Judah's book *Kosovo: War and Revenge* and *Soldier,* the autobiography of General Sir Mike Jackson, both provided invaluable background to the conflict. The staff of Bombardier Business Aircraft in Belfast and Quebec gave serious consideration to the problem of cutting a hatch in the fuselage of a private jet, and then opening it midflight, entirely unaware of what I intended to drop through that hatch. Dr. Frank Barnaby, nuclear-issues consultant to the Oxford Research Group and author of *How to Build a Nuclear Bomb: And Other Weapons of Mass Destruction,* kindly helped me build my imaginary bomb.

Finally, and most important of all, I offer my heartfelt love and thanks to my family, especially my wife, Clare. Many other authors told me that the second book is the hardest of all to write. But however tough it is for the author, it is far worse for the people who have to live with him. Bless you for your tolerance.